M. S. Power was born in Dublin and educated in Ireland and France. He has worked as a TV producer in the United States, but now lives on the Oxfordshire/Buckinghamshire border. His first novel, *Hunt For the Autumn Clowns*, was published to wide critical acclaim in 1983. *The Killing of Yesterday's Children*, which is the first novel in his 'Children of the North' trilogy, was published in 1985, followed by the second and third volumes, *A Darkness in the Eye* (1987) and *Lonely the Man Without Heroes* (1986).

THE KILLING OF YESTERDAY'S CHILDREN

'A high-class, up-to-the-minute job . . . M. S. Power casts a cool yet compassionate eye on the streets of Belfast, "filled with the promise of death", where, as one of the killers says, "there's no sides here . . . there's only survival". The author takes no sides, and this is all the more compelling for that'

Punch

LONELY THE MAN WITHOUT HEROES

'A strangely uplifting and attractive book about "ordinary people trying to survive against the odds"'

Books and Bookmen

THE KILLING OF YESTERDAY'S CHILDREN

M. S. POWER

SPHERE BOOKS LTD

Published by the Penguin Group
27 Wrights Lane, London w8 5TZ, England
Viking Penguin Inc., 40 West 23rd Street, New York, New York 10010, USA
Penguin Books Australia Ltd, Ringwood, Victoria, Australia
Penguin Books Canada Ltd, 2801 John Street, Markham, Ontario, Canada L3R 1B4
Penguin Books (NZ) Ltd, 182–190 Wairau Road, Auckland 10, New Zealand

Penguin Books Ltd, Registered Offices: Harmondsworth, Middlesex, England

First published in Great Britain in hardback by
Chatto & Windus Ltd 1985
Published in Abacus by Sphere Books Ltd 1988

Printed and bound in Great Britain by
Richard Clay Ltd, Bungay, Suffolk

For my friends
Ken and Jeanne

... and it was from the grey and menacing sea that it seemed to come, dark and threatening and evil, moving languidly in that sinister bodeful way that presages only sorrow and death but mostly sorrow, invading the souls of men and planting there the seeds of hate and revenge yet disguising these as good and right, nay as holy and glorious and by this awful deception turning man against his brother, gloating in the grim and terrible slaughter, exulting in the destruction of those who only yesterday were children.

The Visions and Visitations of Arthur Apple

A swirling, ominous cloud of acrid black smoke rose from behind the ornate spire of St Enoch's Church. Seeming to carry in its billows the echoes of the explosion that had just shattered the nervous, expectant quiet of the city, it curled and dispersed into the grey, heavy sky. Almost theatrical, thought Colonel Maddox; the next thing to appear would be a genie with a hollow laugh. Like daemonic incense, decided his companion, Mr Asher, and found the allusion highly satisfactory. The two men stood side by side at the narrow, heavily screened window, watching with curiously detached relief. Both were dressed in civilian clothes and looked ill at ease, the Colonel tugging from time to time at his jacket, straightening imaginary creases; their neat, grey suits invited a familiarity neither of them wanted. It was, appropriately enough, Good Friday.

As the smoke thinned out and the plangent sounds of lamentation and fury (the inevitable aftermath of all explosions) grew louder, the two men turned from the window in unison, as though their remote participation in the privacy of sorrow and outrage were an intolerable intrusion. Only when the screams and wails and the accompanying threnodic keening of the ambulances had diminished, to be replaced by the clamour of dustbin-lids being clattered in protest and the heavy rumble of military vehicles moving in, did Colonel Maddox pour two stiff drinks from a bottle produced, with a wry, guilty smile, from one of the filing-cabinets that lined the small office. He pushed one across the desk to his companion. Mr Asher emptied his glass in one swallow closing his eyes and holding his breath for a few seconds as the liquid burned its way to his stomach. He was a small, thin man in his early fifties, and both his height and age worried him: to compensate for his lack of stature he was excessively aggressive; to overcome any sign of ageing he employed a battery of creams, lotions and dyes which might have tempted one to regard him as effeminate, had not his actions been entirely masculine and his reputation with women such as to dispel any such thought. Although a high-ranking if somewhat maverick officer in the R.U.C., he was always referred to as 'Mr Asher', and in an odd way this civilian title seemed to enhance his rank and endow him with a certain mysterious potency, making him one of those shadowy, slightly sinister creatures more accredited to fiction than fact. Mr Asher, however, was very much a fact, and certainly more than slightly sinister.

Colonel Maddox poured himself another drink. Apparently lost in reveries of his own, he was oblivious to Asher's glass, automatically proferred but quickly withdrawn with a little cough of embarrassment. A deep flush suffused Asher's face, as though the Colonel's unintentional snub had been a conscious chastisement for overstepping the mark of familiarity. He placed his empty glass with exaggerated care on the desk and proceeded to make a great show of blowing his nose.

' – still simply cannot understand it', penetrated Mr Asher's trumpeting.

'I'm sorry, Colonel, you were saying?'

'Oh – that I still simply cannot understand why the wretched man allowed himself to get caught up in such a ghastly business.'

'Ah, that again,' Asher said, sighing with mild frustration. 'He knew exactly what he was doing.'

'Come, now, he can't have known – '

'Oh, he knew,' Asher insisted dogmatically. 'If you ask me he *wanted* to – '

'To die?' the Colonel interrupted in amazement, as if the idea were new to him.

'In a way. He had notions of nobility. Sacrifice. That sort of thing,' Asher found himself explaining, uncomfortably aware that he cared little for such matters.

Colonel Maddox stared into space for several minutes, allowing the remark to mature in the hope that it would decant itself into some semblance of clarity. 'You seem to be saying he *planned* the entire thing.'

'I wouldn't go that far. I think he recognized it as the only possible conclusion to the events he had set in motion. I also believe there was more between him and Deeley than we know.'

'You've read his diary, I suppose,' the Colonel remarked.

'Bits,' Asher admitted, his high-pitched intonation indicating that to have bothered to read the whole thing would have been a waste of valuable time.

'I've read it all,' Colonel Maddox confessed. 'Twice. Every terrible word. Frightening.'

'He was sick. Nothing more, Colonel. Just plain sick,' Mr Asher announced, with that peculiar emphasis that somehow makes illness sound obscene.

Colonel Maddox seemed to think about this for a while, making miniature whirlpools with the whiskey in his glass as his long, bony body swayed to and fro. 'There is an awful sickness, John, that affects that part we used to call the soul,' he said finally, in a vague, distant voice. The idea seemed to awaken something strange and upsetting in him.

'Huh,' grunted Asher.

Maddox finished his drink and returned to the window. Resting his hands on the sill he gazed down and around, his vision blurred by the thick wire screen that protected the glass: the almost deserted streets, rutted and uneven, their paving-stones long since requisitioned as ineffectual ammunition; row upon row of small, mean houses, all lightless, the graffiti on their walls proclaiming hatred and differing shades of patriotism (and demanding freedom, too – little enough to ask); and the upended rubbish truck, remnant of an overnight barricade, where three lean and nervous mongrels now scavenged, unable to believe their luck. Two armoured cars rumbled across his vision, the sound of their grinding motors powerful and menacing – and comforting, too, to the soldiers they carried, as they faced another wet, dreary night filled with the promise of death. What had happened just one week ago should have been forgotten by now amid this constant, continuous tragedy. One would have thought that the death of one insignificant man would be swallowed up and lost in the unending litany of bereavement. It was not so, however. Horror and destruction were now regarded as appallingly normal, but it seemed one was still permitted to single out one individual life, hold it in some regard and mourn its loss. The Colonel fumbled in his pocket, found his cigarettes and lit one. Far to his left, beyond the spire slowly fading in the gloom, a brilliant flash of light shot across the sky. Maddox automatically started counting, waiting for the sound of another explosion. A small, tired smile affected his mouth as he recalled his mother telling him to count between the lightning and the rumbles to know how far away the thunder was. He had reached only six before the noise thudded across the city and rattled the window.

'Bloody boyos are restless tonight,' Asher remarked fatuously.

The Colonel nodded without turning, amazed at the small grin on his own lips.

'Anyway, it's not our worry tonight, Colonel.'

'No.'

'And I must be off.'

'Must you? Have another drink before you go.'

'Well – a quick one, sir. I have someone – ah – waiting,' Mr Asher confessed smugly, always pleased to advertise his prowess.

'God, I wish I could be like you, John,' Maddox said in a quiet voice, his head shaking in disbelief. 'You can switch off just like that,' he said, snapping his fingers. 'None of this affects you one little bit, does it?'

'Should it?'

The Colonel's mouth framed the beginning of a reply, but he restrained himself. He poured two more drinks before finally answering.

'Perhaps not. Perhaps you've got the right idea.'

'I don't know about the right idea, sir, but I can guarantee you this: nobody survives here if he gets too involved.'

'But we *are* involved.'

'No, we are *not*,' Mr Asher interrupted firmly. '*You're* not, at any

4

rate. You've simply got to do your job and get the hell out of here as soon as your tour is up. No attachments, Colonel. And when they send you home, forget Belfast. Throw that part of your mind away.'

'Throw away your mind,' the Colonel heard himself saying. 'Funny,' he continued, looking up and staring at Asher intently. 'Somebody else said that to me once.'

'They were right.'

'Perhaps. And you?'

'Me?'

'Yes, you, John. What do you do?'

Mr Asher pursed his lips for a moment, then allowed them to relax into the semblance of a smile. 'I do nothing, Colonel. I've lived with this chaos all my life. I'd only be lost if it stopped. That's when my problems would start, if it all suddenly stopped.' Asher sipped his drink before adding, 'But it will never end; so I've nothing to worry about, have I?'

Colonel Maddox watched his companion drink again, the slender, well-manicured fingers tilting the glass, the small, hostile eyes peering into it.

'So, in a sense, you have thrown away your mind, John?'

'The day I was born.'

The Colonel nodded, taking the cigarette, long since extinguished, from his mouth.

'Light?' Mr Asher conjured a flaming lighter from his pocket so rapidly it must surely have been ignited there. He moved the flame back and forth under the Colonel's cigarette. 'You're still brooding about Apple, aren't you?'

'He haunts me.'

Asher shook his head incredulously. 'He turned on us, dammit.'

'That's not the point, John. He did what he thought was right. He was honourable,' the Colonel said emphatically, straightening his back. Reference to honour demanded a rigid spine.

'Honour be damned – '

'And he wasn't a coward,' the Colonel remarked irrelevantly, in a tone of vague significance.

'He was nothing but a stupid old fool,' Mr Asher decided, pocketing his lighter at last and glancing at his watch. 'Now I must be off,' he said, joining the Colonel at the window. 'You've been here long enough, sir. Too long. That's what's getting you down. It always happens at the end of a tour. I've seen it a thousand times.'

'I don't think – '

' – and the nights are always the worst,' Asher continued, determined to forestall any further discussion. 'I had an old aunt once. She used to swear night was sent for only two things: making love or reviewing our errors. So I leave you,' Asher concluded, putting on his coat and knotting a dark blue scarf about his neck, 'to the latter. Me, I have high hopes of – '

Maddox rounded on him swiftly and grabbed him by the shoulders. 'You terrify me, John. Nothing touches you. You're just like those animals out there. No compassion. No – no – *feelings*.'

Asher seemed for a moment stunned by this outburst. Removing the Colonel's hands from his coat he held them for a second in his own, without speaking. Then he dropped them and rubbed his own together, saying tightly: 'I'm not paid to have feelings, Colonel. Neither are you.'

Colonel Maddox closed his eyes and nodded like a man willing to agree with anything. Then he laughed, a wry, mournful strained laugh.

While they had been talking the rain had started again, and it now pattered in drops as hard as rice on the window. The demonstrations that always followed the bombings would be postponed, and the soldiers on foot patrol would pull on their waterproof capes and feel a little safer.

'Well, you go on home, John. I'll stay here for a while. I still have a few things that need to be done.'

'Right. I'll see you in the morning. And remember: we're here to do a job. That's all.'

'I'll remember.'

'And try and get some sleep. You look all in.'

'Sleep?' the Colonel asked mildly. 'Ah, yes. Yes. Yes, I will.'

'And forget about Apple and that,' Asher said, indicating the thick exercise-book – several exercise-books, in fact, crudely bound with tape to form one enormous volume – lying on the desk.

'Yes.'

Asher paused by the door and turned. 'Colonel,' he said, in a voice uncharacteristically gentle, 'there's one thing you have to understand. When a man dies here, soldier or terrorist or civilian, it is as though he never even lived. He dies, and that's an end to it. He leaves nothing behind. He takes even the memory of his life with him. They get us or we get them – whichever way it goes, the result is the same. However,' Asher added, his cold humour returning, 'we just have to make sure it's us who get them first.'

Suddenly, the Colonel found himself shaking with laughter. He threw back his head and roared until the tears rolled down his cheeks. Asher was shocked. 'I didn't know I said anything funny, Colonel,' he said softly.

'You didn't, John,' the Colonel confessed, wiping the tears from his face with a large white handkerchief that had his initials neatly embroidered in one corner. 'You certainly didn't. I was just thinking how stupid it all is. Here we are talking so damned philosophically about something neither of us understands, and both of us should be dead.'

'You, perhaps, sir. They never had any intention of killing me. They need me alive to bargain with.'

'Well, me, then. But here I am alive and well, drinking my whiskey and supposed, according to your way of thinking, to have no feelings.'

'You were lucky.'

'Perhaps. Life is not always the greatest favour fortune bestows, you know. Anyway, I'm sorry for laughing. I *am* tired. Forgive me, John. Off you go and enjoy yourself.'

'Good night, sir.'

'Good night, John.'

Alone, Maddox slumped into the old, worn leather chair by his desk and listened to Asher's receding footsteps. As they disappeared with the slamming of a distant door, he leant forward and rested his elbows on the desk, head in hands. His fingers pressed hard into his temples as if to ease some excruciating pain or erase a disquieting thought. And it seemed to work, for he threw back his head and yawned loudly and luxuriously, allowing himself a smile at the mild vulgarity. He was still smiling when his eyes came to rest on the bound exercise-books before him. Slowly, almost reluctantly, like a small child reaching towards a familiar yet still alarming jack-in-the-box, he stretched out to flick open the cover, and started to read again the baleful words printed in large capitals: I AM I SAID. I AM I CRIED; and under these in script so tiny that the Colonel was forced to lean even closer to decipher the words: *The Visions and Visitations of Arthur Apple.*

He started to turn the pages, letting them fall through his fingers as though searching for some particular passage, a passage that would be revealed to him by whatever power allowed the pages to come to rest. 'He was no fool,' he heard himself say aloud. Under different circumstances, indeed, he would have been considered an extremely brave man. An example to us all. Maddox sighed deeply. An example to us all. How he had yearned to hear such words used of him! He decided to risk another small drink and sat for some time unmoving, his eyes fixed on the open book in front of him, the strange horrors and agony it contained seeming to radiate from the pages and taunt him. And yet, he thought, it was not all horror, not all agony. There was hope there, which was good; and comfort, which was something the Colonel knew he could use himself at that moment; and there was even a sense of fun, though whether the writer had been laughing at himself or at some prospective reader was unclear. The Colonel noticed that the pages had stopped moving beneath his fingers, and he leaned forward to read.

... haunted so often by the thought of songs, of warmth, of innocence, of simplicity, of comradeship, of all these and more that you speak of on your journeys here from Tetragrammaton to console me. If only they could know you as I do, understand the wonderful mission you have given me. You have ordained me, created of me a High Priest, nay, a god; through me you have chosen to save so many and I rejoice in the goodness I have been chosen to perform. Ah, my friends, my spirits of light and peace, my souls of Divine and Sefer, in the raising of my petrified spirit you have determined my salvation and through my efforts the salvation of ...

Colonel Maddox, for obscure reasons of his own, refused to turn the page, despite a longing to read again the story of Arthur Apple's attempted salvation. Instead, he closed the book and leaned back in his chair. 'Light and peace'. How dreadful it was that such passages, which held out nothing but the promise of serenity and hope, could be sullied and misconstrued to justify accusations of madness and evil. But then everything decent one did in life was twisted and misinterpreted and held to ridicule, was it not? Suddenly the Colonel felt the urge to cry, in anger more than in sorrow. He sighed as a strange, unfamiliar and overpowering sense of longing possessed him: he longed to have spoken with this shy, gaunt man in different circumstances; longed, too, to have had Arthur Apple explain to him how he had survived, how after all the injustices and belittlements he had remained capable of such great, if misplaced, sacrifice.

2

In the late afternoon of the last day of January 1979 two men, well muffled against the cold, penetrating wind, made their way past the two security guards into the hotel. One of the guards motioned as if to halt them, but changed his mind abruptly when he spotted the tiny warning signal from his colleague, and the hand that he had intended to use in restraint gave instead a salute that hinted at respect and brotherhood.

Inside, the two men walked briskly across the open foyer and made for the residents' lounge: as they entered, the head-waiter's eyes flickered in recognition and he gestured them to a table in the corner. Having taken their coats – each of which he gave a sharp shake to remove the last unmelted snowflakes – he hovered respectfully.

'Oh, a brandy, I think, Declan. Cold as the Arctic outside,' Seamus Reilly, the smaller, older of the two men said. His voice was quiet and precise, but friendly enough.

'A whiskey for me,' Martin Deeley decided. He would have preferred beer, but beer went straight through him when he was nervous.

'Oh – and Declan – '

'Mr Reilly?'

'Something to pick at.'

'Certainly, sir. Anything in particular?'

'Whatever you have handy.'

'Very good, sir.'

The waiter glided away and the two men sat in silence as Reilly took inordinate care over lighting a small, thin cigar. He blew the first lungful of smoke towards the ceiling, watching it as it curled upwards to join the painted clouds inhabited by grim-faced cherubs on the domed roof of the lounge. Finally: 'We're pulling you in for a while, Martin,' he announced casually, but in a tone which warned there was no room for dispute.

'I see.'

Reilly raised his thin eyebrows and smiled. 'You do?'

'No. I don't.'

'Ah.'

Deeley waited a few seconds for an explanation, but when none was forthcoming he leaned forward and said in a low, urgent voice, 'I thought I carried out – '

Seamus Reilly raised a small hand on which he knew he wore too many rings, halting further conversation as though stopping traffic, and gave the waiter the benefit of a thankful nod as the drinks and assorted nuts were placed carefully on the table. When the waiter had left Deeley tried again. 'I thought I carried out – '

'You did, Martin. I can assure you we have no complaints on that score. You have, as a matter of fact, been almost too successful,' Reilly conceded, swilling his brandy in his glass and sniffing it like a connoisseur. 'And so,' he continued, adopting the slightly arrogant, condescending tone he enjoyed using when delivering the orders of his superiors, 'our information is that the Brits are getting a little too interested in you.'

'Oh.'

'Well, to be truthful, not in you precisely; but they've been circulating a description which fits you pretty accurately.'

'Oh.'

'And, as I said, it has been decided to pull you in for a while. In out of the cold,' he added with a little smile, pleased with his literary touch.

'I see.'

'Also, there are some on the Committee who feel – and I am not one of them, I hasten to add – who feel that perhaps you enjoy killing too much, and that a little rest would be in your own interest.'

'That's bullshit, and you know it.'

'Me?' Reilly said in mock surprise and amazement. 'Me? I *know* nothing, Martin.'

'Not much, you don't. Nothing goes on but you know of it. Anyway, so what if I like doing what I'm good at?'

'Like?'

'Well – '

'Let me tell you something, Martin – and this is between you and me, a little friendly information, you can call it. You're supposed to get sick to the pit of your stomach every time you kill. I don't care who it is that's the target. The day you stop puking when you take someone's life you're no use to anyone. Least of all us. You get so you can't stop. You get careless, and that means trouble for everyone.'

'Jesus, I don't *enjoy* it, Seamus. I – '

'I think we'd better leave it there. The decision has been made.'

Martin shrugged his shoulders. 'That's that, then,' he said bitterly.

'Yes. That's that.'

'So what do I do? Sit on my – '

'Oh, don't worry. You are not about to sit on your arse all day as you were about to suggest. Far from it. We have something else we want you to do. Something that needs to be done and will keep you out of the way for a while. Out of the limelight,' Seamus Reilly explained, and gave another thin smile. 'Cheers.'

'Cheers.'

Martin Deeley lay back in the overstuffed, uncomfortable arm-chair and sipped his whiskey, one part of his mind taken up with wondering what job Reilly had in store for him, another, rather more energetic part furiously refuting the suggestion that he had in any way enjoyed performing his successful assassinations. The trouble was, and he was well aware of this no matter how he tried to convince himself otherwise, that although, doubtless, it had not reached the ecstasy that Seamus Reilly had intimated, there was indeed some truth in the accusation: there was, after all, something curiously pleasurable in the sensation of causing death, even if –

' – for the bookmaker's at last.' Seamus Reilly's voice suddenly penetrated his thoughts.

'What did you say?'

'I said,' Reilly replied testily, 'we have found our man for the bookmaker's at last. I wish you would listen when I speak, Martin. You know I hate repeating things.'

'Bookmaker's?'

'You see? You don't listen. We discussed this at length last month.'

'Oh, that. Yes, I remember.'

'Good. Anyway, we have our man to run it and we want you to work there and keep an eye on him.'

'Me? In a bookie's? Me?'

'That's right, Martin. You. In a bookie's. I'm sure you'll enjoy it no end. You will be his assistant, and it will be up to you to let us know if he shows any sign of – eh – changing his loyalties. We don't, of course, expect any complications, but you never know. And we need that shop to clear our funds.'

'Christ, Seamus, I don't know a damn thing about bookmaking. The only time I go near those places is to put something on the National.'

'You don't have to know anything. Anyway, you're a bright lad. You can learn. Think what an interesting interlude it will make when you come to write your life-story.'

'God Almighty! A bloody bookie's!'

'All you have to do is keep a watchful eye on our Mr Apple.'

'Oh, God, no. Not Arthur Apple.'

'Yes, Martin,' Reilly admitted.

'But he's a freak, Seamus.'

'Mr Apple – and you will kindly remember always to call him *Mister* Apple – may have his peculiarities, but he certainly is not a freak.'

'But he – '

Seamus Reilly once again raised his bejewelled hand to command silence, the corners of his mouth twitching peevishly. He was not a man who enjoyed having Committee decisions questioned or criticized.

'Mr Apple may well have left Her Majesty's diplomatic service under a small grey cloud, he may even be regarded as strange – eccentric, if you will – but he is invaluable to us.'

Deeley shook his head in disbelief.

'Furthermore,' Reilly continued, 'the fact that he is widely regarded as somewhat batty places him nicely above suspicion, and that is all that matters as far as we are concerned.'

'He's a bloody freak,' Martin insisted.

'Have it your way. He's a freak. But he's a freak you are going to work with. And you are going to show respect for him. We need him, Martin.'

'Jesus, we must be in a right bloody state if we need the likes of Apple.'

Reilly's eyes went cold. 'We can get any number of young killers to replace you, Martin,' he said, icily. 'It is much more difficult to get the right person to launder our funds, and we have that person in Mr Apple. He is an almost perfect cover for our operation.'

'Well, that's just bloody marvellous. You want me to – '

Reilly placed his glass on the table and leaned forward. 'We don't want anything, Martin. We are simply telling you that this is what you will do: you will work with Mr Apple, you will report to us everything that happens, and you will jump if Mr Apple says jump. Do I make myself perfectly clear?'

'Yes,' said Martin, sullenly.

'Excellent.' Seamus Reilly leaned back, smiling his most bene-volent smile: he was always gratified, if a little surprised, when he managed to bring matters to a satisfactory conclusion. 'One more little thing: naturally, Mr Apple has no inkling of your connection with us and we would like it to remain that way. As far as he is concerned, you were inherited by us with the rest of the fixtures when we took over the shop.'

'Lovely.'

'Yes, I thought you'd like that. Oh, come now, Martin,' Seamus Reilly added, deciding the time was ripe for a spot of largesse, 'it's only for a little while. Then you can get back to your slaughter.'

'When do I have to start this?'

'Oh, not for a couple of weeks. We're having the shop repainted for you – new heaters put in. You'll be very comfortable.'

'Oh, thanks.'

'You're welcome. Very welcome. And who knows, you might end up learning a thing or two from our Mr Apple.'

'No, thanks.'

'It's surprising, really,' Reilly went on, gazing upwards as though summoning his words from on high, 'very surprising, the sources from which one learns. I remember...' Or perhaps he didn't, since he abruptly broke off, finished his drink and stubbed out his half-smoked cigar. 'Well, that takes care of that. I must away. You stay and enjoy your drink. Have another one on me if you like. I'll be in touch next week.'

'Right.'

'Don't look so worried, Martin. You'll love every minute of it.'

'Sure.'

'See you.'

'Bye.'

Martin watched as the waiter glided forward to help Reilly into his coat and bow discreetly as he palmed the remuneration. He suddenly felt very exposed and self-conscious, sitting alone with the potted plants, the cavorting cherubs and whispered conversation for company – and his thoughts, although these were hardly entertaining. All the same, he took them with him along with his drink across the room to one of the enormous windows that boasted panoramic views of the battered city below. He stared out into the darkness, shielding his eyes from the reflection of the room behind. Strange, he thought, how even at night the city failed to conceal its torment, how even the occasional unbroken streetlight seemed to pinpoint some little scene of tragedy. He smiled thinly and studied the rows of abandoned houses, their windows covered with rusting corrugated iron or staring like empty eye-sockets, the barricaded police station, the sandbags and rolls of barbed wire like monstrous hair-curlers protecting the military post at the bottom of the hill, its perimeter lit like a film set by great arclights, and the cars driven recklessly, lights flashing, dipped and flashing again, as people scurried to their firesides and the dubious protection of their homes. To his right, a few yards from the entrance to the hotel, two soldiers, Scots Guards, a sergeant and his inferior, had stopped a woman and were searching her shopping-bag, in a cheerful enough way, it appeared. And it appeared to him then also that all the sacrifices (as he liked to think of them) he had made, all the hardship he had suffered to put an end to just such humiliation as the woman now accepted, had been futile. What had happened to him over the past few years seemed already to belong to a different age, to have been forgotten or, at best, to have sought refuge in some grotesque form of folklore.

And it was from a different age, it seemed, that his mother's face now peered at him from the darkness outside, her features distorted by the thickness of the glass, her grey hair pulled back and curled into her old-fashioned bun, her eyes defiant though not angry: pain dominated her face, and it was this same expression of pain she had worn when she told him, her voice flat, tired, and emotionless:

You're the man of the house now, Martin. Now that your Daddy's gone. It'll be on your shoulders to see to it that somebody pays.

Yes, Mam. I know.

And even if it means the killing of yourself and myself it'll be well worth it in the end.

Yes, Mam.

The evil has got to be driven away, Martin, and you're the one to drive it from this house.

Yes, Mam.

God knows the suffering is only sent to try us, but it wouldn't be right to lie down under it, would it?

No, Mam.

You'll be looking after things, then, Martin?

I will, Mam.

And seeing to it that your Daddy and Steven can lie in peace?

Yes, Mam.

That's my good boy. Ah, sure, God is good to have left me you in His mercy. Are your eggs the way you like them?

16

Martin Deeley left his mother's face to mouth on darkly to itself at the window, and signalled the waiter for his coat. He tipped the man generously (hoping it was more than Reilly had given) and left the hotel, curtly acknowledging the 'Goodnight, sir' of the security guards.

Out on the street, the coldness of the slush already penetrating his shoes, the darkness wrapped itself about him and he relaxed. He walked at a carefully rehearsed pace: not fast enough to appear to be hurrying, not so slowly that he could be accused of loitering, hugging the inside of the footpath, seeking the protection and anonymity of the shadows, his eyes constantly, automatically, darting in all directions, listening for unaccustomed sounds, grateful that the snow, now falling thickly again, offered an extra veil. He had much to think about, but he held his thoughts at bay with a conscious effort, keeping them tucked up warm in his mind until the late hours of the night when he could lie on his bed and summon them one by one from their cosy, secret crevices, dealing with each in turn, being precise and meticulous, using them as a tortuous cure for his insomnia.

3

Arthur Apple thought hard about the noise his feet made on the frost-hardened snow. It reminded him of something, of some other sensation that for the moment eluded him. At six in the morning it was quiet in Belfast, and the sound of his footsteps cracked loudly, painfully, over the snarling of military vehicles returning from night patrols, the friendly clink of milk-bottles and the slamming of doors as the city dragged itself reluctantly to wakefulness. It could, of course, have been construed as the pleasant enough sound of someone walking without a care on sand, perhaps, but the sight of that tall, stooped figure and the mournful, lined face with its grey, red-streaked eyes distorted by old-fashioned steel-rimmed spectacles would have quickly dispelled any illusions of pleasure.

Three soldiers of indistinguishable regiment stood nursing their rifles on the corner of Cliftonville Road, stomping their feet, their breath as thick as smoke in the crisp, sharp air. They stared with obligatory suspicion at Mr Apple until one of them recognized him and said so to his companions: then the tension lapsed in their eyes and they took to stomping their feet again. They continued to survey his progress, however, thinking perhaps that his mournful air of desolation epitomized the wretchedness of the place. Indeed, the appearance of this gaunt, dispirited figure seemed to lift their spirits perceptibly: the awkward, stilted walk and the agony etched into his face spoke of misery on a scale even greater than their own. For a few moments they seemed to forget the cold, the loneliness and the longing for their wives, forget, even, the possibility of imminent, unsatisfactory death that would probably be remarkable only as a misprint on some official communiqué. One of them (oddly, not the one who recognized him by sight) was moved to try a smile as Arthur Apple drew near, and say huskily, 'Cold.'

Mr Apple stopped as if shot, amazed that anyone should speak to him. 'Yes,' he answered quickly. 'Very cold.' He tried to smile in return but could muster only a tiny twitch, and he felt bad about this. He was genuinely sorry for these young soldiers, their youth haunted by the prospect of death; he was sorry, too, for the strange young men who died trying to drive them out; he felt sorry for everyone, but mostly for himself.

As he plodded along down the Antrim Road he passed a trio of gutted houses, the bricks about the windows blackened by fire and smoke, and he thought for one dreadful moment that he heard the screams of someone trying to escape. Abruptly, he shook his head and ran his cold, bony fingers across his brow, as though this physical gesture would banish such disturbing thoughts, if only temporarily; for Mr Apple was pursued by screams of one sort and another, and he was well, if sadly, aware that no amount of caressing could remove them. Still, he told himself, in a small, futile effort to brighten the day, there was something very noble in the way this city managed to survive and carry on.

He narrowed his eyes as the cold, watery sun glinted on his spectacles: then he paused, rocking on his feet, and chuckled to himself at his error: the sun (if, indeed, there was to be any) would not make an appearance for several hours yet, and he gave a small wave of apology to the streetlight as he passed beneath it and continued on his way. Odd, he thought, that he had been fooled like that, especially since he had the painful momentum of his body to shelter him from illusion: nodding, he alerted his mind against similar mistakes. And perhaps it was this conscious effort to stick with reality that sent the sudden searing pain through his head, as though someone had sneaked up from behind and clubbed him. He stumbled forward, one arm outstretched like one deprived of all vision, while horrific images cartwheeled in his mind, images of appalling humiliation, of faces twisted with derisive laughter, of fingers pointing with filthy nails. A small cry escaped him; then he blinked severely and stretched his eyes wide, grimacing wildly, and abruptly there was only the partially lit street again. It was as if nothing at all had befallen him, and he allowed a little sigh to scold his stupidity, his eyes returning to a fixed stare and adopting their customarily wan, morose cast. Seconds later he was his old self again, indulging in his regular morning speculation about what the day might promise. He lengthened his stride deliberately, determined to put a great distance between the present and his dreams of the night before (although he knew only too well that they had not been dreams but actual experiences, journeys and afflictions undertaken in the arms of darkness – but who would understand this?). It seemed to work, and his spirits rose. The withdrawal of the nocturnal phantoms was only gradual, but it was accomplished with a minimum of fuss. The multiple open sores on his memory began to clot and heal, leaving only scars which were thankfully less painful, though he knew only too well that they were liable to open wide again at any moment.

As he made his way down Duncairn Gardens and reached the corner of Lepper Street, at the far end of which stood his bookmaking shop, he paused, and inflicted on himself a moment's recollection of his troubled sleep. It was a silly ritual that seemed to take place every morning and which he regarded now as a kind of soul-cleansing. In itself, he admitted, it was absurd, since he could never remember with any accuracy what his dreams had been about, although they were certainly unpleasant and seemed to warn him incessantly of some tragedy yet to come. For more years than Mr Apple cared to recall he had suffered the nightly visitations of phantoms and ghouls of a most unfriendly nature, but since he had accepted this new occupation of bookmaker they were becoming more frequent. No, that was not altogether true: not more frequent. But certainly the clamourings had developed a new intensity, as though the nocturnal intruders had invited their more sinister relatives to attend and participate in his torment. Cerebral dry rot, I suppose, he thought, smiling wryly. At my age the brain starts to disintegrate. Pieces drop off and puff away like dust. 'Huh,' he grunted aloud, to disparage these unmedical reflections.

When he finally arrived outside the small, drab premises he could not help wondering what had become of the Frederick Bezant whose name was still painted above the shop. FREDERICK BEZANT. LICENSED BETTING OFFICE. EST. 1935, it proclaimed, in that subdued, slightly guilty way that peeling paintwork has a knack of insinuating. He could never quite rid himself of the idea that old Frederick still hovered over the place (envisioned for no specific or justifiable reason as a small, round Scotsman with a wily brain and a kind heart), peering over Mr Apple's shoulder, tut-tutting, appalled by the transactions he saw taking place, appalled, too, that his long-established and, no doubt, respectable firm should now be a clearing-house for currency of dubious origin. Mr Apple's eyes admitted a wintry twinkle: a small part of him could still enjoy a joke at his own expense. So what if this onetime minor diplomat in Her Majesty's service could now be found offering the odds on Her Majesty's horses? It was a living, and it left him time to pursue his stranger destiny; and it was, when all was said and done, the least humiliating joke that life had played on him.

Fortunately, the joke was not entirely on him, he thought, as he unlocked the door with a gigantic key, switched on the lights and picked up an oblong slip of paper urging him to get his mechanical parts from DOBSONS. Indeed, there was a sardonic twist here that some less self-pitying side of him enjoyed: this frowned-upon profession gave him the one thing he coveted: an emotional isolation that allowed him go about without being expected to like people or be liked by them. Indeed, in an ideal existence Mr Apple would have passed what was left of his life as a sort of spectre, seeing but unseen, thinking but unthought of, and almost everything he did bore witness to this quest for anonymity: his house (modest, terraced, identical to twenty others in an unremarkable road); his clothes (plain, discreet, undemanding of comment); even his voice was normally kept modulated to a level that gave no hint of enthusiasm or emotion. His body, alas, the one thing he most wanted to pass unnoticed, gave him away: that ridiculously long, lean, stooped, unwieldy body surmounted by that mournful, grey face with its great beaked nose and baggy eyes, and that awkward walk, stilted, not unlike that of a man recovering from broken legs or polio. Still, his neighbours never intruded: as far as they were concerned, Mr Apple was a quiet gentleman who lived alone now that his mother was dead, lived in comfortable monasticism, alone apart from the whimsical visits of his cat (a white-and-ginger one-eyed creature of erratic loyalty and with a nature as aloof as his own which, perhaps recognizing a kindred tormented spirit, had latched on to him and sometimes answered to the name he had given her: Chloe).

However, unbeknownst to snappy Mr Cahill, who lived on one side and dedicated his life to the culture of Zinnias and cacti, and to the quarrelling Mr and Mrs Bateman, who spent their time dithering about whether or not to quit Belfast and join their son in Australia, Mr Apple had two more lodgers, who dwelt happily enough with him, if only in his mind. They were the perfect tenants, appearing only when he summoned them, always on hand to lend an ear, dole out advice, console him. To Mr Apple they were very real: Mr Divine, a happy-go-lucky little creature, always joking and making him laugh, but capable, too, of penetrating observations; and Sefer, the curiously enigmatic Sefer, rather given to ponderous argument, inclined to pessimism, enjoying forecasts of doom, but entertaining company for all that. They accompanied Mr Apple everywhere, perched as it were on the shoulder of his mind, and he chatted to them quite openly, which presented problems from time to time. Even the unemotional Chloe had looked at him askance on more than one occasion. And just as Chloe depended for food on Mr Apple's weekly visit to the supermarket, so he, Mr Apple, depended for his sustenance on a regular Friday visit from a gentleman known only as Seamus. And Seamus, no doubt, depended on the bene-volence of some more senior shadowy Power for his daily bread, for that was how things seemed to work. Not that Mr Apple dwelt for long on the morality of his income. Far from it. He had discussed it once with his friends, and, while Sefer had warned of implications too dreadful to imagine, Mr Divine had chuckled away and told him to go ahead and enjoy it all. Mr Apple had weighed their advice with considerable care, but, as usual, had made up his own mind.

Eccentric he possibly was, lonely as a wandering ghost perhaps, pained and tormented if only by his own morbid fears and illusions certainly, but he was not a fool. He fully realized that the wages he received and accepted with gratitude were sullied, but only by the grime from the wings of what he liked to regard as his rescuing angels. And rescuing they had certainly been.

Mr Apple had spent most of his adult life shifting from one small diplomatic posting to another, usually tidying up the chaotic, undiplomatic mess left by one of his incompetent colleagues. He was well enough liked, since he was obliging and efficient and suitably insignificant. What had brought about his abrupt and unexpected retirement had been the subject of embarrassed conjecture for a while, but was usually dismissed with something like: Apple? Oh, yes. Something odd, wasn't it? Devils and that sort of thing, I believe. Mexico. All those little civil servants go potty in Mexico. Don't know the details. Can't have been too very exciting knowing Apple. Another drink?

Yet, despite the apparent offhand lack of concern, when Mr Apple returned home to Belfast he soon discovered that his former colleagues avoided him, discovered, too, that he had been placed in social isolation. For a while he lived with his mother, a chronic hypochondriac who fretted continuously that the smoke from explosions was spreading cancer, and was glad that his lifestyle had been frugal and that he had funds enough to keep him going for a while – when they expired he could always see to it that he did likewise. When, however, his mother died, it was as though whatever tenuous strands of reason had held him together had snapped, and he went to pieces. He stopped shaving and only washed when he thought of it, which wasn't all that often. He wore the same clothes day after day until they stank. His hair flowed down his neck in clotted ringlets, and he discovered that sufficient quantities of alcohol made the cast of his nightmares unrecognizable: apart from the haunting, tragic figure of a young man who persisted in dangling, blue-faced and swollen, to and fro across the blurred vision of his mind. Curiously, through all this, Mr Apple set out every second day to the countryside, taking a bus as far as it went and walking from there on until he reached the slowly collapsing wall surrounding a long-since-abandoned farmhouse. Not far from here a small copse stood out in an otherwise bleak landscape, but it was a sad landmark consisting of a few gaunt, dead elms, scrub and wild blackberry bushes the tendrils of which wrapped themselves haphazardly, forming a thorny barrier around a small clearing in the centre. Mr Apple, however, was not deterred: he forced his way through, disregarding the lacerations on his hands, and it was there in that deserted, desolate place that he settled down to have strange and garbled conversations with someone approaching God, assisted by his strange acolytes Divine and Sefer, who chanted obscurely in the background like ephemeral replicas of Tweedledum and Tweedledee. And whatever God he spoke to seemed to have qualms of conscience at the afflictions He had showered on Mr Apple, to have decided that enough was enough, for one day; relenting, He had sent a visitor to Mr Apple in the shape of a dapper, soft-spoken little man who gave his name simply, familiarly, as Seamus, who outlined a plan which, at the time, struck Mr Apple as being something approaching redemption. An unnamed consortium of Belfast businessmen wished to channel unreportable funds through their newly acquired bookmaking establishment, and they would very much like Mr Apple (with his experience in tact and if he would be so kind as to assist them) to manage and be the ostensible owner of that establishment, at least on paper.

And there it was: suddenly Mr Apple found himself needed again and he did not hesitate to accept. The arrangements were made with extraordinary ease. On subsequent visits Seamus worked out all the details, requiring only signatures of Mr Apple; an accountant structured the business and undertook to pay all the bills, and Mr Apple had a bright new future, the shadiness of which never entered his head or bothered him one whit: the consortiums and syndicates of the tattered city could do what they wanted as long as they promised not to violate his privacy – and they assured him they would not. At that stage, of course, the future did not enter Mr Apple's calculations, despite the dire whispered warnings of the morose, despondent Sefer: the immediate present, and, perhaps, on a good day and with the ever-optimistic Mr Divine to bolster him, the second right next to it, were as far as he allowed himself to think.

And that was all there was to it. He was, like Fred Bezant, established. Now, in the small isolated chamber behind the thick glass partition where he spent his days, he began his routine appraisal of the shop. He derived no pleasure from nor felt any sorrow for the patternless conglomeration of characters who wagered their money with him. If they lost, they lost; if they won, they won. It was all the same to him.

He settled himself at his desk, pushed his spectacles more comfortably on to the bridge of his nose, and stared idly at the small pile of betting-slips before him – winning ones that the punters would be in to collect almost as soon as he opened. The lucky ones. The faces that would come in smiling, relieved that they had supplemented their dole. The faces that would be able to confront their wives with a knowing, superior air. Mr Apple was forced to smile wryly to himself: he knew they would give it all back to him, probably that very day. It was, as Sefer had once remarked, not unlike life itself: you think you're ahead and all of a sudden the ground is whipped from under you and you are worse off than you ever were. But, then, Sefer revelled in dismal comparisons.

At the sound of the door slamming Mr Apple looked up, peering over the top of his thick lenses. His assistant – a term of fragile relevance – Martin Deeley trotted across the shop wearing a smile that suggested a truce in their uneasy relationship, suggested that they could, after all, both be on the same side. Mr Apple found himself smiling thinly back, measuring the strength of his smile to match the honesty of the young man's. He sighed inwardly. Perhaps, if it came to it, Martin would be on his side, but he doubted it. He was his watcher. Another shadow hovering over him, put there to keep an eye on things and make sure he fulfilled the obligations of his contract, reporting back with punctilious regularity to Seamus and the mysterious syndicate. Not that Mr Apple was supposed to know all this, and something warned him that it would be prudent to pretend he didn't.

'Morning, Mr Apple. Jesus, it's cold outside. And in here. Forgot the heating again, didn't you?'

'Good morning, Martin. Yes, I'm afraid I did.'

'Not to worry. I'll see to it. I'll see to everything. Just you leave everything to Martin Deeley.'

'Thank you.'

'Oh, that's alright. That's what I'm here for.'

'I'm sure it is.'

' — ?'

' — ?'

'Yes. Well, a cup of tea would go down well, wouldn't it?'

'Thank you, Martin.'

Martin Deeley switched on the heating and busied himself making tea, moving about the place (gathering two mugs and wiping them thoroughly with a cloth, sniffing the milk, selecting teabags) with that strange feline ease that made one wonder if his body was devoid of bone and constructed solely of fine muscle.

'I really don't know what I would do without you to look after me, Martin,' Mr Apple confessed, contriving to modulate his voice and exclude any hint of sarcasm; exclude, too, but from his mind, the uneasy, persistent feeling that his destiny was in some way linked to that of this young man who had been thrust upon him; exclude, also, from whatever region dealt with such things, the feeling of pleasure he experienced when Martin arrived each morning. For Mr Apple found deep and genuine pleasure in anything that was, to his way of thinking, beautiful, and there was little doubt that this nervous, arrogant, boastful, self-assured young watchdog could be seen to be beautiful. No doubt Martin Deeley would have agreed with this assessment, although he would have been the first to admit that his beauty was of an odd, lopsided variety. Each morning as he shaved he regretted – though in a good-humoured, mocking way – that he lacked the perfect features that would have made him outstanding and totally desirable. Still, with a subdued and perverse kind of vanity he was proud that his handsomeness wasn't blatant. He regarded his physical deficiencies as a challenge, and allocated considerable time each morning to making the best of what looks he had. His hair (thick, dark brown and usually unmanageable) was kept brushed in a sort of mini-Afro crown; a small scar from one side of his nose to the right-hand corner of his mouth constrained his upper lip to an almost permanent smile or sneer – which of these depended entirely on the light prevailing in his narrow, green, almost Oriental eyes. His nose, too, had an odd twist to it, and his rare laughter revealed very white but incredibly small teeth, as though nature had made a hash of things or decided, for unkind reasons, that his puppy-teeth would be quite adequate. Taken individually, his features bordered on the monstrous, but collectively they managed to present to a largely disinterested world a lopsided fascination that made his face very dear to him. It had also managed to outwit, or at least sidestep for the moment, the batterings of time's normal dosage of wear and tear, making him appear much younger than twenty-six.

'There you go, Mr Apple. I've even stirred it for you.'

'I don't take sugar, Martin, you – ' Mr Apple began tetchily.

'I know that. I just stirred the milk into the tea for you.'

'Oh. I'm sorry. Thank you, Martin.'

'Service with a smile. That's what I say,' Martin said, smiling extravagantly.

'I'm sure you do.'

'Oh, I do,' Martin insisted, flashing another exotic smile as though offering it as penance for his hypocrisy.

'You don't have to, you know.'

'Don't have to what?'

'Fuss over me. I mean, I can hardly give you the sack.'

Martin Deeley's wide smile froze, hung there for a moment, and was transformed into a grotesque leer as his eyes hardened. A small cruel light like that of a lynx about to make a kill flickered in them.

'I mean, how could I possibly manage without you,' Mr Apple continued, enjoying the discomfort he had created, yet annoyed with himself for having caused it.

27

'Oh. Well, I don't really fuss over you, Mr Apple. I just try to please,' Martin replied, his smile defrosting, and he made a great business of pouring his own tea.

'I see,' sighed Mr Apple. 'Well, it's very kind of you to take an old man under your wing.'

'My pleasure.'

And he almost meant it. There was, indeed, something very pleasurable and satisfactory in being useful to the Cause (as he still somewhat archaically thought of it), if only as what he glumly regarded as an internal spy, particularly since he was certain his current occupation was only temporary: he was, after all, was he not, far too useful and successful at riskier pursuits that called upon his wits and nerve and reflexes and stunning accuracy? Certainly he was. Oh, yes, they would very certainly need his prowess again. Who could replace him, despite Reilly's catty remark about there being an abundance of 'killers'? For more than three years Martin Deeley had been their most successful assassin, with at least seven unsolved killings to his credit. Yet, oddly, despite his reputation of being passionless and cold-blooded, there was a deep-rooted nervousness in him, a sense of vulnerability and terror. He never dared question this feeling or delve too deeply into its roots, for this would have been to admit its existence. But had he questioned it he would, no doubt, have recognized its growth as being nurtured by the memory of that horrific night when both his father and older brother had been senselessly slaughtered (quite mistakenly as it turned out) as terrorist sympathizers. Martin had been only fourteen then, and as the years passed that bloody scene had clouded in his memory. But a sharp residue remained, a lingering web of cold panic that stretched across his mind, and this was sufficient to leave him with his peculiarly callous outlook. All his actions were performed simply as chores to be fulfilled, albeit to the best of his ability, and this applied equally to creating havoc, making love and inflicting death. On those rare occasions when the strain of his curious existence seemed on the brink of getting the better of him, when he became tense – as he described those moments when he broke into a cold sweat and felt like curling up and hugging himself and sobbing quietly – he would trot along to the nearest Catholic church to kneel before the crucifix, not praying, but indulging in a gruesome daydream. He would imagine the suspended Christ as the man who had murdered his father and brother, and he would smile cruelly, gleening an exotic satisfaction from the thought of the murderer's tearing flesh. And this morbid, imaginary little drama, so precisely enacted in his mind, so vivid and lurid that his own flesh would crawl, would exhaust him to such a degree that it diffused his tenseness, calmed him, satisfied any immediate desire for revenge, and allowed him to leave the church, if not refreshed, at least in that frame of mind that allowed him to continue his existence with apparent equanimity.

And so, when Seamus Reilly had suggested that he 'retire' for the moment from his best work and adopt this new role, he threw himself into it and invested it with an importance it hardly merited. Indeed, once there in that sad, squalid little shop that the new coat of paint had done little to prettify, rubbing shoulders with the gentle, mild, rather insignificant man he had so brashly regarded as a freak, he had become quietly obsessed with his job. For it struck him – and he had several times tried to explain this to himself and failed – that there was some unfathomable mystery attached to Mr Apple which linked their lives inexorably.

'Well, it would please me, Martin,' Mr Apple was saying, his eyes fixed on his mug of tea as though addressing some reflection of Martin in the liquid, 'if you would clean the marker-board and get the betting-sheets ready for the day.'

'Right. No sooner said than done.'

'And pin up the *Sporting Life*.'

'Yessir,' Martin said, saluting.

'Go on, then.'

'I'm going.'

But not yet, apparently: he stood by Mr Apple's shoulder, watching as the bony fingers thumbed through the winning slips. 'One of these days you'll go blind counting all your winnings, Mr Apple,' he remarked innocently.

'Losses, Martin. Losses,' Mr Apple told him with equal innocence, aware that this was the overture to their daily little game of pretending neither knew the other's purpose.

'Oh, sure.'

Mr Apple looked up and peered over the top of his spectacles, smiling mischievously. 'I'll have to explain to you how it all works one day,' he said.

'Yes. I'd like that, Mr Apple. I'd like to get more involved.'

'*More* involved – ?'

'Yes. You know – '

'Oh, I know, Martin,' Mr Apple informed him, staring into his eyes.

For several moments neither of them spoke. Finally, wilting slightly, unable to sustain prolonged contact, Martin asked out of the blue: 'Tell me something – does it ever worry you – taking money from all these suckers? I mean, you know half of them can't afford to lose. Doesn't your conscience bother you?'

'Conscience?' Mr Apple asked, feigning surprise.

'Yes. Conscience.'

'Who's got conscience?' Mr Apple asked, quietly mocking.

' – ? Everyone's got conscience!'

'Oh, do they now? Well, that's very interesting.'

'You know everyone's got conscience.'

Mr Apple removed his spectacles and proceeded to polish the lenses with a large handkerchief he produced from his sleeve. 'I'll tell you something you already know, Martin. A man can jettison his conscience with the greatest ease if the fit takes him,' Mr Apple said sadly. 'Or have it numbed and made useless by others,' he added in a soft, distant voice, as though the afterthought struck him as particularly melancholy. Then he shook his head and replaced his glasses firmly on his nose, indicating that the conversation was over.

But as so often before he was wrong. 'That's a pretty morbid philosophy, Mr Apple,' Martin decided to say in the tight, slightly menacing tone he adopted when he felt people were getting at him.

'Philosophers now, are we?' Mr Apple wanted to know. 'Morbid?'

he asked. 'Mmm. Perhaps it is. True, nevertheless. Anyway, everyone gambles one way or another. You gamble everytime you take a breath.'

'That's different,' Martin said, with a small, frustrated sniff. 'You've *got* to breathe.'

'Some people have *got* to back horses. In this business you've got to work on the psychosomatic theory,' Mr Apple announced pompously, suddenly aware that he was enjoying himself again. 'Betting makes people happy if they think it makes them happy. And there are people who are only happy when they are miserable – don't you ever forget that. Besides – ' Mr Apple took off his long-suffering spectacles again and used them to stab home his next point, 'besides, who thinks about me when I lose? Answer me that. Who cares about my misfortune when they collect their winnings? To hell with him, they say. He's the bookie. *I'm* supposed to have all the ethics and all the pity. Huh. Who wants *them* for a monopoly?'

Martin Deeley shifted his feet and laughed nervously. Somehow the conversation had veered away from the course he had set for it and was escaping his control; worse, there appeared to be a darker side to everything Mr Apple said that for the moment eluded him.

'Oh, you're a wicked man, Mr Apple,' he confided, contriving to make his accusation sound like a little joke.

Alas, Mr Apple decided to see nothing amusing in it. 'Me wicked?' he demanded shrilly. '*Me* wicked?'

'I only meant it as – '

'Oh, never mind,' Mr Apple interrupted wearily, suddenly feeling very tired. Then a strange little glimmer came into his eyes and he continued: 'I'll tell you another thing, Martin,' almost whispering, as though in an odd way he hoped Martin would not hear, his voice sad. 'I think there is something, some demon deep inside you, that has turned you upside down. You make no allowances for humanity. White is white. Black is black. That's the way it is with you, Martin. No shades. No variations. You've got to learn to be flexible or you're doomed.'

'I – '

'And there's a – ' Mr Apple hesitated, mouthing, his fingers moving in strange jerky spasms as though assisting his mind to grope for the word, 'there's a hunger – yes, that's near enough – a hunger in your eyes that frightens me to death.'

In the tense, strained silence that followed this grim observation Mr Apple almost regretted having spoken. True, there was certainly something wild and evil in those green, half-closed eyes, a look of malice and unswerving direction; and yet there was an unnerving quality of pain and sadness there too, and both sadness and pain were old familiars of Mr Apple's. It had struck him before from time to time that the young man who now stood so jauntily and defiantly in front of him, his nostrils flared, the blood slowly draining from his face, seemed to have, tucked away in the shadowy and unused recesses of his soul, a disarming innocence, a strange cleanliness of spirit. Undoubtedly he had committed acts of horrendous outrage – the full atrocity of which Mr Apple knew he had yet to discover – and had done so without so much as turning a hair, had committed them brutally and with probable satisfaction. And yet: somehow Mr Apple could not shake off the impression that there was a strong loyalty in Martin that would prevent him attempting certain horrors. To Mr Apple's mind even one redeeming feature stood for a great deal: in his experience there were very few people who could be credited with any limitation of evil.

'No need for you to be frightened of me, Mr Apple.' Martin's voice slipped amicably into his thoughts.

'I'm glad to hear it.'

'I wouldn't hurt a fly.'

'It's not the flies I'm worried about.'

'Hah.'

And with that Martin was around the partition and into the shop, grinning his head off, skipping about, cleaning the marker-boards and pinning up the racing journals with that feline agility that so amazed Mr Apple. A bemused expression crossed Mr Apple's face as he watched the young man – the boy, as he seemed destined to think of him, perhaps because Sefer in one of his more glib moments had commented that he was not unlike the Minstrel Boy. He was trying in vain to recall the distant sensation of youth: his face softened, and for a moment all impressions of pain and sorrow receded from his features. But then they were back. worse than before, as was always the case after such respites, back like a burning darkness folding over his recollections. The deep, jagged lines on his forehead and cheeks returned to their habitual formations, criss-crossing his flesh like welted scars as he frowned over the betting-slips again and tried, as he usually did, to put faces to the writing on them.

How long he was involved in this harmless pastime before he was quickly brought down to earth by the loud slam of the door he could not tell. He glanced up, and made a determined and fruitful effort to keep a bland face as he watched the two soldiers cross the shop with a fretful swagger, their rubber-soled boots making tiny screeches on the linoleum. It struck him, for no good reason, that they could have been two of the Scots Guards he had seen that morning, but he could not be sure. Not that it mattered. They were all the same despite their differences in uniform: frightened (although they would never have admitted it, regarding fear as synonymous with weakness), lonely (usually hiding this in raucous shouts and ribald tomfoolery whenever the occasion permitted) young men who made slightly frenetic attempts to be friendly with the hostile natives.

Mr Apple switched his gaze for a second to Martin Deeley and was relieved to note that he was assiduously wiping yesterday's betting returns from the boards with a damp rag, just wiping and wiping away with a curiously menacing motion, as though erasing somewhat more than the figures before him. Mr Apple felt certain he could see the hairs bristle on the back of his neck.

'You Mr Bezant?' one of the soldiers wanted to know, politely enough.

Mr Apple rose with what he hoped was dignity and came close to the glass partition. 'Mr Bezant is but a name. A name peeling over our door. He is, alas, no longer with us,' he explained, spreading his hands in a curiously Zionistic gesture. 'I'm Mr Apple. Can I help?

You want to place a bet?'

'You the owner?'

'You could say that, yes.'

'I mean, you make the decisions?'

'Oh, I certainly make the decisions,' Mr Apple assured him.

'Ah, well, what we wanted to know...'

But whatever it was they wanted to know was not immediately to be revealed. The soldier turned from Mr Apple (who discreetly contemplated the hidden mysteries of the ceiling) to join his colleague, and indulged in whispered discussion. Mr Apple waited patiently, occupying the lengthening pause with watching Martin Deeley, who had finished wiping and stood motionless by the clean board, the damp rag suspended in mid-air, his eyes unblinking and filled with veiled threats as he, in turn, surveyed the whispering soldiers. Finally a decision was reached, and the spokesman returned to Mr Apple, grinning sheepishly.

'What we wanted to know is if we left some cash with you could we phone in some bets from the barracks? We're not really allowed in here, see?'

Mr Apple felt his breath ease itself from his lungs and pass through his lips in an almost audible hiss, suddenly realizing how tense he had been. With relief he noted from the corner of his eye that Martin, too, had relaxed, and was recleaning the already clean boards. Mr Apple gave a little cough and became businesslike.

'Certainly. We have quite a number of clients who prefer to bet by telephone for one reason or another. And we like to do all we can to help the military, don't we Martin?' he added, on the spur of the moment feeling recklessly mischievous.

'What?' snapped Martin, who had heard well enough.

'Help the military. The good men who are here to protect us from hooligans and suchlike.'

'Oh, sure,' Martin said, and flashed a venomous look across the room.

'I'm glad you think of us like that,' the soldier said innocently.

'But how else should we think of you?' Mr Apple asked, aware that he was perilously close to pushing his luck.

The question seemed to dumbfound the soldier, as though it had never occurred to him that he should be anything but hated. Then: 'Most people don't like us, you know,' he said seriously. 'They seem to think we shouldn't be here at all.'

'Oh, dear, me,' Mr Apple said, shaking his head. 'Did you hear that, Martin?'

'I heard.'

'What strange notions people have, and no mistake. Why, you're only here to keep the peace, to maintain law and order, isn't that all?'

This apparently friendly interpretation of their role seemed to embarrass both soldiers, and they shuffled and grinned to alleviate their discomfort.

'Martin, my very able assistant, will look after you gentlemen,' Mr Apple told them pleasantly. 'Leave that, Martin, and look after these gentlemen, will you?'

Martin Deeley looked as though he could have cheerfully strangled Mr Apple, but he left the board and walked behind the counter to stand facing the soldiers, his face now expressionless.

'How much do you want to leave?' he demanded.

'Twenty – no, make it twenty-five quid.'

'Huh. Big punters. Name?'

' – ?'

'Name?'

'What do you – '

'Shit. I don't want your bloody rank and serial number, just – '

'Martin.' Mr Apple curled the name upwards in mild rebuke.

'We have to have your name so we know who is calling when you pick up the telephone and dial our number and tell us what money you want to put on what horse in what race, don't we?' Martin said, his voice laden with condescension.

'Oh.'

'Yes. Oh. So?'

'Salmon.'

'As in fish?'

'Hah,' the soldier laughed goodnaturedly, though he had heard the remark a thousand times before. 'As in fish,' he confirmed.

'You be making all the bets?'

'Yes. Or him.'

'Great.' Martin sighed with exaggerated exasperation. 'And what's his name?'

'Dukham.'

'As in?'

'Yes. As in.'

'Doesn't he speak?'

'He speaks.'

'But not a lot, eh?'

'Not a lot.'

'Strong silent type, I suppose,' Martin supposed, not bothering to conceal the sarcasm in his voice, nor, indeed, the sneer that crossed his mouth.

'Right. I think we've got that straight. Twenty-five pounds for Salmon and Dukham. Here's your receipt with our phone number on it,' he added, and handed over the slip of paper. 'And, by the way, we don't give credit – when you've lost your twenty-five that's it until you leave some more.'

'*If* we lose.'

'You'll lose.'

'Thanks.'

'Don't mention it. And thank *you* for your business, gents. Now if you'll excuse me I have work to do.' Fucking Scottish bastards.

'Thanks for your help.' Both soldiers, perhaps from force of habit, made as if to salute, but it was a half-hearted effort and fizzled out into something approaching a wave. With that they strode out, trailing another whispered conspiratorial conversation behind them.

'You handled that very well indeed, Martin,' Mr Apple announced without looking up.

'You did that on purpose, didn't you?'

'Did what? Asked you to help by serving the customers? But I thought that was why you were here – to assist?'

'You know I hate the bastards.'

'Really? Good heavens, I had no idea.'

'Like hell you didn't.'

'I didn't even realize you knew them,' Mr Apple said.

'I don't.'

'You don't?' Mr Apple repeated mockingly. 'But how can you possibly hate someone you don't know, Martin?'

'You know what I mean.'

'I wish I did.'

'You know a hell of a lot more than you let on, too.'

'Whatever do you mean by that?' Mr Apple was anxious to know.

But whatever reply might have been forthcoming was forestalled by the door to the shop slamming again. It was eleven o'clock, the hour when the lure of the betting-shop became strongest, and the day's traffic began in the shape of an old, bent man in a flat cap and carrying a plastic shopping-bag, who crept across the shop to the far wall as though pushed from behind by the enormous hand of reluctant optimism. He glued his watery eyes to the prognostications of *Sporting Life*, a rebellious nerve jumping spasmodically below his right jaw. Martin lounged against the counter and watched for a while, then shifted his gaze restlessly, finally allowing it to settle on the small bald patch on the crown of Mr Apple's head, which nodded away, methodically mournful, as he fingered again his accumulating losses.

'Another customer,' Mr Apple said aloud without losing the rhythm of his arithmetic.

' – ?'

'Behind you.'

'Oh.'

Martin turned to the counter and took the yellow slip of paper which the man in the cap offered: a fifty-pence accumulator on nine horses. 'Some bet,' he remarked, trying not to sound patronizing and almost succeeding.

'Jonjo and Francome,' the man pointed out. 'I always back Jonjo and Francome. Don't care what they ride.'

'Good, are they?'

'The best,' the man said with fierce conviction. 'And I've a feeling they'll win for me today,' he added confidentially, as though revealing a dark but profitable secret, as though, too, both jockeys had only his interest at heart.

'Sure to,' Martin said.

'And if not today there's always tomorrow.'

'That's true. Well, good luck.'

'That's all it takes, sonny,' the man told him happily, and shuffled out of the shop. His gait was more confident now that he had sealed his fate.

'Another big punter,' Martin remarked. 'Bahamas this year on the profits, Mr Apple.'

'Don't mock,' Mr Apple scolded gently. 'Every little helps.' There were times when he amazed even himself with the way he treated the business as if it was his own, worrying about losses, cheered by gains – as though any of this mattered to him.

'I nearly told him to take his fifty pence and stuff it – he *can't* win.'

Mr Apple put an elastic band round the counted dockets and patted them flat before turning round. '*I* know that, Martin. *You* know that. So who are we? *He* thinks he *can* win. That's all that matters. Why try and destroy the man's faith in his own judgement?'

'That's a load of crap.'

'Why so? He walked in here and made his choice and had the courage to follow it through despite the odds against him.' Mr Apple peered as usual over his spectacles at Martin, and the solemnity of his tone seemed to suggest there might be something significant in what he had said.

'Some judgement.'

'Yours is better?'

'I don't – '

'Oh, not about horses. You're far too bright a specimen to indulge in that sort of thing. No, I meant about your own preoccupations. You make your own sane judgements and back them up? Of course you do. But you're a very clever chap, aren't you? You want to know something? You're so fierce you can't even see the truth when it stares you in the face.'

'Thanks.'

'The truth is – '

The door slammed again. Mr Apple stopped abruptly and stared at the man in his late twenties who had entered the shop, followed by a woman of approximately the same age. What was remarkable about them was that they were almost identical, even to the haunted look in their eyes; remarkable, too, was the impression they gave of being inseparable, as though the man was doomed to be eternally followed by some transvestite image of himself. As he came closer, Mr Apple put on his glasses and recognized him as a client who had lost considerable money the day before; had indeed lost regularly for several days.

'Mr Apple,' the man said, with a small nod.

Mr Apple came to the counter and waited, sensing unpleasant-ness.

'You know me,' the man stated in a voice that dared contradiction.

'I've seen you, certainly,' Mr Apple allowed, spreading his hands palms upwards and giving a little shrug.

'I'm Terry Duggan.'

'Mr Duggan.' Mr Apple allowed a whisp of a smile.

'My wife.' Duggan indicated behind him without turning round.

'Mrs Duggan,' Mr Apple said, allowing his wisp of a smile to return momentarily, although this time it seemed to be more sympathetic.

'I was in yesterday,' the man began.

'I remember.'

'And he lost everything we had,' Mrs Duggan interrupted. She pushed past her husband and pressed her gaunt, drawn face against the glass. 'He lost *everything*,' she whispered, but with such intensity it sounded like a roar.

So that was it.

'Shut up,' Duggan ordered his wife. 'Sorry, Mr Apple,' he apologized; more, it seemed for his evasiveness than for having been cut short.

'I understand,' Mr Apple told him, and he did.

'Can you help us?'

'Help you?'

'Oh, boy!' Martin Deeley snorted in the background.

'Quiet, Martin,' Mr Apple said quickly. 'How can I help you?'

'Lend us some of the money back until next Thursday.'

'We have nothing to eat,' Mrs Duggan explained with a wail.

'Shut up, Molly,' Duggan told his wife again.

'And I suppose the next thing is the houseful of kids dying of starvation,' Martin put in. 'Hey, this isn't some bloody moneylender's, you know,' he added, on the one hand fulfilling the duty imposed on him by Seamus Reilly, and on the other protecting Mr Apple, whom he felt would be a sucker for this sort of sob-story.

'I'll deal with this, Martin,' Mr Apple said, half-smiling. 'How much do you need?'

Immediately, a small light of greed flickered in Terry Duggan's eyes. He looked away for a moment; when he faced Mr Apple again all trace of it was gone, replaced by his former misery. 'Twenty?' he suggested optimistically.

'I'll let you have five.'

'Five!' Molly Duggan shrieked, her humiliation making her belligerent. 'What can we hope to get for five pounds?' she demanded.

'Can't you make it fifteen?' Duggan asked, prepared to haggle.

'Five,' insisted Mr Apple, who wasn't.

'Ten?'

'Five.' Mr Apple was getting annoyed as he swivelled his face imperviously between the two supplicants.

'You're *mean*,' Molly Duggan screamed at him, as if this was her most appalling condemnation.

'Yes,' agreed Mr Apple. 'I'm mean.' He turned to walk back to his desk.

'All right. Five,' Duggan said quickly.

'Shit!' Martin exclaimed. 'Don't you give them anything, Mr

Apple. Don't you give them a goddam penny.'

But Mr Apple had made up his mind. He reached into the money-drawer, took out five one-pound notes and shoved them across the counter, quickly withdrawing his hand as Molly Duggan lunged at them.

'What the hell did you give in to them for?' Martin demanded as the door slammed behind them.

Mr Apple blinked and gave a little shrug. 'I don't really know,' he confessed, staring at the empty shop that the Duggans' wretchedness seemed to have left even shabbier. He rubbed his eyes in a gesture of weariness. 'Pity?' he suggested meekly.

'Pity, my arse.'

'I really don't know, Martin.' And that was the truth.

'Well, it's five pounds you can kiss goodbye. You'll never see it or them again.'

Mr Apple brightened perceptibly. 'That could be good enough reason in itself, don't you think, Martin?' he asked, keeping his face impassive.

'Very funny. It's no way to run a business.'

'It will come out of my own pocket. My good deed for the day.'

'Huh.'

It was something of a relief after the Duggans when May van Dyke made her boisterous appearance in the doorway. She was small and fat with hard brown skin like tanned leather, and she had long since abandoned any attempt to control the growth of her dark moustache. Her husband, a floundering Dutch seaman whom she had only too willingly befriended, was Jewish, and through her long years of unstable marriage May had taken on many of his mannerisms. Perhaps by so doing she felt she was getting something out of the relationship. 'Here we go again, Mr Apple. Another small donation towards your Rolls Royce.' She passed over an intricate collection of Yankees and Patents that she had worked out with great precision. She had once made a considerable killing and this had whetted her appetite: if she could do it once she could do it again, couldn't she? She was a steady, reliable client, and a pleasant one despite her tendency to chatter endlessly.

'You'll break me one day, May,' Mr Apple told her in mock anguish.

'Sure I will,' May agreed, and there was an edge to her voice, despite her smiling face, that suggested she meant it.

'You'll have to give *me* a job then. I could be your financial adviser.'

'You've got it, Mr Apple. And you can bring that one along, too,' May told him, indicating Martin, who blushed furiously. 'He could advise me on other things,' she concluded, laughing raucously.

'We needn't worry, then, need we?' Mr Apple smiled, enjoying Martin's embarrassment.

'Hah,' said May, and Mr Apple felt she would have tweaked his cheek if she could have reached him. 'I'll be in tomorrow to collect, you hear?

'I hear, May.'

'Byeeeee,' May sang, and waddled out of the shop clutching her handbag (in which, it was rumoured, she kept her more valuable trinkets in a small plastic bag: scraps of cheap jewellery, foreign notes and coinage, and a scapula to remind her of her long-forgotten faith) to her bouncing, unsupported breasts.

'Goodbye, May,' Mr Apple called, stapling the bet and placing it on top of the capped man's optimistic accumulator. 'Twelve eleven,' he murmured, glancing at the electric clock on the wall.

'And thirty-eight seconds,' Martin supplied.

Mr Apple stretched. Just under an hour before racing started.

The Extel had just started its waking crackles when three men walked in: Mr Apple had seen two of them before, but it was the third who claimed his attention. He was not particularly well dressed, but he wore his clothes with the air of a man who should have been. He had a cold, aloof bearing that Mr Apple recognized and associated with many men he would have preferred to forget. With his clean white shirt, his Windsor-knotted, striped tie, polished shoes and neatly pressed trousers the man could have been mistaken for an underpayed civil servant with an interest in, say, moths. Until the immobile face caught your eye: that pallid, stoatlike face dominated by pale-blue, opaque eyes filled with restless, wary suspicion. And in the menacing radiance of that face Mr Apple's situation took on its true meaning, and he found himself dizzy and trembling.

The man, flanked at close quarters by his two companions, crossed swiftly to the counter and summoned Mr Apple's attention by pointing one finger in the air. 'Everything all right?' he demanded abruptly in a surprisingly high-pitched voice.

'Yes,' replied Mr Apple, feeling his chin and sighing inwardly with relief that he had remembered to shave.

'Payouts?'

'A few. Nothing very big.'

'How big?'

'Three hundred, give or take.'

'Not much.'

Mr Apple shrugged his shoulders by way of apology for the stupidity of his clients. 'No. Not much.'

The man pursed his lips and thought for a moment. Finally he removed a thick brown envelope from his inside pocket and passed it over the counter. 'Spread this out,' he ordered. 'Eight, maybe ten bets on losing favourites.'

Mr Apple took the envelope. 'I know how to spread it,' he said. The man looked taken aback by this remark, and he frowned again. He allowed a thin smile to bypass his eyes and make its faltering appearance on his lips. 'I'm sure you do.'

'Yes. I do.'

'Good. Well, I want all that gone by today. There'll be plenty more this week and we don't want any of it hanging about.'

'Very well,' Mr Apple said.

'In fact you'll be seeing a lot of me in the future,' the man went on. 'We have had a number of satisfactory transactions.'

'I'm glad to hear it.'

'So, as I say, you'll be seeing a lot more of me.'

'I look forward to that,' Mr Apple lied.

'I'm sure you do. By the way, the usual for yourself is in there – in a separate envelope.'

'Thank you.'

'You've earned it – so far. We always pay well for a job well done.' There was in his politeness that icy quality of condescension that killers seem to possess, as if their superiority were of such standing that they could afford largesse towards their victims. 'Nothing else you need?'

Mr Apple shook his head. 'Not a thing.'

'Good. If you do need anything, let us know.'

'I will.'

'Good,' the man said again. 'Good. I won't keep you any longer,' and true to his word he left the shop, halting only briefly for the door to be opened for him.

When he had gone Mr Apple found himself with a dreadful headache. He tried to rid himself of it and the memory of those lifeless eyes by fussing about, overdoing his interest in some customers (who now came fast and furious into the shop), disputing nothing, ridding himself of others by pretending to be overworked.

The squawking voice of the commentator filled the shop and Mr Apple's consciousness as he took bets, paid out on winners and forged betting-slips to dispose of the contents of the envelope, his eyes watering as the shop filled with cigarette smoke and the distinctive stench of nervous tension. Occasionally he glanced at the faces of his clients: they wore stoicism like armour, refusing to let even the smallest expression reveal that they were losing. All through the long afternoon they came and went, some staying longer than others, the shop groaning under the weight of their frustrations. And through all this Mr Apple could feel the pale-blue eyes boring into him. Watching him, too, but in a different way, he could feel the eyes of Martin Deeley, who as he marked the prices for each race and wrote up the results wondered to himself what really went on behind Mr Apple's bland expression. There was a secret there, he was sure, and something warned him that he would not like it when he discovered what it was. But discover it he would.

As the last despondent customer left the shop, and Martin clattered about tidying up, the telephone rang, and Mr Apple went to answer it.

'Mr Apple?'

'Speaking.'

'Seamus.'

'Yes.'

'Our replacement man was in today.'

'Yes, he came.'

'Everything in order?'

'Yes.'

'No problems?'

'None.'

'No complaints?'

'Complaints?'

'He was respectful?'

Mr Apple suddenly longed to laugh, but he managed to contain himself.

'Yes, he was respectful.'

'Excellent. We don't want anyone to upset you.'

'Thank you. He was respectful,' Mr Apple said again.

'Excellent,' the voice of Reilly repeated, and went on: 'Our syndicate has come into some rather unexpected profits this week, so we will have quite a bit of business.'

'He told me.'

'Oh. Good.' Reilly sounded peeved. 'The syndicate also wish me to express our satisfaction with your – eh – management.'

Mr Apple said nothing.

'Mr Apple?'

'Yes?'

'Oh, I thought you were gone. I was saying – '

'Yes. I heard. Thank you.'

'Right. Well, if everything is going smoothly – '

'It is.'

'Fine. I'll be in touch. By the way, anything you need?'

'Nothing. Thank you.'

'Sure?'

'Quite sure.'

'Well, if ever there is...' Reilly allowed his voice to trail off, suggesting that anything without reservation could be supplied.

'Thank you.'

And with that the phone went dead.

Mr Apple was still holding the receiver in his hand when he noticed Martin standing by his shoulder. 'Martin,' Mr Apple began, but immediately regretted it.

'Yes, Mr Apple?'

Mr Apple replaced the receiver and sighed. 'Nothing.'

'Oh, come on. You were going to say something.'

'Nothing of importance. It doesn't matter.'

'Christ, it really bugs me when you do that: start something and then stop.'

'The story of our lives, Martin.'

'Shit.'

The two of them stood quietly in the deserted shop, and perhaps it was because both of them felt oddly secure in this atmosphere of despair that they felt an intimacy neither of them welcomed.

'All those suckers,' Martin said, to break the silence.

Mr Apple nodded and started tidying his desk.

'Well, I'll be off, then. See you in the morning, Mr Apple. Have a good night and don't do anything I wouldn't do.'

Mr Apple smiled. 'You can count on that, Martin. Good-night.'

Mr Apple, alone, started to put the shop to bed, as he humorously liked to think of it. He put the takings in the safe and switched on the burglar alarm, feeling, as he did every evening, an intense desire to set it off. Instead, he put on his heavy overcoat, his scarf and his hat, and walked lightly across the shop to the door, tip-toeing almost, absurdly scared that he might stand on someone's shattered illusions and dreams of instant wealth. He put out the lights and shut the door behind him, rattling it to make certain it was securely closed.

Well done, my friend, said Mr Divine gaily. Now we can off home and enjoy ourselves.

Same old boring evening, opined Sefer miserably.

Life is what you take out of it, Mr Divine said accusingly.

Rubbish, declared Sefer.

'He's right, you know,' said Mr Apple, and coughed hurriedly as a passer-by glanced at him curiously.

He stood for a moment in the doorway breathing in the fresh, bitter night air, and braced himself for the long trudge through the snow. Then, straightening his shoulders in the manner of a man about to take the plunge, he began walking away from the grey little street towards his home and the inevitably ravenous, complaining Chloe.

4

Of course, as he might have guessed, nothing was to be as simple as that; how could he have expected it to be? Even what should have been a reasonably unhazardous journey from one location to another was to be filled with frustrations, it seemed.

Mr Apple plodded on, bending his body as though shaping it aerodynamically to cut through the wind, the cold, muddy slush making his poor feet ache, making him think of concentration camps and long marches made by the prisoners. Galoshes would be an answer, he advised himself. And it was while his mind pondered those old-fashioned rubber overshoes and conjured up amusing visions of himself wearing them that suddenly, as he rounded the corner of the Antrim Road, he was pounced upon, and, before he fully realized what was happening, he found himself spreadeagled against the hard, cold brick wall, and was being frisked and searched. Nothing was said: the silence and rapid efficiency of the soldiers gave them a dark malevolence out of proportion to their activities. As one searched, two others, one on either side of him, pointed their rifles in the general direction of his knees. Only when the one searching him was satisfied that he was, for the moment at any rate, harmless did one of the others make a gesture of dismissal with his gun. 'You can go,' he said.

It was this casual attitude to his humiliation that made Mr Apple feel suddenly very angry. For a moment he stood staring at the soldiers (who stared back, bemused, unused to this unaccustomed confrontation), contemplating a protest of some description, but life had taught him the folly of protesting against superior odds. He bathed them instead in a knowing, sardonic smile, and strode away with as much dignity as the slippery conditions underfoot would allow.

Perhaps it was the delayed shock of the assault, or perhaps it was because he felt a small celebration was in order, or perhaps just because he simply felt like one; in any case, he yearned unexpectedly for a drink. And it *was* unexpected, for Mr Apple had long since given up alcohol, abandoning its notorious seduction as a source of consolation. Still, one small drink wouldn't do him any harm, the jovial Mr Divine was hinting, and with the idea implanted it didn't take even that persuasion for the desire to become a craving, despite the persistent tut-tutting of the disapproving Sefer. Mr Apple increased his pace and hurried towards the beckoning lights of The White Bird.

'You look like you could use a drink,' the barman said, with sparkling insight.

'I do.'

' – ?'

'Whiskey. A double.'

'Coming up.'

Mr Apple balanced himself precariously on the edge of one of the stools by the bar.

'Anything in it?'

'No.' Mr Apple spoke with uncharacteristic sharpness. He sensed in the publican's unctuous tones the same bland hypocrisy he showed his own clients, and he had no wish to be reminded of that just now. He had only time to take one sip and feel his nerves recover a little before the door burst open and four soldiers, their faces smeared with warpaint, their rifles at the ready, thumped into the pub. Mr Apple watched their progress in the mirror behind the bar. Good God, they seemed to be everywhere tonight. He glanced uneasily at the barman and for a split second the man's face revealed his loyalty: his lips were drawn back slightly, his eyes glazed over and expressionless, his body rigid as though coiled and taut and ready for firing. Fortunately, he was practised in these things and knew how best to handle such intrusions, knew that it was really quite simple to lull these nervous interlopers into a sense of well-being. He produced a smile under his hostile eyes and ventured a touch of jollity in his voice.

'Hello, lads. Not drinking on duty, are we?'

The soldiers gazed about the empty bar, one of them wrinkling his nose as though sniffing out terrorists, another cocked his head as though listening; yet a third tried a tentative smile until he saw the glower on his superior's face. The smile did not fade: it switched off with electric swiftness.

'Come on, have one on the house. You'll freeze your balls off out there tonight.'

The leader of the pack (as Mr Apple found himself thinking of them, wondering giddily if, indeed, they were following him for some demented reasons of their own; perhaps they were renegades up to no good, *bandidos* – ha! –) jerked his head. What looked like a nervous tick turned out to be an order to withdraw. They retreated in unison, actually marching backwards, their precision endowing the moment with a strange overtone of terror.

'Cunts,' the barman said under his breath, and then quickly looked at Mr Apple.

Mr Apple pretended not to have heard. It was better not to hear anything these days; not to notice anything, either, like the nervous twitches that had suddenly come to life on the barman's face. Mr Apple drank slowly and deliberately: the deliriums and horrors of not so long ago never seemed to fade completely.

'No wonder people won't...a man...quiet drink...a little peace...' The barman's voice floated into his brain and out again, replaced by other voices that gibbered in his consciousness, voices from another time: deceptively friendly voices emanating from flat brown faces:

– *Por qué no?* –

– *Cómo se llama?* –

– *Antichrista* –

– *No se puede vivir sin amar* –

Mr Apple finished his drink with a swift gulp and hurried from the bar, hearing the barman roar for payment, failing to recognize it as such, associating it with those other voices that battered and besieged him. 'Why can't you leave me alone?' he cried.

He was out of breath when he reached home, though he could not remember running, could remember nothing of the short journey: like so many things in his life, it had been conveniently blacked out for the time being by that benign angel who watched over such things. But Mr Apple was well aware that it would be recalled at some future date, recalled and dreaded and used by wild and wilful demons to torment him.

And later, to wash away the thought of future recollections, Mr Apple undressed and took a long, leisurely lukewarm shower. The rattling water drowned the recalcitrant voices that clamoured for attention in his ears. He was sadly aware that the demons and voices would muster during the night to harry him in his fretful sleep, prod him into wakefulness and, by their threats of shattering nightmares, make sleep a dreadful thing. He soaped his body carefully, feeling briefly ashamed at the tenderness he showed himself; feeling, too, like laughing at the preposterous figure he presented. For Mr Apple, undressed, was a sorry sight, the more so as the caressing water from the shower stroked his flesh into unaccustomed contours of relaxation, making him featureless, accentuating the spindly legs that bowed slightly under the weight of his elongated body, which was dominated by a stomach that bulged out and down as though charitably but vainly trying to secrete his wizened little penis. The straight, horizontal, equidistant scars on either side of his chest gave the impression that his ribs had been removed, one by one, with artful surgery. His back, too, was decorated (it was the only word to use) with scars, though these were of more haphazard design, perhaps indicating that the surgeon had made several abortive attempts before finally deciding on the correct location for his incision, or had been drunk, or mad. Across his buttocks a cruel game of surgical noughts and crosses appeared to have been played, the circles like gaping mouths, the crosses like blasphemous crucifixes. Yet when Mr Apple dried himself and, putting on his rather natty spotted pyjamas, concealed his lacerated body, little hint remained of the awful tortures he had undergone except the fear he carried on his face and, if one spotted it, the measured care of his walk.

For several hours Mr Apple lay on his bed writing in an old exercise book. On the shelf above his bed were several more volumes of such writings, stacked neatly between a faded photograph of his mother cuddling a disconcerted Bedlington terrier, and a large stone rubbed smooth and shiny like some dark metal. Indecipherable scribbles covered the pages of these volumes, all written in the same distinctive script, half-crabbed, half-generous, the words sloping steeply downwards, the whole giving the impression of restless movement as if the words had taken on a life of their own and were pacing out some sad and furious misery.

When he had finished his entry Mr Apple glanced back over what he had written, not so much rereading the words as plucking from the pages phrases that conjured up the whole. 'Unusual monotony', 'Mild if inevitable harrassment', 'Oddly disproportionate fear', these were three that disentangled themselves from the blur of writing before him, along with 'Amused at Martin's intrepid practised disinterest', 'Air of chill foreboding as the latest dark avenging angel appeared with instructions', 'Faceless antagonists', 'Plausible and deadly...'

It was, no doubt, this appearance of yet one more sinister angel in his life that made Mr Apple frown and wonder if there was, in fact, anything horribly portentous in his choice of title. And, almost as though he had been waiting patiently in the wings for just this cue, Sefer interrupted with: Verify it, Mr Apple. Always verify. And substantiate, added Mr Divine. Always substantiate.

'Thank you,' Mr Apple found himself saying.

Don't mention it.

Don't mention it.

Mr Apple reached to the shelf above his head and withdrew one of the earliest volumes of his writing, blowing on it gently to remove any dust that might have accumulated. For several moments he held it before him without opening it, staring at the oddly foreign design on the cover. A look of blank, studied trepidation gradually suffused his face: that almost comic, resigned, woeful look beloved of celluloid heroines as they held telegrams from the war office telling them that their loved ones were missing, presumed dead. And, certainly, Mr Apple was aware that something approaching his own death was contained in the book on his lap. With a small sigh of what could have been relief, but was probably resignation, he opened his diary and started reading. The pages he chose were well thumbed, the corners discoloured by constant turning, worn thin and in danger of disintegrating, as if the pages contained some beloved text to be read and reread: the consoling text of a beloved mystic whose wisdom had the power to enlighten the world. Enlightenment, alas, was far from Mr Apple's mind as he dragged himself back over one of the darkest passages of his life.

...and, again, awakening from a fretful snatch of sleep, it seemed still to be night, or if night was still to come I was in a darkness streaked with grey and filled with the sounds associated with daylight and noises that existed in another time; daemonic mariachi bands trumpeting out of key, my name being screamed by instruments of higher pitch, by voices not quite human, screamed in derision, those voices taking shimmering human shapes, floating, and being pointed to by sombre, unsmiling *bandidos* as they dismounted their sweating horses and clamoured to torment me, spectres of the dark; the yelping of pariah dogs, the incessant cacophony of exotic cockerels heralding a never-approaching dawn; the draining heat made all the worse – why, I could not imagine, unless my mind was weighed down under the load of other images – by the stones continually pelted at the walls of that infernal hut wherein they kept me prisoner for what could have been months but was only days. And for all I tried I could not make them understand. How to explain to those flat, hard faces that, yes, I loved them and was sent by princes to save them? How I had reached into the very deepest recesses of my soul and grasped at every branch and root which might assist me in their salvation; how my visions of their redemption brought bright blue summer evenings to my soul, uplifting my flagging spirit, my tormented spirit, and placing it in the wake of a golden scroll of travelling light...

Mr Apple shifted his position and closed his eyes for a moment. Small beads of perspiration gathered on his brow despite the coldness of the room.

...I tried only to make them understand the sadness, the bitter, bitter loneliness of my life before the seven spirits came and raised me; to make them understand that they were the chosen ones on whom I had been told to bestow the everlasting light, to guide them through waterless places, seeking rest which somewhere we must find. I tried to give them dignity, to assure them that every precious stone was their covering, to make them believe they could raise their lives above the stars of God. But when, on what was to be my final visit to that village, that accursed village set in the outrageous glories of the terraced foothills of the Sierra Madre Oriental and protected by those two masters of the earth Popocatepetl and Ixtaccihuatl that rose clear and magnificent though silenced by the power that I was sent to battle above the squalor of their homes, when they welcomed me in the brightness of day and waited only for the shadows of night to attack me (but I, being warned, knew and wept but dried my tears, telling myself, lying again to those factions that lied back, that loneliness and rejection made man stronger, allowing the warm mist that fed on the weeping summits of the great volcanoes to wrap itself about me, conceal me, shelter me from the horror I knew was to come) and drag me through the open street of that village, through the open sewer, and spit on me, curse me, call me pariah and *Antichrista*...

Mr Apple found himself trembling violently, his body damp with sweat. What he read he read for the hundredth time, something urging him to keep the episode alive and vital in his mind. He found himself glancing nervously about the room; strange odours seemed to rise about him, the stench of humid heat and excrement and overwhelming fear that had assailed his senses in the small wooden shed with the corrugated-iron roof into which he had been thrown. Mr Apple continued to read, entranced.

...It was, ominously, the Day of the Dead when they finally pulled me out and manhandled me to the square and dumped my aching body in front of the small church, the bell tolling *Dolente, Dolore* or some such lachrymose incantation, while all I could see, or remember seeing, was the cold, unforgiving eyes of the legless beggar as he squatted outside the cantina, those eyes that mutely accused me of trying to destroy the faith that gave some meaning to his useless life. How wrong he was! I was the saviour! Then, four men grabbed me and held me down: two by the arms and two by the legs. I stared at their faces: faces made darker by the light of the flickering candles behind them, brown, hard eyes, wide, flared nostrils, trickles of saliva running from the corners of their grinning Indian mouths. And then he who appeared to be their guiding spirit (who only days before had welcomed me with open arms, embraced me, said I was his brother, accepted my gifts, swore eternal friendship, insisted his house was mine, shared his bottle of Anis del Mono with me – and refused to wipe the mouth of the bottle after I had drunk lest I be insulted, lest, too, this new found brotherhood be erased by the same gesture) was standing over me, towering in his importance, hatred shining from his eyes as brightly as the candles flashed on the thin, curved knife he held aloft in his hand. I tried, ah, dear spirits of my darkness, how I tried if only with my eyes to tell him he had got it all wrong, that I loved him only as I loved all mankind, and loving him wished to share what I believed to be my salvation with him, that I respected his courage and magnificent dignity in the face of his appalling poverty, but he would see none of this. And just before he started his savage laceration of my flesh do you know what I noticed? I noticed how unbelievably courtly and refined and delicate his hands were despite the grime that lodged so permanently in his skin. And then the pain. Oh, dear and holy ghosts of goodness, the pain! The searing of a million white-hot needles that travelled, not all at once but in procession (like, indeed, these villagers would process later in memory of their dead), slowly, through every fibre of my body to lodge, finally and in agony, in my brain. And through the white-and-scarlet haze of my suffering I saw my erstwhile brother dancing, a sliver of my flesh held high like some heroic trophy, laughing and playing to the cheers and applause of his pathetic audience. He pranced above me like some avenging angel, like the spirit of his ancestors bent on retribution, and I knew that even yet he was not satisfied. His eyes foretold massive mutilation, warned of such disfigurement that I would from then on be regarded with loathing and revulsion. He leaned over me, crouching, the piece of flesh he had already taken dangling from his mouth. Down came the knife again, but this time incising with dainty strokes my chest and through the pain I knew he was using my ribs as guidelines for his attack. Suddenly he stopped and stood erect. Summoning all the saliva he could find in his dry throat he spat at me, whipped my flesh from his mouth and flung it from him. A curious growling and snarling filled my consciousness, a horrible sound that could, I thought, have emanated only from the lowest regions of hell; then it dawned on me that it was only the pariah dogs covetting my body, the smell of blood arousing their instinctive savagery. The true horrific possibilities of this that jittered in my mind were cut short as I was turned on my stomach and the whipping began. It was like a grim satanic party: villagers queued to strike my back and buttocks (as they would queue later to kiss the feet of their protecting saint) as the raw-hide whip was passed from hand to hand, surges of laughter rising each time my body flinched, great roars arising as they sacrificed me on the altar of their hatred...

Mr Apple hurled the book across the room and buried his head in the pillow, clasping it about his ears, his long, scarred body heaving. And it was the best part of an hour before he moved again, dragging himself across the room to retrieve the book, smooth the pages, and replace it on the shelf. Then he climbed into bed and lay there quietly waiting for sleep to release him.

Martin Deeley also lay in his bed, in the small rented room where he lodged, and stared into the darkness, pretending to be endowed with extraordinary night-vision which allowed him to make out the strangely diverse possessions that surrounded him. But each was unidentifiable, anonymous, except for the small wooden crucifix with its white plastic Christ. It was no more than a declaration of his allegiances in the awful struggle that persisted in the province. Yet, lying there, naked but pleasantly warmed by an electric blanket, Martin Deeley seemed at peace with the world, seemed almost an innocent.

As always, however, just when everything held out the promise of a peaceful night, the voices began to gabble in the dark: wholly familiar by now, so familiar that he welcomed their nocturnal intrusion if only because they suspended his isolation...

Mam sat there hugging herself and rocking crazily in her chair, her hair uncombed, her face grey and streaked with tears, his two sisters on the sofa, staring at their fingers that twisted and untwined themselves endlessly, making spires and steeples and churches and all the people in them, everyone longing to comfort the other but none of them knowing how. Only Martin showed no sign of the tragedy that had befallen them. He sat aloof and alone at the table, eating solemnly, chewing each mouthful soberly several times as though recalling some admonition he had been given as a child, each mouthful determinedly swallowed as if the sustenance it gave would strengthen his mind and help him erase or at least accept the grim memories that harrassed him. Curiously, it was not so much the fact that his father and brother had been shot, nor that they had been dumped in a waterlogged ditch, but that their hands had been tied behind their backs before the bullets blew their faces away, giving them, as it were, no reasonable chance of defending themselves, that seared him.

Oh, I knew it would come to this one day, Mam said to nobody in particular, as Cissy and Jo continued to twiddle their fingers with eyes downcast, and Martin forced himself to eat the congealing stew, his thin face close to the plate, shovelling in food in quick darts like a Chinaman plying chopsticks.

Oh, I knew it would come to this, Mam repeated.

So you knew, Martin said between mouthfuls, his voice rough and bitter. The reality of death was easy enough to cope with, but Mam's sing-song lamentations were too much.

And you'll be the next, Mam went on, diving now into the future. Ah, dear Jesus, what a waste. What a waste. All being taken from me. It wasn't worth the pain of having you all.

It wasn't a waste, Martin snapped defiantly. He knew it probably was, but to have admitted it, even to himself, would have left his own apparently inevitable fate perilously open to a similar dismissal, and that was something he had no intention of allowing.

And you could have stopped them, Mam suddenly screamed, her eyes wild and blazing at her son, waiting for some reaction, watching how he ignored her, ignored them all, his thin arrogant face scowling at the empty plate in front of him. They would have listened to you and not gone out, she went on. You know they would have listened to you. They always listened to you and your easy remarks – that was the trouble. Always listening to you and your smooth talk.

I didn't know it was –

You didn't know! Of course you knew. You know everything. Look at you! Mam rattled on, the words possessing her, her voice rising to a shrill whine. Like some wild animal you are. The lot of you. Like wild animals with your fine talk about defending us all and doing it all for the country. Like wild hunted animals, that's what you are, and savage, waiting to kill or be killed. Oh, Jesus, Jesus, Mam concluded, dropping her voice with automatic reverence and retiring into the solace of the holy name.

Shut up, Mam.

And Mam shut up, but only because she could think of nothing more to say. She continued, however, to stare at her remaining son with swollen eyes: sometimes she felt she hated him, hated his cool, unruffled way of dealing with things, hated the way nothing seemed to touch him. She had even taken to believing that some heavenly wrath was punishing her by making her the mother of this monstrous, coldblooded child.

Don't you tell our Mam to shut up, Cissy said out of the blue, more for want of something to say than by way of rebuke.

Martin raised his head slowly and glared sullenly at the two girls, detesting them for taking sides against him. He had the small satisfaction of watching them wilt under his withering gaze. Then he leaned back, clasping his hands behind his head, and closed his eyes with a resigned sigh.

Martin Deeley tossed restlessly in his bed. The memory of that last night at home had become unusually painful. Since then he had suffered the unwelcome intrusion of a loneliness that was both alien and unfathomable. Yet it was this very loneliness, this strange, majestic isolation he continued to impose on himself, that had proved his greatest asset. He could be trusted to speak to no one except in a flippant, shallow way. He would carry out his instructions to the letter, revelling in his attention to detail, and retreat to his room with only the phantoms of his victims for company. He made no friends, though several people thought they had established just such a relationship with him. He carefully limited his sexual activities, imagining on one of his wilder flights of fancy that too much indulgence would bring about some deterioration in his prowess with a gun, and also, perhaps more importantly, because he wanted no intruders trespassing on his private isolation. It seemed a long time since his unerring marksmanship had been spotted at the rifle range of a travelling fair. He had been informed many months later that his craft – as it was put – was needed. He was flattered, his ego bolstered, and he never really thought about his violence, only harboured a vague feeling of power, though sometimes the exquisite sensation created in his loins left him feeling drowsy and peaceful as he dismantled his rifle and vanished into the night. Always the night. Not that he would have hesitated to kill during daylight had he been so ordered; but Martin Deeley was so reliable he was never given instructions as to time or place. So, while his victims determined their own place of execution, he chose his own time, and it was always in darkness. Someone had once told him death should always be inflicted at night so that God would not notice, and he sometimes wondered if, in his case, there was something in this, and that it was to outwit God that he chose darkness. Not that it really mattered, religion had become little more than a sort of tribal definition for him, a symbolism imposed shortly after birth which was mostly a nuisance but, at the same time, created the only identity he knew.

Well, he had been put out to grass (and he grinned in the darkness at the unintentional ambiguity) for a while. But they would need him again, wouldn't they? Certainly they would. Martin Deeley was indispensable, he decided. His mind flickered from image to image, none of them pleasant, and he knew he would be lucky to fall asleep.

5

Spring was particularly slow in coming to Belfast that year, though there were occasional evenings of balmy warmth that gave promise that it was not too far away. On one of those evenings Mr Apple stayed late in the shop. Even long after Martin had waved him a jovial farewell with a warning to behave himself, he pretended to be busy, as though some invisible colleague still hovered in the smokey air to supervise his actions. And as Mr Apple moved about (shuffling papers, opening and closing drawers, picking tiny scraps of paper from the floor, straightening a long, thin line of paper-clips) some instinct warned him of impending pain: pain of an unusual, as yet unexperienced kind, unlocalized, perhaps unreal, more the threat or promise of suffering. Or perhaps it was just that he felt the shop still hummed with noise, the noise of impish shadows abandoned by their masters, doomed to carry tales of woe, cries of triumph. Mr Apple was very clever at picking up such voices, any voices from the past. Indeed, it had struck him from time to time that certain voices were timeless and, though culled from another time, adapted themselves with such efficiency that they became real, and so audible that they could have been uttered but a moment before. And, though many of these voices terrified him and sent small beads of perspiration coursing down his neck, Mr Apple sensed he would be devastated without them. Now, as he tidied up and tidied again what he had already tidied twice before, he muttered to himself, arguing, quite logically it seemed, the necessity of retaining contact with such voices which, in his mind's eye, he saw as little Lowry men and women, gibbering and bickering, not, perhaps, directly for his benefit but loud enough to be certain he heard. In small fragments of broken sentences he allowed them to penetrate his mind, selecting (as he always did when weariness invaded his body) only such snippets as would not upset him too much.

Outside he paused for a moment to accustom his eyes to the gloom. The unseasonal mildness had brought with it the hazard of fog, which now drifted in over the city, wrapping it in drifts of mystery and giving Lepper Street a murderous look made all the more sinister by the jaundiced yellow complexion of the pedestrians as they passed under the streetlamps. Mr Apple turned up his collar, shivered slightly, shoved his hands deep into his pockets, and set out – but not in the direction of his home. Indeed, he walked in almost exactly the opposite direction, and for company he took with him sad little images of people doomed to isolation: off-cuts from *The Third Man* with musical intrusions seemed to predominate for a while, then in rapid succession but with scant regard for continuity the lonely characters of *Death in Venice*, *A Streetcar Named Desire* and *Brighton Rock* insinuated themselves. *Brighton Rock*! Now there was a thought. Perhaps Martin – hardly...

Colonel Maddox opened the door almost before Mr Apple had finished knocking, looking benign in his civilian clothes but nevertheless commanding respect like a bank manager. 'Ah,' he said, opening the door wider. 'Ah, it's you. I wasn't sure.'

'Yes. It's me,' Mr Apple confirmed although his voice suggested he shared the Colonel's doubt.

'Good. Come in, come in.'

All of a sudden I am in great demand: visitors flitting into my life requesting favours. The latest, a senior representative of Her Majesty's forces no less, keen to have the assistance of my wisdom. Well, hardly. Keen that I let them in on the secret of why I should have been given my lucrative new post; even keener to know who, precisely, offered it to me, and to be kept informed as to what is going on. I should, of course, tell them, but I find their appeals to my patriotism a little obscene. In any case I would be cutting my own throat, so to speak, doing myself out of a cosy little job, doing myself, also, in no uncertain way, out of my livelihood! And, to make a clean breast of it, I rather enjoy being the enemy, or, rather, being on the side of the enemy, which comes to the same thing; being that murky character who funnels cash through murkier channels. All very Raftian, I confess, but fun nonetheless. And somehow I still retain that speck of dignity that prevents me betraying those who have helped me, if only for their own ends. What, I ask myself, would have become of me by now had the dapper little Seamus not visited me and lifted me from my degradation? Anyway, it is all part of the scheme of things, is it not? Those that guide me have arranged it, and it is only by my blind submission to their guidance that I can bring about salvation...

Mr Apple walked past the Colonel, down the narrow hall with walls so dark and featureless they seemed to go on for ever. 'The dampness gets into my bones,' he offered the Colonel for no particular reason as he turned into a small room on the left.

'And mine. Do sit down,' Colonel Maddox invited, lapsing for a moment into his garden-party voice. 'I won't be a moment.'

Alone, Mr Apple took stock of the room, as he did on every occasion he visited it. It was just another harmless little game he liked to play: a game of 'has anything been moved?' As usual, nothing had. Not even the dust, he noted, which after lying undisturbed for a couple of months seemed to have lost interest in accumulating and lay in the same thin film on every surface. Clipped British voices penetrated the wall, but Mr Apple ignored them: he did not want, at this juncture anyway, to know more than he was officially told. He settled himself in an old armchair, easing himself down slowly out of respect for the tired, fragile springs, and hissed thinly through his teeth as he lay back. Strange, he thought, strange that all sense of trepidation had flown from him: now that he was actually in the house, was about to carry out the bi-monthly charade, he felt himself relax and view the forthcoming encounter with considerable amusement.

He must have dropped off for a moment, for the slamming of a door brought him bolt upright, wondering where he was. Almost immediately Colonel Maddox, accompanied by a small man who seemed to prefer to remain in the background but towards whom the Colonel showed considerable deference and respect, came into the room and closed the door carefully behind him.

'Sorry about that,' the Colonel began, with a half-smile of apology.

'Tricky business, all this cloak and dagger. Not really my province, you know. Ah, this is – '

'Asher,' the small man interrupted from the shadows.

'Yes. Quite. Mr Asher.'

Mr Apple nodded. Ashers to Ashers, he thought giddily, and cudgelled his bubbling laughter into a small smile, a replica of the Colonel's.

'Well, Arthur,' Asher said from the shadows, lighting a black cigarette. The flame illuminated his features for a moment, then vanished. 'What has been happening?' he demanded from the darkness.

Perhaps it was the impertinent familiarity of the man, or perhaps Sefer's whispered warning in his ear, that made Mr Apple dislike this man more than he had disliked anyone for a long time.

'Nothing,' he lied promptly, with a facility that amazed him.

'Nothing?' Asher snapped.

'Nothing.'

This negative revelation spurred Asher to move into the light. He shared a dumbfounded look between the Colonel and Mr Apple, a confused expression on his face as though for the moment he had been floored by the absence of intrigue. 'What do you mean, nothing?'

Mr Apple raised his hands in a helpless gesture and looked at the Colonel as though appealing for assistance.

'What can I say?' he asked finally. 'Nothing has happened. Not a single thing. I think you must have been misled.'

'Don't be stupid,' Asher said coldly. 'Our information is always correct.'

'Not, it seems, this time,' Mr Apple told him complacently.

Well done, whispered Sefer.

Brilliant, agreed Mr Divine. You have him all tied up.

Mr Apple smiled to himself mysteriously.

'Perhaps,' the Colonel was suggesting hesitantly, 'perhaps they haven't satisfied themselves about Mr Apple yet.'

Asher dismissed the suggestion with a single economical, rather effeminate, flick of his wrist, and screwed his face into meditative lines, his eyes all the while firmly fixed on Mr Apple, who stared back blandly. Only a tiny twinkle in his eye hinted that he was enjoying the discomfort he was creating.

'Now look,' Asher began. 'We know why this operation was set up. We knew even before it started. And you mean to tell me that you've had no instructions to pass money through the – '

'None,' interrupted Mr Apple bravely.

'I – don't – believe – that.'

Mr Apple shrugged, and in his mind his two conspirators danced with glee, Mr Divine bending double with delight.

'You – are – lying,' Asher announced.

Again Mr Apple shrugged.

A new menace entered Asher's voice. 'I would really hate to think, Arthur, that you were keeping anything from us.'

'Why should I?' Mr Apple asked.

'Oh, I don't think Mr Apple would do that,' the Colonel put in. 'As he says, why should he?'

Asher decided to think again: one could almost discern the movements of his thoughts in the twitching lines on his face as he mulled over the various reasons why Mr Apple should or should not.

Outside a siren wailed balefully. Heavy vehicles thundered past the house, making it shake. A pair of small Goss vases with heraldic designs bounced on the mantlepiece; a print of some forlorn Scottish stag bellowing for intercourse shuddered on the wall.

'...*know* that the Provos did the raid,' Asher was saying, 'and that the money was to go to you to be cleaned.'

Mr Apple kept his silence.

'And you still insist that nothing has been passed on to you?'

'Absolutely nothing,' Mr Apple insisted.

'They could be waiting.' Colonel Maddox tried.

'They never wait *that* long. They need the funds. Tell me, Arthur, what did McIlliver want with you the other day?'

' – ? McIlliver?' It was Mr Apple's turn to be dumbfounded.

'I suppose you don't know him?'

'No. I don't,' Mr Apple admitted truthfully.

'I see. You don't, I suppose, remember three men coming into your shop and staying a remarkably short time for anyone wanting to place a bet?'

'Three men. Let me think. Together, were they?'

Asher nodded, somehow making the gesture sarcastic. 'Three men. Together.'

'No. Not offhand. There has been *one* man in whom I had never seen before, but I don't think there was anyone with him.'

'And what did this one man want?' Asher pressed.

Mr Apple raised his eyebrows and peered over his spectacles like a schoolteacher. 'To have a bet, of course. A small bet, I recall. That's right,' Mr Apple agreed, closing his eyes briefly and frowning. 'Yes, that's right,' he said again happily. 'That is quite right,' he said for the third time, determined to keep the objectionable little man waiting. 'He came in and stared up at the prices and then he placed a bet of fifty pounds on the favourite. I would still have his ticket if you want to see it. Lost. The horse, I mean. Fell or brought down early on. But aren't we all?' Mr Apple concluded wistfully.

'Fell or brought down early on,' Asher repeated.

'That's right. He didn't wait for the rest of the race. The man, I mean,' Mr Apple said, smiling at his little joke. 'Just walked out as soon as his horse departed. But then you know he left quickly, if it's the same man you're talking about.'

'Amazing, isn't it, how clearly you remember.'

'I remember the bets. It's my business to remember the bets. . don't remember the faces who put them on. Anonymity is a peculiar requisite of the people I deal with,' Mr Apple explained mischievously, investing his reply with a mild chiding that was rewarded with a light of anger in Asher's eyes. 'Unless they win. Ah, now, that's a different kettle of fish. Now if they *win* they want everyone to know them. They've beaten the system, you see, which is what we're all trying to do one way or another, are we not?'

Asher's eyes continued to flash angrily and, as though his anger was contagious, voices in the street outside adopted its temper, and even the dull thud of running boots pounding on the pavement sounded unreasonably infuriated and ominous. A sudden single sharp crack of gunfire was heard and, without moving their heads, the Colonel and Asher glanced at each other from the corners of their eyes. Mr Apple looked on, for the moment forgotten, while the two men summed up the possible danger of the situation. However, as the shouts and thumping boots grew fainter Asher lit another black cigarette and returned to the matter in hand.

'I'll be perfectly honest with you, Arthur,' he said. 'I don't believe a word of what you've said.'

Mr Apple called upon his neat little hand-spreading gesture to imply that this was, indeed, very sad, most regrettable, that it upset him no end.

'And I don't trust you an inch,' Asher added, as though it might make a difference.

Mr Apple rose laboriously from his chair and stared flatly at his accuser.

'Oh, I do feel Mr Apple would have told us if anything had happened,' the Colonel interjected, feeling it was his duty to ease the tension. 'He really does have nothing to gain,' he added, 'and he has a great deal to lose.'

Asher nodded. 'A very great deal,' he agreed.

'So,' Mr Apple told them, 'I must have been telling the truth.'

'Unless you're a fool,' Asher said.

'Unless I'm a fool,' Mr Apple admitted innocently, and with this solemn observation they were through.

Colonel Maddox ushered him to the front door, herding him protectively past Asher, who had retreated once again to the shadows and had shrouded himself in black cigarette smoke.

'You would tell us if – ' the Colonel began when they were alone in the hall, using that conspiratorial tone that suggested he would have wrapped an arm about Mr Apple's shoulder had he not been wary of rebuff.

'What do you think, Colonel? Would I be stupid enough to defy your Mr Asher?'

'Oh, he's not my Mr Asher, I assure you,' the Colonel hastened to tell him. 'Between you and me he's a bit pushy, isn't he?'

'You could say that, I think.'

The Colonel seemed to feel that this was a suitably amicable note on which to terminate the proceedings. He gave a quick, sharp, barking laugh as he pictured the gaunt, bent Mr Apple doing battle with the brittle Asher.

'Well, I'll see you in a couple of weeks as usual, unless, of course, you have something to tell me in the mean time.'

'In a couple of weeks, then.'

'And, by the way,' the Colonel went on, leaning closer, 'don't let Mr Asher upset you. He's under a lot of pressure.'

'Aren't we all,' Mr Apple said, but mostly to himself.

Mr Apple thought he heard the Colonel sigh as he closed the door and felt a tinge of sympathy for him. Any man who could sigh couldn't be all bad, he decided. Like people who loved dogs and cats and Beatrix Potter.

Perhaps it was his imagination, or perhaps it was just the effect of leaving the mustiness of the house, but Mr Apple felt it had got suddenly colder. He sucked the chilly air into his lungs and felt it creep into his chest. For a moment, it was as though he felt it travel yet further and enter his brain, freezing for future reference the conversation that had taken place. Then he set off through the tangle of backstreets that led to the Antrim Road and from there to his home: they were unusually quiet and uninquisitive. For some odd reason he felt that people should be rushing up to him demanding to know what had happened, but there was none of that: just silence and darkness. All the curtains were tightly drawn across the small windows, even a couple of cats about to fight merely showed their teeth and screamed their defiance soundlessly.

Onwards he trudged, and with each step the elation he had felt at his deception of the detestable Asher receded a little. His imagination started playing tricks on him, conjuring secret watchers from the gloom. Once Mr Apple was positive he heard someone behind him, following him, trying to match footsteps with his own; but when he stopped suddenly and swung round there was nobody there. By the time he reached home he was thoroughly frightened. Still, Mr Apple had been frightened before, had he not? And he had coped, had he not? And he would cope now, would he not?

'Well, Chloe,' he told the cat that pressed against his ankles, mewling for food. 'It looks as though we have taken sides.'

He put a saucer of food on the floor for Chloe, took off his coat and threw it over the back of a kitchen chair. He stood watching the cat devour the chopped liver, then opened the back door for it to go out, standing aside politely and giving a small bow. 'Happy hunting.'

Now what, Mr Divine wanted to know.

'Now what, indeed,' Mr Apple wondered.

He thought briefly about having just one therapeutic drink, but decided against it. He thought about watching television, but decided against that also. Something to eat? Later. Finally, he seemed to make up his mind and left the kitchen, carefully switching off the light behind him. He walked across the hall to a small cupboard under the stairs, a glory-hole as it would have once been called. He opened the door, straightened his back and walked in, closing the door behind him.

6

Almost to the minute that Mr Apple vanished mysteriously into the glory-hole, Martin Deeley pushed open the door of the disco and strode arrogantly in. It was his night of sin, as he laughingly liked to think of it, and the companion in his forthcoming fall from grace was already lined up, willing, and hanging on his arm with an intensity that defied anyone to try and take him from her. Martin suffered her smothering possessiveness simply because he knew she would satisfy his needs and make no demands on him apart from gratification.

The cosmetic eroticism of the disco clattered frenetically about them as they pushed their way through the gyrating dancers towards an empty table in the corner, their faces changing shape and colour under the multi-hued lights rotating from a central glass prism in the ceiling.

Martin produced a half-bottle of whiskey from his pocket and placed it on the table beside the two paper mugs that Daphne Cope had produced from her oversized handbag. She always brought special mugs for herself and Martin; for someone of her risk-laden profession she had an abnormal dread of disease, regarding disco glasses and public toilets in the same light, and she felt it her duty to protect Martin from any infection.

Martin released his arm from her clutch and slung it nonchalantly about her shoulder. He stared about him with half-closed eyes, feigning boredom as he felt was expected of a man of his importance, and he was gratified by the glances thrown at him and the whispered, surreptitious comments. Daphne noticed the glances also, and she was none too pleased: she fixed her eyes on his face and pouted, making odd little inclinations with her head like those she had seen employed by Marilyn Monroe in her successful seduction of Robert Mitchum. Though she would have been shocked and hurt by the suggestion, these facial contortions were about the only way left to her to demonstrate her emotions. She wore her 'special' dress of scarlet brocade, a tight-fitting affair cut low to reveal her full breasts, and these she shook gently at Martin from time to time to attract his abstract attention. But Martin sat still, tense and alert, watching for someone he knew would appear before long.

'Cummon, sweetie, let's dance,' Daphne cajoled in her contrived, deep, nicotine-stained voice, taking his hand and tickling the palm with a long, painted fingernail.

'Uh-huh. I'm whacked,' Martin said, without bothering to look at her.

'Aw, my little babby is tired,' Daphne whimpered. 'Okay. I don't really want to dance if you don't,' she consented, clinging to him again, her long, fluttering eyelashes failing to conceal the yearning in her eyes as she longed for his energetic penetration. In her fantasies she saw some future for herself with him: not that her future as a prostitute was bleak. Far from it. She had a good stable of clients, good and generous and usually undemanding clients, and even her dull mind was amazed at the risks some of the military would take for a quick spot of fornication. But that was their affair, and she was happy to cater for them as long as they continued to pay for their appetites without argument. Still, she promised herself, she would give it all up when her father was released from Long Kesh and she no longer had to support her terrified mother, who now refused to leave her house on any pretext and had taken to doodling, which was fair enough except that she used every wall in the house to practise her art. And it was perhaps because of these intermittent longings to become a 'good' girl that Daphne suffered occasionally from severe depression, even contemplating suicide, but always abandoning such an extreme remedy with a laugh as she lustfully anticipated incredible curiosities in the days ahead. Ah, but Martin, her Martin. He was different.

'You got something on your mind, luvvey?' she asked, concerned by the scowl that dominated his face.

' – ? Huh? No. No, nothing.'

'But you must have something. I mean, you can't have a blank mind.'

'Can't you?' Martin snapped sarcastically.

'Oh, you're funny!' Daphne exclaimed innocently: it would never have dawned on her that Martin would insult her.

'Jesus, I hate this place.'

'We can go, luvvey, if you want. I don't mind.'

'No, we can't. I'm waiting for someone.'

'Oh. Okay,' Daphne said, and snuggled closer. She had become used to these meetings. After all, Martin was an important man and people wanted to consult him. And they treated him with respect; even much older men, men old enough to be his father, showed how important he was by speaking to him with deference. Still, it hurt her that Martin always sent her away when these meetings took place, never introducing her, smacking her bottom as she left and making her feel cheap. These thoughts had barely reached their sad conclusion when she felt his body stiffen and go rigid in her embrace. She gazed up into his face and saw that he was staring across the room. Following his gaze she spotted a dapper little man, dressed darkly as if for a funeral and incongruous for it, making his way sedately through the dancers, smiling, or possibly wincing at the multicoloured shirts and frocks and blouses that swirled about him offending his impeccably conservative taste. Despite his valiant efforts to look friendly, his eyes remained grim and tired.

'You better go and dance with someone,' Martin ordered as the man came nearer.

'Okay, Martin.'

'Good girl,' he told her, and slapped her bottom.

'Sorry to spoil your evening,' Seamus Reilly said, and sounded as if he meant it. 'But it is important.'

'I gathered that. Anyway, you're spoiling nothing. I hate the bloody place. What's up?'

'Trouble – maybe.'

'Oh? What trouble?'

'Our friend Mr Apple,' Reilly announced, looking down at his polished, manicured nails and up again.

'Mr Apple? Don't be mad. He's no trouble. I'm getting on with him like a house on fire. Even getting to like the old bugger.'

'We've heard whispers.'

'Oh, Christ, not whispers again. Seamus, you and your bloody whispers will be the death of me. And you'll be driven mad if you listen to them all.'

'Just hear me out, Martin. There are whispers that he might be playing both sides.'

Martin's face tightened. 'Doing what?' he demanded in a low, grim whisper.

'We don't know anything for certain yet, but – '

'But.what?'

'But we were told that someone who looked like him was seen coming out of the Brits' safe house in – '

'The bastard – '

'Don't fly off into a temper, Martin. It might be nothing. Our man can't be certain. It was foggy and he was too far away. He just said it looked like Mr Apple. He mentioned something about the walk.'

Martin stared at the dancers, shaking his head, unconsciously moving it in time to the music. 'Naw,' he said finally. 'Old Apple would never do something like that. It's not his style, Seamus. He's always on about honour and loyalty and stuff like that.'

'Again, I repeat, it might be nothing. It could have been somebody else,' Seamus admitted.

'It must have been. He wouldn't do anything like that. Anyway, I'd know if he was up to something.'

'Would you?'

'Sure I would.'

'That's really what I wanted to find out.'

'Yeah. I'd know. He'd never be able to hide something like that from me. He'd give himself away for certain.'

'In that case there's nothing for us to worry about, is there?'

'Who says they saw him?' Martin suddenly wanted to know.

'Nobody you know.'

'Reliable?'

Reilly inclined his head and grimaced to indicate moderate reliability.

'Naw,' Martin said again, determined to convince himself, his head continuing to shake for several moments.

'There's been nothing unusual at the shop? No phone calls?'

'No. Nothing out of the way. Clients phone. And you. Anyway, he never minds if I answer the phone, so he can't be hiding anything there.'

'No unusual callers?'

'Uh-uh. But he's not going to invite the Brits in for a chat, is he?'

Reilly ignored the sarcasm. 'Doesn't leave the shop?'

Martin gave a snort. 'Only to go home, and then I follow him most nights.'

'Most?'

'Yes.'

'Not every?'

'No. Not every. Hell, Seamus, some weeks I follow him every night, some weeks just three or four.'

'I see,' Seamus said pensively. 'He doesn't know you follow him?'

Martin shook his head. 'Never even looks behind him.'

A small frown of surprise passed rapidly across Seamus Reilly's brow, but if his thoughts were significant he had no intention, it seemed, of revealing them just yet. 'And he still doesn't suspect you're in the shop to watch him?'

'No,' Martin said, but there was a hesitancy in his voice that prompted Seamus to ask:

'You're certain?'

'Yes. I'm certain, but...well, he's a crafty old sod and you never know what he's thinking.'

'Thinking?'

'Well, he just says things, and you don't know what to make of them. Like he was teasing the whole time.'

'So now you think he might suspect?'

Martin took time off to think about this. He was finding it hard to explain what he wanted to say. 'Not suspect,' he said finally, taking a sip of his drink, swilling it in his mouth, letting it trickle slowly down his throat as though quenching some nagging suspicion that had just struck him. 'Either he definitely knows or he definitely doesn't know. He doesn't do things by halves,' Martin concluded, not quite sure what he meant by the last few words.

'Hmm.'

'Anyway, at this stage, does it matter if he does know?'

Reilly gave a crack of a laugh in which his eyes refused to take part. 'That depends, doesn't it, on what his reactions might be?'

'He wouldn't do anything. I'd stake my life on – '

'You might just have to do that, Martin.'

' – ?'

Reilly smiled. 'So you're happy he's behaving himself?'

Martin nodded. 'He knows what's good for him. He's not a fool.'

'Oh, we know that. He's far from being stupid – '

'He – '

'Let's just leave it at that, shall we?' Seamus interrupted, in a tone that suggested he had settled the matter in his own mind. 'Just be a little more – eh – vigilant, and let me know at once if anything – '

'Of course I will.'

For several minutes the two of them sat without talking, allowing the throb of the music to act as recipient of their thoughts. Seamus Reilly sighed deeply. 'Well, I'll be off and let you get on with your dancing,' he said, rising.

'Huh. I'll see you, Seamus. And don't worry,' Martin insisted, as they shook hands.

'Oh, *I'm* not worried, Martin.'

'Good. Neither am I.'

'I'm pleased to hear it. Good-night.'

''Night, Seamus.'

Martin watched as Reilly squeezed his way through the dancers and left the disco. He poured himself a stiff whiskey and lowered it in one gulp, hoping it would stupefy the nervous twitch in his stomach. Then he closed his eyes and watched jumpy black-and-white images of Mr Apple and himself flicker through his mind like scenes from an ancient silent film, trying, as they jostled each other for screening, to decipher any untoward behaviour by Mr Apple. He was still absorbed with his private viewing when someone tapped him on the shoulder and said: 'Well, if it isn't Martin Deeley. The grand Martin Deeley himself.'

Martin's eyes snapped open and his body froze. He realized the voice was familiar, but he could not for the life of him put a face to it, and it was something approaching terror that prevented him from turning round to see who it was: a gruesome tradition had been established among the many assassins in the province that they would only kill each other face to face.

'And how are you at all?' the voice now wanted to know, its owner moving from behind and presenting himself to Martin's gaze.

'Corrigan! Fuck you, Corrigan, you frightened the shit out of me.'

'Me? Me frighten the great Martin Deeley?'

'Yes, you fucking great shit you. Sneaking up on me like that.'

'Sure I never sneaked up on you, Martin my love. Just came across the room as open as you please to say hello to an old friend.'

Larry Corrigan bestowed the gift of a great toothless grin down and around him, adopting a pose that, in anyone else, would have been seen simply as arrested motion. In Larry Corrigan, though, it acquired a different connotation: with both arms extended and legs wide apart he resembled one of those grotesque figures in early engravings that are only remotely interesting because of their stylized remoteness from life. And Larry Corrigan was a grotesque enough creature: huge and round and flabby and a living denial of the rumour that fat people are jolly and gay. His grey skin told of the many years he had spent in and out of prison. True, he had been free for some time now, and he guarded his freedom with considerable help from his friends: Larry Corrigan was an informer, but an informer of the vagabond breed, reporting to the British such items as he was told to report, always being allowed to deliver sufficient for him to be left at large and in peace.

'And what's all this I hear about you moving into the shady world of gambling, Martin?'

'That's right, Larry,' Martin admitted curtly.

'Bookmaking no less. Dear me, dear me.'

'I'm just helping out.'

Larry Corrigan threw up his hands. 'I'm not prying, Martin. I'm not prying,' he stated hastily, his hands indicating that such a thing would never enter his head. 'Just curious,' he explained. 'Everything going all right for you?'

'Everything's just fine.'

'Oh, good.'

'And you?'

'Me? Surviving.' Larry Corrigan let his eyes rest on Martin's long, delicate hands and seemed hypnotized by the way they clenched and unclenched ceaselessly. 'Relax, Martin,' he said benevolently. 'Just a chance meeting. Nobody wants to know anything. I'm under no pressure. Anyway, you're my friend.'

'Oh, I'm everybody's friend tonight, it seems,' Martin observed wryly.

'You know what I mean. I'd never say anything about you.'

'I know that, Larry,' Martin said, without much conviction. 'I know that. Sorry. Just a bit uptight this evening.'

'It gets that way.'

' – ?'

'Our lives,' Larry said morosely. 'Hadn't you noticed?'

'Never thought about it.'

'It just doesn't make sense, though – '

'I suppose not.'

'You in a bookie's shop.'

'? Oh,' Martin said, finding it increasingly difficult to disentangle the threads of the conversation. 'There's a reason.'

'I'm sure there is.'

Martin stared up at the round, sweating face with a flat, unreadable expression, allowing the pounding music, the shuffling feet and the hands waved in exotic patterns to create some meaning from his blank stare.

'You haven't got into trouble, have you, Martin?'

Martin felt his throat close. 'Shit, no.'

Larry exhaled half a lungful of odorous air and shifted his pyknic body from foot to foot. 'That's all right then.'

Martin was moved by the seeming sincerity. 'You need something?' he asked. 'Money?'

'No, I don't need money,' Larry answered, blushing, his huge body seeming to take offence. 'Even if I did I wouldn't scrounge off you. You know that.'

'I didn't say you were scrounging. I was just asking. Just trying to help. We all need help from time to time. You know that.'

'That's for sure.'

'So you're all right?'

'I'm all right. I'll let you know when I'm not.'

'Good.'

'But thanks for asking.'

'Yeah,' Martin said awkwardly, relieved to see Daphne mincing towards him, her eyes undressing him as she got closer. 'Got to go, Larry,' Martin added, and winked, making this innocent enough gesture brilliantly pornographic. 'Heavy date.'

'Ah. Yes. Well, enjoy yourself, hear?'

'I will.'

'You'll be an awful long time dead,' Larry added. 'A long, long time dead,' he repeated to himself mournfully, as though he had already experienced the hereafter and was none too thrilled by it.

'See you about, Larry.'

'See you,' Larry replied, though sounding somewhat doubtful as he watched Martin and Daphne submerge themselves in the sea of dancers.

Martin had long since dismissed Larry from his thoughts as he allowed Daphne to lead him by the hand up the stairs to her room: one single, pretty dismal room that gave off a corridor with eight doors. Sighs and groans and giggles could be heard through the walls, and Daphne switched on the small bedside radio as if to swamp them. She hummed musically in rhythm with the unmusical voices of some up-and-coming punk group. She had lived in a dozen places since she had left home, but had managed to stamp her presence on each of them in a remarkably short time, putting her mementoes on display, and always managing, somehow, to strategically place, somewhere, a small vase of flowers or a potted plant with extravagant foliage, as though to endorse her femininity and soften any hardness that might have crept into her character.

Martin sat on the edge of the bed and took off his shoes and socks, sniffing the air, hoping his feet did not smell but knowing they probably did. No matter what he did, no matter how often he washed his feet and changed his socks and applied prescribed powders, his feet always seemed to stink. Mam had always been on at him about it. You go straight upstairs and wash your feet and change your socks, you smelly little boy, she'd say.

I'm not smelly.

Your feet are. Like stinky cheese they are. Upstairs this minute with you.

I washed them this morning. And changed my socks.

Well, wash them again now.

That's what's causing the trouble, Martin tried arguing. I'm washing all the natural oils out of them.

Rubbish, Martin, and you know it. No pretty girl will want to marry you if you smell like that. No girl would put up with you.

Then I'll do without.

Well, do without, but get upstairs and wash those feet.

But that had been years ago, and his feet still caused him endless embarrassment. Another of life's afflictions, he thought good-humouredly, lying back on the bed, his head propped on two pillows. He stared about him, his gaze uncritical of the small shabby room with its bulging paintwork. In one corner, on a risky-looking shelf, a small electrified crucifix illuminated a gilt-framed print of Christ, His finger pointing nonchalantly to the blood dripping from his heart, each drop artistically isolated. Other pictures, barely visible in the seductive gloom, hung haphazardly on the walls: a watercolour of a lake, possibly the Bodensee, signed Menzies Jones (whoever he was), two Victorian prints of sugary little girls having animated conversations with, in one, an oversized shaggy dog, and, in the other, with two sharp-snouted terriers, and between these prints, tilting alarmingly, a none-too-clever reproduction of the Goose Girl. Yet despite the overall drabness of the room it was impeccably clean, as though the odour of poverty and aimless love was ruthlessly being kept at bay by the occupant's zealous tidiness. There was a photograph of Daphne's parents on the dressing-table (although dressing-table flattered it somewhat: it was, in fact, a small deal kitchen table, painted a pretty blue with a mirror on top balanced precariously near the back and supported by building-bricks painted white), both of them thin, small people who smiled selfconsciously straight at the camera, obviously embarrassed at being captured in such close proximity and grateful, no doubt, that they were now all but obscured by the conglomeration of perfumes and powders and creams that littered the table about them. Still, Mr Cope gave the impression he was constantly darting little peeps from behind these, a hunted look to his eyes that made a mockery of his smiling mouth, his taut, posed stance filled with a restlessness that gave evidence of his years on the run.

'Come on over here,' Martin said, patting the mattress, putting his arm around her as she snuggled close, her head resting contentedly on his shoulder. Beside them the radio played on, its endless stream of music designed for those who wanted to hear without listening. Martin stared at the ceiling, following the cracks in the plaster, making them into roads down which he had travelled: abandoned, dusty roads upon which he walked alone, wearing sandals, unburdened, a mendicant monk perhaps, and then, as always, inevitably, immediately in front of him, his target appeared, rising spectrelike from nowhere, from within the earth itself, and he was filled with a trembling excitement, not knowing how this particular victim was going to react (and that was always the most interesting aspect – screams or tears? Pleading or disdain? But for the most part they never knew they were targets until the bullet hit them and then it was too late to do anything but die) and he, Martin, aiming, and slowly, slowly squeezing the trigger, and wondering yet again, as he did every time, whether he would feel exalted or, as he knew he should, revolted.

'What you thinking, honey?' Daphne suddenly wanted to know.

Martin jumped. 'Not a lot,' he said finally, closing his eyes. His mind recently had started to stagger at the number of lives he had taken, playing tricks on him, multiplying a hundred times the placid, bewildered faces of death. Too often now he felt terror – the same terror that shot through him that very evening when Larry Corrigan touched him unexpectedly on the shoulder. His whole life, it seemed, was a tenuous, jittery thing linked to the world while he floated, in a wild, disembodied state, in a murky void of uncertainty, forever reaching out and clawing at random for great lumps of reality that glided past always beyond his reach, seeking to get hold of something that would give him an identity, a reason for being alive. Oddly, only Mr Apple with his weak, watery eyes and his gaunt, stooped body seemed to be on offer as a guide to his salvation. It was as though Mr Apple had a monopoly on the knowledge Martin yearned to obtain.

'You've got something on your mind,' Daphne insisted.

'Nothing. Really.'

'You're too good to be mixed up with – '

'Shut up, Daphne. For God's sake, don't go on,' Martin said angrily.

Daphne raised her head and studied him for a moment. 'You're far too good for them,' she repeated solemnly.

'You don't understand.'

'Oh, no. I'm thick. I understand nothing. Huh. What is there to understand? You know, you're just going to end up like all the rest. Locked up or dead. That's what I understand. You think I don't know those creeps you meet with? You think I don't know what they make you do?'

'Shut up.'

Daphne sat bolt upright, her eyes flaring. 'No, I won't shut up, dammit.'

'You don't know the people I deal with.'

'I don't know them? You must be joking, Martin. I've seen everyone of them with their knickers down. I've seen them all trying to be men. So don't tell me I don't know them. You're all I've got to hang on to, Martin. I don't want you to end up on a slab. I care.'

'So you care.'

'What do you do it for? The money?'

Martin snorted.

'Okay. It makes you feel big. I understand that.'

Martin ignored her.

Daphne turned again and stared at him, and her anxiety was not just for his welfare but for the threat to her longed-for, dreamed-of future with him. She looked away as though the sight of him was too sad to bear. Then, 'I love you, Martin,' she announced firmly.

'Sure, sure,' Martin agreed casually, turning to look at her and excluding her love from his life with a tired smile. 'Everybody loves me.'

Perhaps it was the great hurt he spotted in her eyes, or, more likely, perhaps it was his sense of practicality that made him push her back roughly and fondle her thighs, a rage building up in him as he demanded she endorse his masculinity. He crushed her breasts cruelly in his hands and felt that familiar glow of excitement sweep over him as she cried in pain.

'Oh, I love you, Martin,' Daphne sobbed. 'I love you. Love you,' she whispered, biting deeply into his neck as though she wished to devour him and keep him safe within her.

An hour later he lay naked on the bed, smoking a cigarette, frowning, seeing his confidence dissolve like the smoke that drifted away from him in a dim cloud towards the ceiling.

7

There was always the chance that Dr Solomon was wrong, Mr Apple thought with bitter amusement. That would certainly put the cat among the pigeons. Maybe he had a lot longer to live than old, sad Solomon thought; maybe he was going to go on and on, always on the brink of death but never taking the vital plunge. Immediately he began to fantasize about the activity surrounding his own demise, seeing himself, literally, on the edge of some great precipice, about to place one foot over the edge. Strange, he thought, how death could be so familiar, although one had not experienced it yet. Or perhaps one had. Or perhaps not quite: but one had certainly earned the knowledge to recognize it, to be polite to it, to raise one's hat and wish it good morning, but until it came with all its clamouring fanfare of finality one could not, say, address it on first-name terms. Mr Apple sighed, and Martin Deeley – industriously breaking the paper bands that held the betting-slips in neat numerical bundles – glanced up. 'What's the matter, Mr A.?' he asked.

'Nothing, Mr D.,' Mr Apple replied smiling, allowing this recently evolved familiarity to wash some of the despondency from his soul.

'Oh. Thought you were – '

'I was,' Mr Apple interrupted, bringing that particular speculation to an abrupt halt. Immediately, changing tack, he added, out of the blue and with no warning, 'How long do you plan to waste your time on this job?'

'?' Martin raised his eyebrows, his eyes suspiciously bewildered.

Mr Apple raised his eyebrows also, allowing his spectacles to slither half-way down his nose, leaving the question hanging in the air.

Following what was or should have been, on the face of it, a perfectly innocent enquiry, the silence that followed was inordinately prolonged, broken only by the water grinding in the electric kettle as it started to boil.

'I hadn't thought about it,' Martin confessed finally.

'Oh?' Mr Apple feigned surprise.

'Why "oh"?'

'I would have thought you were more ambitious.'

'I am.'

'Well?'

'I'm not going to do it forever, if that's what you mean,' Martin said, annoyed that he felt himself suddenly on the defensive again. 'There's not much work about at present. Got to take what I can get. There's a lot of unemployment you know.'

'True,' Mr Apple agreed, nodding, moving his glasses back to the bridge of his nose with one finger. 'Still...'

'Still what?'

Mr Apple seemed to be losing a wrestling match with his thoughts. Then: 'Do you ever get feelings, Martin?'

'Feelings? Sure I get feelings.'

'I mean premonitions.'

'Like telling the future?'

'Something like that.'

Martin shrugged, disquieted by the turn the conversation had now taken. He was about to throw out some facetious remark when Mr Apple went on: 'I do, you know. Quite frequently, in fact.'

'Good for you.'

' – and I have this feeling about us – '

'Oh, great.'

' – as though – '

'What?'

Mr Apple shook his head in a series of short little jerks, like a watchful bird.

'For Christ's sake, don't stop now,' Martin insisted, crossing the office and switching off the kettle, jerking his hand away as the steam hit him. 'Shit,' he said as he licked his hand.

' – ?'

'Damn kettle.'

'Oh.'

'Anyway, what were you on about?'

'Nothing, Martin. It doesn't matter.'

'Great! Just as I was getting interested.'

'I can't explain it, Martin. Truly I can't. Something, I suppose, to do with destiny.'

'Oh boy,' Martin heard himself saying. It worried him that Mr Apple – yet again! – seemed to be hinting at something significant, something that he himself had sensed from time to time but had preferred to dismiss as soon as it seemed likely to take some sort of shape. And to dismiss it now he busied himself making tea, slopping teabags in and out of the boiling water as though fishing for eels in the mugs, adding milk, and then walking across to Mr Apple holding his mug at arm's length as though avoiding contamination. But Mr Apple appeared to have withdrawn from any thoughts of a common destiny, appeared to have better things to do, and was now busily making dozens of small calculations on a sheet of paper which told him he had another four hundred pounds to lose today. Then he just let the pencil meander, and watched in mild amusement at the amoebic doodles that appeared until he heard Martin's frustrated cough behind him.

'Oh thank you, Martin. Most welcome.'

Martin stared at the back of the old man's head, wishing, absurdly, for one of those sets of scientifically fictitious eyes that could penetrate anything. It seemed to him that many things he wanted to know and understand lay hidden in Mr Apple's brain; things, it struck him now, that were vital to expose; things that were somehow linked with both exaltation and horror. It was as though inside that balding and curiously pointed head were filed precise details of everything he, Martin, had ever done and thought and been afraid of, and from which, now, sallow little one-act plays emanated, depicting moments in his life when he had felt totally bereft and lonely...

...identify the bodies, someone said gruffly in a whirring accent, faintly bored but, at the same time, relieved that two more suspected terrorists could be written out of the records.

I'll go, Mam, Martin said. You two look after Mam and see she doesn't do anything stupid.

Mam doesn't do stupid things, Cissy said.

She's not herself, dammit, Martin snapped. You look after her, that's all.

Let's get going then, the voice commanded without sympathy, though not as strident as before.

I'm coming.

And bouncing over the rutted country lanes (where everything went on as though tragedy mattered not at all, where birds still sang, and bees buzzed and collected pollen, and little insects made a nuisance of themselves, where cattle grazed serenely without bothering to look up) in the back of the military jeep that smelled of oil and sweat and rubber, Martin was shocked to find his stomach heaving with fear. He felt no sorrow, no sense of loss during this drive to identify the bodies of his father and brother, for death seemed to have eradicated all memory of them as people, had in one split second transformed them from loved ones into statistics, into nothing more than another two corpses found by the roadside and reported on the evening news in that same nonchalant voice used to inform the viewers of the prowess of some skateboarding duck or the winner of some Rock and Pop award. If any other emotion found room beside his fear it was simply one that approached resentment that they should have allowed themselves to be killed.

Well? The voice asked.

Martin nodded.

You're sure?

I'm sure.

Right. You can shift them. Come on, jump to it. Get them out of there.

The bodies were hauled from the ditch by young soldiers unused to handling death, placed on large sheets of thick black plastic and lifted into the waiting army ambulance, the muddy water from the ditch oozing from the unfolded ends of the creaking plastic shrouds.

Home?

I'll walk.

Dangerous.

I'm okay.

Up to you.

That's right.

Need you again tomorrow.

Yes.

Still want to walk?

Yes.

Right. Let's get out of here.

They drove off at speed, gears grinding, tyres slithering on the muddy, churned grass verge, the bodies bouncing and flailing on the floor of the ambulance as though they were alive.

Martin crouched by the ditch and stared at the peaty brown water into which Dad and Steven had been dumped. What a hell of a place to die. Nothing noble in that. What was all that shit they talked about the dignity of death? If the ditch had been dry it would have been a little better: the sogginess and slime made it all gruesome and inhuman. One thing was bloody certain: he wouldn't go like that. Not on your life. Oh, no. He'd make bloody certain nobody found his body dumped in a ditch like an animal. Not Martin Deeley.

'...if you're still with us,' Mr Apple's opaque voice was suddenly intruding on the wretched scene.

' – ?'

'Ah, welcome back. A customer. Please.'

'Oh, sorry, Mr Apple. Thinking.'

'A dangerous pastime at the best of times, Martin.'

'You can say that again,' Martin agreed with a small, tight laugh, and turned to the counter to face Peter Taylor, who made the severence from his thoughts complete.

Peter Taylor was a huge man who emphasized his enormity by sporting a sumptuous beard that reached half-way down his chest.

86

Possibly because of his bulk he suffered spasmodically from quite excruciating cramps, which would attack unannounced and leave him, despite his great size, vulnerable and crying in agony, even writhing on the floor as though in the throes of a particulary virulent epileptic fit; as if to compensate for these lapses of weakness he adopted a fearsome and aggressive brusqueness, though this failed in its duty since his voice was ridiculously high-pitched, and he ended up sounding petulant.

'Must win today,' he announced threateningly. 'Bills to be paid. Gas. Light. Rent.'

'It's a hard life,' Martin commiserated.

'How would you know? Haven't lived yet, you haven't.'

'If you say so.'

'I just did. Why doesn't he come?' Peter Taylor demanded, pointing a stubby finger in the direction of Mr Apple.

'Busy,' Martin said. 'Very busy man.'

'I want him. Get him.'

'He won't like being disturbed.'

'Get him.'

'What's wrong with me, anyway?'

Peter Taylor stared at Martin as if suddenly seeing him for the first time. 'You know the business?'

'Sure I know the business.'

'You're certain?'

'Certainly I'm certain.' Martin leaned forward and signalled surreptitiously for the man to lean closer. 'I'm the real brains here,' he whispered conspiratorially. 'I'm the brains behind the whole operation.'

Taylor was impressed. 'Oooooh,' he soughed, and stepped back a pace for a better view of this newly emerged paragon. The shop seemed to creak under his enormous weight as he leaned forward again and submitted his wager with a subconscious sensation of privilege. 'I'd have asked for you every time if I'd known,' he confided.

'Well, you know now,' Martin told him.

'Yes. And you were right. Life is hard,' Taylor went on, a new quality in his voice that suggested he was now discussing life and its attendant hardships with an equal. 'Nothing but bills. Doesn't seem right, does it, just living to pay bills. Pay one and then another arrives to take its place. Pay that and there's another waiting just around the corner. And he doesn't help any,' he concluded accusingly, pointing again at Mr Apple.

'Well he wouldn't, would he?'

The big man laboriously searched out the logic in this. Then: 'He's not like us, you know.'

'Like us?' asked Martin dubiously.

Taylor nodded. 'Haven't you noticed? You can always tell them.'

'Them?' Martin was intrigued, wondering if despite his air of mild lunacy Peter Taylor had discovered something about Mr Apple that he, Martin, had long suspected.

'Villains,' Taylor announced.

Martin shook his head, grinning. 'Oh, I wouldn't call Mr Apple a villain.'

'I would. They're all villains, people like him. You watch out, young man, or he'll have you turning out like him,' Taylor predicted sombrely, and with this he swung away from the counter and trundled his great bulk from the shop, leaving Martin with his mouth open in amazement.

'Hey, you hear that?'

'– ?'

'You're a villain,' Martin told Mr Apple.

'That's right. I thought you knew.'

'Sure I knew, but I've just had it confirmed by an authority.'

'I'm glad. It must be nice to be proved right once in a while.'

'Very funny.'

Mr Apple glanced up from his desk. 'I wasn't really joking,' he said seriously.

'You never do.'

Mr Apple looked aggrieved. 'Yes I do,' he protested. 'I have a wonderful sense of humour.'

'You could have fooled me.'

'I don't think I could, Martin,' Mr Apple said, his eyes quite still and piercing behind the thick lenses. 'I really don't think I could.'

'Oh, I'm sure you could, Mr A. You're a wily old bird,' Martin said flippantly.

'If you say so.' Mr Apple gave in.

'In fact, I would say you could fool just about anyone,' Martin went on, leading up to something, but not quite sure what this something was.

'I think you believe I really am a villain.'

'No,' Martin said definitely. 'No, I don't think that. Not that. I think, though, that you like to play games with people.'

Mr Apple thought about this for a few moments before admitting: 'Perhaps you're right, Martin.'

'That can be pretty dangerous, you know, Mr A. I mean, you can get into a lot of unexpected trouble if people don't see it as funny,' Martin went on, realizing finally that in a roundabout way, and without fully understanding why, he was trying to warn Mr Apple that one particular little game had been observed and was being taken very badly.

'Hmm,' said Mr Apple, keeping his face impassive. 'I can understand that. Ah, well, being misunderstood is one of the hazards of life, isn't it, Martin?' he asked, looking up. Then, as though he only now appreciated the warning thrown for him to catch, he added 'But don't you worry. I won't play any games with you.'

'I'm glad to hear it,' Martin told him.

'In fact, I can truthfully say that games are the furthest thing from my mind when I think of you.'

' – ?'

Mr Apple tried to summon up a friendly smile. 'You're safe with me, Martin,' he said enigmatically.

Martin thought about pursuing the subject. Once again he felt an inexplicable sensation that, somehow, his destiny was hobbled to whatever befell the old man. But enough was enough. He had done his best to warn Mr Apple that he was under some suspicion and that was as far as he was prepared to go for the moment.

Two women from the factory down the road came into the shop, linking arms, giggling to hide a shared boredom, placed an ill-fated yankee, and scurried out. A young labourer, dressed in jeans and wellington boots turned down at the top and caked with cement, wandered from newspaper to newspaper seeking some certainty, failed to find it, and left to continue rebuilding the city. A pensioner came waddling in, the steel tip on his cane and similar tips on the heels of his shoes making three-legged, staccato taps on the linoleum; he wrote out his bet laboriously, making several changes, altering it every time he consulted the views of another tipster. In the end he despaired of ever getting it right and tick-tocked out again. And so it went. Clients came in with reasonable confidence but left soon afterwards looking bewildered, many not daring to risk a bet. Then, just before noon, a slim young man in an anorak rushed into the shop. He was panting, and he approached the counter with an assurance that indicated he was not the type who took chances on horses. 'Mr Apple?'

Mr Apple rose, his face expressionless, his fingers clenched.

'I've been sent to make sure everything is okay.'

Mr Apple stared at the man blankly, raising just one eyebrow in a difficult theatrical gesture he liked to employ from time to time. He kept his eyes fixed on the man's face, but saw, nonetheless, Martin shaking his head, his finger pressed to his lips.

'You know – ' the man said, fidgeting under Mr Apple's stoically uncomprehending gaze.

'I'm sorry?' Mr Apple offered at last.

'Seamus Reilly.' The man mentioned the name in a reverent whisper, as though this would reveal all.

'Seamus Reilly?' Mr Apple all but shouted the name, making the man wince and glance furtively over his shoulder.

'Yes,' he hissed. 'You know – '

'I'm afraid I don't know. I haven't the remotest idea what you're talking about,' Mr Apple lied convincingly. 'Martin? Come here a minute will you? This young man seems to be somewhat confused.

He says a – what was the name? – Seamus something – '

'Reilly,' the man supplied quickly.

'Ah, yes, Reilly. A man called Seamus Reilly sent him in to see if everything was all right. You don't know any Seamus Reilly, do you?' Martin shook his head slowly, his eyes fixed on the young man on the far side of the counter.

'You see?' Mr Apple said earnestly. 'You must be mistaken. I know an O'Reilly, but he's a David – '

The young man hurried from the shop, keeping his hands in the pockets of his anorak, using his shoulder to push open the door.

'Good heavens,' exclaimed Mr Apple. 'We do get some odd ones in here, don't we, Martin?'

Martin nodded, his silence ominous, his eyes still fixed on the door as if expecting it to open again at any minute. And he was not disappointed: suddenly in came the young man again, almost trotting, followed by Seamus Reilly.

'Good morning, Mr Apple,' Seamus Reilly said politely, scrupulously ignoring Martin.

'Good morning, Mr Reilly,' Mr Apple replied with equal politeness, neatly balancing the proceedings by ignoring the young man.

'Ah,' said Seamus. 'You do know me.'

'Of course.'

'Then – ?' Seamus indicated by a lilt in his voice and a vague gesture that perhaps some explanation was in order.

Mr Apple generously decided to oblige. 'How was I to know you sent him?' he asked reasonably. 'In walks this young man, a complete stranger – even Martin didn't know him – and Martin knows almost everyone, don't you, Martin? – and starts asking me questions. How was I to know – ?' Mr Apple asked again, allowing the question to trail away into silence.

Reilly nodded slowly, glancing quickly at Martin. 'Quite right, Mr Apple,' he said finally. 'Quite right. My mistake. I thought you had met.' Mr Apple overlooked the lie, and bowed his head slightly in recognition of his righteousness.

'A private word, then,' Reilly suggested, waving the confused young man away, watching him as he retreated to the far end of the shop.

'As you wish,' Mr Apple agreed, and, adopting an exact replica of the gesture, waved Martin away, giving him what could have been a little wink.

'Now,' said Seamus, pausing to light one of his little cigars and puff the smoke upwards in his slightly effeminate way, '*is* everything all right?'

'Of course.'

'Excellent.'

Mr Apple waited patiently: he knew that men who hold the whip hand liked their victims to wait patiently.

'No trouble at all?'

'No. None.'

'Excellent,' Reilly said again, continuing to enjoy his cigar, his eyes never leaving Mr Apple's face, using the smoke as an excuse to narrow them slightly. 'You haven't had any – eh – interference?'

'Interference?'

'No questions being asked by strangers?'

'Only him,' Mr Apple said innocently, pointing at the young man.

'Apart from him,' Reilly said with asperity.

'No.'

Reilly gave a small, humourless laugh. 'Sometimes, you know, we make mistakes about the people we trust,' he confessed in an oddly paternal voice.

'To err – ' Mr Apple began, his tone overtly human.

'Sometimes they let us down badly,' Seamus went on. 'It can be very disappointing. Very disappointing,' he said, shaking his head sorrowfully. 'And then, you see – ' He paused briefly to create the proper effect, stubbing out his cigar in the small tin ashtray on the counter. 'And then we have to punish them. Regrettably, of course.'

'Of course.'

Reilly shook his head in wonder. 'It is really amazing, you know, how many people think they can let us down and go unpunished. Even God punishes those who let Him down, doesn't He?' he asked.

'He does indeed,' sighed Mr Apple.

'You would tell us if anyone approached you?' Reilly asked abruptly, his voice suddenly sharp and businesslike.

Mr Apple looked suitably shocked. 'Approached? I don't follow.'

'If, say, the British became interested.'

'Oh. I see.'

'You would inform us?'

'I'm sure I would.'

Reilly smiled. 'Excellent. I knew you would. You know, I like you, Mr Apple. I like you a great deal. It would distress me greatly if anything unpleasant happened to you.'

'You're very kind.'

'Yes,' agreed Seamus in a mildly surprised voice, as if the accolade was foreign to him but deserving nonetheless. 'Yes, I suppose I am. Good. Well, that's that all cleared up. Now, about yourself. Are you all right for cash?'

'Thank you.'

'Excellent. Don't hesitate to shout if you need some.'

'I won't.'

'Just keep up the good work and we'll look after you.'

'Thank you.'

'We always look after our own.'

'I'm sure you do.'

'That's how it should be, don't you think? Always look after your own.'

'Quite.'

A well-dressed, middle-aged man came in and placed a hundred pounds first show on the likely favourite in the first race. Mr Apple dealt with him efficiently and thanked him for his custom, making a mental note to lose a couple of hundred on the same horse if it failed to oblige.

Seamus Reilly waited until the man had left the shop before announcing: 'I must be off. I'll be in touch, Mr Apple.' Mr Apple nodded. 'I'll probably drop in next week.'

'I look forward to that.'

Reilly summoned the young man to open the door for him and swept through it in his elegant, well-polished shoes.

'Very funny people coming to see you this morning, Mr Apple. Funny friends you have. I'm surprised at you,' Martin said.

Mr Apple looked up and seemed on the point of saying something significant. But he changed his mind and said instead, 'Just a business acquaintance with a little problem.'

'Oh, I see.'

'I thought you might know him.'

'Me? No-o-o-o. Never saw him before.'

'I see. Nor the other one, either, I suppose.'

'Other one?'

'The young man in the anorak.'

'Uh-uh. Told you. Never saw either of them.'

'Tell me, why did you – ' Mr Apple began.

'Sharp dresser, wasn't he,' Martin interrupted immediately.

'Who?'

'The man. The one with the cigar. Not the yob in the anorak.'

'Oh. Yes. Very sharp.'

'Must be important.'

'Would you think?'

Martin nodded. 'Very important I would say. Used to having his own way too, I'd say.'

'Would you now.'

Martin nodded again. 'Funny how you can always tell them. They're so polite. You know I'd say if that man stuck a knife in you he'd apologize first.'

Mr Apple smiled.

'And send flowers to your funeral,' Martin went on. 'Oh, I wouldn't have him as a friend if I were you, Mr Apple. And I certainly wouldn't do anything that would upset him.'

'I'll remember, Martin,' Mr Apple said seriously, aware that there was nothing funny in Martin's meaning despite his lighthearted manner.

'Must be nice to have power,' Martin went on. 'You ever want power, Mr Apple? Make people jump when you say jump?'

Mr Apple looked genuinely amazed. 'Why on earth would I want to make people jump, Martin?'

'You know what I mean. Make them do exactly what you want.'

'Most people will do what you want if you just ask them politely. You don't have to have power for that, do you?'

'It helps.'

'Only if you want them to do something unkind,' Mr Apple said quietly, the words retracing their steps to chase some incident in his past, gazing at Martin's face.

'Shit,' Martin was saying, as though kindness and power had nothing whatever to do with each other.

'You would have to say that, Martin,' said Mr Apple.

It proved a boring, uneventful afternoon. Mr Apple managed to lose the remaining money and balance his books nicely. It came as a pleasant surprise when Martin finally announced: 'Another day dead and buried.'

'Yes, indeed.'

'And all of us getting older,' Martin philosophized good-humouredly.

'And all of us getting older,' Mr Apple agreed. 'And not a whit the wiser,' he added.

'I wouldn't say that.'

Mr Apple thought for a moment, frowning as if something was eluding him. Then he brightened. 'You're quite right, Martin. Yes. I forgot. Well, no. I didn't forget. I tucked it away so that I could think more about it tonight.'

' – ? What are you talking about, Mr A.?' Martin asked.

'And thank you,' Mr Apple added. 'Thank you, Martin.'

'I haven't a clue what you're on about,' Martin threw over his shoulder by way of farewell, and by the time Mr Apple looked up he was gone.

Mr Apple took his time about locking up. The incidents of the afternoon had upset him more than he would have thought possible. And Martin's warning would have to be heeded: Seamus Reilly was not a man to be trifled with.

He closed and locked the door and set off down the street, his stilted walk very evident now that his mind was occupied with other things. When he had almost reached the end of the street he noticed two men standing on the corner: pretending not to look he recognized the young man in the anorak and, with him, the tall elegance of the nameless messenger who had given him the latest batch of money to lose. Mr Apple buried his chin in his chest and hurried towards the comfortable bustle of the Antrim Road. He was alarmed to find himself shaking. Yet, when he reached the brighter lights and glanced back, the two men still stood where they had been, appearing quite innocent, like any two men who lived in the area calmly discussing the events of the day. And Mr Apple felt a growing anger within him, as though he had allowed his greatest enemy the chance to invade his body and leave him trembling and a stranger to himself.

When he finally reached home Chloe was waiting at the door, mewling impatiently, implying she was starving to death, and how dare he keep her waiting.

'I'm coming, I'm coming,' Mr Apple told her with uncharacteristic impatience. 'You'd swear I never gave you a bite to eat,' he added, watching the tip of her tail twitch in excited expectancy.

And that night Mr Apple was ravaged by dreams of flesh being torn from his body by gigantic claws that ripped him to shreds. But, fortunately, it seemed that whatever spirit was instructed to watch over him could not stand to see him suffer so, and kept waking him every hour with a strange, nameless alarm.

8

Colonel Maddox sat at the head of the long mahogany dining-table (beautifully set with glass and silver, an arrangement of imported flowers in the centre), brooding over his wife's futile attempt at *escalope de veau aux champignons*, trying to exclude from his thoughts the chirping of her dinner guests. When he was younger his undeniable good looks, enhanced by his uniform, had been an impressive focus for women's attention, as had the seemingly limitless horizons of his career. But now his lined, exhausted face was just a joke, his career was almost over and he had nothing else to offer. Words left him in regimented barks, and when he tried to join in the inconsequential chit-chat he sounded absurd: his abrupt military intonation creating havoc with all things floral, theatrical and literary. Once he had dreamed of military greatness, of dying at the front, of leading his men over the top with astounding bravery and scant regard for his own safety, of wielding considerable power in Whitehall; but he had long since foresworn such chimeras. His tired, sagging eyes gave the impression of a once great man resigned to mediocrity, and he carried with him the furtive, nervous shadows and tics that service in Northern Ireland seemed to settle upon anyone assigned there. Yet despite the persistent hovering of death Maddox yearned to return there, and wished his leave was at an end. He sat there prodding the diced mushrooms, longing to return to people he understood and, more importantly, who seemed to understand him: men who said everything they had to say in a few words and with a minimum of fuss. He glanced up at his wife and smiled inwardly as she laughed flirtatiously and tried her wiles on an uninterested publisher of soft-porn paperbacks. He wondered what John Asher would make of her: his smile broadened at the thought of the interrogation he would put her through.

Leading from there, through Asher and on through the tense, panicky nights of Belfast, Maddox thought about Mr Apple and the game he was certain he was playing. The man must be mad. Shrewd enough, but mad nonetheless: only a madman would try the subterfuge and trickery Mr Apple was attempting. Or was Mr Apple the innocent he pretended to be? Was he, in fact, just quietly doing a job with no sinister undertones whatever? Maddox smiled again: what, indeed, if he and the confident Mr Asher were quite wrong, were barking up the wrong tree entirely, were wasting their time? Suddenly the Colonel hooted out loud with laughter.

'Do *tell* us, darling,' Nancy Maddox purred from the other end of the table, leaning sideways to skirt the flowers and get a better view of the remarkable sight of her husband laughing. 'We would all love to share your little joke.'

Colonel Maddox quickly refolded his features into their normal, mournful contours. 'Sorry. Nothing. Just thought of something.'

'Well, *tell* us,' Nancy persisted, flicking her eyes over her guests to glean support.

'It was nothing.'

'Another secret, I suppose,' Nancy sighed, overplaying her exasperation. 'Matthew collects secrets like butterflies. Really, every time he comes home from that awful place he gets worse.'

'I'm sorry,' the Colonel said, his apology halfhearted as if unsure of his guilt.

'I simply cannot understand why he keeps going back there,' Nancy insisted, addressing herself to her guests, avoiding direct contact with her husband in much the same way as she would were she dealing with a cripple.

'Duty,' Maddox offered, feeling some explanation was needed.

'Duty, indeed,' Nancy snapped scornfully. 'Let someone else have the duty. That's what I say. We should pull out and let those savages kill each other off. Like we did in India and places.'

'Quite right,' the publisher agreed, and then coughed as some morsel went down the wrong way.

'We can't,' Maddox said patiently.

'Whyever not, Matthew?' Nancy wanted to know, deciding to acknowledge her husband's presence. 'Nobody wants us there.'

Colonel Maddox studied the small gold signet ring on his little finger, turning and turning it as though seeking inspiration. He cleared his throat and everyone at the table turned towards him, fixing their eyes on his face in anticipation of wisdom. 'We have a commitment,' he said simply.

'Oh God,' Nancy said, flopping back in her chair and throwing up her arms in mock despair. Inwardly she fumed at her husband's fidelity, faithfulness not being one of her strong points.

'That's the cause of all the trouble, of course,' the publisher, recovered and latching on to Nancy's mild blasphemy, announced. 'God. Protestants and Catholics,' he concluded, placing the sects in the order of superiority as he saw it.

'Not any more,' Maddox contradicted, and wished he had kept his mouth shut.

'Really?' a new voice entering the fray wanted to know.

'I thought it was that simple when I was first sent there,' the Colonel confessed by way of atonement, aware that he was about to be launched on the choppy, treacherous sea of explanation. He searched about for the words that would explain the tragedy of Ulster to the greedy, vacuous faces that stared at him, searched also for something that would orientate his thoughts. He felt himself drowning in the confusion of hopes and distortions, fears, truths, half-truths and lies, political wheelings and religious dealings that created the turmoil of Ireland, and the more his mind thrashed about the more he realized he was sinking. 'The problem *is* – ' He stressed the last word unwittingly, and paused as though some clarification was just beyond his reach but attainable nonetheless. His face twisted in concentration, and the heavy silence of the dinner guests was like the murmur of an expectant crowd. Alas, Colonel Maddox was to let them down: how could he get such complexities across to other people? What took mountains of paper, strategic maps and charts, reports, analyzed reports, analyzed analysis, could hardly be explained over a slowly congealing *escalope de veau*. He stared at their

99

quizzical faces, and his mouth closed over air. Slowly he lowered his eyes to his plate and surrendered.

'Well, that explains everything,' Nancy said brightly, flashing her eyes upwards, and her guests commiserated with knowing smiles and shrugs. 'Now that we have solved that, has anyone here seen *Equus*?'

Mr Apple spooned tomato soup into his mouth and alternated his gaze between Chloe, who was playing with a ping-pong ball, and the television, which was showing pictures of another bombing in Belfast. As he watched the building explode in replay, and the injured being trundled away as though for the second time, he was amazed at his own detachment: it was as though it were all taking place a thousand miles away instead of just down the street. Worse still, it could have been fiction: another episode of some thriller with a cast of heroes who never died, were indestructable. Ah, he thought, that is precisely what the people of this violated city are: indestructable, going about their ways, making love at night, smiling, chatting, ignoring death sitting on their shoulders.

John Asher sat in his office, a tiny green-and-beige painted cell, reading through reports with the avidity of a man possessed, the remains of his supper pushed to one side. He read each word, forcing his cluttered, tired mind to concentrate, mouthing some of the words aloud in case his weary eyes were tempted to skip any. Somewhere on the pages before him might lie the clue to the problem that harrassed him continuously: he knew that the Bezant betting-shop was a clearing-house for dirty money; he knew that Arthur Apple was involved; and, most of all, suspected that there was a great deal more to all this than met the eye. The Provo executives who visited the shop so regularly did not do so because they were ardent gamblers. He could have hauled in half-a-dozen men for questioning, but that would have been a futile exercise: he would merely tip his own hand and, in return, receive nothing but the usual dull, gloating silence. No, he simply had to wait until he had proof, until someone made a mistake, or one of his informers came up with something concrete, or he spotted something in the reports that littered his desk: a casual reference to a person who had been sighted somewhere he had never been seen before, a meeting that at first glance appeared meaningless, but which hid a darker motive.

Asher yawned and stretched. Much as he disliked the Colonel's lenient, conciliatory, somewhat offhand attitudes, he wished he was back from leave. If nothing else, he was a useful testing-ground for ideas. No, that was unfair: the Colonel was a good soldier and a good man: like everyone else he was tired, his mind bogged down by the morass of information, the sense of futility and the unbending realization that they were getting nowhere no matter who they arrested, questioned, imprisoned. Stop the terrorists, they commanded from London. Yes, sir! Easy. Just hold up your hand and they stop. Hah. The trouble was that terrorists appeared in an unending stream, generation upon generation, cut one in half and instead of one dead body you ended up with, it seemed, two live ones – both more dedicated and intense than the one you thought you had destroyed. And they blended into the community to such effect that one never knew who was who, the most innocent-looking often the most guilty, and if Asher had learned one thing through the years he had learned that nobody would ever penetrate the complex, unyielding Irish nationalist mind.

Martin Deeley crouched low in his seat in the darkness of the cinema, his knees resting on the back of the seat in front of him, his eyes fixed, unblinking, on the screen. He chewed his thumbnail, spitting offhandedly into the aisle as a sliver of nail broke off. The cinema was holding a Hitchcock festival for that week, and Martin had patronized it every night: last night *Rear Window*, the night before *Dial M for Murder*, tonight *Psycho*. It was the alternatives of death that drew admiration from him as he watched, safe in the conviction that nobody would spot his enjoyment. The fascination of one person killing another completely overwhelmed him. Just as some people aroused themselves from the monotony of their lives by sharing the romantic and sexual escapades of their screen idols, so Martin felt new energy coursing through his veins as he studied celluloid people in their attitudes of death. Indeed, his interest in how people reacted when dying had nearly been his downfall on more than one occasion, as he lingered that minute too long to study his own victims as they came to terms with the fact that life was irrevocably ebbing from them. And as he focused his full attention on the unfortunate Janet Leigh, her body being systematically punctured and mutilated in the shower, he felt the familiar, glorious throbbing in his loins. He closed his eyes and gasped as the warmth oozed deliciously onto his leg.

Daphne Cope led her client towards her room, scrupulously avoiding any mention of the fact that she recognized him as a soldier despite his natty sports jacket and flannel trousers. It was the shoes that gave them away, of course, always the shoes: too brightly polished, too much spit and polish; no *real* civilian ever went to such lengths. Probably a sergeant, she mused: you could tell that sort of thing both from their bulk and the way they talked to you. Not that it mattered: the money was the same regardless of rank, she thought democratically.

As she waited for him to undress she played her usual little game of make-believe and pretended he was Martin. Then, on the bed, she muttered lustful little catch-phrases to him, getting him going: she had researched this well and knew that some worked better than others; married men, for some reason, needed more goading than others. Through it all she kept her eyes shut tight, feeling in his plump, wide body the hardness and slim outline of Martin. And as he heaved and floundered, determined to assert his tenuous dominance (and calling, between gasps for breath, the name Angela – a girlfriend or wife called on to witness his activity, to share his runting passion and possibly to salve his conscience) she groaned with practised artistry, and drew on the memories of her occasional nights with the young man she worshipped and for whose safety she feared.

Somewhere near the heart of the city a siren wailed, and the eerie tintinnabulation of rattling dustbin-lids shattered the night. Catcalls were launched into the air, shouts as venomous as rockets. Fucking English pigs. Para bastards. Youse fucking animals. Then the growling Saracens moved in. Gunfire cracked. Sidestreets were highlit in the evil blue-green glow of petrol bombs. And all over the city hundreds of doors were slammed tight and bolted, thousands of lights switched off as people settled in for a fretful night, waiting for daylight to reveal the destruction of war.

9

Mr Apple eased one eyelid open and viewed the dawn with a jaundiced eye. He always regarded Sundays with a mixture of suspicion and joy, since they meant, on the one hand, that he was forced to insulate himself from the particular sorrows which manifested themselves on that day without the comforting distraction of work and the raw collection of characters this brought galloping into his life, but, on the other, that he was free to visit what he liked to consider his private garden, whether Eden or Gethsemane, depending on the humour of the angels he found waiting for him. Such visits were particularly rewarding now that spring had finally come, the great trees bursting with an energy that was, in some way, transmitted to himself, so that he felt a little younger, a little more capable of fulfilling whatever destiny it was that his spirits had in store for him. It was certainly interesting, he thought, levering open his other eye and staring at the ceiling, how one could almost feel the old body rejoice now that it had survived another winter.

Mr Apple swung his feet over the side of the bed and studied his toes, wriggling them for a while, trying to straighten both small ones, which curved painfully under the others. Spring, he thought (reaching into his mind and sardonically pulling out the memory of a song that seemed to be played to death on the radio about this time of year), is in the air; and even a couple of blackbirds shared his perception and sang tentatively, duly fulfilling their obligations to April. Through the open window also (on the sill of which Chloe sat, busily manicuring her nails with her rough pink tongue) came the sounds of Sunday gardeners energetically mowing lawns with that initial burst of fitness and energy that the first real sun of the year seemed to stimulate. It was all so peaceful. Even violence took a day off on the Sabbath, and explosions and expletives were replaced, for the moment at least, by the soulful peeling of church bells as the denominations vied for attention: *Dolente, Dolore*. Mr Apple glanced at the small travelling-clock by his bed: almost ten. He smiled: the churches had long since ceased to push their luck and now offered alternative services at an hour that allowed their flocks the luxury of a lie-in.

'Time to arise and go now, get the sleep from thine eyes and face the world,' Mr Apple said aloud. Then he chuckled to himself, wondering happily if he was, indeed, manifesting the first signs of madness that talking to oneself was supposed to indicate. 'Rubbish,' he almost shouted. 'Utter tomfoolery,' he cried, falling back on the bed and kicking his spindly legs in the air like a child, building up a skittishness within himself, all the while pretending he was just having a little fun with no particular reason for such actions. But Mr Apple knew very well that there was a very particular reason for his foolishness: the first days of spring – came they early or late – were days of atrocious torment that he dreaded. Each year they brought with them the same long procession of appalling memories which seemed to have planned the invasion of his soul with alarming, seasonal precision, coinciding with that one week that had been the darkest in his life. Strangely, once he recognized that the daemonic images were unfolding their seasonal costumes, dusting them off and shaking the occasional sleepy moth from their folds, Mr Apple found that he could face them with a mildness that was quite fatalistic. He no longer grieved over the mutilation of his body that was a constant reminder of his agony; no longer, either, did the harrassment of his nightmares drive him to the brink of suicide: it struck him that, perhaps, some sympathetic angel had cauterized him from the worst things associated with that time. 'Hah,' said Mr Apple, mildly shocking himself by the sudden exclamation, and he found himself suddenly calmed by the realization that now, lying on his bed, he could even cull tiny memories of happiness from that terrifying time. And perhaps, he thought, that was the secret of man's survival: perhaps that was how everyone in this shattered, battered city survived. You've got to see the funny side, Mr Apple now recalled someone saying to him not so long ago, though what the funny side of death was he could not imagine. And yet people all around him seemed to spot it, to hug it tightly to themselves, and carry on as though reality consisted only of the world that revealed itself to the senses, a world of sight and smell and sound, as though tragedy and all such pains that afflicted the soul could be dealt with by a shrug of the shoulders, treated as vague discomforts, something to be put up with as a veteran might recall and dismiss old war wounds in damp weather. Nothing more. The blackness of pain and death came and went, greeted and waved away, and people continued to exist. 'Faustus is dead, long live the Pied Piper,' Mr Apple said, giggling a bit hysterically at his ridiculous joke, springing to his feet and making for the bathroom. He shaved himself carefully, taking inordinate precautions not to nick himself: for some reason he abhorred those specks of dried blood small razor-cuts left behind – lice droppings, he had heard them called – and he shuddered when he saw them on the faces of other men, treating them like evil fetishes that augured much worse bloodshed to come. Then he brushed his teeth, up and down, doused his face in cold water, dried, and returned to the bedroom to dress.

Clad in what, with dry humour, he referred to as his Sunday suit, Mr Apple made his way down the road, albeit without much purpose in his step. He did not walk aimlessly: it was more as though he was heading towards a sound rather than some more definite destination, a sound that played tricks on him, fading occasionally, leaving him temporarily baffled if not quite lost.

'Morning, Mr Apple.'

' – ?' Mr Apple was taken aback by the burring voice at such close proximity. 'Ah,' he finally managed, eyeing suspiciously the small, stooped, sandalled figure, immaculate and balding in khaki shirt and grey flannel trousers, carrying a watering-can, who regarded him with tolerant distaste through thick hornrimmed spectacles from behind the low, trimmed, crew-cut privet hedge. 'Ah,' he said again, composing himself. 'Good morning, Mr Cahill.'

'Churching?' Mr Cahill demanded as if not approving of religion as a pastime.

'Not exactly.'

'Stopped that nonsense a long time ago. Hypocritical, isn't it?'

Mr Apple shrugged. The last thing he wanted was an argument. But Mr Cahill was in fine fettle and, adopting the same scathing tone he used when dismissing from his mind such riff-raff as niggers, coolies, wogs and Pakis (all of whom he claimed to have had dealings with at some time in his life, though in what capacity he kept a closely guarded secret), he declared: 'All of them. Damned hypocrites. Parsons, priests, vicars, all you have to do is listen to them.' Mr Cahill's words sprinkled over Mr Apple as the water from the can now did over the neat row of primulas. 'All they ever do is trot out the old platitudes. Love one another. Huh. Why should I? Can't stand half the people I meet. Anyway, all their sermons are slanted.'

'Oh, not all, I think,' Mr Apple ventured charitably.

'All of them. What did you mean by "not exactly"?'

'– ?'

'When I asked if you were churching,' Mr Cahill explained.

'Oh. Well, I pray – but not exactly in church. I have my own place, you see,' Mr Apple replied vaguely.

'Your own place? You're not a minister?' Mr Cahill sounded shocked.

'No. Indeed no, Mr Cahill. I just like to get away by myself and chat to – '

'You're mad, Mr Apple,' Mr Cahill announced, turning away and striding towards his house (structurally identical to Mr Apple's, but sporting net curtains, looped and tied back at the sides, and pale blue paintwork which stood out garishly), the last drops from the watering-can dripping on the path behind his impatient footsteps like damp exclamation marks.

For several moments Mr Apple stared at the retreating figure, and continued to gaze at the space vacated by it as it now vanished round the side of the house, seemingly leaving some ghostly vestige of itself in the front garden to guard against trespassers. In an odd way he quite liked Mr Cahill, almost admired the old bigot's outrageous forthrightness, and there was always the possibility he had a point. Certainly (and Mr Apple had noted it with some alarm, the more intense when he spotted himself beginning to surrender to its potent inevitability) the tone of the sermons he occasionally saw reported was subtly overladen with politics. And yet, why not? The fine line between religion and politics had become infinitely finer in Ulster, causing frictions of unidentifiable origin. But Mr Apple (he had turned left at the end of the road and now stood patiently by the bus stop almost directly opposite the church of St Enoch) was content to admit that this was a problem for someone else to solve, and he wasn't very sanguine about their chances of finding a solution.

He glanced across the road at the armoured car parked, in a failed gesture of discretion, at the side of the church, its occupants looking embarrassed as the faithful walked by and headed for the open doors of the church. Their dogged determination to confront the Lord with their problems made Mr Apple think about his own efforts at prayer and wonder mildly why they had been so futile. Possibly it was because he had nothing to pray for, or, more truthfully, nothing to pray to. Still, he acknowledged gratefully as the bus came trundling up the road, there had been comfort to be found in the dark corners he always chose, and an odd communal compassion as the congregation struggled to worship a God who seemed to have better things on His mind. Amazingly, he had noted with wonder, this in no way seemed to deter them; their faces relaxed as though the din of their prayers battering His eardrums formed a noisy, impregnable barrier that released their thoughts from the horrors that were committed around them. In truth, Mr Apple had envied them their faith.

Almost before he knew it Mr Apple found himself at his destination, found himself thanking the conductor who helped him alight, found himself walking contentedly and with a spring in his step down the lane to the abandoned farmhouse, found himself moving through the overgrown farmyard with its collapsing outhouses (the rusting corrugated-iron roof of one swaying in the light wind and making baleful whinnies like echoes of the animals it once housed), found himself clambering over the low stone wall with remarkable agility for a man of his advancing years, found himself quickening as he made for the copse in the centre of the field, found, too, a strange serenity descend upon him as he neared it, found, alas, something like terror invade his soul as he entered under the shadow of the trees. He stood quite still, his head cocked to one side, and listened, but not, as one might have thought, for any natural sound: Mr Apple waited for the voices he knew would come to him, the voices that always came to him in this place.

Be patient, Mr Divine told him kindly.

Yes, agreed Sefer, you can't hurry these things, you know.

'I know,' Mr Apple said aloud.

Ah, said Sefer, you're learning.

'Yes, I'm learning.'

Good, said Mr Divine in a pleased voice.

Suddenly Mr Apple felt a terrible, cold chill penetrate his body. His head began to ache as if several headaches had saved up their pain and now heaped it upon him. A strange, pungent smell assailed him, a stench like burning sulphur or putrefying flesh. He felt himself drifting away as though losing consciousness, and the trees about him shimmered and faded. Small blue lights swam in his brain, blinking in a patternless rota. And then he was floating high above the ground, weightless and unfettered, yet the pain in his head grew worse and that part of his forehead directly above his eyes seemed to puff up, and he felt cold, bitterly cold. The awful pain made him close his eyes, but immediately some antagonistic force made him open them again and look down: he was hovering over the little copse, looking down at himself standing there, a forlorn, lost, abandoned figure. It was as if he had somehow inhabited his soul and left his body to fend for itself for the moment. Then the voices came: they drifted in like the sighs of whispering angels who had abandoned their ancient places, yet, although they permeated him, they did not seem to be audible: they were simply there, coming from a great distance and friendly enough. Birds, too, suddenly abounded, long-winged dark furious shapes, each one a strange embodiment of fierce despairs and dreams, each one a vision of his own suppressed memories, floating on warm streams of air, gliding mile upon mile, then dropping through an entanglement of shapes, an incomprehensible entanglement of geometric silhouettes, alighting on invisible timber ghosts, folding their wings, settling like a black conspiracy.

We have been watching you, the voices cried in unison, half-singing, half-wailing.

'Ah,' Mr Apple heard his body sigh.

We are well pleased.

'Ah.'

Your time is not yet come, but shortly. Soon the salvation of one will be required of you. Soon but not so soon as to give you no time to prepare.

'How shall I know?'

You will be given a warning, and then you will know you must sacrifice yourself.

'What warning?'

Your wounds will open. But you will feel no pain. We will carry the pain for you as you have carried ours.

'Ah.'

You need not be afraid. You will find great peace.

The single word 'peace' echoed comfortingly as the voices withdrew, taking with them the awful throbbing in Mr Apple's head, escorted by the birds that rose suddenly, formed columns, and plunged upwards, great wings outspread but unmoving, giving the impression that they were, in fact, diving, that the world had been turned upside-down and that they were plummeting downwards.

Mr Apple came to himself and shivered. There he stood in the middle of the copse, his feet firmly planted on the ground. He shook his head and smiled: as always after these encounters he felt better, felt as though he had been given some energy which would allow him to carry on, but energy in a limited dosage lest he become impertinent and believe he could carry on for ever. Mr Apple smiled again and, with a small wave towards the sky, he bowed to the trees that surrounded him and set off home, walking briskly until his legs complained.

Had the bus taking Mr Apple to his curious rendezvous been a little less punctual, and had he, while waiting, watched the Sunday worshippers enter St Enoch's, he might have been surprised to spot Martin Deeley (dressed respectfully in a dark suit, white shirt and sober tie) among them. Martin Deeley physically fulfilled his obligations of the Sabbath conscientiously every week: it never struck him as incongruous or perverse that he should remain loyal and obedient to this ecclesiastical regulation while cheerfully breaking every other commandment of his faith. Indeed, he would have been both shocked and furious had it been suggested he might as well abandon this one remaining link. Once, many years ago, the ludicrous disparity of his behaviour had crossed his mind, and, with a feeling of wry, guilty amusement, he had likened it to the Mafia allegiance to family and the compulsory weekly visit to the Godfather's table which he had read about or seen in the cinema: almost everything was forgiveable provided that one precept was faithfully observed, and in much the same light Martin faithfully observed his Sunday visit to Mass. But his relationship with God was certainly spurious: he had a healthy respect for the power He would wield over him when he finally died, but as long as there was breath in his body God's influence was easily curtailed. With monstrous profanity Martin Deeley could never quite reconcile himself to the fact that this Being with all that incredible power at his fingertips could get Himself crucified without at least a show of resistance. All that crap about dying for the sins of man! Hang up there, boyo, and save mankind. Well, He must be pretty disillusioned by now. And yet...and yet, Martin Deeley fully realized that in spite of his bold effrontery, in spite of his casual dismissal of all things religious as not applying to him, he still thought in terms of sin rather than crime. When he killed someone a little sign sometimes flickered mischievously in his brain, accusing him of mortal *sin*: and every once in a while, in those brief seconds before he fell asleep and the innocence of his childhood held centre-stage, he found himself mouthing uncharacteristic apologies to the God he had decided it was mature to disown.

Little silvery bells tinkled in the sanctuary. The Host was raised and the heads of the congregation lowered. Martin bowed his head also, but not so low that he could not observe the mass adoration. The weirdness of it all frightened him, and he felt a strange loneliness, as though he was purposely being excluded from the lucid familiarity of something he had sought and received comfort from in another time. Looking about him, wondering at those genuinely adoring faces, he could appreciate the emotions the ceremony induced in others, yet he himself was stirred only, it seemed, to a reminiscence of sadness: he was, he decided, like an archaeologist recreating the dignified solemnity of some ceremony practised by a defunct but interesting civilization. He smiled faintly, his eyes softening and, as the congregation streamed towards the altar to receive communion, he allowed the chill breezes of memory to blow in his mind and toy with the threads of recollection...

The two coffins lay side by side, the floral wreaths shared equally between them, the flowers crippled and twisted into unnatural shapes, cartwheels and crucifixes, the mourners, also, twisted into the odd contours of lament: the women seeming to have shrunk in their misery, the men grown taller in their anger. Martin stood between Cissy and Mam, feeling embarrassed as Mam sniffed and snorted her griefstricken way through the ceremony, feeling irked and jittery as she flicked her way round her rosary, gabbling her Hail Marys at incredible speed, her head bobbing every time she hit upon the name of Jesus. To pass the time he tried to keep up with her, failed, and decided she was only pretending to pray, just going through a familiar ritual, mouthing occasional words from which she had once drawn comfort.

As the coffins were heaved clumsily on to the shoulders of the four bearers the congregation rose and stood stiffly in the pews, glancing furtively at one another, surreptitiously seeking advice on how to behave, wondering, perhaps, what emotions to reveal, how best to demonstrate their feelings, which signs and signals would confirm their reason for being there. In the end they seemed to sort it out, the men leaving the women to shed the tears, the women leaving the silent outrage to the men.

Martin was impressed by the cortège, which (he thought for one gruesome moment, as he noted the flowers bob gaily over the heads of the adults, the carnations and lilies and imported roses still spanking fresh and colourful) could easily have been some happy, festive affair. And for the first time in his life he felt almost proud of his father, proud, too, but strangely envious of his brother. As the procession made its way through the streets the murmur of the mourners (a mixture of prayer and practical conversation) kept step with the rhythmic stomping of the paramilitary boots worn by the masked guard of honour, defiantly armed, that paraded in front of the coffins and lined them on either side, their presence giving the dead a political importance they hardly deserved. They were victims. Nothing more. Not heroes or cowards. Not terrorists or activists or traitors. Not, in any logical sense, the enemy. Not motivated by anything stronger than a desire to live. Just victims in the true and appalling sense, plucked willy-nilly from the community and shot, perhaps in reprisal for some other killing long since forgotten, perhaps as a diabolic warning, or perhaps just as some horrific show of sectarian might.

And even then, barely sixteen though he was, watching the coffins being lowered into the cold, damp, symmetrical graves, and hearing the crackling rifles as they delivered their premonitory salute (the shots seeming to bounce from gravestone to gravestone, multiplying their deadly homage, the echoes taking an inordinately long time to recede and disappear skyward as though launched to placate some angry, warmongering god), Martin knew he would be expected to join the unending cycle of violence and avenge these two hopeless deaths. Oh, yes, Mam would see to that, making it clear she would be ashamed of him if he did nothing about it, she would, in the grim cold tradition of such things, be happy to sacrifice him for vengeance.

And friends would argue knowingly that two deaths in one family were enough, but their arguments would be couched in words that expected rebuttal; neighbours would express their desire that he would not consider any action that might bring 'further misery and sorrow to your poor mother', but their voices would indicate they hoped he would. 'Ashes to ashes,' the priest intoned, trying hard to make his familiarity with the words less apparent, imparting meaning by the fire in his voice, delivering his homily with extravagant praise for the two dead men, investing them with qualities they never possessed...

Before he realized it Mass was over, and the congregation were filing from the church, blinking in the bright sunlight, the turmoil in their souls assuaged for another week perhaps. But perhaps not: their eyes still carried the haunted look with which they had arrived, and their loathing was still apparent when they spotted a gaggle of Paras patrolling further down the street. As Martin watched, trying to decipher the various reactions written on the faces about him, the crowd immediately to his right separated and allowed the dapper figure of Seamus Reilly to pass through: then they seemed to withdraw a few feet, respectfully, as though they suspected sins were about to be confessed, sins it would be better for them not to overhear. Not an altogether idiotic suspicion, since Seamus Reilly in his black overcoat and black hat, carrying his large black missal with its embossed gold crucifix, gave a distinct impression of something clerical, though one could have been forgiven for imagining there was something more of the undertaker about him.

'Lovely morning, Martin.'

Martin nodded, mildly surprised that Seamus should speak to him so openly.

'Makes you think of holidays, doesn't it?' Seamus Reilly continued mysteriously.

'Holidays?'

'Mmm. Feel like one?'

'Not – '

'Good. I'm glad you do,' Seamus Reilly said, looking away for a moment to acknowledge a greeting. 'They tell me Berkshire is at its best this time of year.'

'Berkshire?' Martin repeated, his voice rising in stunned surprise.

'Yes. Know it at all? Lovely spot. Wide, open spaces. Fresh air. Quite lovely.'

'I don't – '

'Be at home about eight, will you? I'll be round to see you.'

'Tonight?'

'Tonight. Eight. Exactly. I'm always on time as you know.'

And with that Seamus Reilly left him, nodding to acquaintances in his friendly way, shaking a hand, squeezing an arm, frowning in concern as some problem was revealed.

Martin stared after him, his heart pumping rapidly, an old and familiar anticipation gripping his stomach.

True to his word, at eight precisely Seamus Reilly put one neatly manicured finger on the white plastic button and pushed. He had, in fact, arrived three minutes earlier, but so proud was he of his meticulous timekeeping that he had waited in the shadows until the exact time of his appointment before announcing himself.

Martin, coming down the stairs two at a time, raced to the door and let him in, shouting 'I'll get that' as his landlady poked her head around the sitting-room door. She withdrew again willingly, closing the door behind her. 'Upstairs,' Martin said.

Reilly inclined his head in agreement and followed Martin up the narrow stairs that creaked goodhumouredly under their weight.

'Sorry about the mess,' Martin apologized, smiling. 'I'm not tidy.'

'It's as it should be. Lived in,' Reilly conceded graciously, although his lips tightened as he viewed the small room with distaste. 'I always say a home should be lived in,' he added, 'although – ' He waved a small hand in a semi-arc and smiled thinly.

'Yeah. Well, I like it this way,' Martin told him, determined to make no further apology for the chaos about him: his clothes strewn everywhere, books in precarious piles, newspapers, shoes, an incongruous tennis-racket.

'To each his own,' Reilly allowed.

'Exactly.'

'I must confess I don't think *I* could live amid such confusion. I like things to be orderly. A place for everything and everything – '

' – in its place.' Martin concluded the quotation.

'Quite,' Reilly said testily.

'Well, it so happens I think the same,' Martin said, suddenly realizing that Reilly was meeting him for the first time on his own territory and was starting to flounder. 'And everything *is* in its place.'

'I see,' Reilly said, looking about him as though seeking somewhere to sit. Carefully he removed a jacket and soiled shirt from a wooden, high-backed chair (using only one finger and his thumb), placed them on the bed and sat down, but not before flicking any possible contamination from the seat with a white handkerchief he produced from his breast pocket. 'Ah,' he sighed comfortably, crossing his legs. Martin sat on the edge of the bed (enjoying the wince his guest gave as the springs protested shrilly) and waited.

'You don't, I suppose, mind if I smoke?'

Martin shook his head, and waited.

Reilly lit one of his small cigars and spoke through the cloud of smoke as if trying to conceal, or at least veil, the frank brutality of his words, words spoken in a calm, gentle voice that in no way lessened their deadliness.

'You'll be glad to hear we have someone who needs to be punished, Martin. We need your special talents. Just a one-off, however. A chance that is too good to miss.'

Martin made no reply: he stared through the smoke in the direction of the voice and suddenly recalled, from what seemed a lifetime ago, a visit he had made with his mother to a relative who had spent all her adult life as a Poor Clare. He remembered the eerie sound of her voice whispering through the black-veiled screen, a disembodied voice that seemed to come from the grave. And he had the same impression now of Reilly's flat, matter-of-fact tones wafting through the smoke which curled and twisted before his breath and seemed, oddly, to give his words their inflections.

'You will, of course, have to take a few days off. Tell Mr Apple you feel ill. Tell him that tomorrow. Tuesday you go. You should be back by Friday, all being well.'

'Go where?'

'Why, Berkshire, of course. Lovely spot – '

'I know: wide, open spaces and fresh air. You told me.'

'So I did.'

'Why?'

With a brisk wave Reilly cleared the smoke from in front of his face like a magician making his appearance, and leaned forward.

'Well, a certain Colonel Maddox – I think you've heard of him? Yes. Well, Colonel Maddox has his home there. He is at his home this minute. He will be returning from leave on Wednesday. We would be grateful if he failed to reach Belfast.'

Martin nodded, his mind already raking up questions he would need answered.

'He's not really of great importance,' Reilly was saying in a voice close to regret, 'but his demise would serve its purpose. Actually, from what we've learned Maddox is decent enough. Doesn't even want to be here. And he's always been – eh – correct, I think is the word.' Reilly sighed as though saddened by Colonel Maddox's upright reputation. 'It distresses me when we have to punish nice people – so much easier when they're blackguards, isn't it? Anyway, it should be straightforward enough. We don't foresee any problems.'

'Protection?'

'No. They don't seem to see Berkshire as a likely place for us to strike. He will have a driver, of course. His wife is there. One house-guest who might have left by Wednesday. A publisher of romantic novels, I hear.' Reilly grinned widely, as if he found romance hugely amusing. 'There's a maid – a *domestic*, we were told.' Reilly allowed his grin to widen for a moment before it disappeared completely. 'And that's all,' he concluded.

'Dogs?'

'Two. A retriever. Old, deaf and friendly. A pug. Hers. The wife's. Dreadful creature. Fat and wheezy. Nothing for you to worry about.'

'Neighbours?'

Reilly shook the ash from his cigar.

'Nobody close.'

'How close?'

'Quarter of a mile? Something like that. Your best bet would be after he leaves the house. There's an isolated lane he has to travel down before he hits the main road. Plenty of cover for you. The hedgerows should be pretty about now,' he added.

'That'll be nice,' Martin said, and, strangely, there was nothing sarcastic in his tone: it was a simple statement of fact, as though the viciousness of killing was in some way lessened when perpetrated from behind a pretty hedgerow.

'Hmm,' Seamus murmured, apparently sharing the sentiment and already sniffing primroses.

'Weapon?'

'There'll be a selection at the usual place. Take the bus from the airport and go straight there. You're expected.'

'Transport?'

'Tommy Walshe will drive you. You get on well with him.'

'He's okay. What time does Maddox leave?'

'Ah. Well. As to that, we're not quite sure.'

'Great.'

'If you fly over Tuesday afternoon Tommy will drive you to Berkshire overnight, so you will be in plenty of time.'

'So I just hang around bloody Berkshire all – '

'No,' Seamus snapped, not about to tolerate impertinence.

'What, then?'

'When I said we weren't quite sure I was referring to the precise time. We do know Maddox flies out from Brize Norton at midday. Whether he decides to arrive early or on time is up to him. Perhaps you would like us to telephone him and enquire as to his precise movements?'

'Very funny.'

'Tommy has friends in Oxford. You can rest up there for a few hours. Leave about midnight.'

'Okay.'

'Anything else?'

'No.'

Reilly reached into his pocket and produced two brown envelopes. He passed the thicker of the two to Martin. 'Rail ticket to Dublin. Plane ticket to Birmingham. Money,' he said.

'Thanks.'

'And here,' he continued, passing over the second envelope, 'is the only photograph we have of Maddox. It's not great, I'm afraid, but it's the best we could do. He refused to pose, you see,' he concluded, grinning again.

Martin Deeley, however, saw nothing amusing in the remark; nothing cheerful, either, in the face that stared up at him from the small, glossy, dog-eared photograph. Doomed was the immediate impression the face gave. No hint of a smile, eyes both sad and confused, turned inwards on his soul and already dead. It was the face, Martin thought, of a man who had failed, or not quite that: it was more a mask that portrayed an incapability to understand. Not that it mattered a damn what he looked like: in Martin's eyes he was already a corpse, and he comforted himself with the thought that he was probably going to put the poor old bastard out of some longstanding misery.

'You're quite happy then?' Reilly asked.

'Yeah. Delirious.'

'Good. Anyway, you're the expert. We know we can leave everything safely in your hands.'

'Sure.'

'Excellent. Well, I'll be on my way.'

'Right.'

'Sorry to have intruded on a Sunday. I always think Sunday is a private day,' Seamus explained. 'I recall my mother would never open the door to anyone on Sundays. But that was some time ago, of course. Still, old habits die hard, don't they?'

'I'm sure they do.'

Martin took Reilly to the front door and opened it for him.

'Oh, by the way,' Seamus said, pausing on the doorstep, turning to show mischievous little lights dancing in his eyes. 'There's an apt little landmark in Berkshire for you to look out for. When you see it you'll know the Maddox house is just down the road.'

'Well, are you going to tell me?'

'Oh – a gibbet, Martin. High on a hill overlooking the Downs. The very last gibbet in England, so they tell me. I thought you'd like that,' he added, grinning wickedly.

'Oh, lovely.'

'Yes. I thought you'd like that,' Seamus said again. 'I know you feel at home in the shadow of death.'

'You really are a charmer, Seamus.'

'So I've been told.'

'No, really. You're so bloody charming you frighten the life out of me.'

'Me? Frighten *you*? Oh, come now, Martin.'

'Yes. You go about all dressed up like a man on his way to a party, smiling and cheerful, ticking off names on your death-list like they were your goddam shopping – '

'Shut it, Martin,' Reilly snapped, his face tightening, any trace of friendliness wiped away. 'Don't you ever talk to me like that again, Deeley,' he hissed. 'Not ever, do you hear? You know nothing about me. Nothing about how I feel or what I think. You imagine I *like* having people killed? Do you? Only shitty little thugs like you enjoy death. Yes, you *do*. You revel in it. It makes you feel important, gives your grotty little life some meaning. Jesus! You are fucking pathetic. You're as bad as those smug-faced bastards who portray us all as psychopathic murderers who wallow in blood and death. I can tell you this: I hate it. I loath it. I – ' Seamus Reilly glanced at the sky in search of a better word, and, finding it, 'I abominate it,' he said in a whisper.

'So you abom— '

'Shut up. And as to the way I dress, what do you want? Jeans? Grubby shirts? Dirty shoes? Oh, yes. That would fit the image, wouldn't it? I wear the best clothes I can out of respect. I mourn the people I've had killed, whoever they are, and I dress out of respect for their passing,' Seamus concluded breathlessly, the weird preciousness of his remarks making them sinister and frightening.

Martin Deeley decided it would be wiser to say nothing.

'And another thing,' Reilly went on, 'you think it's easy for me to go about ordering punishments, don't you? Just a name on a piece of paper to be struck off. Very clever. You stupid bastard. I *believe* in what we are trying to do, but I am sickened to my stomach at the way we are forced to achieve it. I ordered my own brother killed because he turned informer. I suppose I enjoyed that? I cried for a week. And I still cry when I think of his great pleading eyes. He shouted at me "Not me, Seamus, not your own brother" when they came and took him from the house. Dragged him whimpering and screaming down the garden. But, yes, him, my own brother.' Seamus Reilly paused as if again watching his brother being taken from his home. 'And you say I like it.'

'I didn't know – '

'You know *nothing*,' Seamus informed him. 'Not one damn thing. And maybe,' he added with a sigh, 'maybe it's just as well.' Then his voice changed, returning to its former self. 'Anyway, don't forget to look sick when you see Mr Apple. I'll check with you tomorrow evening,' he concluded, and strode off down the street, his black suit disappearing rapidly in the dark.

'Who was that?' his landlady, Mrs Losey, wanted to know, peering round the sitting-room door, her hair netted and curled for the night.

'Nobody.'

'Oh,' Mrs Losey said, accepting the reply for what it was worth.

'Just a friend.'

'Nice to have friends,' Mrs Losey told him. 'You eaten today?'

'Uh-uh.'

'I have a scrap of shepherd's pie left over you can have.'

'Thanks, Mrs Losey. But no. I'm not hungry.'

'You should eat something. Can't go about all day on an empty stomach and hope not to get sick.'

'I don't want anything,' Martin said sourly, then, seeing the woman's hurt expression, he added: 'Not just now. I have things to do. By the way, I won't be here for a few days. I'm going down to Dublin.'

'Dublin, is it?'

'Just for a few days.'

'I see.'

'You go on back to your telly.'

Obediently Mrs Losey closed the door and went back to her telly.

Alone again in his room Martin counted the money, checked the train and plane tickets, and took another cursory look at Colonel Maddox. Then he lay back on his bed, folding his arms under his head, and stared at the ceiling, thinking:

Hey, someone said, that's pretty good shooting, sonny.

It's nothing.

On the mark every time. I call that something.

It's easy.

Martin bathed in the warmth of the flattery and proceeded to shoot some more, while the stranger stood at his shoulder and murmured continuous praise at his prowess: all about them the noises of the fun-fair continued and gave no hint of the fatefulness of the meeting.

It's just know-how, mister, Martin said.

What's your name, sonny?

Martin.

Martin?

Martin Deeley.

Deeley...Deeley...that rings a bell, the stranger said. Oh, yes, he added, remembering something. Where d'you live, Martin Deeley?

Tiger Bay.

Ah. Brothers and sisters?

Only sisters. Two. My brother was – why all the questions, mister?

No reason, Martin. Just curious.

Oh.

You really can shoot though, the stranger iterated, shaking his head in what seemed to be admiration, though there was something ominous creeping into his voice.

Yeah. You told me that already, Martin said, feeling cocky.

I'll remember you, Martin Deeley. I'll remember you.

And he did, but not until long after Martin Deeley had forgotten him. Eighteen months, perhaps more, perhaps two years later, a man called at the Deeley house in Tiger Bay.

Martin Deeley live here? he asked Mam, who stared at him

suspiciously, squinting her eyes, keeping the thin door on a chain and one foot wedged against it.

Who wants to know?

Me.

And who might you be?

He'll know me.

He will, will he?

He will.

Martin! Mam yelled over her shoulder, keeping her eyes on the stranger. There's someone here who wants to see you.

Who is it?

He says you know him.

What's his name?

Hasn't got one, Mam said.

Coming, Martin called.

Hello, Martin. Remember me?

No – yes. I remember your face but –

The fun-fair. Shooting.

Oh. Yeah. I remember.

I told you I wouldn't forget you.

So?

Some friends of mine want to meet you.

Who?

Friends. They have a job for you.

What sort of job?

A job. It won't take long. Pays well.

I'll think about it.

Nothing to think about, Martin. They want to meet you. Tonight.

Oh.

We'll send a car. Sixish.

Okay.

Good.

Yeah.

Who was that may I ask? Mam demanded.

Just a fella.

I saw that. Who was he?

Someone I know.

From where?

Around.

I see. She didn't, of course, but that hardly mattered. Martin was the man of the house now, and it was neither her place nor was it wise to pry too deeply into his affairs. You'll be careful?

I'm always careful.

I know you are, but still be careful.

I'll be careful.

Don't get yourself used.

I won't.

They can use you without you noticing it.

Not me, they can't.

Don't be too sure.

I'm sure, Mam. I can handle myself.

That's what they all say.

But I know I can.

Oh, you know everything.

That's right.

Well, I hope you know what you're doing this time.

I do.

I hope so.

Don't worry. Like I said, I can handle myself.

I hope so.

I *can*.

And in the months that followed, he showed that he certainly could.

11

'Jesus, Mr Apple, I feel really terrible this morning,' Martin Deeley announced.

'Yes,' replied Mr Apple.

'No, really. Really I do. I think I'm coming down with something.'

Mr Apple looked up from his desk, and nodded. 'Plague, probably. Or leprosy.'

'I'm serious. I don't think I'll make it through the day.'

'Probably not.'

'You think I'm joking.'

'Well – '

'Well, I'm not.'

'Go home then. See a doctor. Go to bed,' Mr Apple advised offhandedly.

'Jeez, you're full of sympathy, Mr Apple.'

'Yes.'

'But I *am* sick, dammit,' Martin insisted.

'I thought you might be,' Mr Apple announced, suggesting by an odd inflection that he had been waiting for some such calamity. 'And I told you what to do. Go home.'

'I can't just hump off like that. Who'll do the board?'

'I'll manage. There's always someone who'll do the board for a few pounds. It doesn't take genius.'

'Well, I'll tell you what I'll do. I'll set up the board and stay until lunch-time. If I still feel like I do now I'll go home then, okay?'

'Please yourself,' Mr Apple snapped, regretting his sharpness but not bothering to do anything about it.

'You're in a funny – '

But whatever funny Mr Apple was in was to remain a mystery, since Martin's diagnosis was interrupted by the arrival of Ursula

Weeks. She stood in the doorway for several seconds, peeping into the shop like a bird deciding where to perch. 'Good morning, Mr Apple. May I come in?'

Mr Apple glanced up, but only with his eyes: he kept his head bent in that petulant posture he had been using on Martin. 'Come in, come in,' he told her, marvelling at the dexterity she showed in cramming her matronly figure into the Salvation Army uniform, her face (clear and innocent and remarkably young-looking for a sixty-year-old, making one think immediately of a nun) framed by her bonnet.

'I thought I'd come nice and early,' Ursula explained, 'before you got busy,' she added with a smile.

Mr Apple nodded, and fussed with pencils and paper-clips on the counter.

'Anyway, people are always in much better humour first thing in the morning, don't you think?' Ursula asked hopefully. 'Before the day catches up on them.'

'Vulnerable,' Mr Apple muttered to himself, glancing away, catching sight of Martin's raised eyebrows. 'And what is it you wanted, Miss Weeks?' he asked.

'Major, Mr Apple. Major Weeks. I'm a major now.'

'What is it you wanted Major Weeks?'

'Oh, the same old thing, I'm afraid,' Major Weeks explained gaily. 'A donation, if you would be so good.'

'Another?'

'Another,' Major Weeks agreed, sighing. 'There's so little money about we have to keep returning to those fortunate few who have it.'

'Hmm. At the rate you keep returning here I'll soon be one of the have-nots,' Mr Apple told her blandly, his eyes softening.

'Oh, I think not, Mr Apple. I'm afraid your business is far too popular for you ever to be short of money,' Major Weeks told him, somehow making her statement suggest that his forthcoming donation would in some way compensate for his ill-gotten wealth.

Mr Apple peered through his glasses, toying with the idea of telling the Major precisely what he was doing there: that could be interesting; interesting, too, to speculate whether she would still accept the money that came from such shadowy origins.

' – just off on my rounds,' Major Weeks was chirping on. 'We have so many people to comfort. And then I spotted the light in the window and I knew you were open so I said to myself it would be so nice to spend a moment or two with someone who didn't need comforting.'

An odd, melancholy breeze seemed to have accompanied her into the shop (or escaped from the bundle of *War Crys* she carried under her arm) and Mr Apple found himself nodding in uncertain agreement.

'Martin's one who needs your comfort,' he heard himself saying, aware that he was up to mischief, indicating behind him without turning round. 'He's very ill, poor chap. Some horrible, bewildering virus has infected his youthful body.'

'Oh dear – ' Major Weeks began concernedly.

'Don't mind that old fool,' Martin interrupted, passing his face through a number of contortions in an effort to disguise the fierce blush that suffused it. 'He's only kidding you. I just feel rough. Flu probably. There's a lot of it going around. And I didn't sleep well.'

'Who did?' Mr Apple asked vaguely.

'Now it's funny you should say that, young man. I'm not at all a good sleeper,' Major Weeks was offering brightly, as if mutual insomnia was a sort of cure. 'You know it simply does not seem to matter what time I go to bed – the very first hint of dawn and there I am – wide awake. The truth is I used to sleep like a baby before I came to Belfast. The way these poor people have to live!' she exclaimed. 'Oh dear, oh dear me,' she sighed, shaking her bonneted head. 'Oh dear me,' she said again, as though hoping repetition would underline her concern. 'The sheer misery.'

But misery, sheer or otherwise, was something Mr Apple had no intention of getting involved with at the moment. He suspected now, as he had always suspected, that people who expressed horror and indignation at misery and suffering were the very ones who knew nothing about it, who recognized it only as some nastiness that affected others, leaving themselves untouched. People who suffered kept very quiet about it, hugged their misery to them, almost guarding it as if it was an investment in future happiness.

'Here,' Mr Apple said gruffly, surprising himself with such pointed rudeness, and pushing a ten-pound note across the counter, 'take this and relieve the misery.'

'Why, thank you, Mr Apple. You are *such* a generous man,' Major Weeks said, her eyes turning dreamy with gratitude while her brow furrowed under the strain of her rapid calculations as to what benefits ten pounds could bring.

'Yes. I'm generous,' Mr Apple agreed, surprised to find he had spoken aloud. And, as though to cover the mild embarrassment that now came over him, he added 'and so is my assistant, aren't you, Martin? You will donate a little something of your considerable wealth to a worthy cause, won't you? A farthing or two perhaps?'

'Huh? Oh, sure. There you go, miss,' Martin said, pushing a crumpled fiver towards her.

'May God reward you both,' Major Weeks implored, casting her eyes upwards, pocketing her takings and blessing them both with a smile.

Mr Apple and Martin glanced at one another, and for a split second there was an awful understanding between them; yet it was not so much an understanding as an unvoiced bond of fear, some telepathic warning that whatever their reward it would certainly not be from God. But almost as soon as this realization came, it was gone, and they were both smiling at Major Weeks, wishing her well, watching her as she waddled from the shop with that fussy gait which made it seem that some eternal, adolescent virgin inhabited her large womanly body.

Whatever aura Major Weeks had brought into the shop left with her. The door swung closed behind her with its familiar bang like a signal to return to normal: the blower crackled and spat, the voice from the speaker sounding breathless as though it, too, had been waiting for the Major to take her leave before announcing that racing at Ludlow had been abandoned due to waterlogging.

'Only one meeting today, then, Mr Apple,' Martin said, as though vindicating his illness.

'Yes. I heard.'

'You'll be able to manage easily now, won't you?'

'Easily.'

'Hey, I'm sorry, you know. I didn't want to get sick.'

Mr Apple turned from the counter and stared at Martin, his face perplexed, worried. 'Are you really ill, Martin?'

'Sure I am. I wouldn't say I was – '

'No. I'm sorry. It's just – ' Mr Apple shook his head.

'Just what?'

'Nothing.'

'There! You see? You're at it again, Mr Apple. Starting something and then leaving it all up in mid-air. I hate that, and you do it to me all the time.'

'You wouldn't understand. *I* don't really understand.'

'Understand what?'

Mr Apple thought for a moment, frowning, fishing among the swarm of forebodings that danced and shimmered through his brain like transparent smigg, hoping to net some explanation for the feeling of impending tragedy he sensed so emphatically. '"And the whirr of their wayfaring thinned and surceased on the sky, and but left in the gloaming – ",' he quoted, his voice as lost as a wayfaring waif, his eyes about to close: suddenly, surprisingly, Martin finished the quotation: '"– sea-mutterings and me",' he said, and Mr Apple bounced back in astonishment.

'Good Lord!'

'That fooled you, eh, Mr Apple?'

'It certainly did.'

'Oh I'm not as thick as you make me out to be.'

'I never thought you were stupid, Martin. I just didn't think Hardy was in your repertoire.'

'Well, you live and learn.'

'Yes,' Mr Apple agreed. 'Do you believe in premonitions, Martin?' he asked suddenly.

'You mean feeling something is going to happen?'

'Yes, in a way.'

'I suppose I do. I never really thought about it.'

Mr Apple nodded, and his slow, pedantic gesture seemed to indicate he now felt Martin's was the wisest course.

'What about them, anyway?' Martin pressed on.

'I feel that –' Mr Apple hesitated again, and took a moment to sigh a sound filled with bewilderment and sorrow.

'For Christ's sake, Mr Apple, you'll drive me crazy. What do you feel?'

'You really want to know?'

'Yes, dammit, I really want to know.'

Mr Apple turned away and shuddered, but only for a second: he swung round and faced Martin and in that twinkling of an eye his humour had changed. It was as though, inexplicably, some part of him had taken flight, had packed its overnight bag with visions of pain and horror and sadness and run off, smiling gaily, waving a hand and promising to send a postcard. And with its departure Mr Apple found he was smiling too, though none too gaily, wistfully more likely than not, and saying teasingly, 'I don't think it would be good for you to know in your present delicate state of health, Martin.'

'Shit.'

Suddenly the shop was full of customers, and for the next hour they were both busy taking bets, paying out on yesterday's winners, explaining that no runners at Ludlow could go into accumulators since racing there had been called off. They were a strangely matched team engaged in an even stranger pursuit: offering hope with a scrap of blue cardboard, stamping TAX PAID across the frail scribbles of people's dreams.

Only near noon did the shop finally empty, resting before the influx of the regular punters who stood about the shop all afternoon, some seeking warmth, others company, most simply preferring to have their losses audibly confirmed by the Tannoy.

'You're quite sure you'll be able to manage if I go home,' Martin asked during this respite.

'Yes. Quite. I'll manage.'

'I do feel lousy.'

'I'm sure you do.'

'You don't bloody believe me.'

' – ? Of course I believe you, Martin. Why should you lie?'

'Right.'

'Well, then?'

'Okay. I'll go.'

'Martin?'

'Yes?'

'If it takes any longer – ' Mr Apple hesitated, wondering what on earth had made him choose those words. 'If you need longer,' he corrected himself, 'to recover,' he added, 'it won't inconvenience me if you take a few days off. Better to be sure you're fully recovered than to risk a relapse.'

Martin stared at the old man with half-closed eyes, but there was an unusual kindness in his voice when he answered: 'Thanks, Mr A. Maybe you're right. I'll see how I feel in the morning.'

'Do that.'

'Now you look after things, hear?'

Mr Apple smiled tightly. 'I will,' he promised.

'Good.'

'And you look after yourself, Martin.'

'That's one thing you can be sure of, Mr A. Martin Deeley will always look after himself.'

Mr Apple watched Martin walk across the shop towards the door, watched him turn and smile a smile that implored response. Mr Apple raised a hand and returned the smile; and before he could stop himself, before, even, he realized he was saying it, he said 'Martin, if you need a friend, remember I'm here.'

Martin Deeley stopped in his tracks, and the brightness fell from his face, leaving his eyes extraordinarily sad. But only for a moment. 'Hey,' he said, smiling again, 'that's really nice, Mr Apple. That's really nice. I might take you up on that. Thanks.'

Mr Apple nodded. 'Off you go to bed.'

'Right. And – thanks again.'

'Don't thank me,' Mr Apple said quietly, somehow managing to make it sound like a warning.

Martin was about to open the door and leave the shop, but then he froze, turned, and came back to the counter, faced Mr Apple, staring at him through the glass. 'That's a pretty big thing, you know,' he said seriously. 'Offering to be someone's friend.'

'Yes. I know.'

'Hey!' Martin said, with a small wry laugh, 'nobody's ever offered to be my friend before. How about that? That's a first for you, Mr A.'

'I'm happy,' said Mr Apple, although he looked anything but. In fact he looked downright morose about his offer, as though his friendship was like the kiss of death.

'You're a nice old man, Mr Apple,' Martin told him seriously.

'Yes. I'm lovely, Martin. Just lovely. Go on home.'

'Okay. I'll see you when I see you.'

'I hope so.'

'Sure I will. I'm not going to die.'

'No,' agreed Mr Apple, with not much conviction. 'No, you're not going to die.'

'Bye.'

'Bye.'

Already, as he walked through the crowds of pedestrians, Martin found himself panting like a terrier. It was a phenomenon that always took place well in advance of an actual killing, as though he was disposing of his surplus energy, energy which might hinder his exactitude, so as to leave himself calm, unshaking, accurate. Yes, it had always been so, and Martin smiled as he thought of it, even on that very first occasion when he had proudly enhanced his status as a brilliantly accurate marksman.

Bye, said Mam.
Bye, Mam.
Be careful.
I'll be careful.

Come home safe, Mam said. She had scrupulously avoided interfering, though she was well aware what was about to happen, aware, too, that there was a strong possibility that she was about to lose her one remaining son; but she knew, also, that what was taking place within her family was inevitable, and, with that peculiar twisted logic of the oppressed, she was proud of Martin, and in her saddened, lonely mind she endowed the monstrous act he was soon to commit with a sort of glory, making it perversely heroic, seeing her callous, amoral son as an avenging angel whose life she might have to sacrifice.

I'll be home safe. Don't worry.

I won't, Mam promised, steeling herself and drawing on television heroines for her expression.

This is Seamus Reilly, he was told. He will look after you.

Mr Deeley, Seamus Reilly acknowledged, bowing his head slightly.

Mr Reilly, Martin replied. That was nice – and as it should be – being addressed as Mr Deeley. Yes. He liked that. Made him feel good. Grown up. Important.

– simple, Reilly was explaining as the stolen car bounced rapidly along the isolated country lanes. He'll be out at eleven exactly. By himself. Checking. Very regular. Like his cattle. Like clockwork. Simple.

What's he done? Martin asked casually. Not that it made any difference: the man was to be punished and that was that.

Nothing, Reilly replied. Not directly. In fact, not even indirectly, he added his voice trailing upwards slightly as though he was suddenly mildly bemused. He's been selected to repay the death of that child the Paras shot the other night.

Oh.

An eye for an eye, Reilly said quietly. It's all they seem to understand.

Oh.

Stop at the next bend, Reilly ordered the driver, and the driver stopped obediently at the next bend.

Reilly rolled down the window and, turning to Martin, placed one hand on his arm: there was something very fatherly about the gesture, and Martin suddenly felt very close to the sinister little man beside him.

You see that clump of trees, Martin? Go through those and you'll have a perfect view of the house. The side door is on the left as you look at it. That's where he'll come from. He'll switch on the outside light before he leaves the house, so you will be warned. Let him walk across the yard. He'll come directly under the light and that is your best chance. He's an easy target, Reilly explained, almost apologetically. You'll have all the time in the world. Come back here when you've done.

Martin settled himself comfortably on the ground, adopting the position he had seen the Paras use, at full stretch with legs splayed behind him, the rifle cocked and pointing towards the dim, shadowy building slightly to the right and below him. It was a very still night, with a watery, half-hearted moon that only revealed itself from time to time. Martin was amazed at how calm he felt: apart from the thumping of his heart and an odd but wholly pleasant sensation in his loins he felt nothing. Then the light was on in the yard below him. A door slammed. A man coughed nicotine from his lungs and spat. Martin aimed the rifle, moving the barrel slowly from left to right, waiting for the man to come under the light. He timed it perfectly: the sights were just in line with the light as the man moved under it. Martin squeezed the trigger. Even, it seemed, before the brittle crack of the rifle reached his ears he saw the man hurtle several feet backwards, saw him attempt to swim, his arms and legs flailing in a grotesque breaststroke, saw him shudder and lie still.

That was nicely done, Reilly told him as the car drove unobtrusively back into the city. Very nicely done.

It was easy.

Easy or not, it was nicely done. Clean. No unnecessary suffering. The committee will be pleased with that.

Good.

Reilly glanced at Martin. You feel all right? he asked paternally.

I feel fine.

No sickness in your stomach?

None.

No – eh – regrets?

Why should I?

Reilly gave what sounded like a chuckle but could have been something else. You sound almost as though you had enjoyed it.

I did. You know that? I really did.

I see, said Reilly.

Don't you? Martin heard himself ask casually, as though discussing something trivial.

I have never killed, Reilly told him tightly.

Never?

Never. It is not my job. I do not have – Reilly paused, searching for the missing requirement, failing to locate it, about to rephrase his words when Martin interrupted generously:

Well, you have me now.

Yes. We have you now, Reilly agreed, a mixture of awe and distaste spreading over the words.

Any time you want a job well done, just call on me.

We will.

Good.

Just one thing –

– ?

Don't become too fond of killing, young man. If you do, your usefulness to us will be over. Good-night.

Good-night.

Mam was waiting up for him, and she hugged him when he came in the door, kissing his cheek and smoothing the hair on his neck with her small, hard hands. You're all right, she remarked gratefully.

Sure, I'm all right. Why wouldn't I be?

Thanks be to God, Mam said fervently.

I'm going to bed. I'm tired.

Have something before you go up. A cup of tea. A glass of milk. I've plenty of milk. I'll warm you some.

No. I just want to sleep.

You should have something to calm you down, Mam persisted, as though she knew all about such things.

I don't need calming down, Martin snapped, feeling oddly insulted. I just want to go to bed and sleep.

All right, son.

Night, Mam.

Good-night, Martin. God protect you.

Yeah.

Do your mother a favour, Martin?

What?

Say a prayer before you go to sleep.

A prayer?

Thank the good God for seeing you safe.

Yeah. Okay. I'll do that, Martin lied.

Thank you, son.

Night.

You're a good boy.

That's right.

Good-night. God watch over you.

Good-night.

And God or some other being had certainly watched over him, for here he was, still going strong, about to add another victim to his impressive list.

As he packed, throwing two changes of underwear, shirts and socks into a small suitcase (take a suitcase, Reilly had told him – not a big one that might be searched, just a small suitcase that one might take for a few days) Martin ticked off in his mind the details of his itinerary. Suddenly Mr Apple loomed up in his thoughts, his long grey face smiling tragically at him, offering him, with hands outstretched, his friendship, but in a way that suggested he was going to need it. Even more extraordinary was the fact that somewhere, somewhere in a dark, unusued cubbyhole of his mind, Martin sensed the truth of this; it was as though the unexpected intrusion of Mr

Apple's generous remark had more to it than met the ear, as though something (perhaps the God that Mam so persistently beleaguered) was on the point of finally linking the destinies of Martin Deeley and Mr Apple together irrevocably. At any other time Martin would have scoffed at such a notion, dismissed it as his understandable nerves playing tricks on him, but now, standing there ready to go, shaved and groomed and polished and scrubbed and nicely dressed, he felt a new and unwelcome element creeping into his life. It was, he thought, puzzled, a sense of foreboding, and he didn't like it one little bit.

That night Mr Apple was assailed by a virulent and terrifying nightmare, the word 'ruination' dominating his fretful sleep. All about him was a scene of utter desolation, dominated by weeds and thorn-bushes: an abandoned orchard, perhaps, filled with terror. To begin with it seemed peaceful enough there, though there was an eerie, hushed and irreverent silence that hinted at unholy places. It was as silent and cold as a grave. No birds, no insects, nothing save himself alone, it appeared, dared enter the dreadful place. All the narrow, crazily paved paths that criss-crossed the enclosure were broken and overgrown. Great thorny tendrils of wild blackberry clawed at the old brick wall over which the spindly nakedness of a dead honeysuckle and dying Wistaria were draped. Currant-bushes, red and black, had capitulated to the systematic onslaught of nettles and cow-parsley and giant thistles. Plum- and pear-trees, once lovingly espaliered, now blossomless and unpollinated, fell forward, their branches buried and rotting in the dank scutch grass. A wooden-framed greenhouse, running the entire length of the far wall, sagged squalidly, saved from total collapse only by the ebbing strength of a tenacious vine, the glass shattered or vanished altogether.

Fearfully he turned his head and stared at the cankerous, gnarled apple tree that grew alone in one corner. At first it appeared to be enveloped in a kind of mist, then he realized that he was crying. He brushed the tears roughly from his eyes, blinking rapidly, and fixed his gaze firmly on the tree. Over the years it had been cruelly mutilated, or (a more optimistic possibility he was pleased to consider) with the passage of time its arthritic limbs had been amputated out of charity, perhaps out of love, so that now its remaining foliage fanned outward only from the top like those thorned acacias of the African veld, leaving its scarred, lichen-covered trunk gaunt and horripilant but for one solitary branch which still protruded at right angles some eight feet from the ground, menacing in its isolation. The tree of death, he thought grimly, forced towards it, hacking his way through the undergrowth with what appeared to be a golfclub, which he wielded like a sickle.

Then it appeared. The instant he saw the apparition he told himself sternly that it was nothing more than another hallucination, and he stood, quite calm, waiting for the object (shaped like a man invisibly suspended by the neck from the sole protruding branch, but faceless, a pale translucent light where the features should have been) to go away. And suddenly it was gone. So he *had* been mistaken once again. Or had he? There it was once more. Or was it? Certainly it seemed to have withdrawn: but no, not quite. There was still something there in some way connected with it, or there on his shoulder, or behind his back, or skipping away and concealing itself as he turned; no...that, too, whatever it was, was going: perhaps, after all, it was only one of those shadows that Blake had so obliquely referred to. Oh, God, he heard himself sigh as he moved closer to the tree, while fully realizing the folly of his supplication: even God seemed unlikely to shed His light in this unhallowed place.

Tentatively he raised one hand as if to touch the branch. At the same time that he realized that the branch was beyond his reach he felt something never before felt with such conviction, with such shocking certainty: it was as though he was surrounded by living, breathing evil. Yet not, it seemed, by a consuming evil, for he immediately became possessed of a curious peace as though the raising of his arm had not, after all, been a wasted gesture, had, rather, become a form of benediction which for some reason protected him. Who are you? he shouted, or thought he shouted, probably did not shout since the words made no sound he could hear. Who are you? he asked again, quietly.

Immediately, suddenly appalled by the realization of what the answer might be, he spun round and hurried from the place, stumbling twice, closing the gate firmly behind him, pressing on it with both hands to make certain it was securely latched, pressing until his fingers ached and small patches of blood appeared on his palms.

12

Colonel Maddox came down to breakfast in a pleasurable frame of mind. At last the ordeal of leave was behind him and he could look forward to the turmoil and hardship of Belfast. The peace of Berkshire irked him; the twittering birds, the hum of the electric lawnmower, the lowing of cattle on the neighbouring farm got on his nerves. Irrationally. It was the sense of being needed he missed, almost as much as he missed the realization that he might, in some small way, be doing something useful, having a hand in finding the solution to the illness that afflicted Ireland.

Nancy Maddox was already at the table, making a great show of scraping low-calorie margarine on to her slightly burned toast, looking dishevelled in a multicoloured wrap-around khaftan that someone had bought her in Suez when Suez was Suez, her hair brushed but purposely tousled.

'What time are you leaving?' she asked by way of greeting, delicately replacing crumbs of toast in her mouth with her little finger.

'Here?'

'Yes.'

'Elevenish.'

'Oh. I see.'

'Anything wrong?'

' – ? No. Nothing. It just means I won't be here when you leave. Jeff is driving me to London.'

'I see.'

'I've *so* much to do,' Nancy sighed. 'I really cannot see how I'm going to get it all done. What with Ascot and Wimbledon just around the corner – ' her voice trailed off like a weak second serve.

'You'll enjoy yourself.'

'I intend to,' Nancy snapped, waspishly defensive. 'Thank God I have some friends who don't want to see me vegetate.'

Colonel Maddox closed his eyes and watched his good humour scarper like a thief. 'There's no fear of you vegetating, Nancy.'

'I would if I depended on you. You really couldn't care less what happens to me, so long as you are amusing yourself chasing bandits with those uncouth, boozy army friends of yours.'

'It's my job.'

'Hah. They seem to manage very well without you. You don't *have* to go back to Ireland,' Nancy urged, wondering all the while why on earth she tried, albeit half-heartedly, to resurrect the contented marriage they once had. 'You know perfectly well that a word in the right place and you could – '

'I want to go back.'

'Oh, I know *that*. The big brave soldier back to the heart of the battle. It's high time you faced it – you're not even needed. And another thing, as far as any of us can see,' Nancy pointed out, indicating vaguely towards the empty chairs her guests had occupied over the weekend, as though their gossiping spirits had remained behind and were now prepared to bear her out, 'you'll never get the better of those dreadful terrorists. They're far too clever for you, my dear. Wily. That's the word. Wily. They flit about on tiny feet while you clomp about in your great big boots,' she concluded, smiling to herself, pleased she had quoted her publisher friend correctly.

'Perhaps you're right.'

'Of course I'm right. And you know it. You fools in smocks and denim are nothing but target practice for those evil men.'

Maddox discovered he was nodding. There was, of course, some truth in what she said, but there was, also, was there not, a matter of duty? He was about to express this opinion, was prepared, even, to elaborate on it, when Nancy rose from the table. 'Well, I must go and get ready. I have to see my milliner before lunch,' she informed him, and frowned as she spotted him smile at her extraordinarily old-fashioned word.

'I'll see you before you go,' he told her.

'Yes.'

Maddox waited until she had left the room (filling the time by wiping imaginary traces of marmalade from his neat, clipped moustache with his napkin) before he settled back in his chair, turning his gold signet-ring round and round on his finger, allowing a varied selection of thoughts to muster their forces and close ranks before marching through his brain, jumbled thoughts of mangled bodies in dingy streets and pretty ladies in the winner's enclosure, the horrendous roar of explosions, the aristocratic applause for a sweating thoroughbred, the flying glass as lethal as any bullet, the clinking of champagne glasses, the wails of anguish as bullets found their target, the oohs of despair as some backhand volley went wide. Dear God, what worlds apart! And who cared? Who really cared?

The Colonel sighed deeply and heaved himself from his chair. In an odd way, he told himself, *he* cared. And it wasn't that he wanted to make a reputation for himself by capturing or killing terrorists – if terrorists, indeed, they were, and he had found himself doubting this occasionally in recent months – in the way the predatory Mr Asher did (I wish I could kill the buggers one by one all by myself, Asher had once said in a moment of conspiratorial frustration, and notch each dead terrorist on the stock of my gun. Better still, herd the bastards into one of their bloody Roman Catholic churches and blow the lot to kingdom come), and if he could have persuaded everyone to sit around a table and make a start on solving the insoluble problem he would have been more than pleased. What he wanted, Maddox now decided, hauling himself wearily up the stairs by the banisters, what he wanted – and at the same time he fully recognized the stupidity and impossibility of his thoughts – what he wanted (and saw in his mind's eye as a sort of dreamy sequence of events somehow linked to daydreams of his childhood, but childish now if only because of his advancing age) what he really wanted –

'We're off,' Nancy brutally broke in upon his reverie, appearing at the top of the stairs, elegantly turned out, beautifully shod, a fawn vicuña coat draped over one arm, her pet publisher draped on the other. 'Tinkle me tomorrow and let me know you got back to war safely.'

'I'll do that. Have a nice time in London.'

'We will. I don't suppose there's any point in hoping you'll make Ascot?'

'I wouldn't think so.'

'No. Not masculine enough for you, is it dear?'

Maddox said nothing, but shifted his gaze to the willowy publisher with the purple neckerchief and back again to Nancy, raising an eyebrow, enjoying his wife's sudden blush, enjoying, too, the odd gesture she made when annoyed or found him tiresome: shaking herself so that her clothes ruffled like a chicken's feathers. 'Is the car full, or do *I* have to get petrol?' she demanded.

'*I'm* taking you,' publishing Jeffrey said. 'We're going in my car.

'Oh, yes. Of course. I forgot,' Nancy admitted, tittering. 'How silly of me. It's just that it's been so long since I've been driven anywhere.'

The Colonel stood to one side and allowed them to pass him on the stairs, wrinkling his nose at the strength of the combined smell of perfume and aftershave, and watched them leave the house, still arm in arm, whispering and giggling, before he went on up the stairs and into his bedroom. He heard the car doors slam and the wheels spin on the gravel, but did not bother to watch from the window: he had seen and heard enough of his wife and her guests during the past two weeks.

Being an orderly man he had almost completed his packing the night before. There had, however, been a few unaccustomed additions to his suitcase this time: a few small items he had never before taken from his home, mementoes of happier times, of less confused, less bitter days, objects of importance only to himself, which he had been prompted to take by some small goblin in his mind hinting that failure to do so would mean their irrevocable loss. There was, for example, an old and tattered, leather-bound biography of Bacon by Dean Church, with an inscription on the flyleaf which had puzzled him since the day he had bought it (along with several other books as a job lot at an auction, longer ago than he cared to remember): 'Ex Libris Denis Redmond (Reverend or, perhaps, not so reverend), suffering banishment of all dimensions', it read. There was also a brown photograph in a circular silver frame, showing a small girl in frilly petticoats and a lace bonnet cuddling a tabby-kitten, and inscribed on the back, perhaps by the man who stood behind the girl and gazed down fondly at her, 'Bishop, Nina and Jo'. Only his shaving-kit and toothbrush remained to be put in the suitcase (an old leather affair with outside straps and brass buckles, plastered with labels of exotic, probably long-since demolished hotels) which lay open on his bed. He now placed these, wrapped in a strip of coloured plastic, beside his shoes, and closed the lid. Then he paced about the room, fingering things, lifting ornaments and other photographs in other silver frames and putting them down again; finally, he took to walking up and down ponderously, killing time, placing his feet in designs on the carpet, his stride awkward, like that of a man trying out new shoes, all the while wondering at the turmoil, the sense of doom that was welling up inside him, trying, too, to recall what he had been thinking before Nancy had shattered his train of thought. To no avail. Alas, it was almost always like that now: memory failed him when he most needed it. He glanced at his watch. In half an hour the car would arrive and that, at least, was a good thing.

Long before the Colonel came down to breakfast in his quiet Berkshire home, Mr Apple was awake and fretting. He had been, yet again, visited by demons with wilful intent who scattered nightmares of the most appalling nature through his sleep, who, worse still, misconstrued just about everything he had written in his diary that night, and threw it back at him, twisting it until the words screamed and crackled as they broke, the shattered letters reforming into meanings and images both lurid and grotesque, making him snap awake, sweating, wondering what could have brought about such an intense affliction. He lay in his bed, quite still, listening, listening for any tiny sound that might explain his awful premonition of disaster. Nothing. Not a sound. Then, suddenly, outside, some distance away, a single bird, a nightingale perhaps, rent the stillness with a stunning cadenza and set its course in search of tetragrammaton.

What was that? a voice seemed to scream in his ear, a voice he recognized as from another time, but to which he could not put a face. Perhaps it never had a face.

Just talking to myself, Mr Apple thought he heard himself reply. Just envying the advantage those small birds have over us – flying off to paradise whenever the fancy takes them.

You think they do? the voice asked, sounding quite like Mr Divine.

I'm sure they do.

Perhaps not so advantageous, Sefer, definitely Sefer was suggesting darkly.

How so?

Striving upwards has its downfalls, Mr Apple was told solemnly.

Ah, was all he managed to get out before 'If thou desirest to mount thou wouldst not be able and in descending thou wilt meet an abyss without any bottom' was being quoted at him.

Yes. I know, Mr Apple heard himself say. I know only too well. But even the abyss can be a source of wisdom.

Or chaos. Don't forget chaos.

Suddenly, as though the elements had been activated by some daemonic force and commanded to assert their ferocious power on his unsuspecting self, all meteorological hell broke loose. Huge purple clouds plunged upwards, thundering against each other. A single ominous shaft of lightning crackled a warning of still worse turmoil to follow. The wind hurled itself across the landscape, bending huge trees, ignoring their awful moans, the screaming of their limbs, and the tragedy that had haunted Mr Apple seemed already to have commenced.

Just as suddenly Mr Apple was awake and all was silent save, incredibly, for the shrill, single note of a lone bird in the garden outside.

Mr Apple eased himself on to one elbow and very deliberately opened the buttons of his pyjama top. There was something comically ceremonious about the way he did this, about the way he folded back the jacket and ran his fingers over the wounds on his chest: he looked carefully at his finger tips and rubbed them gently together. Finally, he lay back with a small sigh of relief, keeping his eyes open lest they turned inwards on his soul and revealed some horrors he could not yet bear to face. But he would, he told himself: he would face them when they came at the appointed time, face them bravely and with confidence in the way he had been preparing himself so to do.

'Oh,' Mr Apple said aloud, his thin voice pitched to almost a cry, and rocked himself on his bed. 'Oh, dear God, help me.'

About the time that Mr Apple (recovered to all outward appearances from the hazards of the night) put the key in the door of the bookmaking establishment, sighing at the prospect of another treacherous day, about the time, also, that Colonel Maddox wiped imaginary traces of marmalade from his neat, clipped moustache with his napkin (sighing at the paucity of his marriage, yet marvelling at Nancy's blatant if petty infidelity), Martin Deeley jogged across the Berkshire skyline and cast a baleful glance at Seamus Reilly's mischievous gibbet. He looked ridiculously small and inoffensive: an isolated little creature in that vast expanse, dressed in a sky-blue tracksuit with natty dark-blue trim and one of those loose-fitting, thin, plastic anoraks with a pocket like a pouch in the front.

Jogger! he had exclaimed, the prospect of such unexpected exercise more surprising, even, than the choice of cover.

Sure, Tommy Walshe told him. Who looks at a jogger? This country is full of them. All ages. All shapes. All running themselves into the ground to stay fit.

Jesus!

And if we do run into trouble there's nothing peculiar about a man in a tracksuit running. You'd look pretty damn stupid galloping across the Berkshire Downs in your Sunday suit, Martin.

Martin guffawed. I suppose you're right.

I'm right.

Martin swung left and headed for the cluster of dead elms, one of which boasted three abandoned rooks' nests. He looked awkward as he ran, swinging only one arm, the other pressed to his side holding the Kalashnikov automatic rifle in place, mistrusting the tapes that secured it to his body. It fitted neatly: tucked under his armpit and resting on his hip; the weapon mechanism and the barrel combined measured barely twenty-one inches. Folded over these, weighing almost nothing, the stock of tubular steel; the magazine in his marsupial anorak, its steady thump against his stomach oddly comforting.

There's a gibbet –

Yeah. Reilly told me.

Hah. He would. He'd like that. Always one for a joke is Seamus Reilly, Tommy Walshe said, shaking his head in wonderment.

Oh, a hell of a joker he is.

Anyway, just below the gibbet there's a bunch of elms. They're all dead. Rot-gut, fluke or something. They're dying all over the place. Soon be no elms at all, Tommy said, giving a little sigh by way of requiem. When you get to the elms you'll see the Maddox cottage. You can't miss it. It's the only house you *can* see from there. Now, count the elms from the left. Under the third there's a hole covered by loose grass and leaves. That's where you bury the rifle before you come back. Easy.

Oh, yes, Martin agreed. Easy.

As soon as I hear the shooting I'll start driving along the road. All you have to do is bury the rifle and your tracksuit and run the fifty yards to the road. You can change into the pullover and trousers in the car, and away we go.

Martin nodded. Like always, it sounded easy.

Any questions?

Martin shook his head. No, except – well, surely I'll be a bit conspicuous running about in my underwear, he said, amused.

Pretend you're a marathon runner. Anyway, who the hell ever shot a British colonel in their underwear?

They both laughed.

Martin reached the trees and immediately counted from the left. Sure enough, the small hole, about two feet deep and packed with leaves and dry grass, was there. Straight ahead, beyond the main road, up a small, winding lane on a rise, was the Colonel's cottage. Some cottage. Bloody great mansion of a place. Down the road he noted Tommy Walshe intently tinkering with the engine of the Vauxhall, his head buried in the gaping bonnet: anyone passing would have dismissed him as yet another lunatic tourist who had overloaded the engine.

Why the bloody boat? Martin had demanded, indicating the dinghy on the trailer.

Aha. Just my little touch of realism, Martin me boy, Tommy Walshe had replied, grinning like a small boy who had just conceived a brilliant idea. Now you tell me: who is going to look for a getaway car pulling a bloody great trailer and boat? We're just a pair of sweethearts on our way to the Lake District for a few days sailing, he explained, giving a camp little flick of his wrist.

Oh, sure. Some sweethearts we are.

It makes it easier for you if I think of details, Tommy said. I have to look after you, you know. Orders from above. You're special.

Yeah. I'm special.

Suddenly Martin froze: a car shot round the side of the house and sped down the lane. Shit. He began ripping the rifle free from his side, wincing as the tape tore at his flesh, his eyes fixed more on the trail of dust in the car's wake than on the car itself. He was still fumbling, trying to assemble the rifle, when the car slowed to a halt before turning on to the main road. Irrelevant details shot through his mind: sports – silver – vintage – Lagonda – or Bristol – top down – powerful – well looked after. Almost by magic the rifle was assembled, loaded, aimed, and the occupants of the car clear in the sights. Martin found himself breathing again, smiling with relief. The driver of the car was certainly not the Colonel and the passenger was a woman, her head thrown back, sitting almost sideways in her seat, her arm across the back of the driver's seat, her hand resting on his shoulder. Martin watched the car as it swung on to the main road, watched it slow as it drew alongside Tommy, saw him wave good-naturedly and shake his head, saw the woman wave back, watched the car gather speed and roar away. Then everything was quiet again. Martin rolled onto his back and gulped in air.

Make sure of this one, Reilly had told him.

I will.

It's important. Let the Brits know we are still in business.

Don't worry.

I always worry, Martin. It's my job to worry.

Well, you needn't.

I admire you, Martin, Reilly confessed, though there seemed to be little admiration in his voice. The way you handle death amazes me.

I don't think about it.

That's what amazes me. I think I would be haunted for ever if I had to kill someone.

Well, you don't, do you? You get someone else to do it for you.

True. And just as well. I would never be able to do it myself. I wouldn't be *afraid* to kill someone, Reilly offered by way of explanation. I just don't have the temperament. As I say, I think they would come back and haunt me. Do they haunt you, Martin?

Who?

Your victims.

Hell, no.

Never?

No. When they're dead they're dead.

Do you feel anything?

Not much. Excited a bit.

A bit excited, Reilly repeated musingly. Marvellous, he said. How you can do something so final and just feel a bit excited?

Well, what do you want me to do? Jump for joy?

No, but I would have thought a little sorrow, perhaps, or –

Shit, Martin snapped.

Yes. Oh, well. We're lucky you're made the way you are.

That's for sure.

But I wonder if you really are –

– ?

Martin stood up and stripped to his underclothes, carefully

placing the anorak and tracksuit in the shallow hole. Then he lay on his stomach, the rifle snug against his shoulder, and waited. He had barely settled into that position when the black Ford saloon appeared on the road below him, braked carefully, swung into the lane and headed for the Colonel's home: Martin followed its progress in his sights and whispered pow, pow, pow to himself like a schoolboy playing cowboys and decimating the Indian ranks.

The Colonel must have been waiting, for he appeared at the door before the car came to a halt. He placed a suitcase a couple of feet from the door and disappeared inside again: Martin trained his sights on the doorway, holding his breath, his finger already tightening on the trigger. It was something that always surprised him, but he was now so proficient at assassination that he could somehow sense the appearance of his victim a split second before he actually came into view. For the moment he had no such sensation and relaxed a little, adjusting the telescopic sights even more finely so that nothing but the doorway was within his vision. He heard Tommy Walshe start the engine of the Vauxhall, gunning it slightly; he heard a skylark take advantage of the silence to demonstrate its vocal prowess. Then, in his sixth sense, the warning came and Martin tensed: the Colonel ambled through the front door and Martin fired. As he fired, however, the driver of the car popped into the picture, standing erect having retrieved the Colonel's suitcase and blocking his superior, taking the bullet in the back of his neck. His head jerked and he collapsed forward into the Colonel's arms, both of them falling to the ground behind the parked car.

'Shit,' Martin whispered. 'You stupid, fucking bastard.'

He leapt to his feet, folded the Kalashnikov and shoved it into the hole, covered it and stomped the leaves and grass down. Then he sprinted down the hill towards the car. He was breathless and panting when he flung himself into the seat beside Tommy Walshe, but immediately started pulling on the pullover and trousers made ready for him.

'See? I told you it would be easy,' Tommy said, grinning.

'Easy shit,' Martin cursed through his teeth. 'I missed the

bastard.'

'You what?' Tommy's voice was suddenly brittle with fear, and for a second he touched the brake pedal with his foot.

'Keep going, for Christ's sake,' Martin shouted. 'I missed the bastard.'

'Oh, Jesus.'

'Oh, Jesus is right. The fucking driver. Up between us. Got *him*. Shit.'

'Why didn't you – '

'I couldn't. Both of them fell behind the car. I had no chance.'

'He would have had to go back in – '

'Yeah, well, I wasn't hanging about to watch for that. How the hell do I know who was in the house? Could have had a phone in the car – he could have reached that without me seeing him. Just you do the driving and let me do the worrying about what I should have done.'

Tommy Walshe obediently drove on in silence, scowling at the road, glancing in his mirror every few seconds, visibly relieved when he saw nothing following. 'They're not going to like it, Martin,' he said finally, obviously concerned.

'That's tough. What the hell do they expect?'

'They expect you to do what you came for.'

'I couldn't.'

'That's all very well – '

'Look, you just get me back to Birmingham and shut up.'

'We're staying in Oxford again tonight.'

'Are we hell. You can dump the boat there if you like but get me to Birmingham.'

'I was told – '

'I don't give a tuppenny shit what you were told. I'm telling you now. Get me to Birmingham so I can get out of here.'

'Okay, Martin. If that's the way you want it.'

'That's the way I want it.'

'You're the boss.'

'That's right.'

They arrived in Birmingham just after five o'clock, amazed that they had not once been challenged on the journey, had not even seen a police car. Martin collected his suitcase.

'Where do you want me to drop you?' Tommy Walshe asked.

'Nowhere. I'll make my own way.'

'You be all right?'

'I'll be fine.'

'Sure?'

'Sure. And by the way – thanks.'

'– ?'

'For being worried about me.'

'Us little guys gotta stick together,' Tommy told him in an extravagant Southern drawl.

'Hah.'

'Watch your step.'

'I will. Don't worry.'

'I do.'

'Don't. Martin Deeley can look after himself.'

'I hope so.'

'See you.'

'See you, Martin.'

Tommy Walshe watched Martin walk away from the car, swinging his suitcase jauntily, but it struck him there was less confidence in the swaggering gait, less spring to the step. It was as though Martin had grown suddenly older, was suddenly unsure, was, perhaps, for the first time in his life, truly afraid.

13

Mr Apple went to his shop at a ridiculously early hour: it was just after five that he sat at his desk, his hands supporting his head, nursing a headache the likes of which he had never suffered before. He had survived another horrible night which in itself would have been unremarkable but for the subtle changes in the actions of the visiting demons, alterations which gave their invasion an unaccustomed heavy-footedness that left his head throbbing, all of which, he felt sure, had been brought about by the news he had watched with disbelief and increasing outrage the night before. *Police in Berkshire are this evening investigating a shooting in which one man was killed*, the dark-skinned female newsreader announced with practised impartiality, clipping her vowels in an effort to treat this item as just another piece of nastiness in the litany of strife she had been given to read. *It is believed that the intended victim was Colonel Matthew Maddox of the Parachute Regiment, who was preparing to return to duty in Northern Ireland. The dead man has been named as Sergeant Anthony Boone, thirty-three, a married man with two small children, from Aylesbury in Buckinghamshire. Peter Haynes sent us this report.* Obligingly, Peter Haynes took over the screen and launched into his report with gusto, determined to make the most of his few seconds of stardom. *Shortly after eleven-thirty this morning Colonel Matthew Maddox came out of this door and made his way to the car that was waiting to take him to Brize Norton for the journey to Northern Ireland. As he approached the car his driver, Sergeant Anthony Boone, bent down to pick up the Colonel's suitcase. As he stood up, a single shot was fired, hitting the Sergeant in the back of the head and killing him instantly. Police are convinced that the bullet was intended for Colonel Maddox and believe it to be the work of the I.R.A. although they stress that so far no one has claimed responsibility. Colonel Maddox, who was alone in the house at the time, had no comment to make, apart from the fact that he would be returning to Northern Ireland sometime tomorrow.*

Mr Apple absentmindedly cleared a small space on the desk and emptied a single aspirin from the bottle he kept near by for just such emergencies, watched it roll, bump into an unopened brown envelope, and settle down. Then he popped it into his mouth, took a sip of lukewarm tea, threw back his head and swallowed, grimacing at the acrid taste. Perhaps it was the fact that he knew the Colonel (albeit it under pretty tricky circumstances) and quite liked him, recognizing in him a kindred lost wayfarer slogging through the intricacies of life, that made him feel profoundly certain that events had now taken a course the navigation of which promised nothing but sadness, a hopeless floundering on the sharp rocks of despair; or perhaps it was just a warning, not yet fully interpreted, left behind in the recesses of his mind by the hooligans of the night – who even now, despite the recent dosage designed to render them immobile, continued to swim along the perimeter of his consciousness, kicking their legs and hollering to each other – that caused him to recognize the doom and sorrow that were lurking just around the corner. Whatever the cause, there was certainly no doubting the unwelcome shafts of piercing cold he felt penetrating every fibre of his body, nor the sudden pain from his wounds which he knew to be his personal, melancholy overture to fear.

But weren't you afraid?

Yes, Your Excellency, I was afraid.

The ambassador, a kindly man, rejoicing in his appointment to Mexico, spending his free evenings writing a thesis on the tragic Carlotta, the dull Maximilian and their twin Miramar castles, shook his head: I simply cannot understand how you managed to *get* yourself into such a mess. What on earth possessed you?

Possessed me, Your Excellency?

The ambassador continued to shake his head, staring at the gaunt, aesthetic creature sitting before him, telling himself to choose his words with greater care, regretting already the word 'possessed' now that he realized it might have special significance. Why in heaven's name did you go to that godforsaken place?

I was sent, I think, Mr Apple said.

Sent? By whom? the ambassador wanted to know, becoming quite confused.

Mr Apple sighed: I wish I knew. Someone, something – I don't know – urged me to go there. I felt I was saving them.

Saving them? The villagers you mean? From what?

Themselves, Mr Apple said obliquely.

But you simply cannot go about trying to save people from themselves, was all the ambassador could find to say.

Mr Apple shrugged.

You realize, of course, that your actions have caused considerable embarrassment to the embassy – not to mention your personal scandal?

Yes, sir.

In the circumstances I think it might be better if you returned to London.

I will resign, sir.

Resign? The ambassador attempted to look surprised.

I think that would be best. I have other things to do, Mr Apple explained, and, anyway, I'm not really very good at my job.

No, no, Mr Apple, you have been excellent up to now. It is such a pity you allowed – you weren't drunk, I suppose? Sunstruck? Overworked?

Mr Apple smiled: I'm afraid not. Maybe you were right when you said possessed, sir.

'Good morning, Mr Apple.'

Mr Apple jumped. He looked up from his desk, half-expecting to see the nodding head of the kind ambassador peering at him through the glass partition. 'Ah, good morning, Aiden.'

'Good morning, Mr Apple,' Aiden Curren said again, and immediately set about cleaning yesterday's results off the board, hissing slightly through his teeth. He was a man of about fifty, pale and jumpy, with a curiously misshapen face that gave the impression one was regarding him reflected in the back of a spoon. He earned a meagre living as a floating boardmarker, floating from shop to shop, replacing absentees, arousing little interest, neither being liked nor disliked, doing his job, taking his money and going on his way, leaving nothing of himself behind, not even a lingering wonder as to what he might get up to in his leisure hours.

'Three meetings today?' he now asked flatly.

'Yes.'

'Good.'

'Why good, Aiden?' Mr Apple asked, without really caring.

'More for me to do.'

'Oh.'

'More customers. That's good. I like to watch their faces.'

'You do?'

'Oh, yes. Interesting to watch people's faces. Especially their eyes.'

'The windows of their souls, eh?'

' – ?'

'That's what they say, Aiden.'

'I wouldn't know about that. Don't believe in souls myself. Never have done. Mumbo-jumbo, if you ask me. Frighten people into doing what you want.'

'Oh.'

'Tell them the devil will get their soul and you'll have them eating out of your hand before you know it. That's what's wrong with everybody these days. All they think about is what will happen when they're dead. They don't care about what's going on around them while they're alive.'

'I see,' said Mr Apple, trying very hard to see the logic in this pronouncement.

'I can tell you this much, Mr Apple: if you took God out of Ireland you wouldn't have half the trouble you have now,' Aiden Curren said firmly, taking to hissing through his teeth again as though orchestrating his beliefs.

'You might be right, Aiden,' Mr Apple admitted doubtfully.

'Oh I am, I am.'

Mr Apple was relieved to see the door open and the first customer of the day come in, though his relief was short-lived. Nobody knew why, but the lady who made her way purposefully across the shop was known as Our Mary Bradley. She was a small woman, comfortably plump, with a kind face and a not-too-secret liking for sherry. She was also regarded as one of the characters of the area, mildly dotty and usually harmless, and as such got away with utterances for which other people would have been painfully incapacitated. She had a passion for badges, and these she sported festooned across her chest, proclaiming her love for Ian Paisley and the Pope, her enthusiastic support for the hunger-strikers and those who incarcerated them, her desire for a united Ireland and her determination to remain loyal to the Crown. Intermingled with these were others which informed the onlooker that she was a member of such diverse organizations as the Staffordshire Bull Terrier Society, the R.A.C., the Barry Manilow Fan Club, the Merton College Debating Society, the Relief Organization for Palestinian Refugees and the Arthur Scargill Appreciation Society.

'Hello, Mr Apple,' she bellowed enthusiastically.

'Hello, Our Mary,' Mr Apple replied, raising his voice an unaccustomed octave.

'I do believe I have a little something to collect.'

'You have indeed.'

'Ah, glory, every little helps, doesn't it?'

'I'm sure it docs.'

'Oh, it does, it does, Mr Apple. How a soul is supposed to manage these days I really don't know – '

'We were just talking about that, weren't we, Aiden?'

'About what?'

'Souls.'

'Oh, dear,' Our Mary said. 'You shouldn't talk about souls in *here*, Mr Apple. God wouldn't like that one little bit. You know He's very fussy where you talk about souls.'

'Huh,' grunted Aiden, holding one finger to the side of his head and twisting it to indicate his low opinion of her sanity.

'Here we are, Our Mary: eleven pounds exactly.' Mr Apple passed the money across the counter.

'Good. That'll buy a titbit for poor Bradley.'

'Ah, yes. And how is Bradley?' Mr Apple asked. It was curious that Our Mary's husband was always referred to by his last name, his Christian name being, it appeared, a dark secret.

'Getting over it.'

'Oh, good.'

'A lot of pain, though.'

'I'm sure.'

'But they're marvellous in that hospital, you know. Putting people back together the way they do.'

'Indeed.'

'I've seen things brought in there that you couldn't really call bodies: bits, just bits and pieces of bodies, carried in and layed out in a line, and the next thing you know those doctors have got everything sorted out and stitched back in place, and those bodies are walking out of there under their own steam.'

'So I've heard,' said Mr Apple, which he had, though not in quite such graphic terms.

'And the lovely thing is, Mr Apple, they don't care who you are or what you are. If the troubles have got at you they'll welcome you in and fix you up like new if they can.'

'But – ' Mr Apple began, about to point out that Bradley had hardly been the victim of the euphemistically-named troubles but changing his mind. A severe scalding by boiling oil from an over-turned chip-pan could not very well be blamed on the warring factions, but his suffering had been real enough, and any pain, however inflicted, seemed to give one the peculiar right to share in the distress of the city. 'But you're coping all right?' Mr Apple managed to switch the question adroitly.

'As well as can be expected. It's not easy, though, is it?'

'No. Life is not easy.'

'Oh, life is easy enough, Mr Apple. I've nothing against life at all. It's the death around us that I find hard. All that killing,' Our Mary said, pursing her lips as though recalling specific instances. 'It means you can't look forward to anything, doesn't it? I mean how can a body look forward to something, if you don't know you'll be alive to enjoy it?'

'Right you are,' Mr Apple decided to agree.

'And what else is there in life besides looking forward?' Our Mary demanded, putting her hands on her hips and resting her case with this extraordinary question.

Try as he might Mr Apple could find no immediate answer. The silence between them grew longer, a silence broken only by the continued hissing of Aiden Curren, who wandered about in the background pinning up the newspapers. Mr Apple found himself becoming mildly frantic, and was on the point of uttering something innocuous and trite when the door opened and Martin Deeley glided into the shop, smiling and giving a comic, exaggerated salute. 'Hiya all.'

'Martin,' Mr Apple heard himself whispering. He cleared his throat and said 'Martin' again, louder.

Our Mary turned and stared at the intruder, eyeing him up and down, while Aiden Curren stopped whistling for a second, glanced across the shop, shrugged, and returned to his papers.

'You look surprised, Mr A.' Martin said.

'I am.'

' – ?'

'I don't know why. I didn't expect – '

'I told you I'd be back as right as rain in a couple of days. It doesn't take me long to shake off the flu. How's everything?'

'Fine. Just fine,' Mr Apple said, eyeing Martin with peculiar intensity.

'Good. You didn't miss me then?'

Mr Apple gave a small smile. 'Yes, I missed you.'

'I must be off,' Our Mary interjected, sensing that the words she was hearing had nothing to do with the sense they made. 'I'll see you later in the week, Mr Apple.'

'Mind how you go, Our Mary,' Mr Apple said, without moving his eyes from Martin's face.

'You do the same,' Our Mary replied, instilling what sounded suspiciously like a warning into her advice as she threw a sideways look at Martin, bathing him in a stare that suggested she knew all there was to know about him.

'Our Mary been winning again?' Martin asked as the door slammed behind her, keeping his voice casual.

'You know Our Mary?'

'Shit, everyone knows Our Mary. Mad as two hatters.'

'Oh,' said Mr Apple. 'You think so?'

'I know so,' Martin affirmed, coming around the counter and setting about making tea as though he had not missed a day. 'So, you missed me.'

'I said I did,' Mr Apple snapped as if he was now regretting the admission.

'Missed the brilliant conversation, huh?'

Mr Apple did not immediately reply: he could not take his eyes off Martin, the pale-blue-lensed stare intensifying by the second. He only spoke when he finally saw Martin starting to wilt under this visual pressure. 'You look remarkably fit.'

'I'm okay.'

'Good.'

'Hey – what did you mean, "remarkably"?'

Suddenly it was Mr Apple's turn to feel uneasy, and he turned away and headed for the confusion of his desk, shuffling papers as he always did when buying time. 'I – ' he began, immediately wondering how to continue, searching for words that would rescue him from the tricky position his mildly sarcastic remark had landed him in.

'You want me to stay now that he's back?' Aiden Curren's thin voice filled the silence in the nick of time. 'They could use me over at Graham's.'

Mr Apple felt himself sigh with relief.

'Or maybe he's just visiting?' Aiden Curren suggested, the question implying disapproval that such a thing should happen during working hours.

' – ?' Mr Apple looked across at Martin and raised his eyebrows.

'I'll stay,' Martin said. 'Be good for Mr Apple to have someone efficient here again.'

Aiden Curren came close to the glass partition and stared through it, opening and closing his mouth like some exotic but stranded fish.

'It's only his little joke, Aiden,' Mr Apple said quickly.

'Jokes I can do without,' Aiden snapped.

'Indeed,' agreed Mr Apple. 'Thank you for coming, Aiden. You've been a great help. How much do I owe you?'

'I'll work it out, Mr Apple. I'll drop back in a day or two. No hurry,' Aiden said proudly, enjoying his moment of largesse, hoping it had made a suitable impression.

'Very well, Aiden. Thank you again for your help.'

'My pleasure, Mr Apple. You're a nice man to work for.'

'Thank you Aiden.'

'Jesus, what a bloody groveller,' Martin sneered as Aiden hissed off through the door. '"You're a nice man to work for"' he mimmicked, emphasizing his mockery with a silly, mincing little dance.

Perhaps it was this ridiculous behaviour that roused Mr Apple, or perhaps he was just suddenly tired of all the pretence, or possibly it was the nagging foreboding that had returned that made him ask sharply: 'Martin, where *have* you been the past few days?'

Martin Deeley froze in a posture that at any other time would have been hilarious, but the transformation in his features was frightening. He stood there, rigid and unmoving, one leg bent, his right arm outstretched, his hand hanging limply in a grotesque attitude of high camp, all of which was the more unsightly when one noted the harshness of his face, the eyes now glazed over with cold fury and suspicion.

'You were in England, weren't you?'

Slowly Martin relaxed. He dropped his arm and straightened his leg. Gradually his face softened, his eyes became sad, taking on an appealing, childlike look of guilty bewilderment and mild shame, like that of a small boy caught with his hand in the sweet-jar. He nodded. 'That's right,' he admitted quietly.

'And it was you who tried to kill that Colonel.'

Martin continued to nod. 'And made a right fucking mess of it,' he said with a wry smile. 'I must be slipping.'

'There were others? I mean – '

'Plenty. Well, seven.'

'My God,' Mr Apple said quietly.

'How did you know?'

' – ?'

'That I'd been in England?'

Mr Apple shook his head violently, as if rattling his thoughts into coherency. 'I don't know, Martin. I can't really explain. I have these visions, you know, and somehow – I don't actually remember – somehow I must have seen you.'

'Jesus,' Martin whispered, the creepiness of Mr Apple's explanation making a shiver course through his body.

Mr Apple also shivered but for reasons of his own, and he sat down heavily. 'Aren't you appalled at what you do?' he asked in an oddly matter-of-fact way, taking off his glasses and polishing the lenses.

'No.'

'Doesn't it terrify you?'

'No. It's just a job. It's, well – well, it's exciting. You wouldn't understand.'

'No. I wouldn't understand. How could anyone in their right mind understand such ruthless killing?'

'They got what they deserved,' Martin said defensively.

'Nobody deserves to be killed, Martin.'

'They did.'

'You decided that?'

'No. The Com— ' he stopped abruptly.

'Ah. So that's it.'

'I said nothing.'

'No, you said nothing,' Mr Apple agreed wearily. He looked up: 'This is one you won't get away with, you know,' he said sadly.

Martin narrowed his eyes. There was something so positive in the way Mr Apple made his pronouncement he was alarmed. 'Huh.'

'It's all falling into place,' Mr Apple was saying, almost to himself, frowning and squinting, trying to decipher those visions of recent nights and reconjure their dreadful warnings. 'It must have been you that was hanging,' he said in a whisper. 'That would explain it.'

Martin felt cold sweat breaking out on his spine. 'What the hell are you on about?' he demanded, surprised at the crack in his voice.

Before Mr Apple could reply the door of the shop burst open and two men hurried into the shop, signalling urgently to Martin. Mr Apple watched as the three of them whispered and gesticulated, watched and felt saddened as he saw Martin grow pale and seem to shrink, the cockiness and bravado that was essentially his disintegrating.

As quickly as they had come the two men left, leaving Martin standing in the middle of the shop; he stood there, quite still and expressionless, for several moments.

'What is it, Martin?' Mr Apple asked, trying to make his voice kind and compassionate.

Martin turned slowly and stared at him, shaking his head. Then he came back around the counter, walking slowly, thinking.

'What is it?' Mr Apple insisted. 'I might be able to help.'

'You can't.'

'I might. I'm a very resourceful man, Martin,' Mr Apple assured him, with a sly little smile.

Martin gave a sad, tired laugh.

'Tell me, anyway.'

Martin sighed. 'I'm to be sacrificed,' he said simply, his eyes suddenly hurt and bewildered.

'Sacrificed?' Mr Apple sounded appalled.

'Yeah. That's it, Mr A. Sacrificed. There's more heat than they can handle over the Colonel, so it's been decided to drop my name in the right place. I'll be done, the heat taken off, and everyone'll be happy.'

'Dear God,' was all Mr Apple could muster up.

'Those were friends of mine warning me. They owe me, you see. Quite a few people owe me, Mr Apple,' Martin said, something of his old assurance returning. 'They told me to stay away from my place. To get out of here, too.'

'Then you must go,' Mr Apple said urgently.

'Hah. Go. Go where? This isn't a game, you know. You can't hide from this. I know. I know exactly what goes on.'

'Then you've got a head start,' Mr Apple said, as he fumbled in his pocket and took out a bundle of keys, dropped them, retrieved them, opened the clip, slipped off a single Yale key and held it out to Martin. 'Now, take this. Go round to my house – you know where *that* is, don't you?' Mr Apple said, smiling thinly at this little jibe. 'Go round the back and let yourself in by the kitchen door. Stay there until I get home. Then we'll think of something.'

'I can't go to your place, Mr Apple. They'll know.'

'I don't care what they know. Take it. Do what you're told for once. It will keep you off the streets for a while. We need time. Take it and go.'

'You don't know what you're getting into, Mr A.'

'I know. I know a lot more than you think. Now take this key and go.'

Martin took the key. 'Hey – thanks, Mr Apple.'

'Will you *go*, for heaven's sake. You can thank me tonight when I get home.'

Mr Apple watched Martin hurry from the shop. It was only as the door closed behind him and he found himself alone in the ominous silence that the full significance of what he had done began to dawn on him.

14

Mr Asher offered Colonel Maddox one of his cigarettes even though he knew it would be refused, accepted one himself, lit it, and stared out at the dark, rainswept streets as the car whisked them into the city from the airport. His face was tense and grey, in total contrast to the Colonel's, which was as usual ruddy, relaxed and calm, if a little mournful. One would have thought (seeing them both, side by side, each, in his own way reliving the events of the past few days) that it was Mr Asher who had so recently escaped the assassin's bullet.

'I still can't believe it,' he said at last, shaking his head.

Colonel Maddox gave a small chuckle. 'Oh, it's true enough, John.'

'God, you were lucky.'

'Yes.'

'The bastards. Right on your own doorstep,' Asher continued, as though the choice of location had been more horrifying than the attempt at murder.

'Anyone claimed responsibility yet?'

'Not yet. They will, though. If only to crow that they can still get at us.'

'Which, of course, they can,' the Colonel pointed out, not without humour.

'Which, of course, they can,' Asher agreed grimly. 'But I'll get someone for this if it's the last thing I do.'

'Not just someone, John. I want no unnecessary reprisals just because it was me they tried to dispose of.'

Asher appeared not to be listening. 'We've pulled in Corrigan for —'

'Corrigan?'

'Hmm. You know him. Larry Corrigan. Big fat lout. No teeth. We use him sometimes. Having him questioned. Knows a thing or two, does Larry Corrigan. I'm going there myself after I drop you off – unless you care to come along. ?'

Maddox frowned. 'Yes. Yes, I think I will. It's a new experience, isn't it? And not without intrigue: attempting to find out who actually tried to shoot one?'

Asher leaned forward and gave instructions to the driver, who responded immediately by swinging the car in a tight U-turn, timing his manoeuvre to perfection, slipping neatly between two oncoming cars without braking.

'Anything exciting over here while I was away?' Maddox asked.

'Not a lot. Routine mostly. You've been the excitement,' Mr Asher said, glancing at the Colonel with an almost envious smile. 'I've had a tighter watch put on Apple's shop, but there's been no activity there. He's got a new assistant, though. I'm checking on that. We'll have to have him in again soon, Mr Apple I mean. I know damn well he's mixed up in something, for all his innocent look.'

Maddox smiled. 'You don't like our Mr Apple much, do you?' he asked.

'No, I don't. Devious little freak.'

'You don't understand him, John.'

'There's nothing to understand. He's just another fool who's been conned or blackmailed into helping – '

'Why do you always call him a fool? I don't think he is, you know. Far from it. And I must say I think you employ the wrong tactics when you question him. I don't think he takes kindly to bullies.'

'I don't have the time for niceties, Colonel. He'll slip up. They all do, eventually. Then we'll have him.' Asher stroked his cheek in satisfaction.

'Unless, of course, they have us first,' the Colonel observed wryly.

'They won't.'

'They might.'

'They won't.'

'They nearly had me.'

Both men swayed as the car pulled sharply to the left to allow a screaming ambulance to pass.

'How did Mrs Maddox take it?'

'Rather well,' Maddox said vaguely. 'I think she was somewhat amused by the episode.'

'Amused?' Asher sounded shocked.

The Colonel gave a wicked little chuckle. 'Yes – in a way. She wasn't there when the actual shooting took place, but they managed to contact her in London. At her milliner's, would you believe,' the Colonel explained, allowing his chuckle to become a small laugh. 'A friend of hers drove her home immediately.' He paused and looked out of the window. He saw again the silver Bristol slither to a stop, sending the neatly raked gravel flying in all directions (and he remembered his annoyance, since he had raked it himself in a pattern of ever decreasing circles), saw Nancy step daintily out on elegant Gucci shoes, noted in her eyes a curious expectancy – but an expectancy of what he could not be sure.

Whatever happened? she demanded, looking about her for signs of carnage. We were told you were shot.

Yes. Someone took a shot at me.

Here? Right here? Nancy stepped quickly to one side as though the possibility of delayed ricochet was imminent.

Yes, dear. Right here. They missed.

I can see that. Why all the police?

Well, they don't really like the idea of someone shooting at me, he told her in his pronouncedly polite way. And I'm afraid my driver was killed.

Here? Nancy demanded again, horrified that her domain had been sullied.

The Colonel nodded.

How dreadful. But you're all right?

I'm fine.

Nancy Maddox shook her head theatrically and tutted. I do wish they wouldn't do it here, she said angrily (and the Colonel recalled her using the same expression and tone when his favourite retriever, now dead, had shat on the lawn). Over there (dismissing Northern

Ireland with a small wave of her gloved hand) you expect it.

I think that's what they had in mind, dear.

What?

That I wouldn't expect it.

Well, all I can say is I wish you wouldn't – Nancy stopped abruptly. Incredibly, she had been about to suggest that he leave his assassins behind him (at the office, so to speak) when the stupidity of this dawned on her.

Wouldn't – ?

Wouldn't get mixed up with such dreadful people, Nancy said lamely.

Colonel Maddox rocked on his heels and laughed until his eyes filled with tears. Even the two uniformed policemen nearest him, who had been unavoidably overhearing the conversation with some amazement, smiled.

Oh, Nancy you are incredible.

Well, you won't be going back there. That's something.

– ? But of course I will. I'll go back tomorrow.

Don't be stupid, Matthew. You can't go back now. They *know* you.

They've *known* me from the first day I set foot in Belfast, my dear.

But they've just tried to kill you.

That's right. So?

You are impossible, Nancy concluded and stormed into the house.

'She made me laugh anyway,' Maddox told Asher. 'I think it was the first time she ever made me laugh,' he confessed. 'The first time for a very long time anyway.'

'Amazing.'

'Yes. She is.'

'They don't understand, do they? Wives,' Mr Asher proclaimed.

'Why should they, John? I don't think we understand it ourselves half the time.'

'Oh, I understand it all right.'

'You do? I didn't think you did.'

Mr Asher rolled down the window a fraction and slipped his finished black cigarette through the gap. Then he rolled the window up again, cutting out the noise of the traffic and wind, and trying to suppress the feeling of resentment that welled up within him whenever the Colonel included him in his inadequacies. He was on the point of making some caustic remark when the car swung left and halted at the gates of Castlereagh police station.

'Anything?' Asher demanded brusquely of the sergeant who met them at the entrance and followed them down the corridor lined with small, anonymous rooms with numbers on the doors, from which issued occasional murmurs.

'Yes and no, sir.'

Asher halted, swung round, and glared. 'What the hell does that mean – yes and no? What the hell sort of an answer is that?'

The sergeant wilted and blushed violently. 'He hasn't exactly said anything – but I think he wants to. He's been insisting on seeing you.'

'Me?'

'Yes, sir.'

'By name?'

'Yes, sir.'

Asher glanced quickly at the Colonel. 'That's odd,' he said, frowning. 'They usually try and avoid me,' he added, his frown broadening and relaxing into a bland smile.

'Yes,' the Colonel agreed non-committally.

'Where is he?'

'Twenty-three, sir.'

'Right. We'd better go and see what he wants, then.'

Asher led the small procession down the corridor and paused briefly at the door of Room 23 to straighten his tie, as though correctness of dress would give him some tactical advantage. 'I'll deal with this. You needn't be here,' he told the sergeant, dismissing him with a curt nod.

'Very good, sir.'

'He has a way of interrupting,' Asher informed the Colonel, as the sergeant retreated up the corridor. 'I dislike being interrupted.'

'Yes,' the Colonel said again, managing to suggest a promise of silence.

'Right. Here we go.' Mr Asher straightened his shoulders and opened the door. He stood to one side and allowed the Colonel to pass into the room first. Then he shut the door firmly.

Larry Corrigan sat on a plain wooden chair which he overflowed, his fat, stubby, nicotine-stained fingers fidgeting nervously on the table before him, his eyes jumping continuously towards and away from the two men.

'You wanted me?' Asher said coldly.

'You Asher?'

'*Mr* Asher. Yes.'

'Who's he?'

'Never you mind, Corrigan. You wanted me and now I'm here. So, what is it you wanted?'

Corrigan shifted his enormous weight painfully in an effort to get his buttocks balanced evenly on either side of the seat of the chair, making it creak. He was breathing sweatily, banging the palms of his hands together silently.

Don't give it to Asher all at once, Seamus Reilly had warned him. Don't seem too anxious to help or he'll know something's up. He's as crafty as they come is Asher, so watch yourself, Corrigan.

I don't like doing this to Deeley, Mr Reilly, Corrigan said. I really don't. He's always been fair to me and didn't laugh at me. He was always willing to help me.

Your affections don't concern us, Corrigan. If you wish to side with Deeley that's your business – and I presume you'll be willing to take the consequences?

Cummon, Mr Reilly, be fair. Can't you get someone else to –

You have always been our source of – how shall I put it – our intermediary with the Brits, Larry. They trust you now. We need them to trust what you have to tell them.

All right, Mr Reilly. But you won't let on to Martin, will you?

Martin will be the least of your worries, I assure you.

Larry Corrigan grinned toothlessly. All right, Mr Reilly, I'll do it. Just leave it to me.

Exactly. We're leaving it to you, Larry. But don't mess it up.

I won't. Hey, why don't you just tell them straight? The Brits *want* to know, don't they?

Reilly sighed. People never appreciated the diplomacy of these negotiations. Because, Larry, he explained, tidying his impeccable clothes, his tone of voice indicating his imminent departure as clearly as if he were donning a hat, because it has been decided that it would be better from everybody's point of view if this information was extracted from you after considerable pressure.

You mean you don't want anyone to know that you set Martin up, is that it, Mr Reilly?

Just do it, Corrigan. Just do it and don't ask so many questions.

'I need a favour,' Larry Corrigan said.

'Well?' Mr Asher asked, and waited.

'I want out. I want to get away.'

'Away?'

'That's right, Mr Asher. Well away. Australia.'

'I see.' Asher seemed to consider this for a moment, glancing once at Maddox. 'An expensive business, Corrigan. Travelling to Australia. Very expensive,' he added, wondering what information Corrigan was about to offer that would warrant such a price. 'It could, of course, be arranged. Anything can be arranged if it's worth my while,' Asher continued speculatively, watching Corrigan's body sag while his eyes brightened in anticipation. 'We would have to learn something very – eh – interesting in return.'

Don't give it to Asher all at once, Reilly warned him.

'I *think* I might be able to find out who tried to hit that Colonel in England – would that be interesting enough?'

'I *think* it might be,' Mr Asher replied, avoiding a look at the Colonel who stood stony-faced and silent by the door. 'When do you *think* you could find out?'

'Do we have a deal?'

'We have a deal.'

Colonel Maddox stared up at the ceiling, trying to concentrate his gaze on the naked sixty-watt bulb, amazed and shocked that the process of treachery and betrayal could be handled with such calm, in such a businesslike way. Despite the fact that it was his own would-be assassin who was being bartered he was appalled by the neatness of the agreements being made.

' – ticket and some cash to keep me going,' Corrigan was now stipulating.

'Agreed.'

'Immediately.'

'As soon as any information you give us has been confirmed.'

'And my name stays out of it.'

'Naturally.'

'Okay.'

Asher sat on the edge of the table and waited. He didn't move a muscle, as if afraid that any movement he might make would distract Corrigan from parting with the information.

'You know Bezant's bookie's?'

'I do.'

'You know the boardmarker there?'

'Apple?'

'No, not Apple,' Corrigan said irritably. 'He's the manager. The boardmarker, I said. Martin Deeley?'

Asher inclined his head, but said nothing.

'He's just back from England. The word is that it wasn't exactly a holiday.'

Asher sucked in air and exhaled it again in a thin, inaudible whistle, controlling his excitement admirably. 'I see. Martin Deeley, you say. And Apple?'

'What about him?'

'He must have had something to do with it?'

By the way, Reilly said just before he left, if they should ask you anything about Mr Apple – it's unlikely, but they might – you know nothing.

Right, Mr Reilly. I'll remember that.

'No,' Corrigan said, shaking his head vehemently. 'Why should he? He's nothing. Just runs the place. Does nothing. Knows nothing. He's not connected with us at all.'

'You're sure of that?' Asher demanded, sounding disappointed and unbelieving.

'Sure, I'm sure.'

'He must have known Deeley was up to something.'

Corrigan shrugged his shoulders, the movement making the chair groan. 'How could he? He's told nothing. Jesus, Mr Asher, he's even a Prod. He just runs his shop, like I told you.'

'Right, Corrigan. You stay here. I'll be back in a while,' Asher said, standing up quickly and making for the door, taking the Colonel with him, an intense, satisfied smile on his face. 'Well, Colonel,' he said as they made their way along the corridor, 'that was nice and neat.'

'Too neat, if you ask me,' Maddox said. 'Can you believe him?' he asked.

'Of course,' Asher replied. 'Come in here a moment,' he added, leading the way into an empty office and closing the door. 'That's the way it works, Colonel,' he whispered, smiling delightedly. 'This Deeley has become a liability, so Corrigan was sent here to unload him.'

'Unload him?'

'That's it, Colonel. They hand over Deeley to us in the hope that we keep the heat off, in case we turn up something more important while we search for your – '

'You mean Corrigan was actually ordered in here to – '

' – to give us the information we want and make a deal for himself? Yes. That's exactly what I mean.'

'Good God.'

'It happens all the time. They're lovely people.'

'How many others have you sent to – Australia?'

Asher laughed, truly amused at the Colonel's naïvety. 'None. And, of course, Corrigan won't be going either.'

' – ?'

'He'll be killed.'

'And you'll allow that, after making an agreement with him?'

'Allow it? Colonel, we'll arrange it. Of course we'll make it look like a punishment for informing, but we'll do it. It's tidier that way, don't you think?'

'But – '

'Just let me handle it, Colonel. I know what I'm doing. You go on. You must be tired after your journey. I've things to do now. As soon as we pick up Deeley I'll let you know.'

'And you call *them* lovely people? John, this is all *wrong*.'

'It's the way we've done things since long before you came here, Colonel. We all have an understanding. Believe me, I know what I'm doing.'

Colonel Maddox shook his head and walked away.

'Jesus,' Asher sighed, watching the retreating figure. 'Jesus, and they expect to beat the terrorists?'

15

Mr Apple shut the front door of his house simply by leaning his back against it, allowing his long body to rest at an angle, giving his eyes time to focus in the gloom, giving his ears a few seconds to retune themselves to the stillness after the noises outside. Then he switched on the light in the hall and made his way to the kitchen, coughing gently to announce his arrival. Using the shaft of light from the hall for illumination he drew the curtains across the kitchen window before putting on the fluorescent light: it flickered belligerently, and in the intermittent blue-white clarity Mr Apple spotted Martin crouched by the back door, his wave of recognition looking jerky and dislocated in the uncertain light. As the overhead tube settled down to a continuous flow of hard brightness Martin said:

'You frightened the shit out of me, Mr A.'

'I coughed,' Mr Apple told him defensively.

'Yeah, I heard that, but I've never heard you cough before, so I didn't know it was you.'

'Oh. Well, it is.'

'Yep. So I see.' Martin stood up and stretched, then leaned a hip lazily against the table.

Mr Apple ignored him for the moment and, with his eyes, searched the kitchen from top to bottom. 'Have you seen Chloe?' he asked suddenly, his voice ridiculously calm under the circumstances.

'Chloe?'

'My cat.'

'A ginger-and-white thing?'

Mr Apple nodded and pursed his lips, peeved to hear Chloe referred to as a thing.

'Yes. She's been at the window for about an hour. I was going to let her in for company, but she ran off.'

Mr Apple appeared pleased with the cat's discretion. 'She's fussy about the company she keeps,' he said, smiling wickedly.

'Very funny.'

'Animals – cats in particular – can always tell what we mortals are like, you know. I never trust anyone who doesn't get on with animals,' Mr Apple explained obscurely. 'And I wouldn't be without some sort of animal myself. Dear little Chloe. Oh, well, she'll be back when she's hungry I expect,' he remarked. 'You hungry, Martin?'

'I could eat something.'

'Ah. Well, let's see what we can rustle up.'

Mr Apple took off his coat and, donning an apron that extolled the virtues of a particular gravy mixture, busied himself getting something for them to eat, opening a can of condensed chicken soup, and, with customary difficulty, a couple of tins of sardines. 'It won't be very fancy,' he threw over his shoulder, licking the sardine oil from his fingers, 'but it will keep you going.'

'Thanks. Anything's fine.'

'By the way,' Mr Apple went on casually, adding milk to the saucepan and stirring the soup, 'I think the hunt has started for you.'

Martin immediately stood upright, his body rigid. 'What makes you say that?'

'We had visitors in the shop. Two strangers. Never saw either of them before. They weren't dressed right for punters. Too – well, too correct, if that's the word. They didn't say anything, mind you. Just looked around, stayed ten minutes, and left. They pretended to be listening to the race. Of course, I could be imagining things.'

'You don't imagine things, Mr Apple.'

'Oh, but I do, Martin. That's my trouble. Anyway, they went. Here, have this while it's hot.' Mr Apple passed Martin a bowl of steaming chicken soup. 'There's bread in the bin over there if you want some. Butter in the fridge. Salt and pepper on that shelf.' Martin shook his head and started spooning the soup slowly into his mouth, blowing on each spoonful before drinking it.

Mr Apple carried his own soup to the table and sat down. 'Then Seamus Reilly came in,' he said. 'You know him, of course, although you pretended you didn't?'

'I know him. What did *he* want?'

'He said he just dropped in to see how I was – and, casually, why I was without a boardmarker.'

'And?'

'And I told him you were still out sick. That you had come in but had felt weak, and that I'd sent you home.'

'Thanks. What – ?'

'I think he knew I was lying,' Mr Apple said, making a quizzical face as he savoured the soup, getting up to collect the pepper-pot from the shelf and sprinkling its contents liberally into his bowl before adding, 'I have a feeling he'd already been to your home.'

Martin nodded, his eyes reduced to thin slits. 'Probably.'

'I thought you two were on the same side.'

'So did I.'

'Oh.'

'There's no sides here, it seems, Mr Apple. There's only survival. You survive anyway you can.'

'I see.'

'Even if it means trading with the army, you have to arrange your survival,' Martin explained, in a voice that suggested he had just worked this out.

'I see,' said Mr Apple again.

'Still,' Martin said with a small laugh, 'I suppose you could say we're on the same side now.'

'We always were, Martin,' Mr Apple told him darkly. 'Even before we met we were destined to join forces.'

'You don't half say some weird things, Mr A.'

Mr Apple nodded. 'I'm a weird person.'

Martin Deeley pushed his bowl away from him and wiped the thin beige moustache from his upper lip with his handkerchief. 'Not weird. But you're different. You're certainly different, Mr A. Although before I met you I thought you were weird.'

'What changed your mind?'

Martin shrugged. 'Knowing you a bit, I suppose.'

'But you don't. You know nothing about me.'

'Yes I do.'

'If you say so,' Mr Apple sighed benignly, scraping the last of the soup from his plate and licking his spoon like a lollipop.

'You don't think I do?'

Mr Apple stared unblinkingly at Martin. 'I know you don't. I don't really exist, you see.'

'Oh.' Martin grinned, but eyed the old man suspiciously all the same.

'I come and go,' Mr Apple went on ponderously. 'Like everyone does, really. We all come and go.'

'Sure.'

'Now you *do* think I'm mad.'

'No.'

'Yes, you do, Martin. You're sitting there saying to yourself that you were right all along. And maybe you're right,' Mr Apple conceded, pausing for a moment before adding: 'But I'll tell you my secret: only my experiences make me exist; when they cease, or even lie for a moment in abeyance, I stop being. Does that make sense?'

Martin laughed nervously. 'Not a lot.'

'It will, Martin. Believe me, it will. The older you get the more you will appreciate that what I say is true.'

'Great. I look forward to that.'

Mr Apple bowed his head and seemed, for the moment, to be lost in unravelling some mystery on the bottom of his soup bowl. Then: 'So what happens to you now, Martin?' he asked suddenly. 'Where do you go from here?'

The abruptness of the question, and perhaps the realization that its simplicity made his predicament all the more alarming, made Martin jump. 'I wish the hell I knew.'

'You're quite certain that you are to be – eh – sacrificed – I think was your word?'

'Yeah. I'm certain. I even know it's Larry Corrigan who's going to drop my name. Poor old bugger. He doesn't know he's as dead as I am. Yeah, I'm certain all right.'

'Well, then,' Mr Apple said, pushing his bowl away and drumming his fingertips on the table after setting his spectacles firmly on his nose, 'we'd better put our heads together and think what we're going to do with you.'

Martin shook his head, a look of amazement spreading over his face. 'You really amaze me, Mr Apple,' he said.

'I don't see why.'

'The way you – never mind. I can't explain it, anyway. I'll just have to disappear, that's all. England for a start, if I can make it. Then God knows.'

'Yes.'

'I can't stay here, that's for sure.'

'Whyever not?'

'And have you dragged into it? Don't be stupid, Mr A. There's a shit called Asher in charge of things – ever heard of him?'

'Oh, yes. Oh, dear me,' Mr Apple was suddenly grinning in delight. 'I know Mr Asher well. Not a nice little man, is he?'

'You've met him?'

'A couple of times. Yes. I was supposed to tell him what was going on in the shop, you see.'

'So they *were* right.'

' – ?'

'You were seen – '

'Yes, I thought I was. I didn't say anything, though. Disliked him a great deal. Mr Asher, I mean.'

'Well, you'll dislike him a hell of a lot more if he finds out you've been hiding me. He'll have you in for harbouring a criminal and *you'll* end up in the slammer.'

'There are worse things, Martin,' Mr Apple said philosophically.

'Oh yeah? Like what?'

'Imprisoning oneself in oneself,' Mr Apple said mysteriously. 'That's far worse, you know, Martin. That really is the most awful thing of all. The constant manacling of the spirit inside oneself.'

'You've lost me.'

'We all lose ourselves...Anyway, you'll have to stay here for a while. I can try and find out what's happening.'

'They'll come here.'

'But they don't have to find you.'

'Hah – you ever seen those bastards do a search?'

'No.'

'Well, I can tell you, Mr Apple, if I'm here they'll find me. They'll tear the place to pieces if they think I'm here.'

Mr Apple smiled cunningly. 'Oh I think we can outwit Mr Asher and his henchmen,' he said cheerfully, as though about to put into operation some enormously amusing game of hity-tity. 'Anyway, they'll only look in places likely to hide a body.'

'Brilliant. So, you going to shrink me? Make me invisible?'

Mr Apple laughed aloud, a strange, cackling, unpractised sound, as though the suggestions tickled his fancy. 'Not quite. Sardines on toast?'

' – ? Oh. No. No, thanks. I've had enough.'

'Certain?'

'Thanks.'

'Right. Come with me, as they say, and I shall show thee things of great import.'

Mr Apple rose from the table with exaggerated dignity and, using his arm like an oar, gestured for Martin to follow in his wake. They left the kitchen and walked down the hall. Mr Apple stopped at the glory-hole and opened the door. 'Now for the wonders of architecture,' he said.

'Jesus, that's the first place they'll look.'

'Yes. I know,' Mr Apple agreed affably. 'It's so obvious, isn't it?'

'And?'

'And, would you believe, the cupboard will be bare. Not a mouse, not a Martin, not a thing.'

' – ?'

'Look,' Mr Apple commanded, switching on the cupboard light. 'Just look,' he repeated.

Martin looked. In the pale forty-watt light he saw only that the cupboard was already as bare as Mother Hubbard's. 'Great,' he said.

'An empty cupboard. So?'

'So they look in here and see nothing,' Mr Apple said, enjoying himself hugely, rubbing his bony hands together.

'You're losing me, Mr Apple. One of us is round the twist – '

Mr Apple indulged himself and enjoyed Martin's confusion for a moment, his eyes glistening behind the thick lenses. 'That is exactly what I intend to do, Martin. Lose you. Behold.'

Mr Apple was suddenly on his knees, fiddling with something on the floor. As he straightened up he lifted part of the floor with him and propped it against the wall. 'Now, then. What do you think of that?'

' – ?'

'Squeeze in and have a peep.'

Martin squeezed in and stared at the opening in the floor. A narrow flight of wooden steps led downwards into darkness. 'What's down there?'

'Your salvation,' Mr Apple told him. 'Your escape, at any rate. Follow me.'

Mr Apple started down the steps, grunting, but manipulating the steep descent with some agility, as though he had practised the exercise frequently. And Martin followed.

'Now, what do you think of that?' Mr Apple wanted to know, switching on a light and waving an arm, as though triumphantly revealing a long lost masterpiece.

'Wow.'

Martin stared about him. It was a tiny room. Immaculately clean. A camp-bed, neatly made and covered by an exotic patchwork quilt stood in one corner. There was a small table and, beside it, one chair with a cushion to match the quilt. A hessian mat covered most of the brick floor, and on the walls hung pictures of beings Martin had never seen before, not even in his wildest dreams. In one, a creature like a black dog, with horns and the face of an ape, straddled a cottage and held a large key in its mouth; in another a succubus reclined, one arm bent back behind her head, her breasts like grinning faces, her stomach and knees portrayed as faces also; there were portraits of

Thomas Darling, Louise Huebner, Aleister Crowley, and a composite of the Monks of Medmenham. Directly over the small table there was a crucifix on which was suspended a negroid Christ, and under it, on a small shelf, lay a scarab, a marble eye of Horus, a bible and a glass bottle containing what looked like dried parsley.

'Christ, Mr Apple,' was all that Martin could find to say.

'Yes,' Mr Apple agreed. 'He has a lot to do with it.'

'It's creepy,' Martin said, shivering suddenly. 'What the hell are all those things?' he asked, pointing at the pictures.

'Ah. Well, aids, I suppose. Symbols of what I must destroy. But don't let them worry you, Martin. They don't effect you.'

'I'm glad to hear that. They're – '

'And, you see, you'll be quite safe here for a while.'

'I'm not so sure about that.'

'Oh, you will. They'll never find you here.'

'That's not what I meant.'

'Oh.'

'Anyway, they'll have dogs with them in case of explosives. You'll be up to your neck in it, Mr A. The dogs will soon sniff me out.'

'Well, now, I had thought of that,' Mr Apple said, tugging at his chin and beginning to look like Merlin. 'That's where the other member of the family comes in. The one you were so rude about. Chloe.'

'The cat?'

'The cat. She has a little tray, you see. To do her nasties in – tee-hee – and I thought if I sprinkled a little of that on the floor upstairs, and, indeed, put poor Chloe in there...?'

'You know, I never would have thought you to be so devious, Mr A.'

'Survival, Martin. That's what you told me. Survival.'

And it wasn't all that long before Mr Apple's survival special was put to the test. He had just settled down in bed to write his diary, and was thinking what words to use concerning the downstairs arrangements, thinking, too, and smiling at the thought, of Martin tucked up under the watchful glare of the daemonic onlookers while Chloe (furious at her restricted liberty and mewling like a mad thing) created feline havoc overhead, when he heard the vehicles skid to a stop outside his house, the muffled orders being given, and the thud of boots running up the path, dividing, some running round the back, the rest thundering up the steps to the front door. Mr Apple leaped out of bed and ran to the top of the stairs, pulling on a threadbare dressing-gown as he ran. He had only managed to negotiate two stairs when the front door splintered and burst open under the onslaught of military footwear. Suddenly, the hall below him was filled with soldiers, all armed. They seemed to freeze for a moment, looking about them uncertainly: then they parted ranks and allowed Asher to make his way to the foot of the stairs and stare up at Mr Apple.

'We have orders to search your house,' he said curtly, somehow making it clear that Mr Apple was privileged to have even this explanation.

'Search my house?'

'Yes.'

'Good heavens,' Mr Apple said, doing his best to look aghast. 'Why on earth would you want to do that?'

'You wouldn't know, of course.'

'I'm afraid I haven't the faintest idea.'

'I warned you some time ago you'd end up in trouble if you tried to cross me,' Asher said complacently. 'And now you're in trouble. Big trouble.'

'Oh dear,' Mr Apple said, switching his expression adroitly to misery. 'Perhaps you'd be so good as to search up here first so that I can get back to bed? I need my beauty sleep, you see.'

Asher narrowed his eyes. 'Right,' he said, and added, sharpening his voice, 'tear this place to pieces if you have to, but make certain you search every inch of it. Get those dogs in here first. And be quick about it.'

Mr Apple sat himself down on the top stair and watched through the banisters as the mayhem proceeded. Two Alsatians were introduced to the scene, great pink tongues lolling, tails wagging high in some anticipation: they were sent ahead into each room before their handlers reported the rooms 'clean'. 'Clean, sir,' was exactly what they said, and Mr Apple gave Asher a little wave to acknowledge this passing of his housework, trying to hide his annoyance and anxiety as the soldiers crashed about in the rooms, throwing everything on the floor, emptying drawers, overturning chairs and tables, pots and pans in the kitchen, books and ornaments in the sitting-room, all thrown willy-nilly into piles on the floor. 'Nothing, sir.'

'Upstairs, then,' Asher ordered, standing aside and letting the dogs and soldiers race up the stairs.

'Hello, doggies,' Mr Apple said to the Alsatians, who ignored him, and 'Good evening,' he wished each soldier as he passed, and they ignored him also, though one did look somewhat embarrassed as he passed the skinny, bent figure smiling benignly at him.

And the routine was exactly the same upstairs as down. 'Clean, sir.' Mr Apple's little wave to Asher. 'Nothing, sir.'

Asher came half-way up the stairs and pointed a manicured finger at Mr Apple. 'You are a lucky man,' he said. 'This time. But don't think I've finished with you yet.'

Mr Apple smiled beatifically.

'Right,' Asher ordered. 'Out.'

Down came the soldiers, followed by the dogs, and passed Asher, making for the door. Indeed, all the soldiers had left the house when one of the dogs started sniffing and growling at the glory-hole door, scratching at it. Asher turned his head and grinned triumphantly at Mr Apple. 'And what have we here?'

Mr Apple peered over the top of his spectacles. 'There? Oh, that's my glory-hole, Mr Asher. That's where I hide things,' he said mischievously. 'I wouldn't open the door if I were you.'

'Oh, you wouldn't – ' Asher said, and jerked his head authoritatively at the dog-handler. 'Open it,' he ordered.

The dog-handler, the dark green of his R.U.C. uniform blending with the shadows and making him appear bodiless, reached out and opened the door of the cupboard, standing behind it, leaving his Alsatian to take the brunt of any attack. For a moment there was silence, the men watching the dog, the dog peering into the glory-hole, its head cocked quizzically. Then all hell broke loose: a small, furry, ginger-and-white missile flew from the dark and landed, screaming, on the dog's face, sharp little claws embedding themselves in the unfortunate animal's eyes. The dog yelped and reared up, shaking itself furiously to rid itself of Chloe, who clung on tenaciously for a few minutes, then jumped nimbly away and dashed out the front door.

'Oh, dear,' said Mr Apple. 'I did say not to open that door, Mr Asher. Chloe does hate her meditation to be disturbed.'

Asher opened and closed his mouth several times, small flecks of spittle forming on the edges of his lips. He cleaned these off repeatedly with his tongue before saying: 'Get that damn dog out and quieten it down.'

'Dear, dear, poor dog,' Mr Apple was saying, coming down the stairs. 'Yet another innocent victim of our times. It's always the innocent who suffer, don't you find, Mr Asher?'

But Mr Asher found nothing, it seemed, but his seat in the car, and by the time Mr Apple reached the front door the invading troops had been loaded up and were pulling out, leaving Mr Apple to gaze into an empty street.

'What on earth have you been up to, Mr Apple?'

' – ?' Mr Apple jumped, taken aback by the unexpected discovery at such close quarters of Mr Cahill, still, it struck him, togged out for gardening despite the lateness of the hour, but at least without his watering-can.

'What brought all this about?' Cahill still wanted to know, standing on tiptoe and attempting to see over Mr Apple's shoulder.

'Sanitary inspectors,' Mr Apple offered by way of explanation, smiling nervously. 'At least, they kept telling each other my house was clean.'

'Not been making bombs, then?' Cahill pursued wittily. 'Can't say I'd have taken you for a bomb maker.'

Mr Apple, perhaps infected by his neighbour's light dismissal of the frightening events, started to laugh. 'You'll never believe it, Mr

Cahill but the combined forces of the R.U.C. and the British Army were driven out, routed you might say, by my cat!'

'By *what?*'

'My cat.'

'That scrawny moggy that steals my milk and – '

'The very same. Who would have thought it? Oh, dear, oh dear,' Mr Apple shook with uncontrollable, jittery laughter.

'You all right?'

'Yes. I'm fine. Thank you.'

'You can stay with me for the night if you like,' Cahill went on, sounding concerned.'

'That's most kind of you, Mr Cahill, but I'm quite all right. They only smashed the lock on the door. Apart from that, no damage.'

'Right. Good-night, then.'

'Good-night, Mr Cahill. And thank you.'

Mr Apple closed the front door and put the little chain across it to hold it closed. He leaned his back against it and started shaking, shaking in sheer terror as the realization of what might have happened sank in. He needed, deserved, a drink. One stiff therapeutic drink was what was called for. He padded into the sitting-room and stared at the mess before him without really seeing it, his eyes seeking out the bottle of brandy he knew should be there somewhere. At last he spotted it, partially concealed by his well-thumbed copy of *The Wind in the Willows*. Mr Apple retrieved the bottle and unscrewed the cap: he was about to take a drink when he changed his mind, screwed on the cap again and went out of the room, making for the glory-hole.

'Was that what I think it was?' Martin demanded as Mr Apple negotiated the steep steps, brandishing the brandy bottle before him.

'That depends what you think it was, Martin,' he said lightly.

'They came, didn't they?'

'We had visitors, yes. Our friend Mr Asher and his entourage dropped in for a moment. But they're gone now, and all's well with the world. Drink?'

Martin accepted the bottle absentmindedly and took a drink,

coughing as the liquid made its way to his stomach. 'I told you they would,' he said, passing the bottle back.

'So you did. Cheers.' Mr Apple drank deeply. 'Aaah,' he said, and belched timidly. 'But they didn't find you, did they?'

'Not this time. They'll be back.'

'Not for a while. By the way, you'll have to show more respect for Chloe in future. She saved your bacon. Attacked like a cat possessed.'

' – ?'

'Drove the invading hordes from our shores,' Mr Apple continued, starting to shake again, taking another mouthful of brandy. 'I thought they had you, though.'

For some time they sat in silence, passing the bottle back and forth.

'Well, that settles it,' Martin said finally. 'I can't stay here.'

'Nonsense,' Mr Apple snapped. 'It's the one place you *can* stay. They've done their search and found nothing.'

'So I just sit down here for the rest of my life?'

'Oh. I see. I wasn't thinking that far ahead. Well – '

Once again they took to sitting in brooding silence, eyeing each other from time to time as though to elicit inspiration.

'Now wait a minute,' Mr Apple said suddenly, brightening. 'I've had a thought.'

' – ?'

'Just let me work this out. You say your name has been given as part of a deal, right?'

Martin nodded. 'That's the way it is.'

'So, what we have to do is to arrange another deal, a sort of counter deal – I'm beginning to enjoy this, you know – to get you off the hook.'

'What – '

'No, don't interrupt me a moment,' Mr Apple said quickly, chewing on his lower lip and frowning. 'Apart from myself, have you anyone else who would help you?'

Martin imitated Mr Apple's frown. 'Yes – well, I think so. Yes.'

'Good. Who?'

'Fergal and Billy – the two who warned me in the first place - would, if they haven't been got at.'

'Good. Anyone else?'

'I can't think of – '

'Surely there's someone else. Someone I could contact to – '

'Hang on a minute. Daphne. That's it, Mr Apple. Daphne Cope. A girl I know – '

'*Can* she help?'

'You bet. She knows everyone. Had most of them,' Martin said, with a wicked grin.

'And you can trust her?'

Martin thought for a moment. 'Yeah, I can trust her. She loves me,' he said, starting to blush.

'Poor girl.'

'Lucky.'

'Huh,' grunted Mr Apple, but smiling kindlily enough. 'Where can I get in touch with her?'

'You can phone her. That would be safest.'

'When?'

'Any time. Now.'

'Now?' Mr Apple glanced at his watch. 'At twenty past one?'

'She works late,' Martin said, grinning again.

'Oh.'

'Shit,' said Martin suddenly, 'what am I talking about. *I'll* phone her. You have a phone, I suppose?'

'I have a phone,' Mr Apple said. 'But I'll phone. You stay down here – just in case.'

'In case of – '

'In case – I don't know. Just in case. You know her number?'

'She won't talk to you, Mr A. She doesn't know you. She's careful.'

'Yes. I hadn't thought of that.'

'Let's do it then. I – '

'Wait, wait, wait,' Mr Apple insisted, waving Martin to sit down again. 'What are you going to say to her?'

' – ? Nothing. I just want her to find out what's happening.'

The phone seemed to ring interminably before it clicked and a tired voice filled with the heaviness of sleep said 'Yes?'

'Get me Daphne,' Martin ordered.

'You know what time it is?'

'Yeah, I know. Get me Daphne.'

'Christ, I'm not – '

'Get me Daphne,' Martin repeated, his request becoming a threat. There was silence for a moment, then: 'Hang on.'

Martin covered the mouthpiece with his hand and winked at Mr Apple. 'Gone to get her,' he said. Mr Apple nodded.

'Hello?'

'Daphne?'

'Martin? Is that you?'

'It's me.'

'Oh, dear God, I've been so *worried*. Everyone's talking about you. I've been going out of my mind. Where are you?'

'I'm safe.'

'Oh, God – '

'Listen. What have you heard?'

'They say you tried to kill that Colonel in England – you didn't, though, did you?'

'What else?'

'Oh. Larry Corrigan was sent to grass on you, to make a deal of some sort. Is that true?'

'I'm asking you, dammit. What else?'

'I can't think, Martin. Where *are* you?'

'I'll tell you in a minute. What else have you heard?'

'Just – just that everyone's looking for you. They've been to your place. And they went to your Mam's. They took her in for – '

'They what?'

'She's all right. They let her go again. Martin, where are you? I want to see you.'

'Hang on.' Martin covered the mouthpiece again. 'She wants to see me. It might be better. Can she come here?'

'If you think it's safe – for you and her,' Mr Apple said.

'Daphne? Can you come now?'

'Of course I can.'

'Right. Here's where you come.' Martin gave her Mr Apple's address, repeating it twice and making Daphne say it over to him. 'And be a bit careful,' he advised. 'They've been here already, so we should be safe enough. But you never know.'

'I'll be careful.'

'See you, then. Oh, hang on,' Martin said, suddenly aware that Mr Apple was signalling wildly at him. 'What?'

'Not now,' Mr Apple said. 'Don't have her come here now.'

'Why not?'

'I don't know, Martin. Tomorrow. Have her come over tomorrow. I have a feeling – '

Martin eyed Mr Apple suspiciously. 'Daphne. Leave it till tomorrow evening.'

'But I want – '

'Tomorrow evening, Daphne. You might be able to find out more by then anyway.'

'Yes – but – '

'No buts. Tomorrow.'

'All right, Martin. If you say so. You'll be all right till then, will you?'

'I'll be just fine. I'm being well looked after. Just find out everything you can and I'll see you tomorrow night.'

'Bye then, Martin.'

'Bye.' Martin put down the receiver and turned to Mr Apple. 'Tomorrow night,' he said. Mr Apple nodded. 'You think they're watching the place, don't you?'

Mr Apple shook his head. 'I don't know. I just don't feel right. I have to follow my instincts.'

'Oh, I won't argue with your instincts, Mr Apple.'

Mr Apple gave a bright little smile. 'Mr Apple outwits the army,' he said.

They both laughed wryly until Martin became suddenly serious. 'Hey, have I thanked you, Mr A.? For everything?'

'You've thanked me, Martin.'

'That's all right then. You're really the first one I've had to thank in my whole life.'

'What is worrying me is that I may also be the last,' Mr Apple said grimly. Then he smiled again. 'We'll get through this together. You wait and see. Together we'll conquer the lot of them.'

'I hope you're right.'

'Good heavens. I'm always right. I thought you knew that.'

'Hah. I'm beginning to believe it.'

'Good.'

'You know I still can't believe I've ended up with you as a friend, Mr A.'

'Strange bedfellows – '

'No, don't joke about it,' Martin said seriously. 'It's a funny feeling. I was sitting down there in that dungeon listening to them clobbering about up here, and it dawned on me that you're the only friend I have in the world. It – '

'You've Daphne,' Mr Apple interrupted, feeling inexplicably embarrassed.

'She's different. She wants something. Me. But you – you don't want anything, do you?'

'From you? No. No, Martin, not from you.'

'Can I ask you something?'

' – ?'

'What made you help me?'

Mr Apple thought about this for a while. Then he shrugged. 'It seemed the right thing to do,' he said at last. 'Hah, it seemed the *only* thing to do. It fitted in.'

'Fitted in? With what?'

'Hmm. That, young man, is what I'm still trying to figure out. "There is a tide in the affairs of men" as the bard said, and I'm trying to stop it ebbing away,' Mr Apple said, his voice trailing off, his face puzzled and all at sea.

192

'You've lost me again.'

'I've lost myself, Martin. That's the problem. Still, we'll muddle through, won't we? We'll come out on top somehow – even if we die in the process.'

'Thanks. Nothing like being cheerful.'

Mr Apple giggled. 'I remember once – oh, a long, long time ago, probably before you were born – I remember someone saying to me – it might even have been my father – no, hardly; he wouldn't, I don't think, have thought along those lines – he worked in the shipyards, you know – a good man, but dull, unimaginative – I think I always held that against him, being unimaginative – anyway, where was I? – oh, yes, someone said to me that the only happy thing about living was knowing you had to die one day. Odd thought, isn't it?'

'Morbid.'

'Only if you're afraid of death.'

'I am. Shit scared of it.'

'Hmm,' hummed Mr Apple. 'I used to be until I died,' he added, closing his eyes.

'Until you *died*?'

Mr Apple opened his eyes again and smiled wistfully. 'In a manner of speaking. Not to worry,' he added brusquely. 'We can talk about that some other time.'

'I don't think I want to.'

'Then we won't.'

Mr Asher sat scowling across the desk from Colonel Maddox, his annoyance intensified by the somewhat mocking smile that played about the Colonel's mouth.

'You look as though you've been up all night,' the Colonel now remarked. 'Don't you ever sleep?'

Asher stretched suddenly and gave a forced, noisy yawn. 'Yes, I sleep,' he said. 'But you're right: I *was* up all night.'

'I hope it was worth it,' the Colonel said, immediately presuming Asher had been having one of his romantic entanglements.

Asher scowled again. 'No, dammit, it wasn't.'

'Oh,' grunted the other sympathetically.

'That damned Apple – '

'Apple?'

'Yes. Apple. Made a fool out of me. Sat there on the stairs gloating. Grinning like a moron.'

'I don't follow – ' the Colonel put in, confused.

Asher stretched again, moving his shoulders in circles to ease his muscles. 'It's a long and boring story,' he said finally, lighting a cigarette, as he always did when about to deliver some explanation that might take time. 'There's something up between those two – Apple and Deeley. I *know* Apple knows where Deeley is. I just *know* it. He was far too smug and self-assured last night. And as for Deeley – he's just vanished from the face of the earth.'

'But what made you go to Mr Apple, John? He's been helping *us*.'

'Has he hell. Colonel, that lunatic has been taking us for a glorious ride.'

'Oh, I don't think so.'

'I tell you he has.'

'But you found nothing at his house?'

'Nothing,' Asher admitted. 'But he knows something.'

'You don't think you're reading more into Mr Apple because you *want* to believe he's involved?'

Asher smiled ruefully and said: 'Maybe I am,' although he was obviously thinking of something else, something that struck even him as rather amusing. 'The damn fool set his cat on us,' he confessed at last, and gave a snorting laugh.

'His cat?' Maddox wondered for a moment if he had heard aright.

'Yes. His cat. Well, he didn't actually set the bloody thing on us, but it leapt from a cupboard and attacked one of the sniffer-dogs. Jesus, you should have seen the chaos,' Mr Asher concluded, laughing snortily again as he remembered the ridiculous scene once more.

'Oh, dear,' Maddox said, joining in the laughter, albeit hesitantly, as though still unsure if a joke was being made or not. Asher could be very touchy about his work, and the Colonel had no wish to offend him at the moment. 'What actually happened?'

'Oh, we searched the place from top to bottom while Apple watched us gleefully. And found nothing. But I still say Apple was just that bit too smug. He let us tramp all over his house as though he knew we wouldn't find anything – no, that's not what I mean. What I mean is, it was more than his knowing there was no one else in the house; it was like he knew we were looking for Deeley and he actually knew where Deeley was.' Asher inhaled his cigarette smoke deeply. 'Does that make any sense, Colonel?'

'I know what you mean, but as to making sense, well – ' the Colonel replied, waving a hand vaguely in the air to disperse the smoke in front of him.

'Hmm,' agreed Asher, somewhat reluctantly.

'You could always ask that chap – what was his name – the one who gave you Deeley's – '

'Corrigan?'

'Yes, Corrigan. You could always ask him again if there was anything between – '

Asher fidgeted uncomfortably for a second. 'I'm afraid we can't do that, sir.'

'– ?'

'Corrigan has been – eh – removed,' Asher said bluntly.

'Removed? Are you saying what I think you're saying, John?'

'I told you that was the way things were done, Colonel. You didn't seem to object then.'

'I didn't believe – You've had him killed?'

'I – yes, I've had him killed.'

Colonel Maddox shook his head, a mixture of outrage and sadness filling his eyes. 'I don't understand you, John.'

'It was the cleanest thing to do. No questions to be answered. No unpleasant repercussions. I had him shot from behind in the head. I had him kneecapped. It will simply be put down as a punishment killing. And the Provos won't deny it. They'll use it as a warning to others who might feel tempted to talk to us, and it will stop Corrigan telling tales that might embarrass them – you follow?'

'Oh, I follow all right. But it disgusts me. I – '

'You know nothing about it, sir. I have told you nothing. You can read about the – eh – punishment if they ever get around to mentioning it in the papers, and what you read is all you'll ever know.'

Asher contemplated the glowing end of his black cigarette for a moment, and for a moment, also, he allowed himself to recall the pathetic, vicious drama he had orchestrated less than twenty-four hours before.

Where're you taking me? Corrigan had wanted to know.

You want protection, don't you? Well, you can't stay here then, can you? Asher asked in his friendliest voice.

Oh.

We've got a safe house to keep you in until we can arrange the papers you wanted.

Oh. Where?

Not far. A short drive. You'll have an escort no less.

Corrigan beamed. An escort, eh?

Well, we don't want anyone taking pot-shots at you now that

you've done us a good turn. We've got to keep our side of the bargain.

Corrigan continued to beam, and he was still grinning broadly when Asher ordered the driver to stop for a moment.

Just a moment, Larry, Mr Asher said. I just want to check with the car behind. Won't be a tick.

Okay, Mr Asher.

Asher stepped out of his own car and walked to the one following. You can go back now, he told the face at the wheel. We'll deal with it now.

The driver nodded, reversed the vehicle into a gateway, then drove away back down the road.

Asher watched the rear lights fade before returning to his own car. Right, Larry, he said. I'm afraid it's on foot from here.

For the first time Larry Corrigan looked worried, but only slightly: Asher's friendly face reassured him. He heaved himself on to the road and stretched.

You lead the way, Asher told the driver. You needn't worry about the car. We won't be long.

The driver led the way. Corrigan followed. Asher brought up the rear. The procession moved slowly, through a broken gate, up a driveway or small lane, it was difficult to tell which in the dark.

The three of them had only been walking for about three minutes when Asher took a revolver from his pocket, aimed carefully, and shot Corrigan in the back of the head. The great mound of flesh seemed to jump several inches in the air before it crashed to the ground, seemed to bounce like a mass of india-rubber, before it came to a hissing stillness.

Here, help me turn him over, Asher commanded in a harsh whisper.

Together, Asher and the driver heaved the body over onto its stomach and then, without a glance at his victim, Mr Asher fired two more shots, one into the back of each knee of the dead Larry Corrigan.

That's it, Asher said, pocketing the revolver. Let's get home. And you weren't here tonight. Remember that. You saw nothing and know nothing, because you weren't here. Understand?

Yessir.

'So all you're telling me,' Maddox was saying, 'all you're telling me is that you raided Mr Apple, had one man killed, and the man you're supposed to be arresting is still free.'

Asher moved uneasily in his chair. 'Yes, but – '

'That's it, isn't it?' the Colonel persisted.

'Yes.'

'Not what you might call the height of efficiency?'

'Perhaps not, sir.'

'I don't think there's any perhaps about it.'

'No, sir.'

Maddox rose from behind his desk and started pacing up and down the office. He stopped suddenly by Asher's chair and asked in a voice that was unusually cold 'What other surprises have you lined up for me, John? How many more people are you going to have *removed*? I want to know. I simply will not be a party to this – this – this abomination.'

Asher looked up at the long, cold face looming over him. 'But that is exactly what I've been telling you, sir. You are not a party to anything. You don't even know about anything.'

'Will you stop playing games with me, John?' Maddox shouted.

'With respect, Colonel, I am not playing games. I am dealing with a situation in the way that that situation has always been dealt with. To deal with it in any other way would, I suggest, be playing games.'

Maddox continued to stare down at the steely eyes that now seemed to penetrate his soul, hearing, but not really listening.

'And, again with respect, Colonel, I would repeat that you are, after all, the stranger here. You do not – do not – understand how things are done, how arrangements and agreements are made. Of course we are trying to stop what you call "the terrorism" in England, but we have to give as well as take. If we did not turn the occasional blind eye, if we did not overlook certain activities, if we did not ignore the occasional sectarian murder – if we did not do all these things we would be overrun in a matter of weeks, months at the most.'

It was probably the sudden silence that followed Asher's lecture that made the Colonel blink and shake himself back from whatever thoughts had been entertaining him. 'I'm sorry?'

' – ?'

'You were saying?'

'Nothing, Colonel. Just thinking out loud. Nothing that need concern you.'

'Oh.'

'Well, if you'll excuse me,' Mr Asher said, making to rise, 'I'd better be getting a move on.'

'Hmm? Yes. Oh yes, of course. No. Wait a moment, John. Sit down again please.'

Asher sank slowly back into his chair, trying to create the impression that he was at ease.

'John,' the Colonel began, speaking deliberately in a school-masterish voice (indeed, with his grey suit, greying hair and hands folded across his stomach he seemed to be assuming a likeness to suit the voice) 'we have known each other some time now. We are, I suppose, almost friends. I haven't all that much longer to go here, and what you do when I'm gone is entirely your affair. But – ' Maddox paused, unwittingly creating a tension, giving his words an edge of importance. 'But,' he repeated, 'as long as I *am* here I want your word that this brutality will stop. And when – heh – *if,*' the Colonel permitted himself a wry smile, 'you do track down this Deeley character and arrest him, I want to be informed immediately. Immediately, mind you. Not the next day. Or even an hour later. Immediately.'

Asher inclined his head by way of agreement. 'If that's what you want, Colonel.'

'That is what I want. That is what I demand, John.'

'Very well.'

'Good.'

'Is that all, sir?'

'Yes, that's all. I suppose you think I'm an interfering Brit, don't you?'

Asher gave a hint of a smile. 'It had crossed my mind.'

'I thought it might. We really are worlds apart, aren't we, the English and the Irish?'

Asher nodded. 'Worlds.'

'And never the twain, I suppose.'

'Never the twain.'

'Pity.'

Asher shrugged. 'It works both ways.'

'Or doesn't work at all. Ah, well, it's not for the likes of us to philosophize, is it?'

'No.'

'Right. Thank you, John. I won't delay you any longer.'

Asher stood up and placed his dead cigar in an ashtray. 'I'll let you know if anything breaks, Colonel.'

'Thank you. Mind how you go.'

'I will.'

'And remember what I said – I want to be told immediately.'

Asher paused by the door, turned, and gave the Colonel a long, hard stare. 'I'll remember. Colonel, you might think about what *I* said: it would make your life a lot easier all round.'

Maddox raised his head abruptly as though startled from a dream, his mind furiously sifting through the gaggle of words that he thought appropriate by way of reply, but by the time they had sorted themselves into some coherency Asher had gone, leaving the door ajar.

Maddox got up slowly from behind his desk and walked across the office, sucking his teeth. He closed the door firmly and leaned against it while Asher's parting shot ricocheted round his skull. It struck him that there had been some elusive subtlety in the words that still escaped him, some impeachment he could not quite put his finger on. Then, suddenly, at last, though the feeling had been nurtured within him for longer than he would ever care to admit, he was humiliatingly aware of what should have been obvious a long time ago, that he, for all his rank and military power, was there to be manipulated, to put a respectable face on things, to demonstrate to a world for the most part bored with the violence and disinterested in the outcome that something was being done. And being done it certainly was, but by others, sinister men who wheeled and dealed in the business of death while he looked on, like the sole spectator of some tatty tragedy, watching the intricate plot unfold.

Maddox sighed, crossed to the heavily screened window and stared out. Slightly to the right and below him, below and in the shadow of the high granite wall topped by strands of barbed wire, a group of uniformed R.U.C. men smoked and chatted casually, while beyond them, beyond the high granite wall topped with strands of barbed wire, civilians made their way through the day. It all seemed so peaceful. It struck him that it was extraordinary that out there, possibly strolling about with his hands in his pockets, nodding affably to his friends, was the man who had tried to kill him, and for an awful moment Maddox wished he had succeeded. How much easier that would have made things! How much 'cleaner', as Asher always put it. A little heroism, albeit somewhat backhanded, salvaged from a useless life. Maddox shook his head and smiled wryly to himself: at least the wretched Deeleys of the world were doing something positive, however unsuccessfully.

Maddox completed the circle of his office and sat down at his desk again. He leaned back in his chair with a small groan, and clasped his hands behind his head, intertwining his fingers. With his eyes closed he watched as his imagination projected images on to the back of his eyelids, images, he instantly realized, of the man who had been sent to kill him, offering for his selection a variety of bodies supporting faceless heads, heads which, although featureless, seemed to smile at him, smile at him sadly, compassionately and say, 'I am sorry for both our sakes that I missed you.' For some reason the Colonel began to dissect this straightforward repentance, wondering suddenly if it might not have another meaning beyond the obvious; and while he toyed with this possibility his mind's eye saw the faceless bodies take on the weightless quality of spirits, appearing to grow more free, yet at the same time more united, more dependent on each other the higher they ascended into a gleaming light. And, perhaps, he thought, there was something significant in all this. Had not his own life become 'featureless'? Was it not true to say that the more disillusion settled on his shoulders, the farther down he sank? 'Aaah,' the Colonel said aloud, and the loudness of his exclamation brought him back to earth; but not before he had time to wonder if Deeley, too, was harbouring thoughts of wastefulness and disillusion.

Martin Deeley was, in fact, having no such thoughts: he stood in Mr Apple's hallway, the phone pressed to his ear, concentrating on the burring noise it made, impatiently tapping one foot. He had spent the morning in the small room under the glory-hole listening to the activity above him as two workmen fixed the front door under the dour, pernickety supervision of Mr Cahill, who had volunteered to see the job was properly carried out while Mr Apple went to work. About eleven Martin emerged, swinging his arms in wide circles to rid himself of the claustrophobic sensations that had tormented him through the night. He glanced at the front door: just like new. He cocked his head on one side and listened intently: silence. Then he tiptoed across the hall and picked up the phone.

'Hello.'

'Is Fergal there?'

'Who wants him?'

'I do. Is he there?'

A clatter descended down the line as the receiver was dumped heavily on a table, and a voice shouted 'Fergal! It's for you.'

'Who is it?'

'Wouldn't say.'

Martin waited, his foot tapping impatiently once again.

'Yeah?'

'Fergal?'

'Yeah.'

'Martin. Martin Deeley.'

'Shit. How – '

'Can you talk?'

'Just a sec. Shut that door, will you? I can't hear myself think.

Right. Martin? I can talk.'

'First, thanks for warning me – '

'Forget it.'

'I won't. Now, what's happening? Have you heard anything?'

'Quite a bit. They found Corrigan this morning.'

'What d'you mean found him?'

'Dead. Kneecapped and shot in the head.'

'Jesus.'

'Yeah. Well, he's no great loss.'

'Who – '

'Who d'you think? Part of the package deal. He shits on you and that done he's no further use.'

'Christ. Anything new on me?'

'Nothing except they're all out to find you – and they're not fussed whether they bring you in alive or not.'

'That's nice.'

'Lovely. An R.U.C. heavy called Asher is in control.'

'I know.'

'And Reilly has put out the word that – '

'The bastard – '

'Yeah, well, that's the way it's been arranged. Where are you now?'

'I'm safe enough for the time being.'

'Well, stay there then. For Christ's sake, don't show your face anywhere. Every motherfucking sonofabitch is looking for you. You're quite a prize. Anything I can do?'

'Not for the moment, thanks. Fergal?'

'Yeah?'

'Can I count on you if – '

'You can count on me. I don't know what I'll be able to do, but you can count on me.'

'Thanks.'

'Okay. Give me a buzz tonight if you want and I'll try and have more info for you. Make it late, though. About twelve.'

'Right.'

'Hey, take care.'

'I will.'

Martin replaced the receiver and stood staring down at the phone. He thought briefly about Corrigan, feeling a tinge of sympathy for the great fat moron who had been chosen to do Reilly's dirty work and who, finally, had been another sacrificial lamb in the long litany of intrigue; and he wondered what Corrigan had looked like in death, if only because he had been told that fat people lost stones in the seconds before they died. Oddly, it was neither fear nor anger that was uppermost within him: Martin Deeley felt a hurt so deep it all but brought tears to his eyes. It was certainly bad enough that Asher and *his* bastards should be after him, but to have Seamus Reilly instigating a similar hunt, Seamus Reilly whom he had always regarded as a friend – as a father, almost – to have him issue orders that he, Martin, should be hunted out and killed was appalling.

Martin left the hall and wandered into the kitchen. He poured himself a glass of milk and swallowed it in one go. Still, he had Daphne and Fergal and Mr Apple on his side, so all was not lost. Between them they would work something out, and when they did the Ashers and Reillys had better watch out.

17

Mr Apple had tidied his desk in rather a hurry but had done his accounts carefully enough, and he was walking across the shop when Seamus Reilly appeared in the doorway flanked by two large young men Mr Apple had never seen before.

'Good evening, Mr Apple,' Reilly said, smiling. 'I am sorry to barge in on you like this just as you're setting off home,' he went on apologetically, 'but there's a thing or two I would like to talk over with you.'

Mr Apple decided to say nothing: he stood his ground and peered over his glasses.

'Can we?' Reilly asked, indicating with a wave of his arm his desire that they retreat behind the glass partition.

Mr Apple inclined his head and led the way.

'I would prefer to have no one overhear,' Reilly explained. 'We must have our confidences. Oh, they're good enough boys,' he confessed, glancing at his young bodyguards (both of whom looked strangely lost and awkward without anything close at hand to guard), 'but the less they know, the better. Isn't that how it should be?'

'I wouldn't know,' Mr Apple told him.

For an instant Reilly looked surprised, then he smiled. 'No, I don't suppose you would, Mr Apple,' he agreed. 'Ah, what a wonderfully untrammelled life you lead.'

Mr Apple stared at him.

'Now,' Reilly said, his voice changing as he got down to brass tacks, 'I understand you had visitors last night.'

Mr Apple nodded. 'You might call them that.'

'And?'

'And?'

'And what happened – precisely,' Reilly asked testily.

Mr Apple shrugged. 'Not a lot. They smashed in my front door, ransacked my house, terrified my cat. That's about it,' he said.

'Why?'

'Why what?'

'Why did they come to you in the first place?'

'Oh, they said they were looking for something – what, I cannot for the life of me imagine. They didn't find it, though. At least, I don't think they did. I wasn't told.'

Reilly stared hard at Mr Apple through half-closed eyes. 'And you have no idea what they were looking for?'

'None at all.'

'Did they ask you anything?'

Mr Apple frowned and thought for a moment. 'No, not that I can recall.'

'No questions about this shop?'

'No.'

'You're certain?'

'Quite certain.'

'I think they were looking for some*one* rather than some*thing*,' Mr Apple volunteered innocently.

'What makes you say that?'

'A feeling. The places they looked. Oh, they turned out drawers and overturned chairs but they didn't *look*: they only searched places big enough to hold a person.'

'You're very observant,' Reilly said. 'Any idea who they might have been looking for?'

'No idea at all. Have you?'

Reilly was taken aback by Mr Apple's question, possibly because it was the first time Mr Apple had ever asked him anything. He was on the point of shaking his head, of denying any knowledge of the affair, when suddenly he changed his mind. He smiled thinly at Mr Apple and said: 'As a matter of fact I do.'

'Oh.'

'Of course, there's very little happens in Belfast that I don't know.'

'Of course.'

'They were looking for your boardmarker, Martin Deeley,' Reilly announced, keeping his eyes fixed attentively on Mr Apple's face.

Mr Apple nearly overacted, but stopped himself just in time and played down nicely his imitation of surprise. 'My boardmarker? Martin? Martin Deeley? Good heavens. You do surprise me Mr Reilly. What on earth has Martin been up to?'

Reilly decided he had confided enough. '*That* I don't know. I think they just want to question him about some minor incident that happened the other night.'

'Oh,' Mr Apple sighed, feigning relief. 'I knew it couldn't be anything serious. A nice boy is Martin. Gentle and kind to a fault.'

'Indeed,' agreed Reilly. 'Very gentle and kind. You haven't seen him I suppose?'

'Not since yesterday. As I told you then, he came in but felt sick, so I sent him home again.'

'He's not at home,' Reilly said sharply, but recovered his composure rapidly enough to smile and add, 'If you do see him you might let me know. I think we should assist him if – '

'Indeed,' said Mr Apple.

'Good.'

For several moments they just stood there eyeing each other before Reilly said: 'Well, I'd better be on my way and let you get home. I expect you've a lot of tidying up to do.'

'Yes.'

'Right. Well, good-night, Mr Apple.'

'Good-night Mr Reilly.'

Mr Apple watched Reilly stroll from the shop, followed by his henchmen. When the door closed behind them he rubbed his hands together and did a strange little dance, a sort of jig interspersed with pirouettes, humming to himself and smiling broadly. One up for us, Mr Divine, he thought and Mr Divine seemed to agree; alas, the pessimistic Sefer wasn't at all sure. I'm not at all sure it is one up for us, Mr Apple, he announced solemnly. All you're doing is getting us deeper into trouble. You really are a very silly old man.

Silly or not, Mr Apple was still in an excellent frame of mind and still smiling broadly to himself as he entered his home by the kitchen door. He switched on the fluorescent light and automatically waited for it to settle down. Then he closed and locked the kitchen door behind him and walked into the hall, coughing as he walked.

'Oh, it *is* you,' Martin's voice said from the shadows before he stepped into view.

'Who were you expecting?' Mr Apple asked with what sounded like a chuckle. 'Your friend Mr Asher again?'

Martin smiled: 'I hope to Christ not. Have you seen him today?'

'No. But your other good friend, Mr Reilly, did drop in for a chat. He's very concerned about you – '

'I bet he is.'

' – and would like to know where you are. He wants to warn you there are nasty men looking for you.'

'He's a nice man,' Martin said sardonically. 'Seriously, what did he say?'

'What I told you.'

'Nothing else?'

'Nothing else.'

'Crafty.'

'Very. Have you eaten?'

'I had a glass of milk.'

'I'll fix us something then.'

'No. I'll do it. I want to do *something*. I'm going scatty just hanging about here.'

'Well, make sure the curtains are drawn. I'll go up and change. See what you can find in the fridge – there won't be much. We don't entertain a lot, Chloe and I,' Mr Apple said, making his way upstairs before adding: 'What time is Daphne coming?'

'I'm not sure. Sometime this evening. Whenever she can.'

'Oh.'

'Why?'

'No reason. Just wondering. Eh – do you two want to be alone?'

Martin laughed. 'Hell, no, Mr Apple. You may as well hear everything now.'

'I just thought – ' Mr Apple paused and gave an embarrassed little cough. 'I just thought you two young things might want – ' he let his voice trail off questioningly.

'Jesus, that's the last thing I'm thinking of,' Martin said, 'but thanks for asking.'

'Yes.'

'Maybe you'd like to have a go, Mr A. She's very obliging.'

'Don't be filthy,' Mr Apple snapped, but he smiled to himself all the same, amazed that Martin could carry on this absurd banter while trying to save his own skin.

'Just asking.'

When Mr Apple came down again to the kitchen, dressed in cavalry twill trousers, yellow shirt and neckerchief, Martin had prepared a reasonable meal of eggs and bacon, sausages and fried bread. He had set the kitchen table neatly and placed a single plastic flower in an empty tonic bottle in the centre.

'Very nice,' Mr Apple commented. 'You missed your vocation, Martin.' He took his place at the table and started to eat.

'All right?' Martin asked.

'Very good. Just how I like them – what the Americans call sunny side up.'

'Yeah – keep your sunny side up, up, keep your sunny side up,' Martin started singing. 'That's what we've got to do, Mr A. Keep our bloody sunny side up.'

'Quite.' Mr Apple eyed the young man concernedly, watching him shovel the food into his mouth in quick, nervous actions. 'Relax, Martin. We won't be disturbed tonight.'

'Jesus,' Martin swore and pushed his half-empty plate away from him. 'It's not tonight I'm worried about, Mr Apple. It's tonight and tomorrow night and every fucking night from now on.'

'We'll work something out.'

'Oh, sure.'

'I'm telling you. Finish your meal. Everything will work out for you. I'm telling you we'll work something out.'

'Oh, sure,' Martin repeated, but this time there was something not far adrift of hope in his voice. He pulled his plate towards him and started eating again. He was wiping up egg yolk with a slice of bread when he mentioned: 'I phoned Fergal – one of the men who came to warn me in the shop. He told me Corrigan had been shot.'

'Corrigan?'

'Larry Corrigan – the shit that was sent to drop me in it.'

'Oh. But I don't quite understand – who would shoot *him*?'

'R.U.C., probably. Asher.'

'But he *helped* them.'

'That's right.'

'So why should *they* shoot him?'

'To tidy things up. Tea?'

' – ? Oh, yes. Tidy things up?'

'That's right,' Martin said casually, getting up and pouring out two cups of tea, adding sugar only to his own. 'They probably promised him the usual crap of a new identity abroad and suckered him into feeling he could trust them. It happens all the time.'

'But why kill him, Martin?'

'That's the price Reilly would have demanded for sending him in. Save him the trouble. I mean he – Reilly – wouldn't want Corrigan out and getting pissed and saying he'd been ordered in to land me in the shit, would he? So Corrigan would have had to be killed. Better the R.U.C. do it and clean up the mess than have some half-arsed Brit officer stumble on – '

'Good God,' was all that Mr Apple could think of to say.

'Oh, you've a lot to learn, Mr A. I told you that you were getting into something you couldn't handle.'

This appeared to annoy Mr Apple. 'Of course I can handle it,' he snapped. 'The more I hear about Asher and Reilly the more determined I am that we'll outwit them. You and I. Dammit, they're maniacs.'

Martin threw back his head and laughed. 'They wouldn't like that, Mr Apple. They think they're very nice men.'

'Shhh,' whispered Mr Apple suddenly, and held up a warning hand. 'Quick. Into your room.'

Martin shot out of his chair and made for the glory-hole.

'Wait,' Mr Apple whispered urgently. 'Take these with you,' he ordered, passing Martin his plate and teacup. 'Now. Quick.'

'What's – ' Martin began, just as the front doorbell shrilled.

'Go,' said Mr Apple, pushing Martin in front of him into the glory-hole and closing the door.

'I'm coming,' Mr Apple announced, raising his voice. 'Who is it?'

A muffled cry came from outside.

'Who?' Mr Apple asked again, opening the door a fraction.

'Me,' the voice said enigmatically.

Mr Apple opened the door wider and was confronted by a vision in black: a long, black, cloak-like affair almost reaching the ground, a black floppy hat, a fedora really except that, of all things, it sported a black veil, black gloves and, as far as he could tell, black shoes. For one awful instant Mr Apple wondered if death had popped in to say hello, and was pleased when the gloomy figure spoke again in a high-pitched, nervous little voice. 'I'm Daphne,' was what it said.

'Oh,' said Mr Apple. 'Daphne. Come in, come in. We were expecting you, but not quite this early. I'm Arthur Apple.'

'Yes, I'm sorry I'm early, Mr Apple, but I thought it better to come now as people may want to see me later.'

' – ? Ah, yes,' Mr Apple agreed, and shut the front door. 'Martin,' he called. 'Your friend is here.'

Martin emerged from under the stairs looking almost sheepish about his appearance from such an unlikely place. The great Martin Deeley skulking under the goddam stairs!

'Hello, luvvey,' Daphne said shyly, casting a sidelong glance at Mr Apple, who immediately called upon his training and diplomatically looked the other way.

'Hi, Daphne. Thanks for coming.'

'How are you?'

'Fine. Just fine. Mr Apple's been looking after me and if Mr A. looks after you you're bound to be fine. Right, Mr A.?'

'Huh,' Mr Apple grunted. 'Let's go into the kitchen.'

Mr Apple sat at the head of the table, Martin on his right, Daphne on his left. 'Get the girl a cup of tea, Martin,' he said.

'No – no, thanks, Mr Apple. I really don't want any.'

'Sure?'

'Certain.'

Martin fidgeted under these politenesses and asked abruptly: 'What news?'

'Corrigan's dead. He – '

'I know that,' Martin told her. He was sick and tired of bloody Corrigan. 'Anything else?'

Daphne shook her head. She had taken off her hat and her long hair flapped about her shoulders. 'Nobody's saying anything, but I did hear there's a lot of money on offer for you.'

'Who's offering it?'

'That's the funny thing, luvvey,' Daphne told him. 'Some say from the R.U.C. Others say the army. Others think it might be – '

'Reilly?' Martin immediately wanted to know.

'That's what some say.'

'Maybe they're all right,' Mr Apple put in. 'Maybe you're more valuable than you ever suspected, Martin.'

'You could be right, Mr A. Could that be the case, Daphne? Could they all be chipping in?'

'It sounds like that.'

Martin sighed, letting his breath loose in a long gasp. 'Shit.'

'Why did you *do* it, Martin? Why – '

'Oh, for Christ's sake, shut up. It was my job. That's all.'

'But I told you – '

'Shut *up*,' Martin shouted.

'Shhh,' Mr Apple warned. 'Now for heaven's sake let's not fight among ourselves. Daphne is only concerned, Martin.'

'Concerned be damned. All I need is her nagging the shit out of me when Reilly's chasing me on one side and Asher on the other – '

'Asher?' Daphne suddenly asked. 'John Asher? R.U.C.? Small man, very smooth? Smokes black cigarettes?'

Martin looked first at Daphne then at Mr Apple, then back to Daphne again, his eyes narrowing. 'Sounds like him.'

'Well, isn't that lovely,' Daphne said, smiling brightly.

The two men stared at her.

'What's so effing lovely – '

'Quiet, Martin,' Mr Apple interrupted. 'Daphne?'

Daphne leaned forward and looked shyly at Mr Apple. 'Well,' she said, 'if it *is* the same John Asher, I know him very well,' she confessed. 'I see him every week. Regular. A sort of standing order. Same time every week. Friday evening at half-past nine.'

'You – ' Martin started, but stopped speaking when Mr Apple again raised his hand.

'Let me get this clear, Daphne. And don't be shy. I understand these things better than you imagine. Now, Mr Asher comes to you every week to make love, right?'

'That's right, Mr Apple.'

'And how long does he stay?'

Daphne shrugged. 'Not long. He just does it and goes. About half an hour.'

'And during that time he is quite alone with you?'

'Of course,' Daphne said, sounding shocked.

'No, what I meant was, dear, he has no escort, shall we call it, waiting outside?'

Daphne giggled. 'Oh, no. He wouldn't want anyone to know he comes to me. I'm not really grand enough for him to be seen with.'

'I see. And he comes to your room?'

'That's right.'

'Do you know how he comes to the house, Daphne? Does he walk? Come in a car?'

'That I don't know, Mr Apple, but I know he walks part of the way. I remember he said one night that he had slipped walking in the snow.'

'And it's every Friday?'

'Yes.' Daphne nodded to confirm her answer.

'Then he would be coming tomorrow?'

'I suppose so. I mean, if he sticks to his usual he'll be up tomorrow night.'

'Has he *ever* missed a week?' Mr Apple persisted.

'Oh yes, but not often. About four in the three years I've known him.'

'And tell me, on the nights he didn't come, did he let you know?'

'I don't understand.'

'Did he telephone and say he wouldn't be coming?'

Daphne gave a wistful little laugh. 'Oh, no. He just didn't turn up.' Then, as though she felt she had in some way degraded herself, she added 'But he apologized the following week, telling me he had been busy.'

'One more thing, Daphne. Does he know that you know he's in the R.U.C.?'

Daphne considered this for a moment, pouting her lips and frowning, before saying 'I don't think he *knows* I know. I mean, nearly all my – ' Daphne stopped and blushed. 'Nearly all the men who come and see me are in some sort of uniform, but they don't seem to care.'

Mr Apple reached out and patted Daphne's hand. 'Thank you, my dear,' he said quietly. 'Now, I know you want to see Martin alone, but I'm going to take him away for a minute. I'll send him right back to you though,' he added with a gentle, understanding smile, standing up. 'Martin?'

Martin got to his feet obediently. He had been listening with, if his face could be believed, something approaching awe and respect as Mr Apple put his questions to Daphne, seeing for the first time a Mr Apple he had never suspected, a Mr Apple who was gentle but self-assured, understanding but persistent, a Mr Apple far removed from the doddery creature Martin had once believed him to be. And through it all Martin had been constantly reminded of yet another interrogation he had overheard, but which had not been meant for his ears; or, on reflection, perhaps he had very definitely been meant to overhear:

He's very young, someone said.

Not that young, Seamus Reilly said.

Sixteen?

That's his age, but he's older than that.

I still think it's too important to be assigned to him.

Trust my judgement, Reilly said. He's good – and he's unknown.

And if he fouls it up?

He won't.

If he does? The gruff, doubting voice went on.

I'll see everything goes according to plan – one way or another.

I don't suppose we have much option.

We don't, Reilly said, immediately pushing home his slight advantage. Anyway, he's got to start somewhere if we're going to use him.

And you're certain you can trust him to keep quiet?

Reilly seemed to smile: I am not certain I can trust anyone, but I take precautions. I usually manage to cover myself.

Ha, yes. You do, don't you? All right. I'll leave it up to you. Anything goes wrong, you're answerable – understood?

Understood.

I still don't altogether like it. He – what's his name?

Deeley. Martin Deeley.

Deeley. He's got no background.

His father was shot – and his brother.

I *know* that, the voice said impatiently. That means nothing. That was just another Brit cock-up.

He – Deeley – doesn't think of it that way.

He wants revenge, I suppose.

No, Reilly said, but with something less than certainty in his voice. Avenge rather than revenge, he added.

You were always a one for niceties. I don't want any young kid using us for his personal vendettas.

Of course not.

And no bloody heroics. A clean job.

Of course.

The voice sighed. Jesus, rid me of romantics, it said fervently.

Romantics?

Hmm. Mark my words, Seamus, they're the curse of every

worthwhile cause. Every revolution, every war is started by bloody romantics and then we have to move in and clean things up somehow.

I see, Seamus said, though he didn't sound as though he did.

All right. Let Deeley do it, and we'll see how it goes.

'We won't be long, Daphne,' Mr Apple reassured the girl, and followed Martin out of the kitchen. 'The front room, Martin,' he whispered and padded along the hall. 'Leave the light off, of course.'

In the sitting-room they faced each other, Mr Apple manoeuvring himself so that the dull light coming from the street outside was behind him. 'What do you think, Martin?'

'Think – about what?'

'About what Daphne said.'

Martin shrugged. 'Not a lot.'

'Oh. I rather thought we might suddenly have found ourselves with a means of solving this unpleasantness, of negotiating our own little deal which would allow you to leave Belfast intact.'

'I don't follow, Mr A.'

'Just think about this for a minute. No, first – how far would Daphne go for you? I mean, would she really be prepared to help you in *any* way she could?'

'Yeah. I suppose so. You better ask her. I think she would, though.'

'All right, let's suppose she would. Now, what if someone was waiting for Mr Asher when he arrived to satisfy his lust?' Mr Apple asked, his tone suggesting a broad grin, though it was impossible to tell in the gloom. 'And what if instead of a romantic half-hour Mr Asher was removed from circulation, kept hidden away in the bowels of the earth, so to speak, and used to strengthen our negotiating position?'

'You mean kidnap the bastard?'

'Not to put too fine a point on it: yes.'

'Jeez, Mr Apple. I dunno. Shit, you'd be getting yourself into very deep water that way. Christ almighty, we wouldn't stand a chance.'

'Oh, dear,' Mr Apple sighed. 'I thought it was a beautiful plan.'

This choice of words struck Martin as unreasonably funny, and he could not control an outburst of laughter. 'You mean, you were really considering it?'

'Why not?'

'Why not? For one thing – '

'Desperate situations need desperate solutions – or something like that.'

'For one thing, where would we keep him?'

' – ? Here, of course.'

'Here?'

'In your little hidey-hole.'

'You *are* mad.'

'But why?'

'We can't just kidnap Asher and hope to do a deal. It's – '

'But you told me yourself that's how things are done. We simply have to play the game they understand – and beat them at it.'

'It's no game, Mr A.'

'I *know* that,' Mr Apple snapped.

'Christ – '

'All you have to do is see to it that Mr Asher is brought back here, and leave the rest to me.'

'Me – bring Asher back here? Oh, sure. That's just great. And how do *I* do that?'

'I thought your friend Fergal might help?'

Martin thought for a moment, and in that split second he realized that somehow he was going to be talked into this crazy ploy. 'He might.'

'I'm sure he would.'

'And then?'

'And then, like I said, leave the rest to me. I spent most of my life listening to diplomats lying to one another. I picked up a thing or two. And I think I know the best man to deal with.'

'Who?'

'An acquaintance of yours actually. Colonel Maddox.'

'Maddox?'

'That's right. I've met him once or twice. He's a reasonable man. He'll listen to me anyway.'

Martin walked slowly across the room and slumped into one of the armchairs by the fireplace. Maybe it *would* work. And what had he to lose? Stay here and he would be found eventually. Make a run for it – hah. Maybe the mad old bugger had hit upon the only way out. Maybe he –

'Well?' the mad old bugger was now saying impatiently.

Martin grunted. 'Okay. It's your neck as well as mine.'

For an instant Mr Apple froze as the flickering image of a faceless swinging body to-and-froed across his vision. Then he shook his head and pulled himself together, rubbing his hands. He gave another of his little cackles. 'I'm quite enjoying this, you know. Who would have thought – '

'Yeah, well, I wouldn't start enjoying yourself yet, Mr A. You could very well end up finding yourself dead.'

'Oh, dear. Ah, well. If that's the outcome, who am I to complain?'

' – ?'

'There are worse things, aren't there?' Without waiting for an answer to his enigmatic question Mr Apple became very businesslike again. 'Now, the first thing you do is tell Daphne more or less what we are going to do – if we can arrange it. Tell her nicely, Martin. We don't want the poor child terrified out of her wits. Just tell her enough so that she can rehearse her surprise when Mr Asher is plucked from her,' Mr Apple instructed, now definitely enjoying himself. 'Then, when Daphne's gone, you'll have to get in touch with your friend Fergal and see how he feels. Then we can make plans.'

'I still think it's crazy, Mr A.'

'That's right, Martin. But that's what's good about it. Off you go and chat to Daphne. I've got some thinking to do.'

Daphne rose from her chair and almost ran to him as he came back into the kitchen. She threw her arms about his neck and pressed her body against him. 'Oh, Martin, Martin,' she whispered. 'What are we going to do?' she sobbed, watching her hopes for the future splinter in her mind's eye.

'Shh,' Martin said, at a loss as to how best to console her. 'That's what I want to talk to you about. Mr Apple's come up with a plan. A crazy bloody plan – but it might work. I'll need your help, though.'

'Anything, luvvey. Anything. You just tell me what you want and I'll do it.'

'Okay. Let's sit down and – '

'No, Martin. Please. Tell me what you want like this. I feel better in your arms. Tell me what you want. I'm listening.'

Martin pulled an exasperated face, and twitched his nose as Daphne's long hair began to tickle. 'Well, you know you told us Asher should be coming to you tomorrow night?'

'That's right.'

'Mr Apple suggested we should have someone there when he comes. That we should kidnap him,' Martin concluded abruptly.

Daphne went rigid in his arms. 'Kidnap Asher?'

'Yeah. Great, isn't it?'

She ignored the question. 'And what am I to do?'

' – ? You? Oh, nothing. You just act all surprised and frightened, and when we've gone you can scream a bit if you like,' Martin told her, smiling to himself at the dramatic touch he had added.

For several minutes Daphne said nothing. She ran her fingers delicately up and down Martin's neck, making a strange little purring noise in her throat. 'All right,' she said finally, pushing herself back a few inches and staring into his eyes.

'Just like that. No questions?'

'I don't want to know anything, Martin. You told me what you wanted me to do and I said I'd do it. That's all there is.'

Martin shook his head slowly. 'You're some girl, Daphne.'

'Oh, yes, I'm some girl.'

'You know it might not work?'

'I know.'

'If we're caught you know they'll fix it so we're killed?'

'Yes.'

Suddenly Martin pulled the girl close to him and kissed her with unaccustomed passion. 'Hey, Daphne. Thanks,' he said finally.

Daphne smiled, her face strangely innocent, as if that one kiss had charmed all the hardness and pain from her mind. 'No thanks, Martin. When it's over – '

'When it's over we'll talk,' he told her gently.

'Yes. Well, I better go.'

'Yeah. And don't be afraid – '

'Afraid? Oh, Martin, I'm not afraid. I told you I'd do anything I could to help you.'

'I know, but – '

'No buts, luvvey. You're the only thing I have in my life. If I lose you, then I've nothing. So why should I be afraid?'

'Okay. I'll see you out.'

Martin closed the front door behind Daphne, wondering at her unsettling confession of love. He was, in his own way, still trying to analyse this when Mr Apple peered out from the sitting-room and demanded, 'Well?'

'Oh. Yes. Yes, Daphne will do what I asked. She'll – '

'Excellent,' Mr Apple said. 'Now, Fergal – what about Fergal?'

'It's too early to ring him.'

'Oh. I think you should try anyway. We don't have all that much time.'

'You're the boss, Mr A. I'll try him. Hey – how come you've taken over, anyway?' Martin suddenly asked.

'I have rather, haven't I?' Mr Apple said gleefully. 'Still, I'm going to make a good job of it.'

'I certainly hope so.'

'I will. Ring Fergal.'

Martin went to the table in the hall and rang Fergal.

'Fergal?'

'Yeah. Martin? You just caught me. I was on the way out,' Fergal told him breathlessly.

'I need a few things.'

'Like what?'

'A car, for one.'

'When?'

'Tomorrow evening. About seven.'

'No problem.'

'And a gun.'

'Rifle, hand or submachine?'

'Hand.'

'Same time?'

'Yes.'

'Done.'

'A woollen helmet.'

'Hah. Easy. Anything else?'

'Yeah. A driver.'

'I'll do that.'

'You sure you want to get involved?'

'Will it help you?'

'It's about my only chance.'

'Then I want to get involved.'

'It's a – '

'I don't want to know, Martin. You need me – I'll be there. Shit, what are friends for?'

'Thanks. I was beginning to wonder.'

'Where you want me to pick you up?'

'Ah. Let me think. Best thing is if you drive past the bottom of Lepper Street at exactly seven. I'll be there.'

'Seven I'll be there. You sure that's safe?'

'It'll have to be.'

'Right.'

'And Fergal – '

'Yeah?'

'Don't carry a gun yourself. If we don't pull it off I don't want you to be – '

'You just worry about yourself, boyo.'

'Okay. And thanks.'

'No thanks. I owed you.'

'Sure.'

'See you at seven,' Fergal said, and hung up.

'That's it then,' Martin told Mr Apple. 'All arranged as per your instructions.'

'You see? I told you things would work out. He must be a very good friend, this Fergal?'

'He must be,' Martin agreed.

'I wonder what you've done to deserve such friendship...' murmured Mr Apple, without really expecting an answer.

Which was just as well, for Martin had no intention of trying to explain the obscure loyalty which had formed the bond between himself and the ever-breathless Fergal. Indeed, now that he thought about it, he could hardly explain it to himself, since the incident that had sealed their friendship was nebulous to say the least, and had, apparently, meant considerably more to Fergal than to Martin...

The never-ending abuse rolled off the backs of the Paras as their heavy boots thumped down the mean little street in the Old Park district, the same boots that would shortly splinter and burst open front doors as the military searched for arms and ammunition, the whole operation mounted as the result of a telephone tip-off – possibly placed by one of their own soldiers out for revenge.

Fucking English cocksuckers!

Youse fucking Para cunts!

Six years ago it had happened, but it could have been yesterday or six years hence, so little had the pattern changed. Inevitably a small crowd of men (braver or more foolish than others) gathered at the entrance to the street, among them Martin Deeley and a young weasel-faced, acne-ridden boy of about twelve. At first they just glared at the soldiers, content to curse them and their mothers. They kept their hands in their pockets, some of them jumping up and down to emphasize their expletives, and seemed harmless enough. But the slow, steady progress of the Paras towards them roused their simmering fury and, as if by magic, petrol bombs appeared – already ignited, it seemed – and were hurled. The Paras, instead of retreating, charged, shifting position constantly, their eyes scanning not only the dozen or so bombers but rooftops and windows. Outnumbered (and perhaps not so foolish after all), the crowd took to its heels. Martin found himself running alongside the boy with the weasel face who was already gasping asthmatically. Come *on*, Martin called to him.

I can't go any faster, the boy wheezed.

Shit. Here. Martin reached out and in one gesture scooped the boy off his feet and threw him over his own shoulder, carrying him through the complex of back alleys that separated the rows of shabby two-up, two-down houses, through the stench of outside toilets, to safety.

Now piss off out of here, he told the boy.

Hey, thanks, mister. Youse saved my life.

Shit, Martin told him.

I won't forget you, mister.

And that was all there was to it.

'I helped him out once,' Martin told Mr Apple. 'Did him a favour.'

'Oh.'

'So what do we do now?'

'Now? Now,' Mr Apple said, 'we go and get a good night's sleep. I have to work tomorrow, don't forget. And you have a thing or two on your plate as well.'

And, strangely enough, Mr Apple slept unusually well that night. He woke only once – not lurching as though from a nightmare, but lazily and with a feeling of well-being. He switched on the light and glanced at his bedside clock: four minutes to three. He was about to put the light out again when something told him to look at his sheets; a peculiar instruction, he had to admit. But he did it nonetheless, and was surprised, but in no way alarmed, to see a pattern on the bottom sheet, a skeletal pattern traced in tiny drops of blood. He reached an arm around his back and felt his old scars, stared at his hand and rubbed his thumb and forefinger together. 'Ah,' he said to himself with satisfaction, as he noted the traces of blood on his fingertips. 'Ah.' Then he lay down again, reached up a long bony arm to switch out the light, pulled the blankets over his head and drifted off into a bright, untroubled sleep.

18

'In there,' Martin said. 'That's as good a spot as we're likely to find.'

'Right.' Fergal pulled over and reversed the inconspicuous Morris into the parking space. 'Which is the house?'

Martin pointed. 'That one. With the light over the door.'

'Oh. What do we do now?'

'Wait.'

'I hate waiting,' Fergal said. 'Always have done.'

'Yeah,' Martin said vaguely. 'You'll remember what I told you?'

'Sure, Martin.'

'As soon as I come out that door with Asher, get this heap moving.'

'I will. I suppose Asher will turn up?'

'He fucking better,' Martin said, and laughed shortly. 'Shit, I've got myself all geared up for this.'

'So've I.'

They slid down in the seats and fixed their eyes on the door with the light over it.

'And don't say anything once Asher is in the car,' Martin warned.

'I won't.'

'I don't want him remembering your voice when all this is over.'

'I won't say a word,' Fergal promised.

'Good.'

A taxi passed them and pulled up a few yards past the house they were watching. Fergal raised his head. 'Is that him?'

Martin said nothing. He stared at the taxi, waiting for the passenger to get out. 'Naw,' he said finally, as a tall figure emerged from the taxi and made for another house, heaving a suitcase from one hand to the other every few paces. 'But that fucking is,' Martin announced suddenly. 'That there is our man.'

'That's Asher?' Fergal asked, surprised that the huge reputation of their victim should be so let down by his insignificant stature. 'Jesus, he's smaller than I am.'

'What did you expect? A bloody giant?'

'No. But I thought he'd be bigger, that's all. I mean, you wouldn't think a little fart like that could be so important, would you?'

They watched John Asher stroll up the street like a man without a care in the world. He went up the steps to the house two at a time, pushed open the door, and went inside.

Martin looked at his watch, holding his wrist sideways so that the streetlamp lit the dial. 'Right,' he said, his voice suddenly hoarse. 'Ten minutes and I go in. He should have his knickers off by then.'

Fergal giggled. 'He'll shit himself,' he said happily.

'That's what I want,' Martin said with a wicked grin. 'I hope to Christ she remembers to leave her door on the latch,' he added, suddenly serious.

'She knows she's supposed to?'

'Of course she knows she's supposed to.'

'Sorry.'

'Shit, I'm dying for a fag.'

'Better not,' Fergal said sympathetically. 'Anyway, you'll enjoy one all the more later.'

'I hope so.'

'Don't worry. It'll all go like clockwork.'

'I hope you're right.'

'Sure I am.'

The ten minutes seemed like an hour in passing, but finally it was time for him to go. 'Don't forget: as soon as we come through that door, get this car moving,' Martin said, and got out of the car.

'Don't worry about that, Martin. I'll do my end.'

'Okay. Well, here goes.'

'Mind yourself.'

Martin crossed the road like a shadow and entered the house, his right hand already holding the gun in his inside pocket. Inside he stood rigid, listening, his eyes constantly moving. When he crossed the hall he seemed to glide rather than walk, his black plimsolls silent as a breath on the worn linoleum. And it was as though he walked on air as he raced up the stairs, his toes barely touching the metal strips on the front of each step. He hugged the wall as he crept down the corridor, stopping every few paces to listen. Suddenly, in a room some way behind him, a radio came alive, making him jump and freeze in an oddly contorted posture which he held for several seconds as he listened to the measured tones fill the wavelength with tales of an air disaster, almost gloating as it told of debris littering a hillside, of bodies scattered in the darkness. It was all too much, it seemed, for the owner of the radio, and the dial was turned back and forth, finally settling for some music that could have been Django Reinhardt or Eddie Lang, but was probably neither.

Martin relaxed and took several deep breaths: four more strides and he was outside Daphne's door. The immediate temptation was to burst in and confront Asher, but Martin resisted this, determined to follow the scenario he had worked out so meticulously in his mind the night before. He gripped the doorhandle and eased it round, using his knee to push the door inwards a fraction. He smiled (although nothing of this showed on his face) as he heard a muffled grunting, and then he was in the room with the door shut behind him, all without a sound. In the dull red glow of the little electric crucifix he could make out Mr Asher runting merrily on the bed, his face buried in Daphne's neck, his naked, round, white bottom bouncing up and down like a distorted balloon. He had not, it seemed, yet reached his climax, and Martin took his time crossing to the bed, gun in hand, his head cocked, listening for the first gasp that would indicate John Asher was about to come: and when he heard it a wide grin spread across his face and he pushed the barrel of the gun into the nape of Mr Asher's neck. 'Well, well, well, and what do we have here?' he said. 'No. Oh, no, *Mister* Asher don't get up. Just stay right where you are. You can even finish off if you want.'

'Oh, dear God,' Daphne started, raising her head slightly and smiling up at Martin. 'Oh, don't shoot us, mister. I haven't done anything. Oh, mister, don't – '

'Shut up, you slag,' Martin told her through his teeth, giving her a wink and sardonically applauding her performance with a thumbs-up sign. 'Shut up, or I *will* blow your stupid head off.'

Daphne shut up.

'Had enough, Mr Asher?' Martin asked.

'What do you want?' Asher asked, attempting to raise his head but finding it pushed down by the gun.

'Not a lot,' Martin told him. 'You, in fact. That's all I want. We're about to take a little trip, you and I.'

'Who the hell are you?'

'Me? Oh, I'm sorry. I thought you knew that. I'm Martin Deeley.'

Asher felt his whole body wince. 'You're mad, Deeley. Coming here. Everybody in the country is looking for you.'

'I still have you where I want you, though, don't I, Mr Asher? And if they find me now – well, that's just tough on you. You won't even have time to get your prick out let alone use it again.'

'What do you want?' Asher asked again, slowly reaching the stage when his embarrassing nakedness was troubling him more than his deadly predicament.

'I told you. We're going to have a little chat.'

'About what?'

'Oh, this and that. About you. About me. About Corrigan. About the prospects of life. About the dangers of death. You know, general things that affect us all. And you can get up now. Nice and slowly, though. I wouldn't want you to injure your little cock,' Martin told him, giving his white bottom a hearty slap with his free hand.

Asher eased himself out of Daphne and knelt over her for a second before gingerly placing one foot on the floor, organizing his balance, all the while feeling the coldness of the gun at his neck.

'Right,' Martin told him. 'You can get dressed. I thought about making you come with me naked,' he went on, moving back a few paces but keeping the gun aimed at Asher's head, 'but you're so fucking ugly I think you better dress.'

'You haven't a hope in hell of getting away with this, Deeley,' Mr Asher said, ignoring his underclothes and pulling on his trousers. 'You're as good as dead,' he added, buttoning his shirt.

'I die, you die,' Martin said reasonably. 'And I don't really care what happens to me.'

'Another bloody martyr,' Mr Asher said, feeling he could afford a sneer now that he was dressed.

'That's right. Me and St Stephen,' Martin said, without really knowing why he had chosen the saint who set the ball rolling. 'Put this on now,' he ordered, tossing a woollen helmet across the room. 'And pull it down over your ugly face.'

Asher caught the helmet and pulled it on, giving one quick glance about him before covering his face.

Martin stepped quickly behind him. 'Now move,' he said, giving him a nudge in the back.

'I can't see,' Asher said, his voice its old petulant self.

'You don't have to,' Martin said, pushing him towards the door, turning briefly to mouth 'I'll phone you tomorrow' to Daphne and make a dialling gesture with his hand. 'And you stay there and keep your mouth shut,' he ordered her roughly, blowing her a kiss.

'Oh, I will, mister. You'll never hear a word from me.'

'I better fucking not.'

Fergal had the car by the pavement and the back door open as they reached the last step, and Martin bundled Asher in and climbed in himself. 'Go,' he said.

Fergal suddenly turned and gaped at him 'Where?' he mouthed, remembering not to speak.

Martin pointed furiously straight ahead. 'On the floor, you,' he said as the car sped away. He leaned forward, cautioning Fergal to slow down by waving the palm of his hand downwards, putting his mouth close to Fergal's ear. 'Make for St Enoch's,' he whispered. 'I'll tell you after that.'

Fergal nodded.

'And for Christ's sake take it easy. All we need is to be pulled in for speeding.'

Fergal glanced in the rear-view mirror and grinned.

For a kidnapping, the journey to Mr Apple's house was ridiculously mundane. Asher remained on the floor, grunting occasionally;

Martin gave directions in a cool, calm whisper; and Fergal drove confidently at a sedate pace, once pulling to the side of the road like a good citizen to allow three armoured cars to pass.

'That's it, there,' Martin whispered finally. 'Just pull in and nip up and knock on the door. Then get back here sharpish.'

Fergal nodded.

Mr Apple must have been waiting within feet of the door, since he opened it almost before Fergal had stopped knocking. He had dressed himself for the occasion: smart suit, white shirt, deep-red tie that contrasted nicely with the grey flannel. He had, however, forgotten his shoes, and he wriggled his toes as he waited for Martin to bring Asher in. 'Welcome, welcome,' he said gaily as the helmeted Asher was pushed past him. 'Your room is all ready. This way,' he added, closing the front door and leading the way down the stairs off the glory-hole. He had been busy: the walls were stripped of their strange pictures and prints and were now quite bare save for the crucifix, which he saw fit to leave. The table and chair had been removed also, leaving only the iron cot. 'You'll be very comfortable here,' he told Asher politely. 'Do take that helmet off him, Martin. We really don't want the good man to suffocate.'

Martin whipped off the woollen helmet and stood back to watch Asher blink, focus his eyes in the light, smooth down his tousled hair and round on Mr Apple. 'I *knew* you were behind this,' he exploded.

'Did you?' Mr Apple asked. 'That was clever of you.'

'You're a fool to have got mixed up with that scum,' Asher went on, licking the saliva from the corners of his mouth. 'You're as dead as he is.'

'Oh, dear,' said Mr Apple, who seemed to be enjoying himself no end. 'I don't think he cares much for you, Martin.'

Martin sniggered. 'That breaks my heart.'

'You'll have more than your heart broken,' Asher told him. 'And as for you – you degenerate,' he spat at the inoffensive Mr Apple, 'as for you, I'll see you wiped off the face of the earth.'

'Oh, dear,' Mr Apple said again, shaking his head. 'I'm afraid you've been beaten to it. I haven't been of this earth for a long time now, you know,' he confided mysteriously.

Martin pushed Asher in the chest, sending him reeling back on to the cot. 'You just sit down and keep your mouth shut,' he ordered. 'We've had enough old shit out of you. Cummon, Mr Apple, let's get upstairs – he stinks this place.'

Together they left the room, Mr Apple giving Asher a little wave before he closed and bolted the door. 'No problems?' he asked Martin, when they finally reached the kitchen.

'None.'

'I knew there wouldn't be.'

Martin stared at Mr Apple for a moment, frowning: Mr Apple stared back, smiling.

'Look, Mr A. I'm worried. You're taking this so – well, you're treating it a bit like a joke.'

Mr Apple drew himself up, appalled at the monstrous accusation. 'I most certainly am not,' he said. 'I am treating it most seriously.'

'But you don't seem to give a damn what happens to you –'

'What's that got to do with it? As a matter of fact, I don't. My fate was decided a long time ago, Martin. The only thing that does matter is that we negotiate a deal that gets you out of trouble.'

'You see? There you go again. Talking bloody rubbish about your fate. We've got to get you out of this too.'

'Oh, Martin, Martin, will you just leave everything to me? I know what I'm doing.'

'I wish to hell I did – know what you are doing, I mean.'

'Well, I'll tell you. I'm seeing Colonel Maddox tonight, to start with.'

'You're what?'

'Seeing your friend Colonel Maddox tonight. At midnight, actually. I thought that would be a good time.'

'How the hell did you arrange that?'

' – ? Why, by telephone of course.'

'You just rang him up and said, "Hey there Colonel Maddox, how about a chat at midnight to make a deal?"'

'Not exactly. I rang him up, yes. Then I told him I had something very important to tell him, and asked him nicely if he would meet me at midnight.'

'And he said yes?'

'And he said yes.'

Martin shook his head in disbelief. 'And why should he agree to meet you?'

'Ah, well. You see, I'm supposed to be spying on you and Mr Reilly. I'm supposed to have been doing it since I came to the shop.'

'And have you?'

'Funnily enough, no. Mr Asher was always there and somehow I never took to him. So I pleaded ignorance on all counts. But the Colonel quite likes me, you know. We understand each other.'

'I bet you bloody do.'

'I'll ignore that, Martin. Actually, Colonel Maddox is a very civilized man. I was very annoyed with you when I learned it was you who tried to kill him.'

'He's a fucking Bri – '

'He's a good man, Martin. I don't care where he comes from or what absurd opinion you have formed of him. He's a good man. An honest man – and there's precious few of those left '

Mr Apple filled a glass with water from the tap in the sink and drank deeply. 'Anyway, he's the only hope *you* have of getting out of this mess.'

'Some hope.'

'Water?' Mr Apple asked.

Martin shook his head.

'Would you like to come with me?'

' – ?'

'I just thought you might like to see the man you tried to murder.'

Martin felt himself growing pale. Perhaps it was this, or perhaps it was the mild challenge in Mr Apple's remark that made him reply, 'Yeah. I'll come. I want to hear what you two get up to, anyway.'

Mr Apple smiled. 'Good. It should be an interesting evening.'

'What about him?' Martin wanted to know, jerking his head in a direction that could have indicated anywhere.

'Oh, yes. You know, I'd forgotten about poor Mr Asher.'

'Well, you better remember him, Mr A. He's a bloody liability now.'

'Hmm,' sighed Mr Apple. 'I suppose we'll have to tie him up,' he said regretfully.

'And gag the bastard.'

'Maybe you're right. I dislike mistreating people, but I suppose in this case – '

'Too damn right. And we better get a shift on if you want to meet Maddox by twelve.'

Together they tied the protesting Mr Asher's hands behind his back and secured the nylon clothesline to the head of the cot. They then tied his feet, looping the rope securely round and round one of the cot's legs. While Mr Apple muttered his apologies for such ungracious treatment, Martin swore under his breath and tied a teacloth around Mr Asher's head, forcing it between his teeth. 'That should shut you up,' he said.

'You're still sure you want to come with me?' Mr Apple asked Martin as they climbed the stairs.

'Yeah, I'll come.'

'I mean, do you think you can face the Colonel?'

'Of course I can face him – if we ever get there. The way you're quizzing me, Mr A., he'll be fed up waiting.'

Mr Apple struggled into his coat and donned his hat at a jaunty angle. 'Are you warm enough? I can let you have a pullover.'

'I'm fine. I'm a hot-blooded creature, you know.'

Mr Apple gave a small chuckle. 'I see.'

Outside, the wind had risen and the forecast of rain seemed to be coming true. Already it was spitting as they hurried along, Mr Apple clinging to Martin's arm, muttering to himself from time to time. As they turned the corner into the street where the safe house was located Mr Apple came to a halt and turned to face Martin. 'Now, I want you to let *me* do the talking, Martin,' he said. 'None of your smart-alec nonsense.'

'I won't say a word,' Martin promised.

'Huh.'

'Honest.'

'Good. I have it all worked out, you see. Up here,' Mr Apple explained pointing to his head. 'And if you start interrupting I'll only lose track.'

'I told you, I won't say a word.'

'Right. Let's get to it,' Mr Apple said, and bustled down the street, leaving Martin standing. 'Come along,' he called over his shoulder.

By the time Martin had caught up, Mr Apple had come to a halt again, and was standing outside a lightless house, his hand already raised to the knocker. 'Not a word,' he whispered.

'Not one,' Martin whispered back, smiling helplessly.

'Right.'

Mr Apple knocked three times, an action that seemed to amuse Martin, who gave a barely stifled laugh.

'What's so funny?' Mr Apple demanded.

'Knock three times and ask for Joe,' Martin said.

'Rubbish,' Mr Apple said, but he smiled nonetheless.

He was still smiling when Colonel Maddox opened the door and reciprocated with a smile of his own.

'I'm sorry to be late,' Mr Apple began.

'Oh, no,' the Colonel said waving the apology aside and ushering them in with a single, sweeping gesture. 'In fact, I'm afraid we may have to wait a while. Mr Asher hasn't arrived yet. I've been trying to contact him since I got your call. I had to leave a message for him in the end. And this is?'

'Oh. A friend of mine. Nameless for the moment, Colonel.'

'Ah. I understand,' Maddox said, and held out his hand politely.

For a moment Martin hesitated, but wilted under Mr Apple's baleful gaze. He took the Colonel's hand and shook it. 'Colonel,' he said.

'Getting up like rain again,' the Colonel said, ushering them into the small, dank, dust-laden front room.

'Yes,' Mr Apple agreed. 'Inclement, isn't that the word?'

'I believe it is, Mr Apple. I believe it is. Do sit down. Both of you.

Do sit down.'

Mr Apple settled himself in the armchair he had always used, while Martin retreated across the room and sat on the arm of the sofa, taking with him an ashtray he spotted on a small table. Mr Apple's eyes followed him intently. 'I'm sure the Colonel won't mind if you smoke.'

'Hmm? Oh, no. Not at all. Please do. You have an ashtray. Good. I do hope Mr Asher comes soon. I dislike keeping you waiting like this.'

Mr Apple rotated his hat on his knee and cleared his throat. 'Colonel,' he said, 'I'm afraid Mr Asher won't be joining us.'

'Won't be – what – how do you know that?'

'Well, we have detained him.'

'You've detained Mr Asher? I'm sorry, I – '

'Yes, Colonel,' Mr Apple said. 'We've detained Mr Asher. I think if I tell you that that young man over there is Martin Deeley you'll begin to understand.'

'Martin Deeley?' The Colonel frowned, confused, repeating the name once more before its significance dawned on him. 'Martin Deeley – the man who tried – '

'To kill you, Colonel,' Mr Apple explained.

'Good God,' was all Colonel Maddox could summon up. He attempted to conceal his loss for words by looking about him for a chair. He spotted one by the door and moved to it, sitting down heavily.

Mr Apple cleared his throat again. 'We have a problem, Colonel,' he said.

If Colonel Maddox heard he gave no sign of it. He stared at Martin as though transfixed, as though he was mesmerized by the cool green eyes that stared arrogantly back at him.

'Colonel?' Mr Apple tried to break the spell.

'Hmm? Sorry. You – '

'I was explaining that we have a problem. But we have a solution to that problem – if you'll agree to it.'

Maddox turned his head. For a while, he said nothing. There was, in truth, nothing he could think of to say. He was aware that matters were getting out of hand, that they had been taken from his control, that what he had expected to be a simple passing of information was rapidly developing into something far too complex for him. And it was probably this frustration that made him ask in a strained, tired voice, a voice that accepted defeat, 'What am I to agree to?'

'I had better explain the problem first, I think,' Mr Apple said. 'As you know, Mr Asher is anxious to arrest Martin – as, indeed, I am sure you are. Well, Martin is just as anxious that such an arrest should not take place. He wants, quite simply, safe passage, I believe the term is, out of Ireland.'

'But – '

'Let me finish, Colonel. In order to ensure that such a passage might be obtainable we have kidnapped Mr Asher, and – '

'You've kidnapped Mr Asher,' the Colonel repeated dully, accepting it simply as a statement of fact, devoid of drama or intrigue.

'We've kidnapped Mr Asher,' Mr Apple repeated, 'and we are willing to trade his safety for Martin's. I think that would be a fair swap, don't you?'

'But why come to me? *I* can't arrange any such – '

'Oh, come now, Colonel,' Mr Apple said. 'You belittle your powers. I am quite sure you could arrange things most satisfactorily.'

'I can't do deals,' the Colonel said firmly.

'You can, you know. Everything is done by making deals – some of which are not carried out. One Larry Corrigan, for example.'

Maddox winced. 'I had nothing whatever to do with that.'

'You knew about it.'

'Yes,' the Colonel confessed. 'But I had nothing to do with it.'

'You could have prevented Corrigan's execution.'

'I don't think – '

'And all I'm asking you to do is prevent another: Mr Asher's,' Mr Apple pointed out frankly. '*I* certainly don't want Mr Asher killed. Neither does Martin. But I'm afraid he will have to be if you and I cannot come to some arrangement.'

Something seemed to strike the Colonel as odd: he perked up

suddenly and frowned. 'What about you, Mr Apple. What deal do I have to agree to for you?'

'Me? Why?'

'Do you want free passage?'

'Good heavens, no, Colonel,' Mr Apple chortled happily at the idea. 'I want nothing for myself. I'll be perfectly all right.'

Maddox found himself forced to smile at Mr Apple's bright and shining optimism.

'Anyway,' Mr Apple went on, 'I am my own concern. What you have to consider is Mr Asher's safe return and Martin's healthy exit.'

Maddox fumbled in his jacket pockets for a cigarette before remembering he had forgotten to buy any, and he was taken aback when Martin offered him one. He was on the point of refusing, but some strange, old-fashioned sense of politeness made him change his mind. He reached out and accepted the cigarette, accepted, too, the light which followed it. He inhaled deeply and allowed the smoke to leave his lungs in company with, 'It would have been so much easier if you hadn't missed.'

'It sure would,' Martin agreed, a touch of sadness in his voice, though sadness for what only he could tell.

'Supposing,' the Colonel said, turning his attention to Mr Apple once again, 'supposing I *could* arrange an exchange,' he said. 'How would it be carried out?'

'Quite simply. I have one or two details still to work out, but basically you would see to it that Martin was escorted to the airport and put aboard a plane to a destination of our choosing. Martin would telephone me when he arrived safely. Within twenty-four hours I would see to it that Mr Asher was returned to the fold.'

'I could, of course, have *you* arrested.'

Mr Apple spread his hands. 'You could. But then, alas, Mr Asher would die. Of starvation, if exposure didn't finish him off first. Poor chap, he's probably feeling wet through already,' Mr Apple lied.

'And how long do I have to agree to all this?'

Mr Apple spread his hands again. 'As long as you like, Colonel. Or rather, as long as you think Mr Asher can survive this – eh –

inclement weather.'

'I need time to think.'

'Of course you do.'

The Colonel rose suddenly to his feet. 'I'll contact you tomorrow,' he said. Then, smiling sheepishly, he asked 'Where do I do that?'

'All day I'll be at my little betting-shop. In the evening I'll be at home. Both numbers are in the book.'

'I'll phone you tomorrow.'

'Thank you,' Mr Apple said politely, and got up from his chair: 'Colonel, I want you to believe me that I regret having been forced to make you the intermediary. I do respect you.'

Maddox nodded.

'Come along, Martin,' Mr Apple said. 'We'll see ourselves out, Colonel.'

' – ? Oh. Yes. Right.'

'I'll hear from you tomorrow?'

'Yes.'

'Good-night, then, Colonel.'

'Good-night.'

'You were bloody marvellous, Mr Apple,' Martin said as they made their way home through the dark, silent streets. 'Bloody marvellous, you were.'

'I'm not so sure, Martin,' Mr Apple replied, his voice troubled. 'There's something not quite right. I have a feeling I underestimated the Colonel's conscience.'

'Conscience?'

'Hmm,' Mr Apple said. 'Some people do still have them. And the Colonel certainly does. And a sense of duty. Queen and country before anything else. Oh, we're not out of the woods yet.'

'He'll arrange it.'

'I wonder if he will. He might, but it will be difficult for him to convince himself he should.'

'He's got no choice.'

'Oh, but he does, Martin. That's the trouble. He *has* a choice. It's a question of balance. Mr Asher's life against his duty as a soldier.

He might very well choose duty.'

'So we've been wasting out bloody time?'

Mr Apple shook his head. 'I didn't say that. I said he had a choice – and he might choose in our favour.'

'And if he doesn't?'

'If he doesn't – well, we'll have to think again. Anyway, look on the bright side – you'll be no worse off than you are now.'

'Like shit I won't! Fucking kidnap round my neck.'

'You know, I don't think that will ever be mentioned. Mr Asher likes to be thought of as a proper man. I don't somehow think he would take kindly to it being broadcast that he was caught – eh – with his pants down!'

Even Martin was forced to laugh at that. 'Christ, it *was* bloody funny, you know, Mr Apple.'

'That's what I meant. Anyway, let's wait and see what tomorrow brings. Tomorrow is, as they say, another day.'

'Yeah, another bloody day.'

'Meanwhile, what we need is a nightcap, and then bed. We'll let the unfortunate Colonel do the worrying tonight.'

'Huh. I wonder what he's thinking now.'

The Colonel was, in fact, thinking about the unholy mess that had suddenly engulfed him. He had switched out the light (trying to conceal, perhaps, even from himself, the aching loneliness, the brooding, cold horror he felt at the intrigue he was now being sucked into), and the darkness murmured and was palpable. It struck him that for the first time he had been made aware of the brutal reality of the terrorism he had been sent to wipe out, a reality drained of compassion and fuelled by hatred and generations of fomented revenge. And now he was part of it: the aloofness of his position wiped away by a few words from a strange old man. Colonel Maddox was not a man given to anger, but he felt a virulent, consuming anger now. It was as though some reckless, murderous power was drawing him on, taunting him, forcing him (while he tried to remain passionless, aware of the all-too-possible consequences) through a bombardment of solutions, only one of which he was to be allowed to accept. Slowly it became clear to him that the only course he could follow was the very one that would necessitate his being as devious as John Asher, as cruel and calculating as John Asher, as conscienceless as John Asher.

Maddox dragged himself to his feet and away from the uncharacteristic thoughts that had so appalled him. He stretched, feeling the twinges of rheumatism in his shoulder, switched on the light and glanced about the room with a look almost of affection: the sort of bewildered, loving–hating look bestowed by celluloid war-heroes on, say, an empty and abandoned hangar that brought back memories of scrambles, and dead friends, and wartime love-affairs. His eye fell on the ashtray Martin had used, and he gave a small sigh. Yes, he thought, perhaps it would have been better if he, instead of his driver, had been killed. A heroic death of sorts. Nancy would have appreciated that, would have made a great show at his funeral, would have adored the military honours, the pomp, would probably have enjoyed even the grief. Oh, military funerals are the most exciting things in the world, she had once proclaimed, as usual displaying a curious choice of words. That trumpet, she exclaimed, when it wails! My God, it makes my flesh creep! Maddox smiled wistfully, and astonished himself for an instant by regretting he had let her down. 'The sick hearts that honour could not move,' he quoted aloud sadly. Then he said the words again, vexed that he could not recall what came next. 'And all the little emptiness of love,' he concluded, and immediately frowned, asking himself why on earth he had thought of the poem in the first place.

As he left the house and made his way back to the barracks on foot he wondered what his friends would have thought, comfortable in their solid English homes, if they could have seen him walking quite unmolested through the streets of what they liked to call 'that demented city'. Probably they would have castigated him, called him a fool – and, he admitted, perhaps he was. Oddly, since the attempt to kill him, he had become unconcerned about his personal safety; it was as though his survival had made him inviolate, untouchable; or perhaps he just felt that precautions were futile. Again (and why should Rupert Brooke suddenly be so dominant in his thoughts tonight?) words that had struck him as being, when he read them for the first time, wholly directed to himself strolled into his mind: 'Unbroken glory, a gathered radiance. A width, a shining peace, under the night.'

Whatever peace under the night, there was, alas, no glory of any sort for him. Inglorious dealings were, it seemed, to be his lot.

19

As soon as he turned the corner into Lepper Street Mr Apple knew that something was wrong. Although the street was empty – as it always was at that hour of the morning – he sensed shunting echoes of movement. He paused, contemplating the foolhardiness of walking into a trap, before straightening his shoulders and making his way with an air of unperturbed determination down the street. He passed no one, yet it was as though the very windows of the houses were eyes watching his progress, glinting at him suspiciously, noting every movement he made.

Still, he arrived at the betting-shop safely, and was quietly scolding himself for imagining things, when he heard a car being started up, it's engine being gunned slightly. He tried to be casual as he glanced up and down the street: nothing, just the continued throb of the invisible engine. Mr Apple frowned and put the key in the door: he was vexed rather than surprised when it would not turn. He fiddled with it, bending down and peering at the lock, pulling the key out and reinserting it several times. He stood back and gazed at the door. He was about to make one final effort, using, as he thought of it, considerable force to gain entry, when the black Ford Escort slid around the corner and came to a sudden halt behind him.

'Mr Apple?'

Mr Apple turned, taking his time, giving himself a few seconds to gather his wits. 'Why, Mr Reilly!' he exclaimed, giving a fair impression of surprise.

'A word, Mr Apple,' Seamus Reilly said.

The back door of the car swung open and one of the young men who had escorted Reilly on his most recent visit to the shop stepped out and gestured for Mr Apple to get in with a sweep of one hand, holding the car door open with the other in the manner of a well-trained commissionaire. Mr Apple raised his hat politely and stepped into the car, immediately followed by the bodyguard, who squeezed in with difficulty, pressing Mr Apple against another man sitting on the back seat (perhaps his brother bodyguard, Mr Apple thought, although it was difficult to be certain without actually taking a good look, and Mr Apple had no intention of doing that for the moment), and slammed the door.

Reilly, sitting beside the driver, gave a flick of his wrist and the car sped down the street, slowed for a moment, turned left, and gathered speed again. For the time being nothing was said, and nobody seemed keen to look at anyone else: Mr Apple found himself counting the gear changes. ' – disappointed,' suddenly filtered into his mind.

'I'm sorry?'

'I am very disappointed,' Reilly repeated.

'Oh,' said Mr Apple, sounding concerned.

'Yes,' Reilly went on. 'Very, very disappointed,' he said in a desolate voice.

'Oh, dear.'

'I had so hoped ours would be a fruitful relationship,' Reilly continued, addressing himself to the windscreen, but allowing himself a fleeting look in the rear-view mirror that he had twisted to his advantage. 'Without complications.'

Mr Apple decided it was wisest to say nothing. He stared glumly ahead as the car continued through the city, taking a circuitous route out to the countryside.

Reilly turned, rested his arms on the back of the seat, and took a long, cold look at Mr Apple before saying, 'I understand you've been meeting with a Colonel Maddox?'

'Oh,' was all that Mr Apple could muster, genuinely taken aback by the abruptness of the question.

'You sound surprised,' Reilly told him. 'Did you really think we wouldn't learn about it?' he asked with a tight little laugh. '*Nothing* happens in Belfast that we don't know about,' he added pompously. 'What we can't find out one way, we find out another.'

'Yes. I'm sure you do.'

'Oh, we do. We certainly do. In fact, you would be amazed how we learn things. Amazed the people who come to us for help when they find they can't solve their problems without us.'

'I'm sure.'

'And you have now created one of those problems, Mr Apple. And you have placed us in a very embarrassing situation.'

'Oh, dear. I really don't – '

Reilly barely raised a hand from the back of the seat, but this tiny gesture was sufficient to make Mr Apple be silent. 'I will explain it all to you, Mr Apple. I always believe that an explanation is due when one's life is at stake, don't you?'

Reilly took a minute to light one of his little cigars, blowing the smoke from the corner of his mouth so that it would not obstruct his view of Mr Apple. 'I was summoned from my bed in the early hours of this morning. I do *not* like being summoned from my bed, Mr Apple. I like to rise when I feel the time has come for me to rise. But, as I say, I was summoned and made to present myself to your friend Colonel Maddox.' Which was not altogether true: Reilly had been awakened by someone breaking the front door of his house down, was hauled from his bed by what appeared to be a battalion of Paras, was, it had to be admitted, allowed to dress, was jolted through the dawn in the back of an army jeep, was all but carried and dumped across the desk from an aesthetic-looking Colonel in full uniform who was told, curtly, that this is Reilly, sir.

The Colonel nodded. 'Right, sergeant. You can wait outside,' he said.

'So you are Seamus Reilly,' he went on, when they were alone. 'You may sit down.'

Reilly sat down, immediately alert, aware now that there was more to this than he had first suspected. 'And you?' he asked tentatively, already in his mind trying to establish some advantage.

'My name is Maddox,' the Colonel informed him.

Reilly's face was stony.

'You've heard of me no doubt.'

'Yes.'

'I'm sure you have.' Maddox gave a small smile. 'And I of you, Reilly. And I of you.'

Reilly blinked coldly, but said nothing.

'You have,' the Colonel told him, 'quite a reputation to live up to. I've been told – correct me if my information was wrong – I've been told that you are the one to deal with if one wishes to make a – negotiation.'

Reilly smiled thinly. 'And who, I wonder, could have told you that, Colonel?'

'Someone who knows quite a lot about you. A Mr Asher.'

'Ah. May I?' Reilly held aloft his packet of small cigars.

The Colonel nodded.

'Thank you. So Mr Asher has been talking to you about me. I suppose I could be of some help in an emergency. Depending, of course, on how the – eh – negotiations were conducted.'

'Strictly between yourself and myself.'

Reilly nodded. 'That would be satisfactory.'

Maddox stood up and paced about the office, his hands clasped behind his back.

'It would also depend – to a lesser degree, of course – on how I would be recompensed.'

'Of course,' Maddox agreed, keeping up his tour of the office.

'And what you wanted me to do for you.'

Maddox returned to his desk and sat down, staring at the man opposite him, aware that he was about to implicate himself inextricably in the shadowy world of intrigue he detested. He put his elbows on the desk and folded his hands under his chin.

'Mr Asher has been kidnapped,' he said simply.

Reilly exhaled slowly, his eyes narrowing. 'I see.'

'He has been kidnapped by two people. I believe you know them both.'

'Indeed?'

'A young killer called Martin Deeley and a bookmaker named Mr Apple.'

Reilly found himself spluttering with laughter. 'Mr Apple? Kid-napped Asher? I can't believe that, Colonel.'

'Oh, I assure you it's true. He told me so himself not an hour ago.'

'Mr Apple told *you* he had *kidnapped* Asher?' Reilly asked incredulously.

'He and Deeley.'

Reilly shook his head, lost for words.

'They asked to meet me – or rather Mr Apple did – and they both arrived and told me. They're holding him somewhere – Mr Apple mentioned something about Asher being in danger of exposure, although I think he may have been trying to fool me – and they want to do a deal.'

'A deal. Yes. Yes, that is understandable.'

'You see, they know that a man called Corrigan was sent to give Deeley's name to us – '

'Why was that?' Seamus Reilly asked innocently.

'Because, as you well know, Reilly, he tried to shoot me when I was in England.'

Reilly looked hurt. 'Why should I know that, Colonel?'

'Because,' the Colonel told him, forced to smile at his effrontery, 'because you know everything that goes on.'

Reilly accepted this. He smiled.

'I suspect you even organized my assassination,' the Colonel said.

Reilly stopped smiling. He stared at the Colonel, saying nothing, his eyes blank.

'Anyway,' Maddox went on, 'they know Corrigan gave us Deeley's name. They know that we are now hunting for Deeley. They want to trade Deeley's safety for Asher's.'

Reilly nodded. 'And is that not reasonable?'

'No. It is *not* reasonable.'

'An eye for an eye? I always understood that was acceptable.'

'Not in this case.'

'Oh. This is special? No. Don't answer that,' Reilly said, holding up one hand. 'So where do I come in?'

'I want Asher found and released unharmed,' Maddox said.

246

'I see. You mean you want *me* to find Asher and release him unharmed?'

Maddox nodded.

'And in return?'

'You can have Deeley.'

Reilly grinned. 'We will have Deeley in any case, Colonel. We really don't have to negotiate with you to have Deeley. Martin Deeley is ours to do what we like with. However – ' he paused to stub out his cigar in the ashtray on the desk, 'however, if Deeley *and* Mr Apple can be disposed of by us and we have your guarantee that no unnecessary – '

'No,' the Colonel said. 'Not Apple.'

'Then – ' Reilly raised his arms to indicate that, alas, he could see no further point in these discussions.

'But why – why on earth would you want Apple?' Maddox wanted to know.

Reilly leaned back in his chair, relaxing for the first time since he had been brought into the office. 'Colonel, you have your way of dealing with things, and we have ours. We have a – a passion for cleanliness. Some people call us the punishment squad, some call us the cleaners. Both have their truth, but the latter more so. We dislike leaving any loose ends, any threads that may unravel and lead to complications. One can't be squeamish, Colonel. Either a job is properly done or not at all, and if any operation is undertaken and not completed satisfactorily, then someone else has to pay. I don't intend to pay, Colonel.'

'And that's why Deeley – '

'Deeley, Deeley. Deeley is a nothing. A thug. A little killer. A good one – usually – ' Reilly presented the Colonel with the glimpse of a smile, 'but we have so many young men only too anxious to prove they can kill. The Deeleys of this land grow in every dung-heap in the city. Look in any house and you'll find one waiting to be discovered.'

'Dear God.'

'Which, incidentally, Colonel, is one of the reasons we will survive long after you have all given up in despair.'

'And if I give you Mr Apple?'

'I will give you Mr Asher – provided, of course, he is still alive.'

'I'm sure he is.'

'I meant by the time we find him.'

'Oh.'

'Do I take it we have reached an understanding, Colonel?'

Maddox bowed his head. 'Yes,' he said.

'We deliver Asher and keep Deeley and Apple?'

'Yes.'

'Excellent,' Reilly said contentedly, rising and straightening his jacket. 'I'd better go and see to things, then. Maybe we will meet again, Colonel.'

'I doubt it, Reilly.'

'Oh, you never know when we might need each other. After all, this is *my* country, Colonel. You are the outsider, and outsiders do tend to find themselves in hot water from time to time.'

'You have it all worked out, don't you?'

'Yes. Yes, I think we do. We have a lot of experience, you know. You can hardly expect to overcome us with a handful of uniformed schoolboys, can you? In a way I feel sorry for you all,' Reilly told the Colonel, and he sounded as if he meant it. 'It must be soul-destroying to be sent over here with no hope of achieving anything and every possibility that you will have to die. Oh, not you, Colonel. Not you. The unfortunate youngsters under your command are the ones I sometimes feel sorry for. We watch them all the time. If only they knew how easily we could kill them if we wanted to – why, you would have mutiny on your hands, if that is the word. Does it apply to the army?'

Maddox did not seem to hear the question: he just sat at his desk and stared unseeing at Reilly, watching him straighten his jacket again and smooth his hair with the palms of his hands.

'In fact,' Reilly went on, 'I suspect you would rather like to die, Colonel. And I understand that. You are not alone, of course. Life is so complicated these days, don't you think? It would be so much easier to shuffle out of it with a little glory than to live on admitting that one had made a shambles of it.'

'Glory.' Maddox heard himself say aloud sadly, and for one frightening second he wondered absurdly if Reilly had managed to penetrate the thoughts he had conceived a few hours ago.

'Unbroken glory,' Reilly went on, his choice of adjective making the Colonel even more uneasy. 'It's what we all seek, one way or another. We settle, most of us, for the reflected variety, but it's not quite the same, is it? It's the personal kind we want, that strange, unattainable something that will make people remember us. How awful it is that most of us will just die, be buried with a modicum of ceremony, and be quite forgotten. In a week it will be as though we never existed,' Reilly said thoughtfully. 'And maybe we never did exist. Maybe it's just the great illusion. It makes one wonder –' Reilly decided to wonder in silence. He stopped talking and looked down at the Colonel. There was something bizarre, something almost piti-able about the pair of them, facing each other, both locked in their cages of wishfulness, both feeling a curious sympathy for the other, both aware that this understanding was fleeting, was already dissem-bling, would, in the twinkling of an eye, appear (if Reilly was right), like themselves, never to have existed.

And perhaps Reilly sensed this; perhaps, too, he realized the danger in such thoughts, and how easily such compassion could be construed as weakness, for he now coughed abruptly and said: 'I will be in touch, Colonel.'

Maddox looked up. 'Yes,' he said. He cleared his throat. 'Yes,' he said again, and watched Reilly to the door. 'I'll have the sergeant see you home.'

Reilly smiled. 'Just out of here, Colonel. Once outside these walls I'll be perfectly safe. Outside here, I'm in my own territory.'

'Of course.'

So much for Reilly being 'made to present himself' to Mr Apple's friend, Colonel Maddox.

'Ah,' Mr Apple said, wondering what was coming next, wonder-ing, too, where on earth he was being taken now that the car had been driven to the outskirts of the city and was making its way back again by a different route towards their point of departure. 'Ah, Colonel Maddox.'

'You *do* know him?'

'Oh, yes. I know the Colonel. A civilized man.'

'Quite,' Reilly interrupted, not, it seemed, anxious to discuss the Colonel's possible merits. 'And you have seen him recently I understand?'

'Yes,' Mr Apple agreed.

'Very recently.'

'Very recently.'

'And attempted to make – to come to an arrangement with him?'

'None too successfully, it would appear.'

'None too successfully, as you say.'

'Ah, well,' Mr Apple sighed, not, apparently, greatly perturbed.

Reilly made a clicking noise with his tongue. 'Why didn't you come to *me*?' he wanted to know, sounding offended, hurt. 'I've always tried to be your friend. You're supposed to call on friends in time of trouble.'

Mr Apple smiled. 'I could hardly have done that under the circumstances. I don't think Martin has a great deal of faith in you, Mr Reilly.'

'Martin? Oh, Deeley. Martin Deeley is not your concern, Mr Apple. You should never have concerned yourself with him. As it is, you have only succeeded in – '

'But Martin *is* my concern, Mr Reilly. He always was. He was my concern long before I met him. Before I met you. Before I was born.'

' – ?' Reilly scowled at this curious pronouncement. But he decided to ignore it, to let it follow his momentary compassion for the Colonel into oblivion. 'As it is, you have placed me in a most difficult, a most regrettable position.'

'I'm sorry,' Mr Apple apologized politely.

'Sorry? Huh. Your sorrow doesn't help *me*, Mr Apple. Your stupidity has forced me to give way to demands from Colonel Ma— '

'Oh, I'm sure you didn't give way too much, Mr Reilly. I'm sure you came out of it very nicely,' Mr Apple heard himself say, heard, too, an angry note in his voice. 'People like you always come out of things nicely. Somehow you manage to exploit the weaknesses and distress of others. You treat people like pawns. You shift their souls about in an evil game, crying brotherhood and patriotism and freedom and every other mindless cliché that fanatics have cried for centuries. And all the time you know what you are doing? I'll tell you what you are doing *Mister* Reilly: you are committing fratricide, you are crippling your country, you are chaining your people to the skeleton of horror and terror and hatred. That's what you're doing.'

If Reilly was taken aback by this unexpected onslaught he gave no sign of it. He seemed, indeed, to be mildly bored by it; he had heard it all before, and the more he heard it the less truth there seemed to be in it. 'Have you quite finished?' he asked coldly.

'Yes. I've finished.'

'Good. I hope you consider those words a fitting epitaph,' he said, and turned away to stare out of the windscreen. 'Pick up Deeley,' he ordered curtly after a moment.

The driver seemed to settle more comfortably into his seat following this order, and even the engine seemed to purr more sweetly now there was some definite destination. Only the men on either side of Mr Apple failed to change their attitudes: they sat stiff, tense and uncomfortable, an uneasy look almost of distaste on their hard, grim faces, as though they sensed that the man between them was doomed, was already dead.

The black Ford slid to a stop outside Mr Apple's house. Reilly gave the driver a wordless command, jerking his head in the direction of the house, making no attempt to move. Mr Apple watched the driver climb out of the car and walk smartly, openly and officiously round the side of the house. He appeared again almost immediately, gave a curt nod, and stood his ground, waiting.

'Bring him in,' Reilly said, without turning round. Getting out of the car, he walked briskly to the house.

The man nearest the pavement opened the rear door and got out, holding the door open, extending his other hand to assist Mr Apple.

251

Mr Apple took the hand and eased himself out, feeling a sudden dampness down his back. He smiled at this, or perhaps he was smiling his thanks to the man who helped him steady himself: whichever, he smiled and followed Reilly.

The first thing that struck him as he came in the kitchen door was that the kitchen table had been overturned. Afraid at what more ominous sights might await him, Mr Apple began to pick out trivial disasters: a cup and saucer, the former broken, on the floor. A pool of milk. Cornflakes, like giant sawdust, scattered near the sink. Slowly Mr Apple raised his eyes, trying, and almost succeeding, to blur his vision as he bypassed the forlorn figure seated on the chair and focusing on the three strangers who stood behind it. Yet, he noted, they were not all strangers: one of them, the tallest – and perhaps for this reason the most sinister – Mr Apple recognized as the man who had delivered occasional brown envelopes to the shop: he had one hand outstretched, holding the hair of the person in the chair. Mr Apple followed the line from the man's shoulder, came to the hand, lowered his eyes another fraction and came to rest on Martin Deeley's face. Immediately he flicked his eyes away (but not before he noticed the red weal running down Martin's jaw) and concentrated on John Asher, seated in the corner, a look of mixed apprehension, fear and defiance on his face, shifting constantly in his chair as though these slight movements would defend him from any attack from the man who stood behind him. Mr Apple turned his head and stared pointedly at Martin. He was touched to receive an exaggerated wink.

Reilly also looked about him and was displeased at what he saw. He snapped his fingers. 'Pick that up,' he snapped fiercely without indicating anything. Immediately one of the men behind Martin moved forward, looked about for aid, got it from the driver, and between them they lifted the table and set it upright. Then they retreated, looking absurdly humiliated.

Reilly balanced himself against one corner of the table, thinking. As usual, to help himself concentrate he lit a cigar, taking an inordinately long time about it, and it was not until he had inhaled and exhaled the smoke several times, had left the table and crossed the kitchen to the refrigerator, had leaned against this and satisfied himself that he had a clear view of the entire room that he said, shaking his head like a disillusioned father about to scold recalcitrant children, 'Why, oh, why do you fools *put* me in a position like this?'

In the silence that followed Mr Apple removed his hat and placed it on the table. This done, he paused, perhaps waiting to see if anything more was to be said; but as the silence continued he took off his overcoat, folded it, and put it on the table beside his hat, patting it a couple of times as though it were a friendly, nervous animal. 'Jesus!' he heard someone behind him exclaim. 'He's covered in blood!'

Reilly was immediately alert. He sprang forward, touched Mr Apple's blood-sodden jacket, rubbed his fingertips together and peered at them. 'Which of you – ' he began, looking furiously at the two men who had sat either side of Mr Apple in the car, both of whom glanced at each other, both shaking their heads in terrified bewilderment. 'Mr Apple – ' Reilly tried again.

Mr Apple turned to him and bathed him in a strange, contented smile. 'It is nothing,' he said. 'Just some old wounds. I had been expecting them to bleed soon,' he added enigmatically.

'Expecting them to?'

Mr Apple nodded 'Hmm. A small sign I've been promised,' he confided.

'A sign?'

'A sign.'

'A sign of what?'

'Ah, as to that, I'm not altogether sure. Death I think, but it hardly matters.'

Reilly took a couple of paces backwards, recoiled almost, a look of suspicious discomfort showing momentarily in his eyes. 'If this is one of your tricks – '

'Tricks?' Mr Apple swung round in amazement. 'Oh, no. It's no trick, Mr Reilly. As I said, it's my old wounds. Sefer always warned me they would bleed when – ' he stopped as Reilly demanded:

'Sefer?'

Mr Apple heard himself chuckle. 'A friend of mine. You wouldn't know him, Mr Reilly. He comes and goes. He's always on hand when I need him, though, aren't you, Sefer? Of course you are. Always there when I need you.' Mr Apple dropped his voice to a whisper. 'Thank you for the warning,' he said, gazing upwards.

Automatically, everyone looked upwards, and they were still gaping at the kitchen ceiling when Reilly shouted furiously: 'Shut up, Apple!' His whole body was shaking.

'Oh, I'm sorry,' Mr Apple apologized. 'I thought you asked – '

'Shut *up*,' Reilly said again more quietly, making a considerable effort to compose himself.

'Certainly,' Mr Apple told him, turning away, belatedly returning Martin's encouraging wink.

'You,' Reilly said gruffly to John Asher. 'Are you all right?'

'Yes,' Mr Asher replied.

'Take him out,' Reilly ordered. 'Is there a front room? Take him there,' he said, 'and keep him there. Don't let him out of your sight.'

Asher was lifted by his collar from the chair and frog-marched from the kitchen. As the door closed behind them Reilly crossed the room and took up a position in front of Martin, legs spread, hands clasped behind his back. Bending slightly, he said, 'Martin, Martin, dear, oh, dear, we had such high hopes for you.'

'Yeah,' Martin said, sneering. 'Real high.'

Reilly didn't like that, didn't like it one little bit, and a glint of bitterness entered his eyes. 'You know we cannot allow this random activity. We can't have people taking actions on their own without consulting us first.'

Martin shrugged.

'It disrupts the balance of things, Martin,' he went on. 'Makes everything so untidy.'

'Shame,' Martin volunteered.

'Yes. Yes, Martin. You're right about that. It is a shame. As you know, it always grieves me when I am forced to inflict punishment,' Reilly told him, shaking his head mournfully. 'But, as you also know,

I have my job to do.'

'Some job, Seamus.'

Reilly blinked several times. 'Yes,' he said. 'Painful, but quite necessary, as you well know. I had hoped you would be more understanding, would help me – '

Martin gave a huge guffaw. 'Jesus, Seamus, you really are something else. Look, I know fucking well you're going to kill me, so just get on with it. You don't have to give me all that old shit about how sorry you are. I've heard all that crap from you before.'

Reilly gave something approaching a smile and nodded his head several times. 'Yes,' he said finally. 'Yes.'

'Good,' Martin said, his voice defiant but the blood already beginning to drain from his cheeks. 'You all right, Mr A.?' he asked suddenly.

Mr Apple turned and stared at him, stared and nodded before coming over to him. 'Yes, Martin,' he said. 'Yes, I'm fine. I'm sorry – '

'Sorry? Why the hell should you be sorry, Mr A.? You said everything would work out. Well, it has, hasn't it?'

'Yes, I suppose – '

'No supposing, Mr A. It's worked out fine. I think this is what I wanted to happen. And I'll tell you something else, you mad old bugger. I bet you knew this was what I wanted all along.'

Mr Apple thought about a denial, but changed his mind: he smiled at Martin, bent down and took hold of one of his hands. 'Maybe,' he said, an odd crack in his voice.

'Hey, cummon, Mr A.,' Martin said gruffly, squeezing the bony fingers, 'I don't want any shit out of *you*.'

'No.'

Martin laughed. 'Jesus, I don't half choose my friends,' he said. Then he suddenly leaned forward and impulsively kissed Mr Apple lightly on the cheek. 'And thanks for being my friend,' he whispered.

Mr Apple knew he was crying, and he was content to let the tears course down his cheeks.

'Hey, quit that, you old fool,' Martin told him kindly. 'I feel terrific. You know, it's the best thing that ever happened to me in my life!'

'Oh, Martin – ' Mr Apple began. There was so much he wanted to say, but as he searched for the words he noticed one of the men behind Martin start to screw a silencer on to the barrel of a revolver. He saw him point the gun at Martin's head and glance at Reilly.

' – and free,' he heard Martin say happily.

Mr Apple had just time to kneel down and extend his arms as the man fired. *Pfffft*, and Martin collapsed forward, the wooden chair slithering sideways and cracking against the wall.

Mr Apple cradled the warm body in his arms, pressing it against him, rocking it gently as though sending it into a comfortable and untrammelled sleep, muttering to it, only occasional words decipherable. 'Peace', was certainly one of them. And 'joy'. Then, strangely, 'with you soon'. And 'unafraid'.

Reilly turned away: he believed in grief, believed, too, that it merited respect and privacy. Grief, he thought, was a noble emotion, far surpassing such jaded ideals as love or honour. It was, he now told himself, grief that made people and countries great, set them apart, made them worthwhile, and he admired it all the more, he knew, because it was an emotion of which he himself was incapable. Mild sorrow was as far as he went: anything deeper had long since been gouged from his soul. Mildly he wondered about this, and was no nearer discovering a reason for it when he heard 'Christ!' exclaimed behind him. He swung round, half-expecting to see Martin Deeley standing upright, grinning at him defiantly. For a second he was relieved to see this was not so, yet what he did see was, for some inexplicable reason, more frightening, more – he could not find a word – more sinister. Mr Apple had keeled over, still clutching Martin Deeley's body in his arms, and now lay staring into space, unmoving.

'Jesus, he's dead,' the man who had killed Martin said in awe.

And he was almost right. Mr Apple was not dead, not quite, but he was certainly dying. Or perhaps he was, indeed, dead, and it was his gentle spirit that lingered for a moment, taking, as it were, a last, sad, baleful look over its shoulder. We have been watching you, voices said. We are well pleased, they added, as great black birds swooped in and seemed to raise him up, flapping their gigantic wings, causing the gathering mist to swirl about him. Ah, Mr Apple thought he heard himself sigh. He thought, too, that he could make out shapes, familiar shapes, hovering over him. Faces loomed, dark Mexican faces, pale Irish faces all appearing together, disintegrating, withdrawing. Hey, I feel terrific, was whispered to him suddenly, and he smiled, the smile freezing on his lips, remaining behind.

Reilly leaned down and felt Mr Apple's wrist. Rising, he nodded. 'Yes,' he said quietly. 'He is dead.'

'What do we do with them now?'

'Leave them be,' Reilly said, and walked to the window, gazing out, fixing his attention on a ginger-and-white cat that stalked an unsuspecting sparrow. 'Wipe the gun and put it in his hand,' he ordered without turning round, watching the cat crouch lower and cover the ground almost on its belly.

'Whose hand? Apple's?'

Reilly swung round, his face livid. '*Mister* Apple's,' he spat. 'It's *Mister* Apple to you, you thug,' he said vehemently, and turned back to the window.

He heard the shuffling behind him as one of Mr Apple's hands was released and the gun placed carefully in it; he heard, too, and winced at the small, helpless cries the sparrow sent up as the cat grabbed it, secured it in its mouth and loped off into the bushes.

'It won't fool anyone,' Reilly said quietly, glad that he had been able to compose himself. 'But that hardly matters.'

'We've done that, Mr Reilly. Anything else?'

Reilly turned and looked down at the two bodies, almost envying them their peaceful attitudes.

'You two take Asher and leave him outside St Enoch's.'

'Do we – '

'Just do what I said. Take him and leave him outside St Enoch's. Nothing else. And you,' he added, turning to his driver, 'you wait in the car.'

Alone, Reilly crossed the room until he stood directly over the bodies. For a while he seemed content just to stare down at them, unable to see Martin's face, which was buried in Mr Apple's shoulder, but seeing clearly and wondering at the smile on the old man's face. And there was something in that smile that made him feel it was directed at himself, not in any cruel, taunting way, but with a friendliness that moved him. It was as though Mr Apple was smiling in gratitude at an old friend, an old and trusted friend who had done him a great and wonderful favour. Reilly bent down and smoothed Mr Apple's hair and fixed his spectacles at a correct angle on his nose, making him, as he thought of it, respectable. Then he stood upright again and a smile came to his lips, perhaps in satisfaction at the neatness of his handiwork, perhaps just returning Mr Apple's. Then he turned on his heel and hurried from the house.

20

Mr Asher sipped his neat whiskey and eyed Colonel Maddox balefully: he was worried about the Colonel, worried that he seemed so morose, so distant, not at all what he had expected from one whom, he felt, should be in jubilant mood and celebrating his, John Asher's release. But it was not so. Maddox had welcomed him well enough and offered him a drink, but there was something about his manner that Asher could not quite put his finger on, and he thought about this as he waited for the Colonel to speak again.

'You say Mr Apple was *not* shot?'

'No, Colonel. Just Deeley. Apple seems to have died of a heart attack. I'll know more definitely in the morning.'

'And Mr Apple had the gun in his hand?'

'Yes. Put there, obviously. Made to look like *he* killed Deeley. Quite neat, really. Trust Reilly to give us a way out.'

'A way out?'

'Of course. We can write it off as a lovers' tiff. A pretty serious tiff I grant you. But – '

'Lover's tiff? Good God, John, they weren't – '

'No, of course they weren't, Colonel. But that's not what matters. We will simply *say* they were. Who's going to deny it?' Asher asked, pleased that things had worked out so well.

'But you can't go about saying that. It's so unfair,' Maddox said, sounding ridiculously petulant and proper.

'Would you prefer the truth to come out, Colonel? No, I thought not,' said Asher, noting the look of sudden consternation in the Colonel's eyes. 'Don't worry, Colonel. Leave it all to me. You won't be involved in any way. I owe you that much.'

'Yes,' the Colonel said, indifferently. 'And he was smiling?'

' – ?'

'Mr Apple was smiling?'

'Yes. Yes, he was,' Asher confirmed, smiling himself in surprise as he remembered the strange look of peace on the face. 'Beatifically, I suppose is the word.'

'Ah.'

'Holding Deeley in his arms – but I suppose that was another Reilly touch.'

'But you said something about blood? A lot of blood on his back, you said.'

'Hmm. Odd, that. We had a look at that in the mortuary. Very odd. He had a lot of little criss-cross scars on his back, and they all seemed to have opened for some reason.'

'Criss-cross scars?'

'Yes. As if he'd been whipped.'

'Reilly didn't – '

'Oh, no. They were old wounds. They had just split open. No obvious reason for it. Maybe it happens when you die suddenly. Like ejaculating when you hang?'

'Do you?'

'Do I what, Colonel?'

'Do you ejaculate when – '

'So they say.'

'And you think – '

'I don't know. A possibility, I suppose.' Asher sipped his whiskey again.

'And this is all you found of interest?' Maddox asked after a while, indicating a collection of exercise-books bound with tape that lay on his desk.

'Hmm. That's all. Seems to be a diary of some sort. I just glanced through it. Mad ramblings, if you ask me. Talks about his dreams and that sort of drivel.'

Maddox nodded, and stared at the exercise-books.

'I wouldn't bother with them, Colonel, if I was you.'

'No?'

'No. The best thing you can do is put the entire incident out of your mind. It's over and done with. I'll tidy up what needs to be done.'

'And that's all there is to it?'

'That's all there is to it.'

'Dear God. Two men die and are dismissed without a second thought.'

'That's the way life goes here, Colonel. Anyway, it's two we don't have to worry about any more. No more potshots at yourself,' he said airily.

'And now?'

'Now? Like I said, I'll tidy up.'

'You'll tidy up,' the Colonel repeated, but mostly to himself.

'Yes. I must say you arranged things very nicely, Colonel. It's very satisfactory to have someone like Seamus Reilly where we want him.'

'Seamus Reilly where we want him?' Maddox asked. He knew that he was repeating almost everything Asher said, but he succumbed to this willingly since it saved him a lot of thinking.

'That's right.'

'But I gave him my word there would be no repercu— '

'Ah, yes. You gave him *your* word, Colonel. But that hardly affects me, does it? I mean, I can't be held responsible for what you promise,' Asher said smugly. 'You don't really believe we could let that shifty little bastard get away so easily, do you?'

'Yes, John, I'm afraid I did.'

'Oh, dear,' Asher said. 'You are an innocent, Colonel. Anyway, not to worry, you'll probably be long gone from here before we have occasion to benefit from Reilly's situation.'

Maddox stared at the man across the desk. He suddenly felt very sick and very tired. His weariness outweighed his feeling of sickness, though, and in an odd way this consoled him. It numbed his thoughts, leaving only traces of sorrow – sorrow for what, he was not sure. 'I think I'd like to be alone, John, if you don't mind,' he said quietly.

' – ? Yes. Yes, of course, Colonel,' Asher said, finishing his drink and standing up. 'I've a lot of things to see to anyway.'

'Tidying up, I suppose,' Maddox said, immediately regretting his mild sarcasm.

Asher grinned. 'Yes, tidying up. I spend my life tidying up.'

'That's what Seamus Reilly told me. Cleaning up *he* called it, though.'

'Indeed?'

'Yes. You two seem to have something in common.'

'We do, don't we?'

'Yes, you do.'

Asher gave a short, sharp laugh that was really a snort. 'That's quite amusing when you think of it,' he said.

Maddox looked up at him with a long, mournful gaze. 'That must be what's wrong with me, John. I can see nothing remotely amusing about it. The two of you revel in deceit and corruption. I have never held either in very high regard.'

'Only because you've never before had to resort to them, Colonel,' Asher told him. 'Your nice, comfortable, Berkshire lifestyle doesn't lend itself to devious ways. We, however, have extraordinary lifestyles that demand extraordinary measures. You call it corruption and deceit, we call it merely wheeling and dealing. Wheels within wheels and deals within deals. It leads to only one thing – survival. Survival, if you want, of the fittest. The fittest in this case being the one who can deal the better hand, deal himself the aces. Seamus Reilly is now one ace in *my* hand, and I would be fool if I failed to use it,' Asher concluded.

Maddox closed his eyes and sighed, hoping that when he opened them again Asher might have gone. But: 'In a sense we play games,' Asher continued. 'Rather vicious, dangerous games, I agree, but games nonetheless. Games,' he added, 'that we know we really cannot win. That nobody can win.'

Maddox opened his eyes slowly and nodded.

'Yes. Well. I must be off,' Asher said. 'I'll let you know the results of those tests on Apple tomorrow.'

'Thank you.'

'Good-night, sir.'

'Good-night, John.'

And that was that: an official report would be on his desk in the morning, neatly typed, objective, inhuman, uncaring. As inhuman and uncaring as he himself had been when he agreed to Seamus Reilly's terms. But that had been done in the name of duty, had it not? Had been done for reasons beyond reproach, had it not? Certainly. Colonel Maddox leaned forward and stared again at the bundle of exercise-books before him. Poor old Arthur Apple, he thought. And poor old Matthew Maddox. Fools, the pair of them. Dreamers. Believers in ideals long since extinct.

Maddox pulled what John Asher had scathingly described as a 'diary of some sort' towards him, and flicked it open at random. He gazed at the words, letting them float up to him, it seemed, rather than actually reading them.

'...gloating in the grim and terrible slaughter, exulting in the destruction of those who only yesterday were children.' Immediately he closed the manuscript and pushed it from him roughly, feeling an unwelcome chill travel down his spine. He rose and walked to the window, to stare out at his reflection staring back: a gaunt face, grey and haggard. Death, he thought, death staring me in the face. He shuddered, shaken by his morbid thoughts.

Away across the city a milk churn, standing unobserved in the back of a parked lorry, exploded, sending shards of jagged metal screaming in all directions, ripping into flesh, rendering limbs useless, flicking life away with elegant precision.

'Sir?'

Maddox jumped and swung around.

'Sir. Another explosion, sir. A bad one. Some of our lads were caught in the middle of it.'

'Dear God.'

'At least five dead, sir. A lot injured.'

'The destruction of those who only yesterday were children,' Maddox heard himself say.

'Sir?'

'Nothing, sergeant. Nothing. Nothing at all. Just thinking what a

263

useless, useless mess this all is.'

'Yes, sir.'

'You think so too, sergeant?'

'Sir?'

Maddox smiled sadly. 'Never mind. Never mind,' he said quietly, almost as though he were offering comfort to himself. 'It doesn't seem to matter.'

'No, sir.'

'I'll be down directly.'

'Sir!'

The Colonel indeed made as if to follow the sergeant down directly, but then he hesitated. He reached out and laid a hand on Mr Apple's strange manuscript, stranger now that he had read a few of the words. Those few words, though, had suggested that it contained nothing but a horrible truth, and for a time he seemed to be praying. Then he pulled himself together, straightened his shoulders, and marched smartly out of the office: out and away from the white shadows that haunted him, that tormented him and would, he knew, be there waiting for his return; out and away into the shrieking, frightened city.